By the same author:

TARGET: BATTLESHIP

COASTAL

BARRY COWARD

WILLIAM KIMBER · LONDON

First published in 1988 by
WILLIAM KIMBER & CO. LIMITED
100 Jermyn Street, London SW1Y 6EE

© Barry Coward, 1988
ISBN 0–7183–0693–7

Typeset by Scarborough Typesetting Services
and printed in Great Britain by
Biddles Limited, Guildford and King's Lynn

The Battle of the Atlantic was the dominating factor all through the war . . . for the individual sailor or airman there were few moments of exhilarating action to break the monotony of an endless succession of anxious, uneventful days. Vigilance could never be relaxed. Dire crisis might at any moment flash upon the scene with brilliant fortune or glare with mortal tragedy . . .

WINSTON S. CHURCHILL

I

Mick Hargan picked up the pint which had just been placed before him, held it up to the light to survey its contents, raised it to his lips and took a long, deep draught. Slowly he lowered the glass to the table, wiped a trace of beer from his mouth with the back of his hand and only then did he look at the man who had just sat down opposite him. Raising a forefinger with which to jab the air between them, he continued a conversation which had been developing for the last half an hour. 'Look, Dinger old mate, I'll drink this warm gnat's piss they call beer, I'll put up with their frigid women, I'll forego the sunny beaches of Australia, I'll survive somehow on their bloody awful rations, I'll even help fight this bleedin' war for them, but I'll not put up with that Pommie prick Tomkins for another day longer. Either he goes or I go, that's straight!'

Geoff Bell, although it was a long time since anyone had called him Geoff – it was always Dinger now – had heard it all before. When Mick was in one of these moods, usually around the third or fourth pint, it was better just to let him have his way. When Mick Hargan, second generation Australian, was sounding off about his favourite subject – the English, or more precisely those Englishmen who wore RAF uniform, it was better not to say anything.

'What do they do?' went on Hargan. 'They put a bunch of Aussies in a squadron, call it an RAAF squadron at that, and then put a Pom in charge. I ask you! Don't give me any of that claptrap about there not being any Aussies senior enough. There are plenty of good blokes I would be happy to have as CO. Better than Tomkins any day. "Hargan, I'd like a word with you."' His imitation of an English accent still had a lot of Australian in it. '"Hargan, I notice you call your NCOs by their first names. Not done, old chap". Not done! 'Course it's bloody done, 'cos I do it.' He chuckled quietly to himself.

Dinger Bell took a sip from his own glass and surveyed the scene around him. The pub was crowded, mainly with other Australians. There were a few locals sat in the corner, their corner, from which not even a bunch of Australian aircrew could shift them. It had been their corner for many years and the passing phase of a world war was not going to change that. These young lads could come and go but they would always be there, West Countrymen and proud of it.

Another crew was crowded around the next table. Bill and George were together at one of the window seats. It was much like other evenings they had spent there, when breaks from flying allowed. But at least the goddamn awful winter seemed to be over. Outside the last light of a glorious spring evening was fading. Inside the pub, it was growing dim. Mick had only been able to inspect his beer by holding it to the window's light. Any minute now, the landlord would pull the blackout curtains and switch on the electric lights.

'And he knows we've got a good crew. Dinger, you're the best bloody navigator I know.' Mick was in full cry now. 'Bill — good first pilot, knows what he's doing with an aeroplane. And young George there,' he nodded to the pair sitting in the window, 'may be green but he's coming along nicely. And the other lads . . . couldn't be better.' He paused to pick up his pint but did not drink from it. 'Tomkins knows we do a good job. We've put the hours in, rain or shine, night and day. We've done our bit. Only had to come home early twice with snags. And we got ourselves a possible U-boat. And what praise do we get from Tomkins? "Hargan, could you have a word with your engineer? His logs are a bit scruffy. Try and get him to tidy them up, will you, there's a good chap?".' Now he did wait long enough to take a long drink from his glass.

Across the room, Bill Newton and George Kemp leaned aside as the barmaid came round to pull the curtains behind them. The last of the evening was shut out and the dim lights of the bar took over. As she moved on, a faint whiff of her cheap soap lingering over them, they resumed their quiet conversation. In this case, it was Bill, the experienced 21-year-old who was listening to the young 19-year-old beside him. 'Coastal Command, they said. Oh, good, thought I. No getting my arse shot off in some bomber over Germany. Sunderlands.

Big aeroplanes. Fight the war in comfort. Nobody told me that U-boats shoot back. Nobody told me that Jerry sends out Ju88s to have a go at you. Apart from that, nobody told me how bloody awful a British winter can be.'

'Look on the bright side, George,' replied Bill. 'At least we're down here in the West Country. If you were in Northern Ireland or somewhere like that, it rains there all the time. Here it just rains most of the time.'

'Yeah, maybe, but at least those blokes in Northern Ireland don't do the Biscay patrols like us. They don't take on the U-boats on the surface who seem to have a lot of guns. They don't have to keep their eyes skinned for a Junkers appearing out of the clouds.'

Bill Newton let the lad have his way. He did not like to point out that a surfaced U-boat sighting was a very rare thing and when it did come, you did not have time to think about whether it was going to fire back or not. However, privately, he would concede that keeping your eyes skinned for a Ju88 did make you a bit twitched at times.

'What about Mick? Is he a good skipper? I'm not sure about him yet.'

'How many ops have you done with us, George?'

'Only the two.'

Had this lad really only done two ops with them? Is it that short a time since Jack went off to Martin's crew? It seemed an age.

'Yeah, Mick's OK. Doesn't go in for a lot of bullshit. Likes a pint or two but then don't we all? Bangs on a bit about the Brits from time to time. Sure . . . he's OK. Bit of a character, really. Provides a laugh or two.'

Mick Hargan would have been pleased to have heard himself described as a bit of a character. It was an image he had been working on ever since he left Australia. Mick Hargan, hard-drinking, hard-flying Australian character. That was how he wished to be known. Asked where he came from, he would answer Western Australia. In fact he came from a suburb of Perth, a city boy. Asked what he did before volunteering, he would say this and that. In fact, he had worked in an insurance office. And indeed his name was not really Mick or Michael. He had been christened Edwin Maurice. He thought Mick sounded better.

What Mick did not know was that Dinger Bell knew most of this. They had been together a long time and little snippets had come out which Dinger had quietly filed away in his mind. He now knew quite a lot about Mick Hargan. But what he did not know, did not realise, was that what had once been a thin veneer over Mick Hargan's true self was fast becoming the real Mick Hargan. The war had changed them both. They had come from the remote lands of Australia into the brunt of the war in Europe. They had arrived young and green. Now they were old and wise, Mick an ancient twenty-three, Dinger a year younger. The war, the responsibility of flying a Sunderland, of running a crew, had matured them and changed them. What had once been something of an act now came naturally to Mick Hargan. He had become a bit of an Australian character. If he were able to stand back and look at himself, he would have been proud of the job he had done.

*

A little over a mile away, in a small hotel which did not get much trade now there was a war on, Leading Wren Jilly Johnson would have objected strongly to Mick Hargan's description of English women as frigid. As she was in bed at the time, wearing nothing other than black stockings held up by garters, she would have felt the generalisation unjustified. John Williams, sergeant, senior air gunner, would also have objected to his skipper's statement, although at that particular moment he was distracted by the sensation as his finger tips slid slowly up a cool, smooth thigh.

'Whoever decided on black stockings for Wrens was a genius,' he whispered, slightly muffled as his lips caressed her left breast. 'But where did you get nylon ones from?'

Jilly giggled as his hand slid a little higher. 'We girls have our secrets, you know. We keep them for special occasions. And we don't . . . ooooh . . . normally wear garters either. And where do you think you're going?' she added quickly.

'Nowhere,' he replied, his hand stopping its slow progress.

'Oh, how disappointing,' she giggled. She moved her legs a

little further apart and, encouraged, his hand moved a little higher, his fingertips brushing her skin lightly, sending tingles up her spine. His lips brushed against her nipple and she stroked the back of his head, her fingers ruffling his hair.

His fingers reached their goal and his gentle caressing suddenly made her feel incredibly randy.

'I want you,' she whispered, urgently. Then, as an after thought, she added, 'Have you got a . . . you know, thingy?'

''Course I have. Always prepared. Boy scout's motto,' he replied as he deftly slid on the condom and moved on top of her.

Afterwards, as they dressed, he said, 'And where are they sending us tomorrow, sweetheart?'

'You know I don't know.'

'But you work in the ops room.'

'Maybe, but all I do is plot the areas on the wall map. I don't know which aircraft is going where, or indeed which crew is going when.'

'Yeah, but you know what's been planned. Are we going to the Bay or to some quiet convoy out west?'

'John!' she whispered, 'you know you shouldn't talk about such things. Walls have ears.'

He laughed. 'Here! You're joking. Come on, love, what's on the board for tomorrow?'

'I can't tell you.'

''Course you can. I'm one of the jokers that's going, aren't I? I'm not going to blow it.'

'All I know is there is a convoy coming up from Freetown which will need support and the standard areas in the Bay are on the board. There are at least six sorties tomorrow so, Johnnie darling, you could be going anywhere. And if that is the only reason you took me to bed, to get information out of me, then you didn't really succeed, did you?'

John patted her bottom. 'All I want is to get my hands on that neat little bottom of yours,' he answered.

'Huh! That's about the only thing you didn't get your hands on. They were everywhere else but on my bottom,' she tried to say indignantly but her grin gave her away. She picked up her watch. 'Come on, I've got to be getting back.'

*

Not a mile away but nearer two hundred, to the south-east in occupied France, was a man Mick Hargan would have enjoyed drinking with, if there had not been a war on. He would also have enjoyed having him as his squadron commander, for that is what Helmut Schafer was, or to be more strictly correct, he was a Staffelkapitän, of a Staffel of Ju88s. Helmut was, at that moment, engaged in business similar to Mick's, although it was wine in the glass before him, not beer. Around him were some of his men. However, he had something Mick did not have, and which was not likely to occur in a West Country pub – Helmut had a girl sitting on his lap, a French girl.

Helmut was speaking, '. . . and what we need to do is get at least two pairs of aircraft up against a Sunderland. They've got guns, lots of them. Flying Porcupines, they are. But if you can split their fire, come in from different sides. . . .' He moved one hand from where it had been stroking the French girl's leg to join the other in formation over the table as he demonstrated his tactics against a large white flower which stood in a slender vase in the middle. 'Come from opposite sides, then whichever way he turns, one of you can get him!' His hands swept in, shattering the white flower and spreading petals over the table. The men around laughed.

Continuing in German, he turned to the girl. 'And what do you think of that, my little Yvette?' The girl looked blank. He switched to French: *'Ah, ma chérie, tu compris?'* The girl shook her head. *'Très bien!'*

He pushed the girl off his lap. As she straightened her skirt, he held up the empty wine bottle to her. She took it and moved off towards the bar.

The men around the large table started talking amongst themselves. The Staffelkapitän had said his piece. The murmur of conversation increased. 'I had a letter from my wife. . . .' 'They say the raids. . . .' Did you hear what happened to Willi the other. . . .' The man next to Helmut turned to him. 'Helmut, my friend, is it wise to talk of these things in front of the girl?'

'Hans, *Kamerad*,' replied Schafer, slapping him on the shoulder,' you don't think a simple French girl like that understands anything we talk about, do you?' He emptied the last of the wine out of his glass and looked towards the bar in anticipation of the next bottle. Then he turned back to his companion. 'And now, Hans, when are you going to finish the engine modifications on the aircraft? I need higher availability. I cannot use my crews fully at present whilst you take the aircraft off me to play with the engines.'

'Just another couple of days. It is an important modification. We should not have so much trouble with salt corrosion once it is done. Bear with me.'

'OK, Hans, OK. I know, I know. But I have to keep the pressure on you engineering chaps or you would spend all your time taking the aircraft to bits to find out why they work. According to you, aeroplanes are there for engineers to tinker with. Pilots are allowed to borrow them from time to time. And you complain when they come back with bullet holes in them!'

Hans' look turned serious. 'Helmut, I never complain when pilots come back with bullet holes in their aircraft. I know there is serious work to be done out there, out over the sea. If a pilot has holes in his aircraft, then I know he has been getting in close.' He paused. 'Can we move to another table . . . there is something else I must discuss with you.'

'Hans, you take things very seriously. You want to talk now?' He raised a questioning eyebrow. The other man nodded. Helmut picked up his glass and, as an afterthought the new bottle as well, just placed there by Yvette, pushed back his chair and moved across to an empty table against the wall. The short, rather rotund, engineer followed him. They sat down facing each other.

'Now, Hans, what troubles you?'

'Helmut, I am an easy-going man – I let a lot of things pass me by. I have a job to do. I do it as well as I can. I let other people do their jobs. But I am proud of my mechanics. I make them work. I encourage, I teach, I father them. From time to time I kick their arses too. They are good men. Some not too intelligent but they are willing and they work hard for me . . . and for you too.' He sipped from his glass. 'This new man, this pilot . . . Bruckner. He is driving my men crazy. He struts around like the Prussian he is. "Do this, do that! Now! Immediately!" He tells my men they are scruffy. He tells them to get haircuts. He comes and complains to me when all is not perfect with his aircraft. He's driving me crazy. Doesn't he know we are fighting a war? All is not perfect in war. We try but we are not preparing for some magnificent parade through the streets of Berlin. We are trying to hold together an outfit in western France, where the natives are not exactly friendly and where we are one hell of a long way from the supply bases. Yesterday he was complaining that his pilot's seat was rather worn. He wanted a new one right away. I ask you! It took us two months to get a replacement when Karl's seat had a bullet hole or two in it! Where the hell has he been, this man Bruckner? Flying for Hitler or something?'

Helmut could not help grinning. The other man looked askance. 'I'm sorry, Hans, but that is exactly what he has been doing, flying one of the Führer's courier aircraft. I think perhaps things were a bit different there.' He picked up the bottle and topped up both their glasses.

'Well, I don't care where he has come from, Führer's pilot or not, if he goes on the way he is going, one of my men is going to hit him. Then we will have to have a court martial with all sorts of trouble. Has this man Bruckner done any operational flying?'

'Yes, Hans, he has. Back in the days of Poland. I think things were a bit different then. He has only been with us a short time. He will learn.' He could see in the engineer's face that such an answer was not enough. 'And I'll have a word with him as well.'

'Thanks, Helmut. I wish you would. It will save a lot of trouble all round.'

The group at the main table was getting noisy. More wine had arrived on the table. What the hell, thought Helmut. We do not unwind too often. A few sore heads in the morning maybe but an hour in the cockpit on the way out to the search area will sort out those who are flying tomorrow. He noted that the crews who were on at dawn in the morning were not represented in the bar that evening. Karl, Franz, Big Fritz, all tucked up in bed . . . hopefully.

*

'Time, Gentlemen, please!' The traditional cry of publicans rang out to a jeer from the aircrew filling the bar. The locals, much against their will, quietly finished their beers and slipped out with a nod to the man behind the bar. After the war, they could resort to their old ways. Just lock the front door of the pub and open the back. . . . Even the local policeman would pop in for a pint after hours. But now, with coppers from outside the West Country sent down here, they had to be more careful. Always prowling round, checking on the blackout. So the locals made their separate ways back to their homes, before there was any trouble from the Aussies.

'Come on, landlord! Just one more quick round before we go?'

'No, lad. You know the rules.'

'Rules, Bert? Here I am, a regular customer of yours. . . .'

The landlord had heard it all before. The young pilot before him was just one amongst the hundreds of faces which had passed through his pub. Some of them he got to know – some were around for months. They were the regulars. This lad? Could have been in once or twice before.

'I've told you. That's it. Time, it is. Now drink up quick. I've got a bed to get to, like you.'

Mick was half way down his last pint. He was not going to be hurried. He could never figure out the English licensing laws. Bloody awful beer it was, anyway, he thought to himself, taking another mouthful from his glass. He had run out of steam. He had had his say. Now Dinger and he would walk slowly back, down the lane. Good job it was downhill all the way. . . .

'Come on, Mick. Time to go.'

'OK, Dinger, OK. Just finish me beer.' Mick drained his glass and put it down before him. Just then, the barmaid reached their table, her hands already nearly full to capacity with glasses. She picked up the two empties. Only then did Mick notice her presence. 'Maureen, my love! Where have you been all evening? And what are you doing for the rest of the evening?' Playfully he patted her bottom.

'I'll thank you to get your hands off, Mick Hargan! As for the remainder of this evening, I've a stack of glasses to wash up and then I'll be heading for bed.'

'Now, it's that second bit that interests me. . . .'

'Well, don't hold out too many hopes. . . .' She moved on quickly.

She, like the landlord, had heard it all before. At least Mick was a face she knew. Usually it was some spotty-faced youth in a uniform a size too big for him. Mick was OK. Not bad-looking in a rugged sort of way. But hardly tall and dark. A bit short really, with fair hair, already a bit thin on top. Not exactly slim either. Stocky, he was. Not fat, just stocky. She placed her handfuls of glasses carefully on the bar and turned back for another lot. The landlord was starting to move through the bar, getting people moving. Men were standing. 'Who's pinched my bleedin' cap?' 'You got my wallet, Ginger?' 'Maureen, you beaut!'

Mick stood up, looked around for his cap, could not see it, muttered 'Sod it!' to himself and headed for the door. Dinger, watching his skipper's slightly unsteady progress, headed after him. He paused for a moment as he went 'Bill, find the Skipper's hat, will you?' he said to the two who were just standing up from their window seat and straightening their tunics, and then hurried after Mick. Behind him, Bill Newton said something about 'Oh, shit, the Skipper's lost his hat again' to his companion and started to look around the bar. The surge of bodies towards the door blocked his way. Why was it always he who had to find Mick's bloody hat?

Dinger found Mick standing across the road from the pub, looking down at the sheltered water at the foot of the hill. The moon was rising above the hills across the water. The harbour was calm. No light came from the houses off to their right, although there was a chink of light to be seen from a cottage lower down. Men were making their noisy way down the lane, down towards the base. Home. A few wooden huts hurriedly constructed eighteen months before. Freezing cold in winter. Roofs leaked in the rain. Not much privacy. But a good bunch of mates.

*

In another land, in another bar, another girl washed up the last of the glasses. The Germans had gone. The tables were cleared, their tops wiped. A slight haze of cigar smoke still lingered. Yvette wiped her hands dry. At last, all was done.

She ran her fingers through her hair and paused for a moment, hands clasped behind her head. Slowly she stretched and yawned. But her night was not yet finished. Not quite. She could hear Monsieur Albert moving about in the cellar below. It was time. She turned to the door behind the bar and pushed it open.

The man was sitting there as always, a glass before him. She knew him just as L'Hibou, the Owl. An appropriate name as he had large, round spectacles. He nodded as she came in. Yvette took the chair opposite him and sat down. Without waiting for any preliminaries, she started to speak. Yvette, 19-year-old daughter of a French father and half German mother, brought up in Strasbourg who used to visit her German grandmother across the border until she died, Yvette the fluent German speaker, told the man, in low whispers, what she had heard discussed by the Germans in the bar over the last week. She had a good memory. So did he. He wrote nothing down — it was all committed to memory. Then the Resistance presumably, somehow, got the information back to England.

Tomorrow she would have to go to the market. She would have to run the gauntlet of the whispers behind her back. '*Quelle coquette!*' might be the mildest she would hear. '*Colla-boratrice!*' certainly. And whispers about 'How is she in bed with the German swine?' 'More like a rabbit than a sow, I hear. Always at it!' In fact, this small, dark, rather plain girl had never been to bed with a German. One day, she would hold her head high when all was told, when this dreadful war was over. Meanwhile she would accept being spat at, being taunted, defiled. Quietly she talked on as the man sat and listened.

II

Although it was early in the morning, Peter Tomkins was at his desk. Get the business of the day done early, that was one of his mottoes. His office might have been at the end of a hastily constructed wooden hut which offered the barest of amenities but, within his private sanctum, all was neat and tidy. He was a meticulous man. His desk was carefully arranged, with In and Out trays. He prided himself on not having a Pending tray. Do it now, was another motto. A small set of bookshelves contained reference books, a dictionary, a bible, a book of quotations and an atlas, plus Air Force manuals, King's Regulations, pilot's notes and so on. They were arranged in order of size, tallest on the outside, shortest in the middle, like men on parade. On the walls were photographs, photographs of aircraft, of groups of men posed in front of aircraft, and one of a dog.

He sat at his desk, bolt upright in his chair. Even seated, it was easy to see that he was a tall man, thin but with rather large and angular features. His nose was particularly prominent and he had rather narrow-set eyes. He was not a handsome man. Before him was the routine paperwork of the squadron. He picked up the record sheets for the squadron's pick-up truck, maid of all work. Of course, there was a base transport pool but this pick-up was for the exclusive use of the squadron. He noted that the sheets had been neatly filled in, the mileages carefully entered, all journeys logged. To him, such a document was indicative of efficient administration. What he would never understand was that most of it was a pack of lies.

'Hey, Nobby, when you go up to the station, turn off and call in at Smith's farm will you and see if they've got those chickens for the sergeants' mess.'

'OK, Sarge, but what about me log sheets?'

'Don't worry, my son, we'll just put it down as an extra trip for luboil. The mileage is about the same. I'll fudge the times for you, don't worry.'

He signed the sheets and placed them carefully in the out-tray. Next were some stores requisitions. A demand for engine spark plugs. Priority. It needed the CO's signature. He signed. Must keep the supply of spark plugs flowing. What he did not know was that the transaction was already complete.

'Nick, this is Spike here. Look we've got a crisis with plugs. If I send the van over, can you let me have some?'

'I'm a bit tight myself but I could let you have six sets. How would that do?'

'Marvellous. If you're happy, we'll square the paper work later.'

'Sure. Just get your boss to sign and send the forms over in the next few days.'

For Peter Tomkins had been brought up in a cloistered environment. Prep school, public school, holidays with his family, then straight into the Air Force. He did not understand men who were not from the same background as himself. He did not understand the ways of the men of his squadron. He did not understand the way they did things largely through personal contact, by knowing someone who . . . by a bit of wheeling and dealing. For him, it was done through official channels, by the book. His men did not work like that. He would never know that the paperwork which crossed his desk was just the tip of an iceberg, a small sample just to keep him happy, whilst his officers and men got on and ran their particular parts of the squadron largely without his help or guidance.

Next in the small pile of papers was the form giving the details of a man who had been charged with being absent without leave. Tomkins had dealt with the case two days before. He felt he had heard all sides of the story, listened to the man's excuses for being late back from his leave, heard what his superior officer had had to say about him and he was proud of the fact that he took infinite care over such matters. The man had been dealt with fairly. The punishment was also fair.

What Tomkins did not know was the reaction of the warrant officer who had brought the charge, discussing it in his mess afterwards. 'What a palaver! You'd think the CO was trying a murder case at the Old Bailey instead of an open and shut case of absent without leave. Ages, he took. Could have been done in five minutes. I shan't bloody well bother next time. . . .'

There was a knock at the door. 'Come!' called Tomkins. He knew who it would be – Smiley, the Operations Officer. It was a daily ritual, except when Tomkins was flying. Smiley entered.

'Good morning, Ops. Do sit down.'

'Thank you, sir.' It was the same each time. Very formal. No. 'Hello, Dickie, how are you?' just 'Good morning, Ops.'

Smiley placed the flying programme on the CO's desk. It was a list of all the sorties Group had ordered for the next twenty-four hours, by squadron. Then, against their own squadron's allocation, Smiley had pencilled in his suggested allocation of aircraft and crews. He took into account who had flown what sorties recently, to ensure each crew got their fair share, that one crew was not always doing the night take-offs for a dawn on-task and so on. It was comparatively easy, just cycling through the crews. From time to time, a new crew would join. Crews dropped out of the roster. Some had finished their tours. Some, sadly, just failed to come back from a trip.

Tomkins picked up the list and studied it carefully. He checked to see what the other squadrons were doing, although the allocations were always similar. The Liberator squadrons would get the convoys furthest from UK, out in the Atlantic. They had the range. The Sunderlands worked a bit closer in, as the convoys neared British shores. And the Sunderlands also took the brunt of the patrols in the Bay, the Bay of Biscay. His squadron knew the Bay well. He went carefully down Smiley's allocation of crews to sorties. Smiley knew he would change something. He always did. That is why the plan was in pencil. Tomkins did it because he thought it showed he was taking a close interest. It annoyed Smiley intensely every time Tomkins reached for his rubber and pencil, but he said nothing.

'Ops, I'd just like to change a couple of names. I'll take the early sortie in the Bay tomorrow morning.' Now this did surprise Smiley, for the sortie was due to brief at 0130 for a

0330 take-off. A bastard of a trip. All the way down the Bay, almost to the Spanish coast, and back. What he did not know was that the only reason Tomkins was taking it was so he could be back in time for the Commodore's dinner party.

It was going to be a combined Navy and Air Force do. The local naval commodore was hosting it. Some of the brass from Group would be there. 'Ah, Tomkins, how's that squadron of yours? Not working your chaps too hard, are we?'

'No, of course not, sir. We can hack it. As a matter of fact, I've just got back from a trip myself. All the way down the Bay.'

'Splendid, splendid. Now, tell me, what ideas have you chaps got for finding these damn U-boats. . . .'

The other advantage of putting himself down for that trip was that it was a long one. Long trips put up the flying hours more quickly. 'Tomkins, you've done your share, done your hours. We need chaps like you on the staff at Group. . . .' For Tomkins saw command of a squadron as an interlude in his career, a very necessary one but he knew his place was on the Staff. A job at Group, then perhaps in the Air Ministry. Promotion, hopefully.

He finished changing the allocations on the list and handed it back to Smiley. Only then did he first refer to the morning's biggest problem, the fog. It was really only early morning mist. The sun would burn it off later. But, with high pressure sitting just to the west of Britain, the air was slack and conditions ideal for fog and mist patches. 'Did this morning's sorties get away on time?'

'No, sir. They went out to the aircraft but they are still swinging round the moorings waiting for a break in the weather.'

'Right. Well, as soon as the weather breaks, they must be away. I expect the sun will burn through shortly. Make it clear over the radio that they must go as soon as they can.'

Smiley just nodded. It was, as the saying goes, teaching Granny to suck eggs. None of the crews liked swinging round the buoys waiting to go. They were all keyed up, nerves a bit twitched. There was nothing worse than waiting. They would go as soon as they could. 'Is there anything else, sir?'

'No, Ops, that's all, thank you.'

Richard Smiley, veteran of the First World War, who now

walked with a limp from a leg injury – but who was the father confessor, comforter, adviser, consoler to the young pilots and navigators, known throughout the squadron, except to Tomkins, as Uncle Dickie, ten years older than Tomkins, recalled to do his bit in this war too – left the room.

*

Jilly Johnson opened the door of the Ops Room and stepped out into the chill, misty morning. It had been a long watch. Slowly she made her way back through the rows of huts towards the female accommodation. WAAFS and Wrens shared a hut. When the base had grown from an occasional stopping place for Channel escorts and patrol craft to a Sunderland and MTB base, the brass had decided to set up a joint Ops Room. 'No point in having two Ops Rooms, old boy. You run your Sunderlands, we'll look after the MTBs. We'll get some Wrens in too. They can help out.'

There were only eight of them, eight girls from a wide variety of backgrounds who wanted to do their bit, who had volunteered for the Wrens. 'What do you want to go into the Wrens for, my girl?' She could hear her father even now, in his broad Yorkshire accent, one evening after he'd cleaned up from his day in the pit. 'The only time you've seen the sea is a day trip to Bridlington.' What he did not know was that she saw it as an opportunity to break out of the stifling existence of a small pit village, to see the world maybe. Well, Cornwall was not quite seeing the world but it was a long way from Yorkshire.

She pushed open the door of the hut. The room was in its usual state at this time of the morning. Some occupants had already left, one of them being the girl who had relieved Jilly on watch. Janet, who had shared the long night in the Ops Room, was getting ready to get into bed. Irene and Linda were just getting up.

'Ah, here she is. And how was your night out last night?' Irene always wanted to know what everyone had been up to. 'How was the handsome Sergeant Williams?'

'Fine, thank you,' answered Jilly noncommittally.

'Ooooh, please yourself,' said Irene with a bit of a huff, and headed for the bathroom.

As soon as she had gone, Jilly stepped across to her locker, opened the top drawer and pulled out a pair of garters. 'Thanks!' she called as she tossed them across the room to Linda, who was just wrapping a dressing gown around herself.

'Is that John Williams, the dark one with very blue eyes?' Linda asked in a whisper so Irene in the bathroom would not hear.

'Mmmm.'

'Ooooh, you naughty girl. He's scrummy. He can get his hands on my tits anytime.' She giggled. 'When you've finished with him, chuck him over to me.' She giggled again, winked at Jilly and herself headed off for the bathroom.

Jilly was glad they had gone, for a moment. She was not used to living so closely with other girls. She only had brothers at home. Did girls always talk like this about men? Then she realised Janet was still there, in the corner behind the lockers, putting her shoes away. But Janet was very quiet. It was Irene that was always talking, always prying. Linda was OK. Bit coarse at times but OK. Slowly she undid the buttons of her jacket. It had been a long night. What would her mother say about what she had been up to?

*

Dawn on the Biscay coast of France came, by the laws of the motion of the sun, twelve minutes earlier than in Cornwall. This morning it had made no difference. You could not see the sun coming up. Forthe coast of France was also influenced by the same high pressure that lingered out in the Atlantic. The coastal fog and mist did, in fact, stretch from south Wales all the way almost to the Gironde.

The moisture in the air clung to his running vest as Bruckner continued on round the perimeter track. His breathing was steady, the rhythm of his legs constant, his arms moving easily as he ran. He was a good runner, always had been. No war was going to stop that. A man could find time to run. If it had to be in the early morning, so be it. There was a slight rise in the wide concrete track ahead, almost imperceptible in the poor visibility. But the slight change in effort required to keep up the steady pace told him he was climbing. He did not yet know the airfield well enough for, if he did, he would have known that this particular rise needed just a bit more throttle when taxiing. But if you were not careful to take off the throttle at the top, the dip on the other side caught you unawares. This might be a flattish corner of France but the war time rush to build the airfield had not allowed time to level out such minor perturbations.

When was he going to get an operational sortie? He had been here, what, six days now. Six days of practice flying, of circuits, of formation flying, of gunnery practice. He wanted to get on with operational flying. It was what he had volunteered to do. Coming to a Staffel stuck out in the wilds of western France was not quite what he had in mind. What do they do out there? Shoot down Sunderlands and Liberators and Whitleys. Is that all? It's not so easy, my friend, you'll see. Anyway, why do you wish to leave the Führer's service and return to operational flying? It is a great honour to fly for the Führer. I appreciate that but I feel it is my duty to fight for the Fatherland. What he had not told them was that it was starting to become embarrassing with the smart women of Berlin. And what do you do? I fly in the Führer's personal service. Oh, is that all? Why aren't you at the front, earning some medals? He was very conscious of the fact that he had only a Polish campaign medal. That did not count for much these days.

He reached the furthest point of the airfield. The perimeter track turned through ninety degrees and crossed the end of runway 24. Bruckner pounded on down the long straight, the next corner hidden in the mist. There would be no flying for a few hours yet, not until the mist had gone.

*

Whilst there was something of a lull in the affairs of two air bases, one in France, one in Cornwall, another group of men were wondering if they would ever see land again. Two hundred and fifty miles west of Finisterre, in the grey light of another dawn, but one not affected by mist or fog, a U-boat staggered to the surface. A welter of foam poured from her casing, from around the bridge, as the last of the compressed air remaining in her air bottles forced the water from her ballast tanks.

As the water cascaded from the drain holes around the

bridge deck, the upper lid crashed open and the captain scrambled up. Behind him, ignoring the last of the water on the deck around them, came the officer of the watch and two lookouts. Below them, at the foot of the ladder, poised, were the guns' crews. The captain took a quick look around. Nothing. He put his binoculars to his eyes and swept the sea out to the horizon. He did it twice. Behind him, the other men did the same, taking their allotted sectors. They swept the skies above as well. Only after a minute was the silence broken, by a single word. *'Gut!'* declared the captain.

At the captain's word, the officer of the watch gave a crisp order and the gun's crews scrambled up the ladder and moved swiftly to man their guns. Quickly the 37 mm and 20 mm anti-aircraft guns were made ready. Now they were committed to remaining on the surface, aircraft were the biggest threat. And with the cloud down quite low, as it was, an aircraft could appear without warning at any time.

Below, men were staggering back into activity. After the nightmare hours after the attack on the convoy, with depth charges raining down around them, the men were exhausted. In U-boat terms, they had not been held down for long by the escorts. It was the damage that had been done which had driven the men to the limit. Foul fumes filled the submarine. Broken glass crunched underfoot. Water swilled around the decks, mixing with the oil from the numerous hydraulic leaks, making movement treacherous. The attacks had been short but devastating. Only by using valuable reserves of battery had the captain wriggled them clear so, at last, the depth charges dropped further away and then petered out. Only by using precious air to blow the tanks with the main vents open to create giant air bubbles in the sea had they managed to confuse the asdic operators in the escorts above. And now these precious reserves were gone. The last of the air had pushed them to the surface. They would need to run the compressors to fill the air bottles again. But, only now, the engineers were finding that neither air compressor would run up. They had no means of replenishing the compressed air. And without compressed air, they could not dive again.

But the diesels were intact. A cooling water leak here, a small fuel leak there, but nothing to prevent them starting. As the first one burst into life, the rocker gear on the cylinder heads building up momentum as the pistons below moved in their cylinders, the injectors sprayed the first of the fuel, and the engine fired. Great draughts of clean air were sucked down the tower and through the submarine. Men vomited at the sudden change in the atmosphere. Above them, on the bridge, six men had already been sick.

The captain checked that all was well on the bridge, that the gun's had not been damaged, that their defences were intact. A quick burst from each gun, kicking up a line of spray in the sea a hundred metres away, had ensured all was well. Then he wearily descended the ladder to the shambles of a control room. His navigator was hunched over the chart table. As the captain appeared at his side, the navigator had only one question. The captain answered it before it was asked. 'No sun.'

Without a sun sight, they would have to rely on dead reckoning. Well, was nothing new in the grey wastes of the Atlantic. But down here, at 44 degrees north, surely there should be a glimmer of summer, a chance of some sun?

The two men leaned over the chart, a battered chart with oil stains and dirty marks on it. A line ran across it, a bold pencil line, due east across two hundred and fifty miles of open sea until it almost joined the coast of Spain. From there it zigged slightly north to parallel the northern coast for another hundred miles. Then it struck boldly north east, cutting the corner of the Bay, towards the mouth of the Gironde, towards Bordeaux, towards sanctuary.

The navigator had his pencil on a spot just north of the north-western tip of Spain. It represented the end of the first leg of their journey home. 'Twenty-fours, Captain.' The bearded, old, weary, hardened, veteran of twenty-four at his side nodded. The captain knew the dangers of the Bay, knew of the air patrols by the British, had dodged the patrolling aircraft before. Could they do it again?

III

For Mick the mist and fog was not a problem, was not a feature of his day. By the time he was up, late in the morning, it was a warm spring day with glimpses of sun through scattered, medium level cloud. He wandered slowly over towards the mess. It was about the only good thing about this base, the mess. For the base stood in the grounds of what had been a lovely house overlooking the sheltered waters where the aircraft swung at their moorings. It still was a lovely house, on a slight rise above the beach. The huts occupied the slightly lower ground and then, down by what had been a fine sweep of sandy beach, was the maintenance area, the slip for pulling the aircraft out of the water, the small jetty for the tenders which ran backwards and forwards between the aircraft and the shore. Further along was the navy's pier, with eight or so MTBs alongside, their ensigns hanging limp in the still morning air. It was the warm sun which had evaporated the mist. There was still not a breath of wind.

It was early for lunch but the bar had just opened. There were a couple of brand new chaps just coming in but Mick ignored them. He ordered just a half and took it out through the French windows onto the lawn. The garden chairs were out, for the first time that year. It was warm enough to sit out so he selected a seat on the far edge of the lawn, looking down towards the water, perched his half on the arm of the wooden bench and sat down. Not a bad spot, seen from here. The Sunderlands were in a neat line at their buoys, a line broken by the gaps left by aircraft which were on a sortie or by the one which was up on the beach for maintenance. The aircraft on the water were in a neat formation, all swinging to the tide so that they formed a smart echelon port. Pity about the gaps. Close up, No. 3. Get in closer! The thought took him back to his flying training days. Hell, it seemed a long time ago. Look at him now. Sunderland pilot. Sunderland captain indeed. Insurance clerk to Sunderland captain. That's what wars did for you. He'd never go back to an office when this lot was over. But would they want flying boat skippers after the war? Who could tell. Let's get the bloody war finished first.

A tender was heading out towards one of the Sunderlands. He could see men working on one of the engines. They were perched out over the water, working on the small platforms which let down from the leading edge of the wing. Dead clever, the bloke who thought of that. The platform was a neat arrangement, fitting flush into the wing when not required but forming a couple of steps and a working platform so a mechanic could step down off the wing to get at the guts of an engine. Bloody cold out there in the winter. Bastard of a job. He'd seen them rigging planks between platforms so they could get under an engine. Dead dodgy, that one. But much quicker than pulling an aircraft up onto the slip to work on. The men leaning over the engine had spotted the tender, coming to pick them up for dinner. They stowed their tools in their boxes, pulled down the engine cowling and climbed onto the wing to make their way back along to the flight deck hatch, to climb inside and down to the door where the tender would come alongside. It was so still he could even hear them calling to each other.

Mick had enjoyed his lazy morning. He had known the day before that he would not be flying until at least the evening. Despite the official programme which had to be endorsed by the CO, Uncle Dickie kept them informed of what was likely to happen. 'Mick, you should be OK if you want a few beers at the pub tonight. I shouldn't need you until at least late tomorrow.' 'Oh, good on yer, Dickie, thanks.'

Thank God that system of Tomkins' about hours off after flying had died a death. So many hours rest after a sortie, depending on the time of day and length of sortie. Then he had expected the crews to be up and about. It had not worked. You couldn't regulate the men like that. There were some trips where you got back absolutely knackered and wanted to crawl into bed. There were others where you wanted to have a few quiet drinks with your mates first. There were other times when a party developed and then you crawled away to bed in the small hours. Tomkins soon got the message. But woe betide anyone in Mick's crew who was ever the worse for wear, or lack of sleep, come the start of a sortie. It had happened once. One of the gunners had been to a birthday celebration in the pub. Early next morning he was in no condition to fly. They left him behind. But when they got back, the senior gunner had taken him quietly round the back of the hut. 'How did you get that black eye, son?' 'Walked into a door, sir?' More like a sergeant's fist.

The peace of the scene before him was shattered by the sound of an engine running up. One of the aircraft was swinging at the mooring as the pull of the newly-started engine spoilt the symmetry of the formation of aircraft, pulled the Sunderland out of line. The revs went up and down a bit, steadied for a while then died. Just the ground staff doing a check. Down at the pier, the tender had arrived back from picking up the small group who had been working on the other aircraft. Now it was waiting for a whole crew who were walking together down from the huts towards the pier. The next sortie was preparing to go. It would be a while before they would actually be on their way. It took a long time to get a Sunderland ready.

As he sipped slowly at his half, his gaze wandered over this peaceful spot. It must have been great here before the war. Wide, sheltered waters. Ideal for sailing. A long expanse of water. Pity it did not point in quite the right direction. The longest run was nearly always slightly across the wind. But you got used to that. And you had to be a bit careful coming in over the low hills to the north. Better to come down the valley and turn onto finals as you came over the last point of land. And if the cloud was low, let down over the sea and then come in at low level. If necessary fly all the way up the harbour, stand on one wing tip at the other end and land from there. Some of the hills just a couple of miles inland went up to 350 feet or so. Stay above 500. Give yourself a bit of a margin. Allow for altimeter setting errors. Allow for a tired pilot. Yeah, come in from the sea low down if the weather clamped. But not today. Today was OK.

Across the water, the green rolling hills of Cornwall rose to country which time seemed to have passed by. Forget the

Sunderlands at their moorings, the MTBs at their jetty and the scene might not have changed for a hundred years. The small villages, the cottages, the narrow lanes and small fields. It was a good land. Pity about the winters. Hell, I could be flying bombers. Probably be dead by now. If not, I'd have frozen my arse off stuck up there in East Anglia, in Lincoln, in Yorkshire. He'd been there once. In January. Bloody cold wind from the east. They said it came all the way from Siberia without a stop. Felt like it too. Russia's secret weapon. That's what the Germans had found out.

'Penny for them.' The voice brought Mick back from his day dreaming.

'What? Oh, hello Dinger, old mate. Nice day, i'n'it?'

'Want another?' asked Dinger, nodding to Mick's glass.

'No. I guess we're on sometime. Any news?'

'Oh, yeah. Dickie says we're briefing at 0100 for a 0300 take-off.'

'Oh, shit! What a bastard. Still it's a while since we've done one of those. Any idea where we are going?'

'Convoy out west.'

'Great. Cushy ride. No sweat. No, I won't have another, thanks, Dinger.'

So Dinger made his way across the lawn and in through the French windows. The bar was starting to fill. Others were coming out onto the lawn.

'Hello, Mick. I heard you setting the world to rights last night.' It was Frank who had also been in the pub the night before.

'What, me mate? Never 'appen. Few quiet beers with me mate Dinger. Quiet discussion of the ways of the world, an appraisal of the political situation, that's all.'

'Yeah, sure thing Mick. Now, can I buy you a beer?'

'Sure. A Foster's would go down well right now.' They both laughed. Frank knew Mick's opinion of English beer. 'Yeah, a real, cold Fosters with frost on the glass, sitting at the back of some Aussie beach would go down a treat. Know what I mean?'

'Certainly do, Mick, certainly do. My Susan back home says they've had a real scorcher of a summer. Down on the beach most days, she was. I'm glad. It's no fun for her with two young kids to bring up on her own. She's finding it tough but she's managing.'

Mick just nodded but said nothing. He did not really understand the problems of the family men, for he was not married. He didn't have any parents even to drop him the odd letter. They had both died a couple of years earlier. Pretty young they were really. Sad. Aussie he might be, but home, just for the moment, was here.

*

'Come in, Hans.' Another squadron commander was in his small office seeing to the administration of his men and their aircraft. Helmut Schafer stood as his engineer came in, indicated the chair the other side of the desk and sat down as Hans sat down.

'What's the damage?'

'Port undercarriage a write-off. We'll have to change the complete unit. Wing tip a bit bent but we can sort that. Otherwise, nothing else.'

'How long?' asked Helmut.

'We think we have the parts. If so, twenty-four hours.'

'Twenty-four hours! Hell, you've changed an undercart in half a day before now.'

'Yes, yes, we have. But I've got men working long hours on the engines. I can give you an aircraft with the engine mods complete faster than I can do an undercarriage change. Bear with me, it's aircraft you want. I'll give them to you my way, if you'll let me.' There was a note of irritation in his voice, a note of 'get off my back'. Helmut let it go. He knew Hans too well. He was a good man.

'OK, Hans, OK. We'll do it your way. But Gruppe are putting the pressure on. We need all the aircraft we can get. How many tomorrow?'

'Eight.'

Helmut was about to question this figure. Eight! How could he fight the war with that number, with Gruppe wanting almost continuous cover. But, again, he let it go. Hans said eight so eight it would be. 'Right. We'll manage, Hans, we'll manage. Now, where's that young idiot?'

'He's outside.'

'OK, I'll let him stew for a bit longer. Thanks, Hans.' He nodded to indicate the exchange was at an end. As the engineer got up to leave, he turned back towards Schafer.

'Have you spoken to Bruckner yet, Helmut?'

'No, not yet, not yet.'

'I wish you would . . . real pain in the arse he is.' With that, he opened the door and stepped outside.

Helmut went back to his desk after seeing the engineer out. He had two interviews to deal with. The first would be short and one-sided. But he would let that clown Elman wait for a while. Then he would have to see Bruckner. Better, perhaps, just an informal chat. Not an interview in the office. A word in Bruckner's ear at some convenient moment. Problem was, he would probably have to make the moment.

He turned to look out of the window. He had a wide view across the airfield. He could see what was going on. He enjoyed watching the activity. He could see the runways stretching out across the undulating land. Off to the right he could see the hangars and the dispersal. And his men knew he could see what was happening from this window. The ballsed-up landing. The maintenance crew stopping for too long for a cigarette. The scruffy fire crew racing round the perimeter track in their wagon. OK if they were going to a crash. But they seemed to think that their job gave them the excuse to speed everywhere whether there was a crash or not, and to dress how they liked when not in their fire suits.

But his technique would have been a complete mystery to Tomkins. A quiet word hear, some encouragement there. Occasionally a short, sharp phone call, or interview. He might meet a pilot walking back to the mess 'My friend, your landing today, perhaps a little fast. . . . Slow down, get your speed right on finals. . . .' 'Hans, I know your men work long hours for us but perhaps they could finish the job sooner if they did not have to stop every five minutes for a cigarette?'

'Your bloody firemen nearly hit one of my aircraft racing round the field today. They're here to sort out crashes, not cause them! If I have to tell you again, I'll have your bollocks for a neck tie!'

Right, time to see Elman. He walked over to the door and

opened it. His clerk was at his desk outside in the outer office. 'Is Lieutenant Elman waiting?'

The clerk sprang to his feet. 'Yes, sir, he's just outside,' the man replied, indicating the outer door.

'Send him in!'

With that, he went back into his office, shutting the door behind him. Let the little bastard knock. He knew the feeling when you had to knock at the door of a superior, knowing you were in deep trouble. It had happened to him at school, more times than he would like to remember. It had happened when he wrote off an aircraft during training. Fortunately, the engineers had bailed him out. They had identified a problem with the fuel pump from the slightly shattered remains which he had managed to get into a ploughed field when his engine failed.

There was a knock at the door. A little too firm for his liking. A timid knock might have got a fatherly chat. A confident knock would get a firm dressing down.

'Enter!' The door opened and Lieutenant Elman entered, came smartly to attention and saluted. Schafer left him standing at attention. There was no 'Sit down, my boy.' Not with this one, he was too cocky.

'Your aircraft, Lieutenant Elman, will be out of action for twenty-four hours. We have enough difficulty stuck out here in a corner of France keeping aircraft serviceable without clowns like you writing-off an undercarriage. It's a big task. The engineers have enough to do without that sort of job. Next time you run off the taxiway and get bogged down, wait for the ground crew to come and tow you out. You know full well that trying to get the aircraft out by applying full power only puts a lot of strain on the undercarriage. It is not designed to take those sort of strains.' This was getting too long. Keep it short, sharp. 'Clear?' He did not give the other man time to answer. 'You are confined to the air station for a month, except for flying of course. You will have no leave. And tomorrow you will help the men finish putting a new undercart on your aircraft.'

The last bit would hurt. This lad did not like mixing it with the ground crew. He would learn the hard way. Helmut would have a word with Hans – make sure Elman had to get amongst it, get his hands dirty. It would do him no harm.

'*Jawohl!*' The man continued to stand at attention, his eyes on Schafer. Bloody hell, these ex-Hitler Youth really frightened him. They lived in a dream, the Führer's dream. Could they not see the realities of the world? He would make sure Hans put his biggest, most coarse, greasiest, smelliest mechanic to work alongside the upstart product of the Third Reich.

'Dismissed!' The man saluted and left.

Helmut turned back to the window. Two aircraft were taxiing out. The first pair away today. The sea mist had lingered all morning. Even now the visibility was not good. Two aircraft! They needed to be out there in fours, fives, more. Out over the Bay, looking for the prey. It was the law of the jungle out there. The U-boats preyed on the convoys. The Liberators, the Sunderlands preyed on the U-boats. And the Ju88s preyed on the English aircraft. Who would come along to prey on them? English fighters? Mosquitos? Now there was a thought. Mosquito versus Ju88 over the Bay. Bloody hell, what a bastard of a war! And they expect me to do it when I am down to eight aircraft. At least he had the crews. It did not take long to turn an aircraft round. He would have a word with Hans about speeding up refuelling, re-arming, topping up the oxygen. If they could turn round just a bit faster, they could improve the sortie rate over the Bay. He picked up his cap and made for the door. Time for a walk around.

*

Jilly Johnson was also out for a walk. She was down by the water, throwing stones. She picked up some flat ones and tried to skim them across the surface of the sea. Her throwing action was a bit awkward and the first one splashed once and disappeared from sight. She never could throw things. The second was better. Two skips and it sank. She was bored. She had managed a few hours sleep in the morning but the general bustle of the place made it difficult to sleep. Door banged, people shouted, an engine was run up for test. OK, the hours were long in the Ops Room, but it was interesting in there. After sleeping and eating and washing clothes and ironing, and baths and washing hair, and the very occasional evening out, there was not a lot of time left. But the time that was left could get very boring. She was not a great reader. She had never had much encouragement at home to read books. There were occasional films to watch in the canteen. There was the wireless. But it was the afternoons after a long night watch which were the problem. The winter had been even worse. At least now she could get out in the sun and walk down by the water. Perhaps they would be able to swim a bit later on? That would be nice. She had never really learned to swim properly. Splashing about in that filthy river at home had not been the best place to learn to swim. Perhaps one of the girls would teach her? Or even John Williams?

The thought of him sent tingles up her spine. She thought back to their brief hour in bed. They said he went to bed with lots of girls. Was she just another scalp on his belt? What the hell, it was fun. The other girls did it, or so they would have you believe. Was it true or did the others make up tales about what they had been up to? She was pretty certain Irene did. If Irene's stories were true, she would have been to bed with the whole camp, the way she went on about men. She wasn't sure what Linda got up to. It was Linda who had the silk underwear hidden away in her locker. It was Linda who had loaned her the garters. It was Linda who knew someone who knew someone who could get them nylon stockings. But poor Janet, she was so quiet. Very shy. She hardly knew how to talk to men or so it seemed. But hadn't she said something about seeing a bloke from stores? Jilly would have been very surprised to learn that, of the group she lived with, Irene was, in fact, still a virgin and Janet was two weeks pregnant. But then even Janet did not know that yet either.

Jilly walked on along the beach, along to the wide slip where they pulled the Sunderlands up for servicing. She had watched them do it one day. They fitted legs under the wings with wheels on the bottom and then towed the Sunderland in to the slip. There a rope was attached and they winched the aircraft slowly out of the water until a tractor could be hitched on. Then they towed it up onto the level area at the top of the slip. There was one there now, one engine missing. The engine was sitting in a cradle under the wing. Or perhaps that was a new one they were putting in. There was always chat about engine changes in the Ops Room. Perhaps this was one of them.

She was standing idly just looking at the Sunderland when a group of men appeared from round the front of it. It was half a dozen sailors, led by a RAF flight sergeant. The sailors would be from the MTBs. Groups came along from time to time to be shown a Sunderland. Airmen went to have a look at the MTBs. She had been to see one a couple of months before. As the sailors noticed the petite, auburn-haired Wren, there was a stirring of interest amongst them.

'Hello, love,' one of them called. The flight sergeant, however, did not pause in his commentary.

'. . . Sunderland Mark Three. Big bastard, i'nt it. Wing span one hundred and twelve feet. That's ten feet more than a Lancaster. Or put another way, you could park three Spitfires in line abreast across the top of the wings. Twenty-five tons of her when she's full of fuel and bombs and things.'

Jilly found herself on the edge of the group. One of the sailors gave her a grin and a wink. But the commentary continued: 'Three gun turrets, one in the nose, one on top, one in the tail. Four Bristol Pegasus engines, air cooled radials.' The group had moved round towards the door and was about to climb into the aircraft. Jilly decided to move on. She might not be welcomed by the sergeant if she climbed in with them. But just as she went, one of the sailors asked a question.

'Sarge, what are those things up on top?' He was pointing to the aerials sticking up above the top of the fuselage, above the tail section.

'Those, my son, are radio direction finders. Now let's climb inside.' The sailor accepted that answer and the group moved on. But Jilly knew that the sergeant had glossed over the true answer. She knew they were radar aerials, in fact ASV Mk II aerials. They were along the top of the fuselage and along the side as well. The main beams went out to the side of the aircraft. She also knew there were other aerials in the nose which looked ahead. She heard them talking about the radar quite a lot in the Ops Room. She was allowed to know about it. Perhaps the sergeant thought the sailors should not?

She left the small group to continue their tour and turned

to walk back towards her hut. She must write to her parents.
She had been putting it off for too long. If only they would
write more frequently!

*

'Ah, Bruckner! I'm glad I've found you. You'll be flying
operationally tomorrow.' Helmut had found him in the crew
room, carefully reading through intelligence reports.

'Good. Thank you. I was getting tired of waiting,' Bruckner
replied rather curtly. Was there a touch of insolence in his
voice?

'Now, my friend. How are you finding life here?' He did not
wait for a response but went straight on. 'A bit of a change
from your last job, I expect?' He raised an inquiring eyebrow
but again did not pause long enough for Bruckner to answer.
'You will find things rather different here. We are a long way
from the supply bases. We have to make do with what we have
got. We also have a war to fight here. So maybe our aircraft are
not all bright and shining. Perhaps they are a bit tarnished
here, a scratch there. We have to put up with that, my friend.
We concentrate on the main things. Instruments. Flying
controls. Engines. Guns. The rest is unimportant. Remember
that when the mechanics have been sweating to turn your
aircraft round. Forget the gloss. You only need the essentials.
We are not here to transport VIPs around. We are here to get
out there,' he was pointing towards the sea, 'and shoot down
Tommies. That's all. We don't have parades, we do not line the
aircraft up in nice straight lines, we do not wear our best
uniforms. We are here to fight a war.' He had kept his tone
mild, his manner friendly as he chatted. Surely this Prussian
would understand? Or would he really have to spell it out for
him?

'Very well,' was the only response he got. 'And when will I be
flying?' At least Bruckner appeared keen to start operations.

'Ummm, probably tormorrow afternoon. Check the flying
schedule this evening. We'll know how many aircraft there will
be by then.'

'Jawohl!' Bruckner gave a curt nod and made to leave the
room. Hell, who was in charge here? thought Helmut to
himself. But he let the other man go. Probably a mistake. Oh,

balls, there were other things to worry about besides a stuck-up Prussian pilot. Time for a call at the met office, see if those clowns were going to produce sea fog again in the morning.

*

In England the met men would say that the chances of sea fog were remote. There was a slight breeze from the east. The indications were that the high pressure was drifting north-east and that an easterly air flow would set in along the English Channel and across France. But Mick Hargan was not concerning himself with such things yet. That would come later, at the briefing.

He was more concerned about the gnawing feeling in his stomach, the cold sweat on his hands, the twitch in his left eye. Pre-sorties nerves, that was all. But he had never felt this bad before. Bloody hell, mate, cushy trip this one. Out to the west, stooge around a convoy for a while, motor back home. No dicing with effing Junkers in the Bay. No wondering if you'll come across a U-boat on the surface who'll start shooting back instead of diving the hell out of it. If you find a U-boat round a convoy, he's not going to hang around on the surface 'cos he knows you're going to call in the Fifth Cavalry from the surface escorts. So what are you getting so bloody twitched about? You've done it all before.

That's the bloody trouble. I've done it before too many times. How many trips was it? Twenty-six times, mate. Two hundred and sixty-two hours. Near enough ten hours a trip, on average. Some were long, some were short. But near enough ten hours a time. And now they wanted him to do it again. How many more times? He'd done his bit over the last few months, when Group had piled on the pressure. First there was Operation Enclose. Then there was Enclose II. Then Derange. Who the hell thought of a name like that? Hour after hour they'd been out there, Sunderlands, Wellingtons, Liberators, Halifaxes. Someone had said something about some of them having a new sort of radar. But they plodded on with ASV Mk II. They did their bit. Down the Bay. Keep your eyes skinned, lads, there might be Ju88s about. Oh, while you've doing that, watch out for U-boats too. That's what we're really here for. All part of the big picture. Keep the pressure on the Jerries. We won't get a U-boat. It's always some other bastard. But we'll play our part.

Come on, Mick, not you getting the twitch? You, the great Australian character? Just give us a decent beer and we'll hack the bastards. Stuff your Pommie pricks. We Aussies can do our bit. We'll win the war for you. Colonials you may call us but we'll go out there and find U-boats for you. And sink the bastards.

It didn't quite work out like that. Long hours, just looking. I've had a go at one for you, Pommie bastards. But he saw us coming and dived out of the way in plenty of time. I dropped me depth charges and made a bloody great bang. They called it a 'possible'. I know I didn't get him but it must have rattled his coffee cups. Did they drink coffee in U-boats? he wondered.

It was no good lying down like this, trying to get a couple of hours sleep early in the evening. Hell, the sun wasn't even down yet. You've tried it before when on a night trip, tried to get in a couple of hours. Never works. And here you are, sweating, getting twitched. But when were the buggers going to say, 'Mick Hargan, you've done your bit, done your tour. Take a break, mate. We can fight the war without you going down the Bay again. It's someone else's turn now.' When were they going to say that?

Meanwhile, Mick, old son, you are going to have to keep on going out there. You're the skipper. The lads look to you to show the way. What would they think if they saw old Mick had the twitch? It's called leadership, mate. That's why they put stripes on your shoulder. King's Commission and all that. All so you can go out there and pretend to be brave and convince a bunch of young lads a long way from home to be brave as well. And what's it all for? Who is winning this bloody war anyway. It's starting to look a bit better, admittedly. Monty's chased the Afrika Korps halfway across North Africa. The Russkies have stopped the Jerries short of Moscow. They tell us we're bombing the shit out of Germany. But what about the Atlantic? Sink a few U-boats but more keep bobbing up. Ships are still getting sunk. Where do all the bloody U-boats come from? They don't seem to be getting any fewer. And we're the

poor bastards who've got to go out there looking for them.
Don't mind that. Take on a U-boat any day. It's those runs
down the Bay that get me. Wondering when a bunch of Jerry
fighters is going to appear out of the clouds and shoot your
arse off. All that way down the Bay, France not too far away to
the east. Jerry fighters stooging around. Aircraft missing.
Guys not coming back from trips. One day you know a bunch
of boys. Next day they don't make it back. There's a gap in the
list of aircraft on the stateboard. Just rub out the aircraft
number – it's only in chalk anyway. Not meant to be permanent. Aircraft are expendable. So are the crews. There's a
war on. People get killed. But not me, someone else.

'Bollocks!' Mick climbed from his bunk, slipped on his
shoes, tightened up his tie, ran his fingers through his hair. No
point in lying here worrying about it all. Waste of time trying
to get a couple of hours in. Go over to the mess. See some
mates. A glass of orange squash. Bit of a chat. Real sods, these
0100 briefs. No chance of any sleep but all bloody evening to
think about the trip. Do it with some mates. Might even listen
to something on the wireless . . . Mick threw open the door of
the small room which was home, grabbed his cap and stuck it
on the back of his head. Slamming the door noisily behind
him, he set off at a brisk pace for the mess.

*

The sun was below the horizon. Night was coming. Would it be
a shield? Four men clustered on the bridge of the U-boat
wondered what the night would bring. The captain stood
slightly apart from the officer of the watch and the lookouts,
leaning over the side of the bridge, watching the bows lifting to
the sea. A wave caught the side of the bow as it rose, hung for a
moment and then cascaded across the submarine's casing. But
it was a kind sea. There was hardly any wind, a gentle breeze
from the south-east and the motion of the boat was more from
the low swell coming from the west, from the wide open
Atlantic. White water ran along the side of the submarine, an
ever changing pattern of swirls and eddies where the submarine cut its way through the sea. The bow dipped into the next
wave, throwing water in an arc out on either side, and then the
bows lifted again and the submarine shrugged off that wave,

ready for the next one. How many hours, how many waves, how many miles until they could stop, until they could say 'Finished with main engines', until the men on the casing could secure the final line which would attach them to the land?

Below, the chaos of the morning was turning into some form of order. The men had worked without a break. The mess was cleared up, water pumped over the side, oil leaks tightened up, broken lamps replaced. The diesels thundered on, their minor leaks cured. But back aft the air compressors were both in pieces. Neither of them would run again on their own. But make a whole out of the remains of the two and they might get a working compressor. Then they could put the vital air back in the bottles. And then they would be able to dive again if threatened. But for now, they were committed to remaining on the surface. Dive again and they had no reserves of air with which to surface. They had tried to think of ways of doing it, but it didn't work. There was no other way but to compress air into the huge air bottles fitted in groups around the submarine. That was the only way.

So the guns' crew remained closed up, men changing round every so often. They backed up the lookouts, watching the skies above, guns cocked, waiting . . . waiting for an aircraft to appear out of the cloud and descend on them. But that should not happen without warning, for the aircraft had to see them first. It had to see them either by eye, in which case the U-boat should see the aircraft too, or by radar. And they should know if there was a radar looking for them, for above their heads, fixed to a raised periscope, was the *Biskayakreuz* – the Biscay cross, a simple wooden frame with an aerial on it. The aerial was for the Metox receiver, designed to detect the transmissions from the radar of hunting aircraft, in the 113–500 Mhz band. ASV Mk II transmitted in that band. The U-boat would have warning of the approach of an aircraft. Or that was the theory. The captain did not know it, because they had been at sea too long, but there was talk back in the submarine bases along the French coast of aircraft appearing without warning at night, homing in accurately on the surfaced U-boats. A few had lived to tell the tale. How many had not? How many had found their final moments consisted of an aircraft roaring across the sea at them, pointing straight at them, a bright light coming on at the last moment to illuminate the startled men on the bridge and then depth charges raining down on them, to explode, to crush, to shatter, to end their days? Some had survived to tell the tale and now the scientists were saying that perhaps the Tommies had changed the frequency of their radar? There was a whisper that, perhaps, the Metox equipment was radiating some weak transmission which the aircraft could pick up. But these uncertainties were talked about in hushed terms ashore, and only in the last few weeks, the weeks since the U-boat had sailed.

So a lonely man, the captain, stood on his bridge and pondered these thoughts and hoped and prayed, if there still was a God, that the simple cross above their heads would protect them through the night, a night in which the coast of France grew nearer at the rate of ten miles every hour, a night in which the coast of Spain would draw abeam, unseen to the south, a night in which they might run across some Spanish fishing vessels, which would be a blessing for a fishing vessel looked much the same as a U-boat on a radar screen. But he was alone in his worries, his concerns, his responsibility for these men. They toiled for him, they swore, they cursed, they fixed things, they cleaned up, they worked away on the compressors, individuals working for the common good, small teams working together to solve problems, guns' crews chatting quietly whilst their eyes scanned the skies, all for him, for themselves, for the crew, and to save their own skins.

*

The peace was shattered by the roar of Packard engines bursting into life. Night had fallen. It was time for the MTBs to be about their business. Time for them to set out across the Channel towards the French coast, to seek and probe around the coast of Brittany, to take the war to the enemy's waters. Tonight they were later than normal. Normally they would be away before night had fallen. But they had just had two days in harbour for maintenance. Thus they had made full use of the daylight to do those thousand and one things that needed doing. Apart from maintenance of the engines, plugs to change, oil filters to clean, cooling water strainers to remove and check, there were guns to clean, torpedoes to charge, a radio aerial to change, a new mounting for a machine gun to fix, a compass repeat to move 'cos that's where the Skipper wants it, and no arguing. A spot of paint here, a bit of varnish there, not so much to look smart, more to preserve the wood of the hull and decks.

Now it was time to go hunting. One by one the lines were let go and the boats manoeuvred slowly out astern, picking their way carefully out into the more open waters, there to form up into two lines and head down harbour. In the very last of the light, their bow waves stood out, smudges on the darkness of the sea. The sound of their engines came across the water, thirty-one engines in unison. There should have been thirty-two but one engine had a fuel pump problem. Four per boat at a 1000 revs. Just ticking over. 12 knots. Wait until we do thirty. Then you'll see us go. But we don't go to France like that otherwise we'll never get back, 'cos thirty knots really burns the juice. So we'll motor over at a steady twenty-one or so. Four and a half hours should see us in the convoy route along the Brittany coast. We'll sweep along to the east for a couple of hours. Find what we find. Coastal convoy. E-boats. Minelayers. Patrol craft. Take on what we find. I mean, it's eight of us against them. 'Cept if it's E-boats there might be eight of them. Then we'll run for home before the dawn, put a few tens of miles between us and the fighter bases, get well on the way before the fighters come sweeping out to find us. They went that way, cries the convoy, as the MTBs leave the burning wrecks and sunken ships. They came and attacked us and then ran off towards England. Bloody right, mate, 'cos we don't like mixing it with a bunch of Jerry fighters. A few Me110s, some Ju88s. Nasty things. Fast, powerful, firing cannons at you. Go right through our wooden hulls then burst inside. And when you've still got 500 gallons of petrol in your tanks, one cannon shell can turn you into a bonfire. So, as I say, we run like hell for home before they turn the lights on, before the sun is up. And, some days, the Spitfires come out to welcome us home as well, some days when it's been a bit hot over the other side and we need a bit of help to run away.

So the eight boats felt their way out of the darkened harbour, finding the gap between the headlands which marked the entrance, a shaded light on one side showing the way, and headed off across the Channel.

*

In a bar in France and a pub in Cornwall, it had been a quite time. No aircrew had been in. Yvette had only seen four Germans all evening. A few ground crew had come in for a while. Maureen had had only locals in all evening. For both of them, it meant they would get an early night. They could keep up with washing glasses as they went along. And then to bed. That would be nice. As long as they were not kept awake by aircraft taking off in the middle of the night. For two girls seeing the war through in not dissimilar circumstances, the realities of everyday life were much the same. Except Maureen was free to run her own life. For Yvette there was one vital difference. She was in occupied France. And the threat of the Gestapo was never far away.

IV

Jilly picked up the signal which had just been placed in the In basket. It was a report of a sortie from another squadron, a sortie which had covered the convoy to the south-west. She scanned it briefly. It told of some U-boat sightings in the vicinity of that convoy but no successful attacks. She stepped across to the Operations Officer's desk and placed it in his signal file. He looked up from where he was writing and nodded and smiled at her. Uncle Dickie did not say much but he was a fatherly figure who looked after the girls. He seemed to spend hours in the Ops Room. When did he ever sleep? Here it was, half past midnight and he was still here. In fact she knew he would stay on to brief two crews which would be in around one o'clock. One of them was John Williams' crew.

She lingered by Uncle Dickie's desk for a moment. 'Cup of tea, sir?' she asked.

'Thank you, Jilly. That would be nice.' He paused for a moment, then, as she turned away, he added, 'I thought you had this shift last night?' She turned back. Golly, how did he remember these little things?

'Yes, sir, I did but I did a swap with someone else so I get two night shifts on the trot. It gives me a long day off tomorrow. I want to go to the cinema in town. There's a new Clark Gable film on.'

'Good . . . good.' He smiled again and returned to his paperwork.

Jilly walked across to the corner of the room and filled the kettle from the tap Dickie had had installed. Then she lit the small gas ring and put the kettle on top. While she waited for it to boil, she put the tea in the pot – not too much, Uncle Dickie did not like strong tea.

The Ops Room was like a thousand others around the

country. A large map, stretching from Northern Ireland all the way down to Portugal and from the coast of France well out into the Atlantic, dominated one wall. On it were plotted the routes of the convoys, the patrol areas of the Coastal Command aircraft, their routes to and from patrol, safety areas where British submarines were on patrol and bombing and depth charging were not allowed. Also the routes of British submarines on the way to or returning from their patrols. There used to be a lot of those off Brest but after the *Scharnhorst* and *Gneisenau* had escaped up Channel, the number of patrols off the French coast had decreased. And also on the board were the U-boats, or at least the best estimates of where the U-boats might be. Some positions came from aircraft, from the signals like the one she had just handled. Some came in intelligence summaries issued by Group. They put the picture together and sent it out to the various squadrons. She did not know how they did it but sometimes they seemed to have a pretty good idea where the U-boats were. Other times the plot was a bit blank.

To one side of the main map was a larger scale plot of the Channel. This was the one the Navy used. The MTBs planned their raids from it. Included on it were the known minefields, British and German, British Channel convoy routes, the best guess at German convoy routes along the French coast, the positions of shore gun batteries, the positions of fighter airfields, navigational dangers, submarine patrol areas, exercise areas, danger areas, everything the MTBs had to consider out there in the Channel.

The various stateboards were also duplicated a thousand times over, at air stations in Britain, in Germany, in Italy, in the Pacific, in Russia. Lists of aircraft, their readiness, captain's name, time of take-off, time of return, callsign, armament, remarks. It was kept in chalk. From time to time an aircraft did not come back and the entry had to be rubbed out. She hated doing that. Missing in action. Just rub the name out, they don't exist anymore. Another aircraft, another crew arrives, just fill the gap. Write in the serial number, take the captain's name. Give it a callsign. A-Able, this one. Write it in, fill the gap, keep it neat.

And then there were intelligence reports on clips, weather

forecasts, times of high and low water (you didn't see that any many air stations), recognition posters, photographs – there was one of depth charges erupting around a U-boat, clocks in Greenwich Mean Time and British Double Summer Time, with a notice saying 'Wind me at 0800', recognition codes for the day, convoy escort callsigns, radio frequencies, lists of duty officers, lists of where people slept – CO, Hut 6, Room 2, telephone numbers, candles in case the lights went out, tin hats in case a raid came over, the tea boat, the cupboard where they kept the mops and brooms, a rack for coats and hats, and a big curtain to pull across the wall maps in case anyone who was not 'cleared' had to come in, like the electrician to fix that bloody light switch by the door which was playing up again.

And in the middle sat one man, the squadron Operations Officer. Uncle Dickie. He ran it. He was always there when something was going on. Always there to brief the crews, whatever the time of day or night. Everything you ever wanted to know about running Sunderlands out into the Atlantic or down the Bay was in his head. How long does a Sunderland take to get to a patrol area just north of the Spanish coast? Dickie would know. How long does it take to pull an aircraft up the beach, change an engine and get it operational again? Ask Dickie. How many times had the squadron sighted U-boats, attacked U-boats, sunk U-boats? Dickie would tell you. Not as many as you might think. Takes a lot of long boring hours of patrol after patrol even to see a U-boat, or that's what the statistics say. Some crews did a whole tour and never saw one. Some saw several in one sortie. Turn a sighting into an attack? Not so easy. Say you spot him at five miles. Two and a half minutes in a Sunderland. Time enough for a U-boat to dive and get out of the way.

Dickie had never done it himself but he listened to the crews, listened to the captains chatting, debriefing. He had accumu-lated the folklore, the wrinkles, the tricks of the trade. Never done it himself but he knew it all. He could tell you the chances of getting in an attack. Get spotted at five miles, you'll miss him. Get into two miles before he knows you're there, then you've a chance, my lad. And he had seen the crews who had done it and come back to tell the tale. Attack a diving U-boat – that's easy. Or as easy as precision flying of any twenty-five ton

aircraft a hundred feet above the sea can ever be. Attack a
U-boat that stays on the surface and shoots back. Now that is
something else. He'd seen those crews as well, bringing back
an aircraft full of bullet holes, an aircraft damaged by cannon
shells. And he'd seen the crews who had brought back their
wounded and their dead. And he had told the girls to wipe
another name, another aircraft off the stateboard. It's too late.
They won't have any fuel left. I've given them a few extra
hours just in case. No distress signal. No, they haven't put
down somewhere else. Sorry. Leading Wren Johnson, rub off
B-Baker, they're missing, I'm afraid.

He it was who turned the requirements of Group into the
realities of an aircraft taking off at the right time to be at the
right place to relieve another aircraft from another squadron
who would be coming back another way. He it was that got the
crews to the aircraft, allowing for Tomkins changing the plan
slightly every morning, crews to aircraft which were serviceable, which had been fuelled, which had been bombed up,
which had all the gear on board. He it was who ordered the
routes to fly out to patrol, not going too close to France but not
spending too much time getting back and forth. Send a
Sunderland 600 miles, it could only stay there two hours. Cut
50 miles off the route each way, it gets another hour or so on
patrol. He it was who told Group the weather was too bad and
they really could not get a sortie away. And he it was who told
Group when an aircraft failed to return. To them it was just
another statistic. 'Sorry, old boy. We'll send you another lot in
a couple of days.' Plenty of aircraft coming off the production
line. Just about getting enough crews. They'll be some chaps
on a train soon. Fill the gaps. Another name on the board.
Keep doing our bit.

The kettle boiled and Jilly picked it up and poured the water
into the tea pot. Dickie's opposite number, the Naval Ops
Officer, had just come in as well. It was different for the
MTBs. Different way of doing things. Go out in a bunch, all
come back together. As a Wren sharing the Ops Room with the
RAF, doing shifts with WAAFs as well as Wrens, she actually
felt more connection with the RAF. There were names on the
RAF stateboard. Names of captains of aircraft. Dodds, Pre-
ston, Birch, Collins, Hargan, Smith and others. She saw the

aircrew when they came in for briefing. There might be a bit of light-hearted chat, a joke or two, a smile and a wink. But the Navy were just numbers. MTB this and MTB that. The COs came in from time to time but they did not need the same sort of briefing before each trip. They knew their parish, their patch of the ocean.

She poured out four cups, including one for Brenda, the rather large WAAF who had just finished plotting a route on the wall map, and added two sugars for Uncle Dickie, and one each for the rest. You got to know those sort of things as well.

*

Mick Hargan pushed open the door of the Ops Room and stepped inside, pushing aside the blackout curtain as he did so.

'Evening, Dickie!' he called as he turned to hang his hat on the hook.

He also shrugged off the jacket he was wearing. American jacket it was. Acquired, somehow. Nice and warm. He stuck that on the hook as well, and walked across towards Dickie's desk. He glanced at the clock. Five to one. Not bad. Early for once. His mood of nervousness, the tight feeling in his guts, the sweating palms had passed. Now it was Mick the character, a joke here, a laugh there. 'Come on, lads, let's get out there and hack the bastards!'

'Hello, Mick,' greeted Dickie. 'Rest of your lads coming?'

'Sure. They'll be along in a minute.'

As he spoke, he turned towards the wall map. There was no triumphal opening of the curtain before the assembled crews, no jeering if the bomber crews saw it was Happy Valley, the Ruhr again, no cheers if it was a cushy target. Here the crews came in one at a time, not as a squadron en masse, saw what had to be done and went out and did it. So the plot was there for Mick to see. And he could see his route out and where he was to meet the convoy. Bit further to the south-west than expected but no problem. His route took him well clear of France. But some other poor sod was going right down the Bay, his route dog legging out around Ushant and then the long run south.

'Who's going down the Bay, Dickie?' he asked, turning round.

'Tomkins. About thirty minutes after you.'

'Is he, by hell? Tomkins. Well, well. Good luck to him.'

'Cup of tea, sir?' The little Wren had appeared at his side. Nice kid. Small but nicely formed, as the saying went. Nice auburn hair. Freckles, little turned up nose. Bit of a cheeky face really. Yeah, nice kid. Never really noticed her before. Must have seen her in here before.

'Yeah, thanks, love. That would be nice. Just one sugar.'

He turned back to the board and eyeballed distances, working out times in his head. About three, three and a half hours to get out there. Depends on the wind. He glanced at the weather forecast, at the map attached to it. Bit blank over France – they had to guess some of that bit, unless a high level Spitfire had been over for a look-see before the bombers. But the high pressure was moving north a bit with an easterly flow setting in along the Channel. Bit of wind to help them out up their tail, bit slow coming back against it. It was usually the other way round.

The door opened and Tomkins walked in. Oh, shit! thought Mick.

'Ah, Hargan,' called Tomkins as he put his cap down on the edge of one of the desks. 'Thought I'd come along to your briefing before I do mine. How's it going?'

'Oh, fine, fine, no problems,' answered Mick, as civilly as possible, and wondering what triviality Tomkins would pick on tonight.

'All set to get out there and give the Hun what for, then?' went on Tomkins, his Pommie accent grating on Mick's ears. Mick thought he saw Dickie wince but he was not sure.

'Yeah, sure . . . sure, we'll go out and . . . and do our bit.' Hell, what was he saying? He sounded just like Tomkins himself. Doing our bit!

'Splendid, splendid.'

Tomkins turned to look at the plot himself. Mick noticed his uniform was immaculate, his shoes shined. Mick had put on a nice warm sweater under his tunic top. At least Tomkins did allow that relaxation to dress regulations. But it was a good job his desert boots were out in the aircraft. Bloody comfortable they were. Wear them all the time flying. But I got a bollocking last time Tomkins found me wearing them for briefing. I'll put them on when I get out there.

Jilly came across from the corner and handed him a mug of tea. The mug was a bit chipped and it was powdered milk but never mind. He gave her a smile and a wink. 'Thanks, love.'

Tomkins gave her a stiff 'Thank you, Leading Wren Johnson.' His mug did not have a chip. Jilly had been told off when she accidentally gave him a chipped mug a couple of weeks earlier. She did not like Tomkins. Bit stuck up. Not like the Aussies. She wondered what they thought of him.

The door swung open and Dinger Bell, Bill Newton and George Kemp burst in, '. . . and you know what you can do with your parrot . . .' just audible from Bill's lips. But his joke died when they caught sight of Tomkins looking down his nose at them. 'Evening, sir. Evening, Skipper.' Tomkins glanced at the clock. Two minutes after. In the shit again. And where was Sparks? Just as George was pushing the door shut, it was opened from the outside and Sergeant Jim Bailey, wireless operator, came in, having just finished stubbing out his cigarette on the side of the building. He was about to put the nub end behind his ear, saw Tomkins, thought better of it and slid it into his trouser pocket.

'All here?' asked Dickie, knowing the answer. Pilots, navigator, Sparks. Some crews brought the senior gunner too. Not Mick, not usually. Mick nodded anyway as Dickie moved up to the plot, a pointer in his hand. 'Convoy SL 168A. 27 ships. 6 escorts. Ten knots along the route shown.'

He pointed to the track marked on the plot which pointed towards the southern end of the Irish Sea and Liverpool. 'Not doing too badly, so far, as best we can tell. They've kept HF silence, of course. Lost only two ships but we have indications of up to four U-boats in the vicinity.'

What the hell were these 'indications'? wondered Mick. Where did they get all the information from? Some times they seemed to have a pretty good idea just where the U-boat packs were, or where they were forming up. Other times the picture was a bit blank. Dickie was continuing, Tomkins nodding at each point that Dickie made '. . . last sortie from Mountbatten reported sighting two U-boats to the west of the convoy which dived as soon as they spotted the aircraft. By the way, there are indications,' that word again, 'that U-boats, particularly in the Bay, are choosing to stay on the surface and shoot it out.' Oh, shit, thought Mick, but I'm not going that way tonight. But you, Tomkins, you bloody-well are. Tomkins was just nodding again. He had read the intelligence report already.

Dickie was pointing to another line on the plot, a line which joined the base to the convoy, via a slight dog leg. 'Route out via Point Oboe Jig. Same route back. Nothing along your route but be aware there is a convoy rounding Land's End and if they are a bit ahead of time, you may see them on the way out. No danger areas affecting you, no British submarine movements. You will be relieved by X-Xray at 1200, if your fuel lasts that long. But, as usual, come home at PLE.' Good phrase that, thought Mick. Prudent Limit of Endurance. Stay as long as you dare but don't run out of petrol on the way home.

'Standard joining routine for the convoy. I'll give Sparks the frequencies and callsigns, plus the recognition codes as usual.' Tomkins stopped nodding and butted in at this stage. 'Make sure your joining routine is absolutely correct, Hargan. We can't have the Navy accusing us of sloppy drill.'

Mick said nothing. Dickie let the remark pass and moved over to the weather chart.

'High pressure moving north . . . here. Easterly airstream. Winds pretty moderate. Cloud base, well, about three thousand here, bit higher further west. Layer of stratus, pretty solid but clear on top if you get that far.' He let out a little laugh and the boys grinned back. Sunderlands were strictly for lower airspace. 'Visibility good all the way, with a possibility of the odd shower. No fog or mist forecast. Freezing level might be as low as four thousand so watch it if you do have to go into the cloud. Sea state moderate, wave height three to five feet, from the east, but probably the usual Atlantic swell from the south-west. High water here was just after midnight and its springs. Take-off is to the south.' He stepped across to his desk and handed Dinger a summary of the weather with the forecast winds at the various heights.

Dickie stepped back to the plot and continued, 'Full fuel load on board your aircraft plus full depth charges and ammunition. Try to get away by 0300. P-Peter will be about thirty minutes behind you.' Or in other words, thought Mick, get away on time or bloody Tomkins would be wanting to know why you were late. P-Peter! Tomkins had insisted on changing his aircraft's callsign when he arrived at the squadron. 'Peter Tomkins flies P-Peter.' It had been in the local paper, a bit about what the boys in the Sunderlands were up to. Tomkins had arranged it all. There he had been, posing in front of his aircraft, splashed across the front page. What he did not know was that his aircraft was known to all and sundry, except him, as P-Pom.

'Any questions?' asked Dickie, his brief complete. Mick's crew knew the routine, they had been around a while. He just ran through the normal things. No need for fatherly advice, not like with the new crews. Briefing them could take half an hour. But not Mick's lot. They knew the drill. Sparks had a query about one of the frequencies on his briefing sheet. Dickie sorted that out. Mick, meanwhile, finished the last of his tea whilst his eyes ran over the plot. Easy, wasn't it. Draw a line on the map, put a few times on it, write a callsign by it and that was a Sunderland on its way out over the sea for twelve hours or so. Bunch of lads out over the cold, grey Atlantic. Just a line on a wall map.

'Hargan, all well, then?' Tomkins interrupted his musing.

'Yeah, no problems.' Keep it noncommittal.

'Good, good.' Tomkins turned and leaned down so he could talk quietly in Mick's ear. 'How's that new second pilot of yours coming along?'

'Oh, fine. Just fine. Doing well,' answered Mick in a normal voice. 'Right, we'd better get going.' Then as an after thought, he added to Tomkins, 'Have a good trip.'

This remark caught Tomkins by surprise. 'Oh, thank you, Hargan. Errr, you have a good trip too.' Mick was already on his way towards the door and was addressing himself to Dickie. 'Thanks, Dickie, old mate. See you when we get back. Come on, lads!' He picked his hat off the hook, grabbed his jacket and was out of the door, hopefully before Tomkins noticed the jacket. The night was cool outside. He slipped on the jacket as the lads followed him out of the door.

They walked together down towards the jetty, picking their way carefully until their eyes became accustomed to the dark, Dinger was carrying his bag of tricks, as he called it, all his navigator's gear in one hand. The others were carrying their

flying helmets and Mae Wests. Young George was also loaded
down with the binoculars, a new Very pistol they needed, his
gear and the Skipper's gear as well. Second pilot's perks, old
mate, carry the Skipper's gear. Old tradition in this crew.

Down at the pier the others were waiting. A full crew.
Skipper. The boss. Navigator. Be nice to him, look after him,
give him cups of tea when he asks 'cos he'll find the way home.
Skipper and the first and second pilot might fly it but Dinger
had to know the way. 'Cept of course the pilots could navigate
if the navigator bought it, but we don't talk about that. First
and second pilot. Take three pilots then you can take it in turns
on the flight deck, take a break from time to time, let the
Skipper stretch his legs, take a pee, grab a sandwich in the
galley. Wireless operator mechanic. Sparks. He would do the
talking to the convoy, or to base if need be. Fix the radio if it
broke. Engineer. Quiet one, the engineer. 'Hank' Jones. Quiet
but dependable. And the four wireless operator/gunners.
Sparks was boss of the radio but the other four could operate
it. But their main job was the guns. Ginger, Tiny, Ray and
Banjo. And the senior air gunner, John Williams. All there,
eleven of them, clustered round a dim light which marked the
end of the pier. The tender was waiting, its engine ticking
over.

'Evening, lads!, called Mick as he joined them. 'Nice cushy
run this one, out to a convoy. No problems. Right, what's the
rations this time?'

'Steak tonight, Skipper,' replied John Williams out of the
dark. Wonder which WAAF or Wren he's chasing around at
the moment? 'Steak, eggs, beans, bit of bacon, spuds. Usual
stuff.'

'Good on yer, Johnno. And a few bottles of Fosters?'

'Yeah, sure thing, Skipper. I'll put them in the ice to cool
when we get on board.'

The lads had started filing down to the tender and passing
the gear down. Mick slapped his senior gunner on the
shoulder. 'We'll have a couple of those Fosters on the beach
when we get back. Couple of Sheilas. We'll be all right.'

Mick was the last one into the tender. The girl in the bows –
he assumed it was a girl, he could not really see she was so
wrapped up against the cool of the night – let go the line, the

coxswain kicked the gear into reverse and the tender moved slowly out from the pier. The coxswain let her swing as the boat moved out astern and then gave a kick ahead and put the tiller hard over to complete the turn. 'D-Dog is it?' he called to no one in particular. He was greeted by a chorus of 'Yeahs' and 'Sures'. The tender picked up speed and headed out across the water, the breeze of its movement ruffling their hair and sending a chill through their bones. At least it wasn't like the middle of water. And it wasn't pissing with rain.

They saw the first aircraft looming out of the dark. The coxswain turned the tender to run up the line of aircraft. Dog should be fourth one along . . . two . . . three . . . there she was, you beaut. Dog was no name for a female aircraft. Good, she was. Nice aircraft, and she was all theirs. Home from home. Had to be when you spent twelve hours at a time out there.

The tender swung in under the wing, missing the port float, and headed in for the door, the speed coming off rapidly as the coxswain kicked her into neutral and then gave a quick burst astern. Does this thing fly? It looks bloody big out here, especially in the dark. Hell, it's enormous. Look at that wing. You could play a game of football on that. And the fuselage, standing twenty odd feet above the water at the top. The tender bumped alongside and Ginger grabbed onto the door's frame to hold them there. They started to scramble out and pass the gear into the aircraft. They had done it before. They knew the routine.

Mick climbed up on the side of the tender, called a quick 'Thanks, mate,' to the coxswain and climbed inside. The lights were on, just for the moment. Turn them off later, get used to the dark again. But not just yet, we've got to get her ready to go first. Not a fighter this one where you jump onboard and press the start button. Got to check her out first. Engineer to take a walk down the wings. You can't do that in a fighter. Bilges to be pumped. Guns to check. Radios to check. Long list to go through. Takes time. The lads know what to do.

Mick climbed up through the cavernous fuselage. He could never get over how much space there was inside. It went back to the Sunderland's pedigree as a passenger aircraft before the war. Spin off from the C-Class flying boats. Travel in luxury, bags of space. Now the aircraft was stripped of any frills. It was just a workhorse military aircraft. But it was still big inside. It had decks, ladders to climb up and down. A galley even. The earlier Marks had a wardroom. Bunks and room to stretch out and take a break. But not the Mark III. They put extra bombs in the space now.

He arrived on the flight deck. They called it the bridge as well. Confusing, all this nautical terminology. That was big too. Familiar territory. Know every knob and switch, blindfold. How many hours have I spent with my backside in that seat? he wondered, looking at the left-hand seat, the captain's seat. Bloody long time. He leaned down and extracted his desert boots from underneath the seat where he had stowed them after the last trip, sat down on the edge of the seat and changed his shoes. That was better!

Bill and George were busy stowing things away. Dinger was establishing himself at his table just behind the flight deck on the starboard side. He had the chart in his hand and was just getting it folded to cover the right area before he stuck it down on the table. Then he would sit down with the weather forecast and his calculator, the thing that looked like a short, wide slide rule, and starting working out the courses required to take them out along their route. Via Oboe Jig. That was the way to go.

Hank Jones the engineer appeared at the back of the flight deck. Time for him to take a walk along the wing. He had a torch in his hand. He opend the hatch above his head and scrambled up. Doesn't say much, does the engineer. He'll take a walk along the wing and check it's all there. Seriously. It only needs a fitter to leave a panel loose which comes off in the air and you've got a problem. And he'll check the engine cowlings too. They are the most likely things to be left undone. The fitters were always in amongst the engines. Don't leave it to chance. Check they've secured the cowlings properly. Or as best you can in the dark with a torch.

Down below there was the sound of the bilge pump, removing the small amount of water which had accumulated. No riveted hull could be absolutely watertight. Get the water out before you go. Heavy stuff water. And it moves around in flight and plays merry hell with the trim – that is if you were silly enough to leave any in the bilges. Always a bit of a musty

smell down there. Higher up, the aircraft had her own smell.
Fuel, cooking, and whatever she was made of. They all
combined to give the Sunderland her own smell. Lancaster
would smell different. Spitfire would smell even more
different. Something familiar about the smell of a Sunderland.

There was a clanking and crashing from the galley as one of
the boys stowed the food away and sorted out the utensils.
There were the massive RAf issue frying pans and kettle and
saucepans. Built to withstand being dropped from thirty
thousand feet. And there were the cups and plates and knives
and forks and spoons and mugs, all acquired from various
sources. So a local hotel was short a few things. It was their
contribution to the war effort. Put a kettle on, lad. If we're
quick, we'll have a brew before we go.

Up in the nose two of the men were struggling to get the slip
rope rigged. The tender was round by the bow now giving
them a hand. Let go the bridle from the buoy. We don't need
that anymore, 'cos we'll be going soon. Just get a slip rope on.
That'll hold us in these conditions. No gales to worry about.
Then when the Skipper's ready, we just let it go with a flick of
the wrist and we're on our way. 'Cept there's a hell of a tide
running past that damn buoy and it's dark and a bit cold and
why is it always me who gets lumbered with this bastard of a
job? But at least it's not pissing with rain.

Sparks was at his radio checking things out, setting up the
frequencies, writing the callsigns on his board in big letters so
he could see them and did not have to fumble around for a bit
of paper. The gunners, those who were not in the galley or up
in the bows, were checking out the guns. Give them a test burst
over the sea later. Here, make sure the breeches are clear and
that the ammunition feed is correct and that the belts of
ammunition are free to move. If you need them, you want
them to work. But make sure the safety is on, just 'til we get
going. Check out the depth charges too. Hanging on racks
above your head in the belly of the aircraft. Kept inside the
aircraft until you needed them. Then the big hatches in the
side just aft of the galley were opened up and the depth
charges went out on rails under the wings. Clever that. No
drag until you needed them. As long as they went out when

you wanted, to hang poised under the wings until you were down at a hundred feet above the sea and racing in towards the U-boat at a hundred and twenty knots. Then you hoped they dropped off in precisely the right sequence when you pressed the tit, to drop in a pattern which straddled the submarine and blew its guts out. Depth charges they were, although they looked like bombs at the moment. They had tail fins. Those broke off when they hit the water and then they became depth charges, just like you've seen the Navy using on the newsreels.

And so it all came together and the checks were done and completed. And the skipper was told they were ready to go. The hatches were shut and locked. The door was shut. They were ready in the bows. The five gallon water drums were stowed away so they won't move around. We've had a brew and we've turned the cooker off and tucked the kettle in its slot so that it won't go rattling round the galley. The Aldis is plugged in and young George has it ready so we can see where the buoy is and anything else around us. The engineer had been up on the flight deck to bleed the throttles. Funny arrangement, that. Hydraulic 'extractor' throttles. You need to bleed them before you go. Make sure the fuel is off first though or you find you've pumped a lot of juice into the carburettor and then you get a fire in the engine when you try to start it. Not nice that.

'OK, lads, let's get going,' called Mick over the intercom. 'Port outer first, engineer, then starboard outer.'

'OK, Skipper.' Hank was back at his panel. Fuel gauges, ammeters, luboil pressure, temperatures, that was his world. He primed the port outer, ready for starting. 'Port outer primed, Skipper.'

'Right!' Mick pressed the start push and the far engine on the port side could be heard turning over. Come on, baby.

The engine fired, missed a beat, then caught and roared into life. And as the engine roared into life, the aircraft came alive as well. An aircraft without its engines is an inanimate object. Start an engine and life blood starts to flow. Luboil pressure coming up. Generator running to charge the battery. Now we can get some hydraulics to the turrets. Instruments coming alive. And, most of all, the noise and vibration. That was what brought her to life. The steady roar, although muted as yet. Wait till she's up to full power, mate, then you'll hear her go. And then the vibration will get you. Everything shakes. In a ladylike way, 'cos she is a lady, this aeroplane. But it will all shake gently for the next twelve hours, all the way until we turn the engines off again.

The starboard outer joined in. Then the two inners. Won't need them for a while. Taxi on the outers. But we need the inners nice and warm before we go. Never try taking off on a cold engine. You're likely to blow the thing to pieces. So start the inners but keep them ticking over, just for now.

'Captain to Engineer, all set?'

Hank ran his eyes over the engine instruments one more time. No point in telling the Skipper he could go if there was a snag with an engine. Pressures and temperatures looked OK. Electrics were fine. Fuel line up OK. Fuel pumps on.

'Set to go, Skipper!'

'OK, George,' called Mick on the flight deck. Standing just behind him, George blew on the whistle he had poised at his lips. This was the signal for the nose to let go the slip rope. Up in the bows, Ginger and Ray let go the rope and the Sunderland was free.

Mick was a competent pilot but he was never fully at home when it came to handling a Sunderland on the water. Line him up for take-off and give him the controls and he handled her nicely. It was getting out there lined up which was the problem. His plan was to let her drop back off the buoy with the tide pushing them and then swing to starboard to take them out into the open water, clear of the other aircraft. The trouble was, the tide was running much more strongly than he estimated. It was two and a half hours after high water at Springs and there was one hell of a lot of flow that night.

As soon as she was released from the buoy, the tide caught her and started pushing her down towards the next aircraft astern. At the same time, the wind was now able to play its part. The restraining force of the buoy holding the bow was released. The huge tail fin could now act like a giant weather vane. A gust of wind from the east caught her and she started to swing, swing more than was needed to ease her out of the gap.

'Shit!' called Mick as he watched the buoy, which George was now illuminating with the Aldis, disappearing rapidly as it seemed to move across the nose and then disappear into the dark out on the port bow.

But it wasn't the buoy which was moving, it was them, being set down sideways towards the next aircraft astern. Except the next aircraft was now on their starboard beam and closing rapidly. Mick shoved the starboard outer up to full power to kick her round, saw that it was having only a minimal effect and wound up the port outer up as well. If she won't turn, then let's just get some space between us and the line of aircraft swinging at their buoys down tide of us.

She started to move. She started to move out of her slot in the line but she was still being set down towards the next aircraft. Tiny was in the rear turret and suddenly saw the nose of the next Sunderland appear out of the dark to his left. Shit! They were going to hit it! But the propellers gripped the cool night air and D-Dog moved forward just in time for the nose of the next Sunderland to pass three feet clear. Its mooring buoy must have gone under the tail. Bloody hell, Skipper! thought Tiny quietly to himself. Good job that wasn't P-Pom astern of us. You'd've had Tomkins walking across the water to give you a bollocking.

As she picked up a bit of speed, the rudder started to help, just a little and Mick was able to ease her round to point up the harbour towards the flare path, half a mile away.

'Bit of tide running there, Bill,' was all he said, glancing to where the first pilot was sitting on the right hand side.

Bill said nothing. He knew Mick's limitations. They'd had a few hairy moments before. They seemed to get away with it each time, just.

They taxied slowly up the harbour, only the distant lights of the flare path to show them the way. The other aircraft at their moorings were hidden in the dark to port. Up in the bows, the lads were stowing away the mooring bollard and then they would wind the turret forward to its in-flight position. Mick steered her mainly on the engines, keeping the starboard outer with the power on to stop her weathercocking into the easterly wind. Going to be a bit tricky, this take-off. Quite a lot of crosswind. Well, we've done that before. Wind Mick could handle, it was just tide that caught him out.

The Sunderland reached the end of the flarepath. Mick had come up slightly over to one side so he had room to turn. As they got set up ready to turn, the boys were strapping themselves in. Final check all hatches shut. Forward turret was wound out. Propellers to fine pitch. Flaps down one third. Elevator trim . . . just a touch of nose-up trim. They would be heavy tonight. But then they always were.

'Turning for take-off now, lads,' Mick called over the intercom.

He clipped the microphone up to his flying helmet and left the microphone switched on. If he needed to talk during take-off, he would need to talk fast and would need both hands free as well. He pushed the port outer throttle all the way forward, eased back on the starboard outer, kicked on full rudder and heaved her round through the wind. He lined her up down the flare path, the line of lights bobbing on the water before them, pointing down the harbour. Don't stop now, keep the momentum going. Keep full power on the port outer to stop her swinging into wind. Full right rudder to hold her as well but you need more speed to use the rudder effectively. She started to move more purposefully, starting to cut a line down the flare path. Ease up on the starboard outer. The speeds coming up. Hold her straight on the starboard outer. Don't let her swing into that wind. That's it, Mick, she's doing nice. Full power starboard outer. She's running now, mate, OK, you can give her the inners as well now. Don't do it too early otherwise the spray from the bow wave goes through the props at full power and does them a lot of no good. But she's OK tonight. It's pretty calm. The spray should be blowing behind the props by now. You've got her running. So he pushed the inner throttles all the way forward. Full power. 4,260 horse power. Not much to spare, particularly when she's up to her maximum load, and a bit beyond, because this is war, boys, and you push things to the limit.

The rudder was biting. He had the stick full back. Got to get her on the stop. Got to get her planing. Can't drag this hull through the water all the way up to flying speed. Got to get the hull up like a speed boat. Only way to get flying speed, otherwise we're just going to end up on the beach at the far end. The roar of the engines penetrated every nerve, the power straining to get them into the air. Come on baby, up you come. And like the lady she was, she came. Slowly the great hull lifted up onto the step, to sit on its own bow wave, the bulk lifted from the water, the drag reduced. And then the laws of physics took over. As the drag reduced, the speed came up. And Mick eased the stick forward to hold her level on the step whilst the speed came up. She was really going now, straight as a dye down the flare path, the rudder biting and holding her straight. No more problems with the crosswind. She'll hack it now, mate. Full power all round. Engineer watching the dials. Temperatures and pressures OK. And then she was there, waiting to fly, so he let her.

Slowly he eased back on the stick, the nose lifted, the angle of attack changed a couple of degrees and she flew. Like the lady she was, she lifted gracefully from the sea and took to the air. 2,300 revs all round, pulling her into her natural environment. Light on the controls, now she's flying. Let the speed come up a bit, then ease her into the climb. Feel rather than see the headland pass a hundred and fifty feet below. Ease her up, let's be on our way.

In the Ops Rooms, they heard them go. Jilly went across to the stateboard, glancing at the clock on the way. She picked up the chalk and, in the column marked Take-Off against D-Dog she wrote 0258. Two minutes early. Good luck, boys, she thought quietly to herself.

V

Tomkins might not know how to handle his Australian squadron, but he could handle a Sunderland. He could handle it in the air, he could handle it on the water. He had judged the conditions as the tender brought him and his crew alongside P-Peter. There was the strong tide running along the hull and there were gusts of wind blowing from the east. Wind blowing across the tide. Tricky. He judged distances as best he could in the dark.

So when Tomkins and his crew left their buoy half an hour after Mick, Tomkins had the buoy round on the port bow and the outer engines already holding the aircraft against the tide before he gave the order to slip. As he gave that order, he eased up the starboard outer, caught the swing which started as soon as the slip rope was released and eased her out diagonally from her slot, keeping level with the buoy as he stemmed the tide and let the angle of the aircraft move them sideways out of the gap. It was nicely done and even the most hardened of his Aussies would acknowledge that, quietly and to themselves.

'Know anything about boats, about the sea, Tomkins?'

'Oh, yes, sir! Done lots of sailing. My family has a cutter moored at . . .'

'Good, good. Then you'll have no problems with Sunderlands.'

'Sunderlands, sir? But I want to go and fly Spitfires!'

'Yes, but we need good men to go into Sunderlands, Tomkins. You're just the chap.'

Tomkins took them up harbour and thirty one minutes after Mick had wound on full power to take off, Tomkins did the same.

*

Dawn came clear and bright at thirteen west. The low cloud

which Mick had found as they climbed away from base had moved higher as they flew south-west and then had started to become broken. So from starting out under a low roof of solid stratus, they had found open skies with only occasional patches of cloud as they neared the convoy.

The transit out had been routine. But never forget there might be the odd night fighter around, boys. So we'll keep the midships and tail turrets manned, just in case. It's not like trying to take a Lancaster over Germany where there certainly are night fighters about, but you never know as we do our slight dog leg around Ushant, there might be one out there prowling around for chaps like us. So we'll keep our eyes open, just in case someone appears out of the dark who wants to shoot our arses off, to fill us full of cannon shells.

But I don't think the danger is that great that I can't put her on autopilot and let the old girl fly herself for a bit. We'll change the watches on the hour as usual, let everyone shuffle round, take our spells, take a break from time to time. And one of you lads off watch can put the kettle on and make sure that we get a good brew up here on the bridge. Not your stewed stuff like they serve in the railway stations, something I can enjoy, something which won't make me feel like throwing up.

So Mick took them out over the Atlantic. When it was George's turn to take over the right hand seat, Mick stayed on the left hand side and made him fly her manually. 'Bit of time on instruments will do you no harm, young George! She's all yours.' And the four gunners swapped around on the hours, taking it in turns to keep the watch in the tail, for that was where the greatest danger lay, or up in the midships turret where a burst from the guns might help put off a night fighter. Trouble was, would you ever see one before he started shooting? And once he did, would it all be too late? But you feel very naked if you don't keep a lookout, and we'll do our spell in the galley as well. 'Cept we usually get a bollocking when we do the galley for making the skipper's tea too strong.

And Dinger kept track of where they were, taking Gee fixes whilst they were in range and checking the wind, for when they went out of range of Gee, he would have to rely on dead reckoning or, if the cloud broke up, get the occasional sun line. And the cloud did break, so he would not have to rely entirely on dead reckoning. Meanwhile Sparks listened into the radio, ready to receive any messages which might be broadcast from base. He would not acknowledge such messages, for to transmit on HF might indicate their position to listening stations in France. But he would listen in to the set frequencies which would be used to pass any urgent messages, like a change of tasking, listen in to the faint morse, sometimes broken by interference, sometimes fading altogether, and try to make sense of what he heard. And Hank Jones kept an eye on the engines. All readings steady, all temperatures OK, luboil pressure fine. And he would take the fuel readings and check consumption and keep a record of how much was left. Then he could tell the skipper when they had to turn back. Or rather he and the navigator would work it out between them, he with the fuel figures, the navigator with the distances and speeds and wind.

So they arrived out of the east, out of the dawn to join the convoy. Never easy finding a convoy out there. The convoy had its route but might not have been able to get a sight from the sun or stars for days, might be running on dead reckoning, might be miles out of position. Or they might have had to dodge some U-boats, or heave to in heavy weather. But the radar helped, and they picked up the convoy out on their starboard beam, echoes coming in at nine miles and then a cluster of ships showing up. Mick turned towards but not too close. Let's tell them we're here first, boys. They get a bit trigger happy down there. Sometimes not too good at telling a Sunderland from a FW Condor.

'Sparks, give the convoy a call!'

'Call the convoy, Roger, Skipper.' There was silence on the intercom for a minute, ninety seconds, two minutes. Don't ask Sparks what's going on. He knows his job. He'll tell you when he's in touch. He'll be calling them on short range voice radio. Sometimes you have to get a bit closer to establish contact.

'Radio operator to Captain, in touch with the convoy escort leader!'

'Good. Radar, what's the range of the nearest ship?'

'Radar. Seven miles, Skipper.'

'Roger. Sparks, tell the escort leader I am orbiting seven miles north-east of the convoy.'

And so they went through the joining routine, about which

Tomkins was so meticulous. Make sure they know who you are, identify yourself, establish your position, then receive your instructions from the escort leader. He'll tell you what's going on and what he wants you to do.

'Radio to Captain, I've got our tasking. Passing it to the navigator now.'

'Roger.'

The lads took up their positions. Radar was already manned. Radio would stay manned. Now they manned up the nose turret as well. You never know when a U-boat might suddenly appear and you had to go roaring in at a hundred feet and the nose gunner had to try and shoot the gunners on the U-boat before they shot him, that is if the U-boat stayed on the surface to fight. And it was a good lookout position as well anyway. Even if you've been with the crew a long time, we've never had to fire the guns in the nose in anger. Not yet.

Dinger's voice came over the intercom. 'They've given us a search plan to the front of the convoy. Steady up on north for a starter. There are U-boats around. They've been picking up HF from U-boats during the night but they've not been attacked in the last twenty-four hours.'

'Roger. Captain to crew. Time to start earning our keep, lads. You heard what the navigator said. Keep your eyes skinned.'

As he spoke he eased out of the turn, bit of left rudder and caught her neatly, the compass exactly on north. Mick might be a bit dodgy on the water but he could handle her in the air. Thousand feet will do us, he thought to himself. Best place for radar, down low. Reduces the clutter. We'll see how it goes, might have to go a bit lower. As he steadied up, his eyes ran over the instruments. All well. Engines working hard as usual. But then they always did. Load a Sunderland up to maximum, and then squeeze in a bit more because its war time, and accept that she was never very powerful in the first place, and of course the engines are going to work hard. No wonder they have to keep changing them. Someone was talking about putting Pratt and Whitneys in. There had been a suggestion one night in the mess for a Merlin-engined Sunderland. Give it the power of a Lancaster, or four Spitfires. But that had led to a long discussion about whether you would prefer to have a rugged, simple air-cooled engine when you were five hundred miles out over the Atlantic or a sophisticated, liquid-cooled one. There was a consensus that the Merlin was vulnerable to bullet holes and cannon shells. That had settled the argument, until someone had pointed out that Lancasters and Spitfires got shot at regularly as well . . .

*

As the dawn turned to day, they could just pick out the convoy, eight miles over the left shoulder. Dinger took them into their imaginary box, centred some ten miles ahead of the convoy, a box represented only by four pencil lines on a chart, a box which moved across the map at the speed of the convoy, a box they would move back and forth across. They came round to port for the first leg across the front of the convoy. Now eyes were sweeping, in the turrets, on the flight deck, sweeping the sea below for the tell-tale sign of a U-boat, for a feather of wash from a periscope, for a swirl in the water which might mark the position of a submarine trying to go deep to avoid the aircraft. Keep your eyes open, boys, we're here for about five hours.

*

Far to the south-east, close into the northern coast of Spain, one U-boat continued towards France. There had been no alarms in the night, no tell-tale whispers from the Metox to indicate the presence of a searching aircraft's radar, nothing appearing out of the night with engines roaring to hurl depth charges at them. The dawn here was similar to that seen by Mick and his crew. Broken cloud, a bit lower than it was further west, but promise of some sun later, certainly enough for a sun sight or two to check their position. The wind had come round a bit more to the east, round onto the nose, but it was still a gentle breeze, with a swell still from stern, lifting them gently as the engines pushed them east at a steady twelve knots. As the small leaks on the engines had been fixed, they had been able to ease up the power and now they were running at twelve knots. Every bit of extra speed reduced the time to reach the sanctuary of harbour.

Repairs were coming along, but still the air compressors remained the major problem. Even if they could fix them, they were in no position to return to patrol, to turn again out into the wide sweep of the Atlantic, to hunt along the convoy routes, for they had no torpedoes. They might have been hammered by the escorts but they had got two ships, what, only thirty hours before. And they had got another two, three weeks earlier and a lot further west, right out in the middle of the Atlantic, a long way from the air bases. Just this one day on the surface and then we'll be too far east for the Tommies to come looking for us, too close to the fighter bases in France, into relative safety. Just today we need. Give us this day, Oh Lord, and we'll do the rest.

The officer of the watch scanned the horizon for the hundredth time. How much longer until the end of the watch? Must be another hour. I hope that lazy sod Bernard is on time or I'll give him an earful. Hello, what's that! His sweep stopped, swung back a few degrees and steadied on a spot on the horizon. Nothing. But he waited. Let the sea do the rest. Let the waves run across the horizon, let a dip form in that distant line between sea and sky and I'll see it again . . . if there was anything there.

'Captain to the bridge!' There was something there. A mast, on the horizon, just off the starboard bow.

'Control room! Look through the periscope on a bearing of Green One Zero. There's something there.'

'*Jawohl!*'

Above him, he could see the periscope rotating. Raised on the surface, it gave a much greater height of eye. Even as he checked that it was turning to the right bearing, the captain appeared at his side.

'A mast, Green One Zero, sir! You can just make it out from time to time.' The captain said nothing but put his binoculars to his eyes and scanned that same horizon, searching. Got it! What is it? Could well be a Spanish fishing boat. But it might be something else.

So they watched and stared and tried to pick out the detail as the range closed at a mile every five minutes. But it took another ten minutes before they could be sure that it was a fishing vessel, ten minutes in which the first lieutenant looked through the periscope from below and the officer of the watch and the captain stared from the bridge. Ten minutes in which the upperworks of a fishing vessel became visible through the periscope, ten minutes after which the first lieutenant could tell the captain that all was well.

It took another thirty minutes for the fishing vessel to come abeam, a mile and a half away, a seine netter hauling her nets, her Spanish flag fluttering in the breeze. And after her, others appeared, shapes on the horizon to the south, shapes which told them that Spain lay that way. Spain, a neutral country. If we get into real trouble, we could go in there. Might be interned but that would get us out of the war. But that is a thought we keep to ourselves. But it's a thought . . .

*

Once in the air, Tomkins' crew worked just the same way as any other Sunderland crew. OK, Tomkins insisted that the intercom drill was by the book 'Captain to Navigator, Engineer to Captain'. He insisted that they were correctly dressed, although the concession of a sweater under a uniform tunic top was allowed. He insisted that everyone reported in when they had changed round on the hour. But they did change round on the hour, they had a breather from time to time, could stretch their legs. And they ran the galley like everyone else. And Tomkins was partial to a fried egg sandwich about three hours out from base.

'Captain to Galley, how's my egg coming along?'

'Galley to Captain, be ready in about two minutes.'

However, despite the fact that Tomkins was prepared to relax enough to eat a fried egg sandwich, and drink the cup of tea which would come with it, he rarely gave up his seat on the left-hand side. Let the first and second pilots, Bannister and Lane, change round in the right-hand seat, let them do the flying, but he would stay in his seat. He might relinquish it if they were on a long transit out to the west, but certainly not today, not today when they were going down the Bay. Ushant had passed abeam somewhere in the dark to port, a hundred miles clear. But now the dawn was up and they were well down the Bay. Fighter country. And U-boat country.

All the way from Ushant south, their search had been continuous. Not much to see in the dark, but the unseen beams of the radar probed into the dark on either side of their path. ASV II. Main beams out at right angles either side. Like a blind man going along with his arms outstretched. Search out to the sides, because the aerials on the tail are designed to do it that way. Use the much weaker ahead looking beams just for homing in on a contact. Get a radar contact in a beam to the side, turn ninety degrees towards and switch to the nose aerials, that was the drill. But don't expect to pick something up in the ahead beams right away. Much smaller aerials, they are. Turn and close the range, expect to pick it up pretty close. Oh, by the way, have the depth charges ready too. Once you get contact ahead, there's not much time left.

But as they searched southward down the Bay, the depth charges nestled inside the aircraft. Only run them out on their rails under the wings when you need them. Too much drag otherwise. We have enough trouble just cruising down here at about a hundred and ten indicated without having the depth charges out as well.

As the dawn came up, and Tomkins' fried egg sandwich arrived, the visual search started in earnest as well. All turrets manned. Flight deck keeping their eyes open. Surprising how many times the pilots saw things first. Radar might not see it. Fickle thing, this ASV II. Needs nursing, and even then you never really know if it's working properly. So keep your eyes open as well. The visibility was good so they might spot a U-boat at long range, a U-boat on its way out to patrol, ideally, or one coming back. Get them all if you can but the one on the way out is a few ships saved. The one coming back has already done his dirty business. But if you get him, he won't be going out again.

Oh, by the way, whilst you're scanning the surface of the sea, watch the sky as well, for that is where the German fighters come from, and radar cannot see them. Air to Surface Vessel, the radar. ASV. Looks for ships and submarines on the surface, not for aircraft in the air. And it doesn't look astern anyway, which is where the fighters come from if they are going to get you.

*

Runway 06, the opposite of 24. The easterly runway, to face the gentle breeze from the east. No fog this morning. The sun an hour above the horizon. Two aircraft reaching the end of

the taxiway and turning onto the runway. Two Ju88Cs.
Fighters. They had been used as a bomber over the hop fields
of England in 1940, the Ju88As. But they were versatile
aircraft and now two of the C versions sat on the runway. Solid
noses, not the greenhouse nose of the A for the bomb aimer.
No bombs in this one. Guns for this version. Three fixed
20mm cannon and three fixed 7.92mm machine guns. No
radar, not like the 88C-6b which hunted in the bomber
streams over Germany by night, weighed down by the
cumbersome aerials around its nose. No, this was sleakest of
them all. No bombs, no aerials, just guns. And two powerful
Jumo 211 engines.

Bruckner was approaching the point where the taxiway
crossed the end of runway 24 for the second morning in
succession. He could hear the two aircraft at the far end of the
runway but the slight rise in the centre of this, the main
runway, hid them from view. But he paused to watch the first
pair go. After the disruptions of yesterday, the sortie programme was back into some sort of shape today. First pair
away shortly. He would follow them later in the day.

He heard the roar of engines building up to full power and
waited, his gaze down the runway, watching for the dark
shapes to appear over the rise. Some startled seagulls took to
the air. Keep clear, boys, we don't want to be hitting one of you
just as we take off. A bird strike in the wrong place could have
even a Ju88 ploughing into the ground, into the fields just
beyond the perimeter fence. Suddenly they were there, two
aircraft rising above his sight line, running balanced on their
main wheels, tails up, building up speed, air speed indicators
edging up until they reached flying speed. Then the first one's
nose lifted a fraction, the wings took the weight and she was
airborne. The second, tucked in on the port quarter of the
first, followed. As they lifted from the ground, the undercar-
riages started to move, to tuck the wheels away. We won't need
those for a few hours.

The roar increased to a crescendo as the two aircraft swept
over him, big, dark shapes against the sky, two birds of prey
going hunting, hunting out over the wide waters of the Bay of
Biscay. This was not the war he wanted to join. Flying over the
sea in a fighter? Knocking down defenceless anti-submarine

aircraft – Liberators, Sunderlands, Halifaxes. Easy pickings, surely? The first pair away were now turning, banked hard over to port, a steep climbing turn as they swung round to the west. No good going east, no good carrying straight on after taking off on 06. The sea is out to the west. That's where the hunting ground is.

Bruckner watched as they completed the turn, watched as he picked up his rhythm again as he ran on around the perimeter track. They steadied up on a westerly heading and roared on out towards the sea, just two miles away to the west. But that was not where the hunting ground was. That was much further out, out where the Tommies searched for the U-boats, a hundred miles or more out over the Bay. That was where the hunting ground was.

*

Mick was relaxing in the left-hand seat. He had his pipe in his mouth. As he put it, he didn't really smoke it, more sort of chewed on it and occasionally tried to light it. At least there was the time and space on the flight deck of a Sunderland to sit back and have a smoke. But even as he has went through the motions with his pipe, his eyes were roving, roving over the sea below and, from time to time, scanning across the instruments. Bill Newton was in the right-hand seat. He had control, but he had her on autopilot. The less time he had to spend flying the aircraft, the more time for looking out. And it was not so tiring either. Mick scanned the instruments from time to time as well, more out of instinct than anything else; Bill would be running his eyes over them more frequently.

The sun was higher in the sky now, right ahead of them. They were on an easterly leg of their search across the front of the convoy. Occasional patches of cloud still marked the sky but the sun shone through the breaks and there was clear blue above the cloud layer. Below, the sea looked almost inviting. There was a hint of blue in it. It often did look inviting from a thousand feet. But down low, the slight ripples of the waves would turn into walls of water feet or tens of feet high, walls of water which would stop a Sunderland dead if they tried to land. There had been a time when Sunderlands did try to land to pick up fellow crews who had had to ditch. No more. Too many aircraft, too many extra dinghies in the water as one ditched crew was joined by another, had put an end to that. They were not allowed to try anymore. Mark the position, drop dinghies, supplies, yes, but do not, repeat not, try to land. But from a thousand feet, it still looked almost inviting.

'Radio to Captain! From escort leader, investigate huffduff bearing two eight five from me.'

Trade at last! Mick acknowledged the call, and nodded to Bill who had already flicked off the autopilot and was hauling them round to the west. Mick pressed the klaxon push and the alarm sounded throughout the aircraft. Get everyone's attention, get everyone plugged into the intercom. Huffduff, a direction finding bearing of the HF transmission from a radio, almost certainly a U-boat's radio. Somewhere out to the west was a U-boat talking to its base or talking to other U-boats. And it could be one who was in sight of the convoy and reporting its position. They knew something about how the U-boats worked. If one of them found a convoy, it would shadow and pass reports which would allow others to home in. The wolf pack at work. Gather around the convoy and then attack from different directions at the same time. They all knew a little about how the system worked. Mick was allowed to know more. So was Dinger. They were the brains of the crew. Captain and navigator. They knew how the U-boats would be formed in long lines across the convoy routes, lines at right angles to a convoy's track. A line of searchers across a wide sweep of sea. Then the first one in the line to spot a convoy would call in the rest.

The Sunderland steadied out on a westerly heading. They could not come all the way round to two eight five. They needed Dinger to draw a line bearing two eight five from the escort leader, then let him con them onto that line on his chart. Already he was working on the problem, talking to radar to get the ranges of the ships. 'Navigator to Captain, make it two six zero to start with.'

Dinger took them out to a point about five miles on the port beam of the convoy and then ordered a turn to two nine two compass. Allow for the wind, allow for the difference between true north and magnetic north, allow for the small deviations in the compass on the flight deck, deviations which were marked on a small card on the panel in front of him, juggle it all on the slide rule-type calculator every navigator carried and give the captain the course to steer. 292, to make good two eight five as measured from the escort leader's position. Lines on a chart, that was all it was. Except at the end of this one there might be a U-boat.

All eyes were now alert. Young George was standing up between the pilots, sweeping ahead with the binoculars. In the nose, John Williams had the watch; dark, handsome John Williams was searching the sea ahead. The two pilots searched as well. Four pairs of eyes, sweeping backwards and forwards across the sea before them. A lump of wave would rear up some miles ahead, casting a shadow behind it just for a fraction of a second, a shadow which would catch the eye. Was that it? Look again. Then the shape would go, the wave would fade away, the shadow gone. Keep looking, the bastard's down there somewhere.

'U-boat, right ahead!' George screamed it out, his voice rising in excitement.

'Range? How far?'

'Oh, err . . . five, six miles.' Golly, it was difficult to judge distances from the air.

'You sure, lad? I can't see anything. Which way's it going?'

Even as he asked the question, Mick went through the drill they had practised so many time. His right hand went out to the throttles and pushed them all the way forward. At the same time, he called 'I have control!' to Bill and pushed the control column forward. Get her down to attack height. Five miles. Two and a half minutes. As he let the nose drop, he could feel the slight change in drag, the slight flutter as the depth charges moved out along the rails.

'Engineer to Captain, bomb doors open, bombs are out.'

The hatches in the sides of the aircraft under the wings would now be gaping open, the depth charges had run out through them on their rails and now hung ready. The indicator lights beside him came on. Let's give the bastard six, he thought to himself and selected six on the panel. Now when he pressed the tit, if he pressed the tit, a pattern of six would drop, fractions of seconds apart, set to explode 25–30 feet below the surface. It was all designed to catch a U-boat just as it was diving. That depth setting would also blow the shit out of one on the surface. The boffins had worked it all out.

'Radar to Captain, contact right ahead, four miles!'

'I think . . . I think it's diving, Skipper!' Young George was still the only one who could see it. Mick concentrated on getting them down to a hundred feet. He would see it soon enough if it was there. Just don't fly into the sea while you're doing it, boyo. Could make for a bad day.

'Yeah, it's definitely diving!' Bollocks!

He held her down at a hundred feet and roared on at full power. Might just get the bastard. Ninety seconds. Shit, a U-boat could get a long way down in ninety seconds.

'Radar contact faded!'

Yeah, they were going to miss this one. His left hand went out and turned the depth charge selector to two. If there's a swirl in the water, I'll drop two. Rattle his coffee cups, put the bastard off his stroke, show him we know he's down there.

But as they roared over the spot, there was not even a last ruffle on the surface, not even that little calm patch you see when a submarine's propellers have kicked up a whoosh of water towards the surface as they force the boat deeper. Not a thing. Not even worth dropping two to give him a shake up. They roared over the spot and then Mick took them up in a gentle climbing turn to port. They circled the spot, or where they thought the spot was, for five minutes, for ten minutes. Nothing.

'Captain to Navigator. Mark the spot on the chart. We might just tiptoe back here in forty minutes or so, see if he's chanced his luck. And give Sparks a report to pass to the convoy.'

He took them back to the north-east, back to their box in front of the convoy. The depth charges were wound in, he eased back the power and climbed slowly back to a thousand feet. We'll go away for just a while, then we'll sneak back and see if he's stuck his nose up.

'Well done, young George, good sighting!'

Hell, two and a half minutes! A young lad, on his third sortie sees a U-boat. He's now seen as many as me. It takes us two and a half minutes to close the range. But he's seen us so down he goes. By the time we close the range, he's gone. Nothing on the surface to mark the fact that a U-boat was there. But somewhere down there a bunch of Germans had, perhaps, been cowering in their submarine, wondering if the depth charges were going to come raining down. Perhaps we'll get the bastards next time.

*

Helmut Schafer was in the briefing room. Before him was a wall map, very similar to one in the West Country of England. The eastern Atlantic, the Bay of Biscay. Here the roles were reversed. On it were the known routes of U-boats moving to and from their bases, not the guesses which appeared on the English wall map. But here the positions of the convoys were estimates, and the most uncertain part of all was a series of lines which marked routes running down the Bay and search areas just to the west of the Bay. The best that they could make of the routes and areas used by the Tommies. An idea of where trade was to be found. Somewhere out there, the Tommies would be searching, flying low, looking for U-boats. It was a hell of a big sky out there. Bloody difficult to see another aircraft against the sea sometimes. You had to get closer than most people imagined to spot one. They might be big, but they looked very small from five miles away. Draw a five mile circle on this map and you can hardly see it. But that's about the area we can see at any one time. It was all a game of chance. Some days you were lucky; many days you weren't. You just played the statistics. Fly enough sorties in roughly the right place and, from time to time, one of the boys would find a target. Not that it was all one-sided after that.

He glanced to the left of the map where a cartoon was pinned to the wall. It had been there quite a few months now. It showed a large porcupine with wings. The caption across the top read *'Fliegende Stachelschwein'* – Flying Porcupine, otherwise known as a Sunderland. Underneath it said, 'If you want to get him, get underneath. His belly is soft.' And so it was. There were no guns under the hull of a Sunderland. But someone had added in a scrawl 'If you don't mind flying in the sea'. This referred to the Sunderland's trick of getting down low over the sea if threatened. The Tommies knew they had a soft underbelly. So get down low and the Hun will have to come at you from the same level or above. Then you can shoot back.

He looked again at the stateboard on the wall. No little, freckle-faced Wren to fill this one in. Only a rather fat clerk with glasses. The numbers were much the same as on the stateboard which showed D-Dog and P-Peter. The names were different. It was those names he was looking at, looking at the flying schedule, working out if there was any better way to get more sorties in that day. Still not enough aircraft. He had the crews but not the aircraft. Work the aircraft hard. Turn them round quickly. But you still had to plan the crew schedule. The best he could do that day was pairs or threes. Hell, Gruppe had given him a lot of sea to cover. What he wanted was to get out there in fours, sixes, maybe more. Then you could virtually guarantee a kill. Pairs of aircraft had been known to come back to tell tales of how the defensive fire had been amazing and that the *Stachelschwein* had survived to stagger back to England. Some days only one of a pair made it back, the other lost in the sea somewhere, shot down by a Tommie. Once a pair had been lost completely. Took off one morning. Never seen again. It had happened to other Staffel too. There were no easy pickings out over the Bay. Porcupines had nasty spines with sharp points.

Bracketed with his own name on the flight schedule were Bruckner and Elman. One new boy, one still pretty green. Give them to me, I'll take them out there, show them the way, nurse them back home if they get into trouble. Me and Ernst, Ernst the faithful observer. Only two crew in a Ju88C. Don't need a bomb aimer. Don't need a radar operator. Just a pilot and observer. Observer to do the navigating and help with the lookout, and reload the cannon down in the nose if need be. Hell of a job that but it did not take long to fire off a load of ammunition. No point of spending all those hours out over the Bay if you could not put enough cannon shells into a Tommy when you met one. So the observer had to be able to reload the cannon as well. Hell of a job.

The door opened and Hans, the engineer, came in. Helmut had been waiting for him to arrive.

'Morning, Hans.' He wasted no time but got down to business. 'How many?'

The engineer hung his cap on a peg by the door, turned to Schafer and nodded a good morning.

'Just eight, as I said,' he answered.

'Elman's undercarriage?'

'Coming along. I've had him working on it since early this morning with a couple of the lads. They've got the aircraft up on jacks and most of the damaged gear off it. It's coming along.'

'OK, Hans. Give him a break in about thirty minutes. I need him for flying.'

Two mugs of coffee appeared beside them. The routine of Ops Rooms the world over. There's always someone there just to make the tea or coffee, depending on nationality. Not that it was anything like decent coffee, but you could put plenty of sugar in and then it did not taste so bad. Hans had sat himself down in one of the chairs which faced the wall map. It was where the crews sat to be briefed, just a half circle of wooden chairs of all shapes and sizes, begged, borrowed and stolen. Behind them were a couple of desks. At one of them sat the German equivalent of Uncle Dickie. They would have found much in common. Both flew in the First World War. If they did but know it, they once passed within a mile of each other over the western front. Now they were each playing their part in this war, two old hands trying to help out the young men, the boys who had to fight this war.

Bernard was a tall, slim man, with very little hair left. He was busy writing a message for Gruppe, rather awkwardly with his left hand. Even after all these years, he had not really mastered writing with his left hand. Pity about that crash all those years ago. His empty right sleeve was pinned neatly to his jacket. Sometimes he imagined his right arm was still there. There was a medical term for it. Sometimes he was sure he could sense his arm and hand in place, but when he touched the sleeve it was always empty.

Hans and Helmut sat silently for a few moments. In the corner, the clerk was emptying the ash trays into the rubbish bin. Then he would take the bin round the corner to the line of big oil drums which served as temporary homes for the rubbish. The lorry came round each day to empty them, a French lorry, driven by Frenchmen. Hell, you had to use local labour for so much, even if they did work as slowly as possible.

Then to make conversation, Hans asked, 'What time are you off?'

'Me? Oh, about eleven. It depends how long it takes those idle engineers of yours to fill her up. If they're slow, I'll set Lieutenant Bruckner on them!'

Hans did not take the joke at first 'That's all I need.' Then he relented and a grin spread across his face. 'What a hell of a war,' he mused as he put his mug of coffee to his lips.

*

The gyro repeat was steady on zero eight five, just a touch to the north of east. Get some more miles under us to the east before we turn north-east for the Gironde. The navigator had the watch on the bridge of the U-boat. He was starting to feel a little more relaxed. At least he knew where they were now. Two sun sights, two hours apart had been enough. Not the world's best fix, but good enough. Within fifteen miles of his dead reckoning position. Not bad after so long without a fix. The presence of the Spanish fishing vessels had been reassuring, a confirmation that they were heading along the north coast of Spain. Twelve knots now. Good news. But still cannot dive. Compressors still in pieces, engineers cursing and swearing over them. Still no air in the bottle groups. Stay on the surface and fight it out if an aircraft appears. Keep the guns manned. Keep the crews alert. Those were the captain's orders.

He turned to look at the guns' crews. The guns were pointing at the sky, ready at a moment's notice to open fire at an attacking aircraft. Ammunition was ready. The crews were relaxed but could spring into action at a second's notice. Their eyes roamed the sky above, continuously sweeping over their allotted arcs, watching for that tell-tale little speck in the distance. Hoping it was just a sea bird. Watching its movement. A dark speck, steady, unchanging could be an aircraft. One that wheeled and dived and swooped amongst the waves . . . that was OK. Just keep looking.

The captain says if we can just make it to darkness tonight, we'll be OK. Next we'll be heading up the Gironde, watching

the French landscape pass by. Not this evening, but tomorrow evening, we should be tucked alongside. The base
engineers will come onboard to help us. They'll have brand
new compressors for us, and all the other things we need.
And there'll be a bath ashore, and clean clothes, and fresh
food, and beer and French wine . . . and women. They'll be a
bunch of us at La Chatte Verte and we'll show those French
whores what we've been missing all these days. They won't be
able to walk by the time we've finished with them!

The navigator turned to look forward again, to watch the
bow rise and fall to the sea. He took up his binoculars from
where they were hanging against his chest and swept the
horizon ahead. Then he swung to sweep the sky to the north,
and then round to the west. Nothing. All clear.

He let his thoughts wander to his parents. No news for
several weeks made life difficult. Hopefully there would be
letters waiting for him. How were they surviving the bombing? Living on the edge of the Ruhr was not a nice prospect.
They had to stay for his father's work. Tool maker. An
important man in a factory. A skilled hand. They were short
of those. Anyway, his father was too old for military service.
But he was still in the front line. The Ruhr was a regular
target for the British bombers. Were his parents still alive?
They could have been killed in an air raid for all he knew.
Perhaps the officer who was always on the quayside when
they got back would this time call for him. 'I am sorry,
Lieutenant, your parents were killed in an air raid whilst you
were on patrol. Your sister too.' It could happen to him. It
had happened to others in the crew. The captain's grand-
parents had been killed. The engineer's sister. And a number
had lost brothers on the eastern front.

That must be a hell of a place to be. It could be bloody cold
out in the Atlantic in winter, on the bridge at night, trying to
survive an Atlantic gale, the wind screaming from the north-
west. But the eastern front! That really must be one hell of a
place. Who was better off? Who had the most chance of
surviving? How many of them would actually survive the
war? Where was the safest place to be? Was anywhere safe?
Those fat cats in the base staff in France had it pretty easy.
No bombs, no Russian winter, no depth charges in the night.

Their only concern was whether they had caught a dose from that French tart the other night.

Come on! He realised he was staring out into nothing. Hell, he was the officer of the watch. If he had seen a lookout doing what he was doing, he'd kick his arse. Quickly he picked up his binoculars again and once more scanned the horizon, once more swept the skies. How many more times before safety?

*

Tomkins took the mug of tea and set it in the holder he had had fixed to the throttle pedestal. Might as well have a few creature comforts. Like Mick Hargan, his eyes were constantly looking, looking out at the sea around them, looking at the sky above, looking occasionally at the instruments. Flight Lieutenant Bannister, first pilot, had control but, like Bill Newton, he had the autopilot clutched in. Both pilots were playing their part in the search, looking down on their respective sides, under the great sweep of the wings. They had the best view out to the sides, especially out to the sides and down. The turrets could see best ahead, astern and on top; the pilots covered the sides.

It was amazing how many times the first sighting was made from the flight deck. Suddenly the aircraft would bank steeply and the klaxon would blare. What's that down there, just under the wing? Let's have a look. Sixty seconds later they could be roaring in across a U-boat, guns firing, engines at full throttle, depth charges dropping. They could be. Statistically you had to put in a hell of a lot of hours just looking, and looking again, and again, and again. Looking at the restless sea below, never still, always changing. Waves blown by the wind, sometimes just gentle white horses, sometimes whipped to a fury by a gale, spindrift sweeping across the surface. Swell born of far away winds, perhaps thousands of miles away. Shadows of clouds, and of aircraft. Their own aircraft. Birds, and sometimes whales or dolphins. They were the worst. A whale blowing could look like a submarines. A dolphin breaking the surface. What was that?

All was quiet on the intercom. Tomkins did not allow chatter on the net. If you want to gossip, do it in the galley when you're off watch. When you're on watch, you look and listen. That's the way we do it in my crew. That's how we do it in P-Peter. So he sat in silence, except there was no silence on the flight deck. On either side, the engines roared their deafening cacophony. Except there was no discord in their steady beat. Get them synchronised or you'll drive us all crazy. There's a knack to it but I can't stand nine, ten, eleven hours of that. So the engines roared in unison, and the whole aircraft vibrated and shook in sympathy, and the instruments blurred slightly in your vision, and the tea in the mug was never still but had patterns of ripples running across its surface.

He picked up the mug and put it to his lips. This could be tricky too. Remember the vibration. Make sure it's not too hot or you can burn your lips before you know it. Not a bad brew! 'Well done, galley. Good cup of tea!' Remarks about food and drink from the captain were allowed over the intercom, he'd just decided. Orders for food and drink from the captain were always allowed over the intercom.

'Galley, how long before lunch is ready?'

'Galley to Captain,' (don't want another bollocking for intercom drill so do the 'Galley to Captain' bit), 'about thirty minutes. The spuds are just about to go on.'

'Captain to Galley. Roger!'

Even as he slipped his mug back in its holder, his eyes were doing one more search. Start at the nose and work down the side and out under the wing. One more search. One day they'll be something there.

*

The watch had changed round again. George Kemp was in the right hand seat. Bill Newton was standing at the rear of the flight deck. Mick turned to him and called, above the noise of the engines.

'Bill, take my seat for a couple of minutes, will you? I want to have a look at the plot with Dinger.'

Bill nodded and waited whilst Mick unstrapped himself and climbed out. Bill slipped into the seat.

Mick stretched his weary muscles and then turned to the rear of the flight deck. He moved across to the navigator's table on the starboard side. He leaned over the plot and looked at it briefly. 'Where's where we spotted the U-boat, Dinger?'

Dinger took up his dividers and pointed to a neat cross on the plot with the points. Beside it was a time – 0925. Mick glanced at the clock on the panel above the plot. It was just on the hour of ten. 'Dinger, as I said earlier I'd like to go back and see if he's stuck his head up again. Get Sparks to call up the escort leader and ask permission to re-investigate our lost contact.'

He waited whilst Dinger spoke into his microphone, talking to Sparks who was only just behind them across the other side of the gangway. Nevertheless, the roar of the engines was making their conversation difficult; it was easier to use the intercom to the radio operator.

'What's the best way to approach, do you reckon, mate?'

Dinger pondered the problem for a moment. 'The sun's too high for us to come out of it. I reckon the best we can do is not come directly from the direction of the convoy, perhaps swing out a bit to the east and come in this way.' He drew a faint line in an arc ending at the cross on the plot.

'OK, Dinger. You take us round there. I reckon I'll go in low – about two hundred feet maybe.' Dinger nodded and Mick slapped him lightly on the shoulder in acknowledgement.

Mick stepped back onto the flight deck and nodded to Bill, who slipped out of the left-hand seat. Mick slotted back in to his familiar position, plugged back into the intercom and strapped himself in again. He was plugged in in time to hear Dinger saying, 'OK, got that.' There was a pause then Dinger came up again. 'Skipper, you back on the net?'

'Sure.'

'Escort leader says that's OK. In fact he wants us to do a search round the back of the convoy out to thirty miles.'

'Roger.' He turned to look at George. 'OK, young George,' he continued, still speaking over the intercom, 'She's all yours. Just do as the navigator tells you.' He could see the reaction on the young man's face. What, me? Shit!

Dinger ordered a turn to the south to take them round to the stern of the convoy. The leg would take them only about two miles clear of the ring of escorts. Not that it was exactly a ring of steel. There were never enough escorts. All they could do was spread themselves out around the merchant ships and do their best to protect them. In the early days it had largely been a matter of reacting to U-boat's attacks, searching out the area where ships were blazing in the night, seeking the U-boats who came boldly in under cover of darkness. But radar was changing all that. The escorts could see in the dark . . . within the limitations of the early radar they were being fitted with. And the aircraft who, in increasing numbers and for increasing periods of time, reinforced the escort, were helping to change the pattern as well.

As the convoy came abeam, they were able to look out on the ships they were helping to protect, the regular lines of the merchant ships, the small dots which marked the escorts around the neat lines and columns. Time to get everyone on their toes. Mick reached for the klaxon push. After it had sounded for a few seconds, he waited long enough for everyone to get on the intercom net. 'Right, lads, we're going back to where we spotted that U-boat. We'll have a look, see if he's stuck his nose up again. We'll be down low this time. Everyone keep their eyes skinned. Once we've checked out that position, we'll be going for a wider sweep around the back of the convoy.' He paused. 'OK, who's back there on radar at the moment?'

'It's Ginger, Skipper.'

'Right, Ginger, lad, what I want is radar on the nose aerials. If we run in to the right position, you may be the first to spot him. Who's in the nose?'

'Tiny, Skipper.'

'OK, mate, you know what to do . . . Right, we're going down to two hundred feet now.' He turned to George and nodded. Again he could see the What me? look on George's face. A little tentatively the control column went forward and the nose dropped. They might have done low flying on OTU but there's nothing like the real thing out here over the Atlantic, is there, George? thought Mick quietly to himself. But he glanced across to make sure George was following the radio altimeter. Don't try the pressure altimeter here. You never know how accurate the pressure setting is.

The altimeter crept down through five hundred feet, then the rate of descent slowed. George was easing her down. OK, lad, I know you haven't done this before but if it was an attack we were going in for, you'd have to be getting her down faster than that. The needle crept down, stopped at 250 feet and then slowly moved down to 200.

'Navigator to Captain, two four zero.'

George acknowledge the new course and gently eased on some bank, his right foot moving in unison to apply rudder and slowly D-Dog came round to the south-west. He overshot the course by five degrees, caught her and steadied. Meanwhile he had lost fifty feet. Mick let him sort it out for himself. The nose came up slightly. Good boy, keep it coming. Now, Mick, don't watch him too much, you're supposed to look out of the window as well.

'Eight miles to run, Skipper.'

Eight miles to a spot in the ocean, which may or may not be where the U-boat last went down, give or take the inaccuracies of navigation, allowing for wind, plotting errors, and other balls ups. Anyway, the U-boat had had nearly an hour. Might have moved five miles, maybe more. Call it a five mile circle. Area of a circle? Call it three times five squared. Seventy-five square miles of sea. Bloody hell, that sounds a lot.

The sea had much more shape and form down here, just two hundred feet above it. The waves were heaps of water beneath them, not just ripples seen from on high. The splashes of white where waves broke had shape and form. It was moving by pretty quickly too. About a hundred and twenty miles an hour. Two miles every minute. Must be about three and a half minutes to go. Check height. Check course. Search to port. Check height, search. Check height, check heading, search. Let George fly her but just watch where he's going. Bill was covering the search to starboard. Check height . . . just make sure young George is not trying to fly us into the sea. Just a sneeze at this height, that's all it needs. He glanced across at the right hand seat. George was a study of concentration, his eyes moving round the instruments then glancing at the horizon ahead, then back to the instruments. Good lad, keep it going.

'Five miles to run!'

In the circle now. Keep your eyes open, boys, thought Mick. We might catch the bastard back on the surface legging after the convoy. Check height, check heading, search. Eyes out right ahead, then down the port side, out under the wing, that bloody great wing that is holding us up two hundred feet above the cold Atlantic. And do it again, and again. A shape, caught in a glance of the eye. Blink, look again. Shit!

'U-boat, port beam! I've got her!'

He grabbed for the controls, shoved the throttles all the way forward and stood the Sunderland on one wing. Two hundred feet above the sea, he banked her hard over. Even as he did so, the image of what he saw came back to him. A U-boat, beam on, with a plume of spray above it. A plume of spray which submarines make when they open their main vents, vents which allow air out of the ballast tanks so the water can flood in. Oh, bollocks, the bastards were diving!

'About three miles, moving right to left, and diving!'

Enough said. The lads know what to do. The depth charges would be on their way out again. Leave that to Hank. Watch the height, keep the bank on, hold her hard over. Check heading. The U-boat had been under the wing. Ninety degrees. Call it a hundred by the time we've turned. Hundred degree turn. One four zero. Passing two zero zero. Keep her coming, plenty of left boot to bring her round. Check height. Half a sneeze at this bank and you'll have the left wing tip in the water.

As the compass passed one six zero, he hauled her level, kicked off the rudder, bit of opposite rudder and steadied. One four five. Near enough. He could sense Bill standing between the two pilots, binoculars in hand, searching the sea ahead.

How long since he'd seen it? Thirty seconds max. Mick glanced ahead. Nothing! But then the U-boat was on its way down. You get her down to one hundred feet, boyo. The depth charges are going out. You can feel them. Let the other lads do the looking.

'Got it!' shouted Bill's voice in his right ear. 'Come left five!'

Mick pushed on a bit of rudder and brought her round five degrees. Out of the corner of his eye, he saw the depth charge indicator lights come on. He glanced at the switch. Still set to two. Careless, Mick my boy. He took his left hand from the controls for a moment to wind it round to six.

'It's gone!' Not again!

Again they raced across the intervening gap, a gap

measured in miles across the sea, seconds, minutes of flying time, and, for a U-boat, metres, metres of depth between it and the surface. Get deep, dive out of the way, avoid the depth charges, leave no trace of your presence. And again the Sunderland swept over the spot in the ocean, and again no trace remained. The restless waves hid any mark the U-boat might have left. They roared over at a hundred feet and could see nothing. Mick climbed gently away and went through the motions. Circle the spot, just in case, but you know this one will be down for a long time. If it's the same one. If it is, he's not going to stick his head up for a long time to come. We'll go through the motions so I can say in my report that we did, and I won't get a bollocking from Tomkins when he sees my report and we'll do our bit for the war. At least I've now seen two U-boats in my flying career. Twenty-seventh sortie and that's only the second one. How many have dived before I've seen them. That's the real question.

*

'Bridge! Contact on Metox. Aircraft radar. Faint!'

Before the officer of the watch had time to react, the captain was at his side. He had heard the report being passed to the control room and was immediately on his way up the ladder to the bridge.

'Gun crews! Aircraft radar in our vicinity!' They needed no second bidding. Immediately all eyes turned to the sky. An aircraft, somewhere around. Keep your eyes skinned, lads, because the bastard's looking for people like us.

The captain stepped to the voicepipe. 'Control room! Report the contact!'

'Still faint!'

All around him, his men were searching, searching the sky for the first glimpse of an aircraft. What to do if they see one? Turn beam on to it. That way, the guns have freer arcs of fire. Also the aircraft cannot run down the length of the submarine dropping depth charges. It has to come from the beam where it is a target for all the guns.

'Contact still faint!'

How long had they had it? Fifty seconds. A minute, maybe. Still faint. Not getting any stronger. Not getting any closer.

Could be searching well away from them. If it was faint on their receiver, the aircraft should not detect them. They would be out of range. The pulse only had to come one way to be received on the U-boat's Metox. It had to get there and back to paint an echo on the aircraft's screen. What sort of screen did they have? He had only seen some pictures in intelligence reports, but what did a U-boat look like on a radar screen?

The U-boat shouldered her way through the waves at a steady twelve knots whilst ten men on her bridge searched the skies around for the first indication of an aircraft. Would this one pass them by? Would they stay out of the reach of its radar? Silently men prayed to whatever god they worshipped.

*

P-Peter was steady at five hundred feet, the compass heading showing south. Another leg of the search. Move ten miles east between legs. Search out the corridor off the north coast of Spain where the U-boats try to sneak through. Don't go too close to Spain though, just as close as you dare. Spain's neutral, you see.

They had seen the coast of Spain in the haze ahead at the end of the last leg. A blue line on the horizon – a different world, a world where the war could pass them by, where life could go on undisturbed. Was it really like that? Probably not. The whole world was affected by this bloody war. No country could live in isolation from it. But at least Spanish men and women were not dying daily from guns, bombs, torpedoes, mines. No, but Spain had had their war, a bloody civil war. They were probably glad to sit on the sidelines of this one.

Not much longer to go. Bring a Sunderland all the way down to the bottom of the Bay of Biscay and you can't stay all that long. Three, four hours or so, depending on the winds. Strong wind against you going home and you allow plenty of margin for error. Prudent limit of endurance. Make it real prudent, navigator and engineer, and then we'll get home with a bit of fuel left in the tanks.

'Navigator to Captain, end of leg in two minutes.'

'Captain, roger!' Two minutes, then they would turn to the east, fly ten miles and then turn north. That would be it. Head north all the way home. But we'll keep looking all the way north across the Bay as well. The sortie is not finished just because we have turned for home. Keep looking all the way across the Bay.

Tomkins finished the last of his lunch, except the Aussies called it dinner. Steak and beans and potatoes. Then there would be some tinned plums. Rare treat, but then the Aussies were sent comforts from home. Things like tinned fruit. One advantage of commanding an Australian squadron. He placed his knife and fork neatly on his plate and placed the plate on the flight deck floor just behind his seat. His precision was for nought; the vibration started the knife marching slowly across the plate and the neat formation was broken.

'Navigator to Captain, end of leg, next heading zero eight five.' Tomkins nodded to the first pilot, Phil Bannister, who was already setting the new heading on the autopilot. As the figures moved under his fingers, the autopilot responded and the aircraft banked to the left. Left rudder was applied and slowly she came round onto the new heading.

On the U-boat, the Metox contact faded. The long fingers of the radar beams from P-Peter no longer touched them.

VI

'Any questions?' Schafer looked at the other two pilots. Had he told them all they needed to know? No, of course not, because the only way to learn all they needed to know was to get out there over the Atlantic and learn for themselves. Bruckner – aloof, believing there was nothing he could be taught about flying aircraft. Had he not coped with all the vagaries of winter flying in Germany, Austria, Poland? Had he not flown in weather where other aircraft were grounded. The Führer's aircraft must get through. But tackling the weather of northern Europe might make you a good pilot but it did not teach you about combat flying over the Atlantic Ocean. There was no training for that.

Elman – arrogant, all-believing in the Third Reich. The master race could do it all. How could he, Helmut Schafer, get the message across to these two men? The answer was, he couldn't. They were not going to listen to him. They knew it all. They were both shaking their heads. There were no questions.

'OK, let's go!'

He led the way to the door of the briefing room, glancing at his watch as he did so. Twenty minutes before they were due off. Bit tight. Outside Ernst, his observer, was waiting. As Helmut came down the steps, Ernst passed him his parachute pack.

'Come, my friend, let's get out there and show these two what it is all about,' Helmut said quietly into Ernst's ear as they walked together out towards the aircraft.

The other two pilots were branching off towards their own aircraft, except the aircraft they were flying were not exclusively theirs. They had already been flown on one sortie that day. The riggers and fitters and armourers had turned them round in quick time and now they were ready to go again, fully fuelled, oxygen topped up, engines checked, oil levels OK, tyre pressures, electrics, hydraulics. No need to re-ammunition. They didn't find anything on the last sortie. All guns still fully loaded, except for the few rounds they fired off as test bursts once they got over the sea.

Helmut reached his aircraft. The maintenance chief was waiting for him. As Helmut approached, the other man saluted. Not a very military salute, more a sort of greeting and acknowledgement that Schafer was the Staffel commander.

'All set?' enquired Helmut.

'All set, *Kapitän!*' the man reported. 'No problems.'

'Good.' In that brief exchange, the aircraft became his and Helmut headed purposefully for the hatch under the nose. He pushed his parachute up through the hatch and scrambled up afterwards. The familiar smell hit him as he climbed up into the belly of the aeroplane. He ducked and made his way forward and slipped into the all-too-familiar seat. At least he was flying his own aircraft today. Ernst followed him and slipped into his own seat. On the ground, they did not mix, were not really compatible. In the air, they approached their jobs with experienced professionalism. No bullshit but let's do it right. It's pretty unforgiving out there over the sea if we get it wrong.

Helmut strapped himself in. Get the straps right. Don't hurry. You're going to be in them for a long time. Be as comfortable as you can in these damn-awful seats. And then he started his checks. His eyes and fingers started on the familiar litany, running across the instruments, the knobs, switches, levers, dials, and gauges. He checked the altimeter, compasses, gyro direction indicator, turn and slip, artificial horizon, rate of climb indicator. His fingers touched each dial and gauge as his eyes ran across them. He checked every switch, every knob, every lever. He checked his oxygen was plugged in and checked the pressure. He tried the rudder pedals and the control column. Full and free movement. An expression drilled into every student pilot's brain. And made sure they go the right way. It has been known for a fitter to connect up ailerons in reverse. Make sure they go the right way. Leave nothing to trust. The air, like the sea, is unfor-giving of any mistakes. If you have got to fly an aircraft over the sea, you face both unforgiving elements together. Do it all, check her out before you go.

Five minutes later the port Jumo 211 burst into life. The peace was shattered by the engine and the aircraft came alive. Luboil pressure built up. Switch to internal electrics. Rev counters wound up and steadied. The starboard engine followed, and on the other two aircraft, parked to starboard, their engines burst into life as well. After another two minutes whilst he did the final checks that all was well with the engines, Helmut waved away the chocks, released the brakes and eased the throttles forward. He let her roll forward a few yards and then turned her, braking the right wheel and giving a burst on the port engine to wing her in front of the other two aircraft. He straightened up on the centreline of the taxiway and lead the way out towards the end of the runway.

In a neat line, the three aircraft trundled steadily out towards runway 06. Not far to taxi today. Helmut rolled onto the wider expanse of the runway and turned to line up just to the right of the centreline. He let her run on a short way so the other two aircraft could tuck in behind. Once lined up, he ran through the final engine checks. Let the engine warm up taxiing out, then do your engine checks. So he wound on some power, checked pressures and temperatures were OK, checked the magnetoes. Then he eased back to idling revs, and went through the final vital actions before take-off, a drill he had learned from the first time he had sat, rather nervously, at the controls of an aircraft. Trim was set for take-off. Mixture set. Flaps. Fuel, Instruments. All hatches were shut. Everyone strapped in tight. He gave the little side window one last check. That damned catch was always springing open. All set to go. But he waited a little longer, give the other two aircraft just a bit more time. Don't hurry them. They might think they know it all but . . .

He glanced across at Ernst who nodded and pointed a finger down the runway. Helmut's right hand moved to the throttles and eased them all the way forward. The note of the engines rose to a roar and she was rolling. He glanced at the engine instruments to make sure they indicated that he was getting full power as his feet moved instinctively to catch the initial swing. A touch of brake just to straighten her up until the rudder bites. But once she's rolling, tweak the throttles to control a swing if you have to.

Then the airspeed indicator started to respond, the needle moved off its stop and, with an initial twitch, moved steadily upwards. He let the tail come up, felt the controls responding, knew he could hold her straight on the rudder. The rise in the runway obscured his view to the end of the long strip of concrete but they were climbing up the slight incline. The airspeed came up, he held her a little longer, and then eased back on the control column. The nose lifted and they were airborne. His right hand moved to the undercarriage lever and he felt the slight thump as the wheels started to retract. He glanced over his shoulder to make sure that Bruckner was not tucked in right under his wing. He wasn't – he was about a hundred metres astern. So Helmut led them round in a climbing turn to port.

Two mintues later they crossed the narrow stretch of sand that was all that remained of the beach at high water and headed out to the west, still climbing. Bruckner was tucked in neatly to port of his leader. Elman had swung wide on the initial turn and was lagging the other two aircraft. He'd catch up. There was plenty of time, they had a long way to go.

*

Phil Bannister came from a little place called Borroloola in the Northern Territory of Australia. When people asked him where it was, he used to say 'about four hundred miles south-east of Darwin'. Then he found not many people even knew where Darwin was, so he just said he came from somewhere near the top of Australia. He had never seen a city until he volunteered to join up. Even the journey to get to Brisbane had been a major adventure in itself. Even to a lot of his fellow Australians, it was difficult to explain just how big the Northern Territory was and how remote places could be. A hundred miles was nothing. That was just down the street.

Now here he was, out over the Bay of Biscay, doing his bit for the Mother Country. He was not quite sure whether or not it made sense for Aussies to be out here trying to help fend off the stranglehold of the U-boats on Britain's lifeline. Shouldn't they be doing their bit against the Japs? No matter. There was a job to do and he was here to do it. Pity he had such a prick for a captain. Professional enough. Just couldn't get on with the chaps. Didn't make too much difference. They did not have to see much of him when they were not flying. Tomkins had the squadron to run so Phil was largely left to run the crew. That was great. Good bunch of lads. Fair mixture but they all mucked in together. They tolerated the Skipper but that was about all. In some ways they were glad he insisted on tight intercom discipline. That way they did not have to talk to him. They could have a natter amongst themselves when they went down to the galley for a break and a quick fag.

His eyes glanced at the compass. Steady on 015 magnetic. Height steady. Engine readings OK. All the needles were in their familiar positions. The patterns was not broken. All was well. His gaze moved from the instruments to the horizon ahead. Unnoticed by him, his eyes refocussed to infinity and, in a fraction of a second, his view moved from the panel just a few feet in front of him to the distant sea seven miles ahead, where the slight haze blurred the line between sea and sky. His gaze steadied for a moment and then moved slowly to the right. Take it slow, keep looking. We've seen a couple of fishing boats earlier on but that was on a southern leg. They were tucked in towards the Spanish coast. There shouldn't be any out here. Move along the horizon slowly, then come in closer and look out to the side, under the wing. Then do it again.

Oh, my God! A shape, a dark smudge in the haze ahead.

'Contact ahead!'

He grabbed for the binoculars, hanging by the throttle pedestal. He put them to his eyes and searched the sea ahead. Where was the bloody thing? He took the glasses from his eyes, peered ahead. Its gone! No, it hasn't – there it is. Trying to keep his eyes on the same spot, he put the binoculars back to his eyes. Got it! He adjusted the focus slightly and the picture leapt at him.

'U-boat!' he screamed.

Tomkins had waited, not hurrying his first pilot. He had looked ahead but could not see anything. Let the first pilot sort it out. Might only be a fishing boat, but, if it is, it's a long way from the others. But as the cry of 'U-boat' came forth, his thumb was on the klaxon push. At the same time, he flicked off the autopilot and grabbed the controls. 'I have control!'

*

The cry on the flight deck of P-Peter was almost in unison with a shout from a lookout on the bridge of the U-boat. 'Aircraft!' The officer of the watch, still the navigator, turned to follow the man's gaze. His binoculars to his eyes, he swept the sky in the same direction. Where was it? There's nothing there. No . . . yes . . . yes. Oh, hell!

'Captain to the bridge! Action stations!'

Already the guns' crews were at their guns, the barrels were swinging to where the lookout was watching. It was too far away to see with the naked eye yet. For the hundredth time, they checked the ammunition feed, checked that the gun was cocked and, now, the safety catches went off.

*

He could see it with the naked eye now. Four – five miles. A minute or so since Bannister had first seen it. And it was still there. Not diving, but then intelligence reports were starting to indicate that U-boats were prepared to fight it out on the surface. Perhaps this was one of them. It was heading east, heading for home.

Tomkins was not a cowardly man. Neither was he a particularly brave man. He saw the necessity to attack the U-boat in terms of duty. Duty, and a sense of getting in amongst it learned on the rugby fields of his public school. He had never been very good at rugger. Always the wrong shape. Tall, but not heavy enough to be effective, but, again, not fast enough to be a good three-quarter. But cries from the touchline, from his masters, of 'Get in there, Tomkins. Get stuck in, don't hang back!' had coloured his view of things even into adult life. There was a loose ball in the ruck – get in there with the others and get it out. Here was a U-boat which had to be tackled. Just get in there and do your duty.

'Engineer to Captain. Bomb doors open, bombs are out.'

'Captain, roger.' He paused. Bombs were ready. Check settings. he glanced down and checked that six depth charges were selected. Gun turrets manned. Second pilot ready on the flight deck, in case he or Bannister was hit. Sighting report? Hell!

'Captain to Navigator. Give the radio operator our position. Radio, transmit a sighting report!' They both acknowledged but Tomkins was not to know that they were already ahead of him. His Sparks already had the position on a slip of paper in front of him and was quickly setting up his transmitter. Thirty seconds later he would be tapping out the morse at the key on his desk.

Camera! Must get a photograph. 'Captain to Tail. Stand by with the camera.' Oh, shit, here we were about to run in over the top of a U-boat and he wants the photographs! But he's right. That way, the attack can be analysed afterwards.

Two miles to go. Down at three hundred feet. I won't go all the way down yet. If I dive at him, I can fire the fixed guns in the nose at him as well. Do I go straight in or wait? No point in waiting. I can't call up any help. There are no other aircraft in this area. Ops briefed me on that. We've got to get him on our own, and we havn't much fuel to spare to hang around either. I am on his beam, though. He can bring all his guns to bear. Can I get ahead of him? Can I get round him faster than he can turn? Probably not, but I ought to try. No point in going in through the mass of his gunfire if I can get ahead of him where some of his guns cannot bear.

'OK, chaps, I'm turning starboard to try and get ahead of him. We'll try and attack from his bows.' Intercom discipline was gone in the heat of the moment. And even Tomkins had his moments.

*

Below and two miles away, a young man who commanded the U-boat watched the tactics of a slightly older man. The aircraft was turning. A Sunderland. Big aircraft. He'd never seen one before but had examined hundreds of intelligence drawings. He knew they were big but this was much bigger than he expected, even two miles away. It looked big and lumbering but he did not underestimate it. Guns and depth charges. That's what it had. And he and his men had to fight it off, had to put up a wall of steel to force it away, to stop it coming in over the top and dropping its deadly charges. Stay beam on, that was the way. Keep turning as the aircraft manoeuvres. As the Sunderland steadied up, the captain ordered the rudder over to swing the U-boat.

*

Tomkins could see the U-boat start to turn. As the Sunderland started round on its circle, the U-boat matched the turn. If Tomkins had had time to sit down and work out the mathematics of the situation, he would have found that P-Peter was covering 60 degrees of a circle every minute. The U-boat could easily turn that quickly to keep up with the Sunderland. Tomkins did not have time with paper and pencil but he could see that the U-boat was staying beam on.

But logic dictated that, if he got in closer, but not too close so as to be in gun range, he would, perhaps, outpace the U-boat's rate of turn.

'I'm going in closer, try to outpace his turn, chaps!'
He banked sharply to port, towards the U-boat.

*

'He's coming in!' yelled the captain. He steadied the U-boat on course, passing his orders down the voicepipe, but watching the aircraft all the time. Below, he knew his men would be ready. There was nothing they could do in the fight which was less than a minute away, but they were there to leap to contain any damage, to shut off valves, to stop leaks, to isolate electrics if the depth charges damaged them. If. There was nothing they could do if a depth charge tore through the pressure hull and the water came pouring in.

Then the Sunderland banked the other way and turned beam on. So, my friend, you are going to circle a little closer, hope to out-turn us. Trouble is, you might succeed this time.

*

In the nose of P-Peter, an eighteen-year old was contemplating the fact that he had just wet his trousers. He could feel the warm dampness spreading. And his legs and hands were shaking. Tony Scott felt very vulnerable in the nose turret, knowing that he would be at the front when they did turn into attack. What was the Skipper doing, pissing about out here?

Why wasn't he getting on with it? What was he waiting for? I'm the poor bugger who's got to sit right out at the front of this aircraft and be the first one the U-boat's guns get to. And you want me to fire back. I will if you'll get on with it but otherwise I'm bloody scared and I've just pissed into my trousers.

Despite being bloody scared, one part of his brain was following in automatic and, in response, the guns were tracking the U-boat precisely.

*

Phil Bannister could not see the U-boat from his side. He could only imagine what was going on. Oh, shit, any moment now, the skipper was going to turn in and then the bloody U-boat is going to start shooting and those bullets are going to be coming straight at me. I know it. One of those bullets has got my name on it. I'm a pilot and I have to sit at the front and watch it all happen. I can't even fire back. I just have to sit here and watch the skipper do it and take over if he gets hit. But he's not going to get hit – it'll be me.

Tomkins watched the U-boat out of the port side window. They were winning. The U-boat could not turn fast enough. Just a bit more . . . try and get ahead. Then go for it. Bit more . . .

'Attacking now! Turning port!'

He heaved the aircraft round, willing her to turn. The port wing tip dipped towards the sea. Plenty of room. Still at three hundred feet. Haul her round. But not all the way. Let's attack in an arc, make the job of his gunners more difficult. He glanced at the U-boat. Sixty degrees off the nose and they were twenty degrees off the U-boat's bow. As good as we'll get.

Tomkins was a good pilot. He handled the Sunderland with precision. He brought her neatly out of the turn, still pointing slightly ahead of the U-boat. Instinctively his hands and feet moved in unison on the controls, holding the aircraft exactly where he wanted her. Just hold her there . . . just a bit more. Then he eased on left bank, followed through with the rudder, but not quite enough so that, as he intended, it was not a perfectly balanced turn like they taught you at flying school but the aircraft side slipped slightly as well, slipped to the left and started to lose height. And he brought her round in an arc, the height bleeding off, to line up for the final half-mile, the final fifteen seconds.

*

Cunning, very cunning. The Sunderland had out-turned them and was now coming in from on the bow. He kept full rudder on. In the time it takes the aircraft to complete its run, we'll turn another twenty degrees. It'll be enough. The aircraft was swinging in an arc, lining up for its attack, and dropping down closer to the sea. A difficult target for his guns. By chance, the U-boat had ended up beam on to the long swell coming in from the Atlantic and an occasional burst of spray came over the bridge from the waves coming at them from the east. She was rolling and turning, and the aircraft was turning and dropping. Bloody difficult for the guns. Moving target from a rolling deck.

The staccato roar of the 37mm broke the silence. The gun opened fire, its barrel angled forward so the cannon shells were passing, unseen, close up the starboard side of the bridge. The noise was tremendous. All rational thought was drowned. Now the guns were in action, the next few moments, next half minute, were just raw animal survival, fighting back, hoping your bullets would get him before he got you.

*

Now that the moment was upon him, Tony Scott found cool detachment taking over. His guns followed the U-boat as the aircraft swung. Don't fire too soon. You've only got .303 machine guns. Pea shooters in this game. Get a bit closer. Steady up on the guns' crews. Get those bastards and they won't shoot back. Just a bit closer . . . Don't worry about the fact that one of those guns seems to be firing. Probably cannon. You won't know about it if it hits you so don't think about it. Ah, the other gun seems to be firing now as well.

Suddenly the Sunderland steadied. Tomkins was hauling her straight and level, a hundred feet above the sea. Over a runway ashore, it would have been a beautiful peace of precision flying for an air display. Here it put a 25 ton aircraft in position for its run-in over the U-boat. It could be the last thing P-Peter ever did.

*

The 20mm gun aimer squeezed the trigger and his gun roared forth. The noise did not penetrate his brain. He was just conscious of the power that he controlled with one finger. Squeeze the trigger and cannon shells pour forth at this bloody great aeroplane. Problem is, the boat's rolling around and the last dash of spray is still running down my face and I'm having a hell of a job to stay on target. Just keeping squeezing and aiming. Swing the gun around a bit. Something ought to hit this bloody great shape that's roaring in across the sea at me. Squeeze and pray.

*

Tony Scott continued to watch with detachment. Then their own 0.5 inch machine guns opened up, the ones in the nose. They were fixed, fired by the pilot. The skipper could not really aim them, just sort of spray lead in the right general direction. He could hear the sound of the guns firing on either side of him. Almost time . . .

He squeezed the trigger and his own guns opened fire. Watch your own aim. Forget everything else. A line of spray kicked up in front of the U-boat. Falling short. Never mind. We're almost there. He watched as the little spurts of water which marked where his bullets were hitting the sea moved across the surface towards the U-boat. And then they were there, hits climbing up the side of the U-boat. A touch to the left. Then his bullets were amongst the guns' crews. Compared with the U-boat, the Sunderland was a stable gun platform and he was able to follow with his guns as the Sunderland raced on and the U-boat moved in under the nose.

The captain watched rooted as the aircraft came on. There was nothing more he could do. He had done his part. Now, either his gunners hit the aircraft in a vital spot or it would come in over the top and drop its depth charges. Then either it would be a good aim and they would all die, or no charge

would drop close enough to cause lethal damage and they
would live a little longer.

Suddenly the aircraft's bullets were amongst them. A
lookout fell to the deck, blood pumping from his neck. Then
the bullets moved aft and were amongst the guns' crews. A
loader staggered back, clutching his arm. He bounced against
the rails, and then slumped down. There was a pause, a long
pause, at least two seconds, and then the 37mm stopped firing.
There was another pause, and then the men realised what was
happening. One man grabbed at the lifeless body which
occupied the aimer's position, ignoring the fact that the corpse
had a hole in the side of its head. The man pushed the body
clear and moved into position. He grabbed the controls and
madly tried to swing the gun upwards to keep up with the
aircraft as it came in over their heads.

*

Of the last three shells which the 37mm fired, all three hit the
Sunderland. One struck just below the nose turret. Splinters
sprayed over a limited area. It made a bit of a mess of the
mooring ropes stowed there. It also made a mess of the turret
hydraulics. The nose turret stopped moving. And one splinter, half an inch longer, penetrated the turret, penetrated the
gunner's seat and hit Tony Scott in the backside. He was aware
of a jolt beneath him, of a thump in the bottom of his seat. But
he was firing at the U-boat and that was what mattered, except
his aim was going wild and the gun was not following. Oh,
bollocks!

The second cannon shell struck the nose on the starboard
side, aft of the turret but forward of the flight deck. It did
minimal damage except one pane of perspex in the starboard
flight deck window was shattered. Minute splinters sprayed
aft. Most of them missed Phil Bannister. Some caught him on
his earphones and flying helmet and did not penetrate. One
caught him just over the right eye, embedding itself deeply.
Blood started to run down his forehead and into his right eye.
The third shell struck the starboard wing between the wing
root and the starboard inner engine. It tore a large hole in the
leading edge of the wing but missed the engine and fuel tanks.

Tomkins was aware of a slight change of drag, a slight yaw as the flow of air over the starboard wing was disturbed. The aircraft swung slightly to the right, he caught her, swung back and steadied up on the U-boat. He was conscious that his aircraft had been hit. He was just concentrating on his aim. Forget the guns. Forget he is firing at us. Forget the nose guns are firing back. Keep your finger on the tit for the fixed machine guns. It does not matter now where the bullets are going. We are committed. There is no turning back. The only way out of this thing is over the top of the submarine. It's them or us. His finger moved to the depth charge release.

*

The aircraft was upon them. Its great mass was above them. He could see the rivets, see the scars under the wings caused by the engine's exhaust, see the individual panels under the fuselage. And then, in a detached way, he saw the depth charges drop. One after the other, six charges fell clear of the aircraft. He watched them as they fell in a neat line. Black shapes against the sky, appearing to hang for a moment then dropping rapidly towards the sea. Not bombs these. Depth charges. They'll hit the surface then sink. You have to wait until they go off underwater. Then you find out whether you will live another day.

The first one went in forty metres from the bow. Too far. The second seemed to be a bit erratic in flight and was not far from the first. The third splashed in just off the bow. The fourth . . . He ducked instinctively as the fourth came over his head. Oh God . . .

*

The tail of the Sunderland shook and jolted. In the tail turret, Paul Irving was aware of a series of bangs behind him. He had been hearing the front guns firing for thirty seconds. They were running in over the U-boat. He had the camera ready. How the hell was he going to get a picture with the back end bouncing around all over the place?

Suddenly the U-boat appeared beneath him as the Sunderland swept over it. Blimey! He could actually see the Germans on its bridge and around the guns. And he could see the splashes where the depth charges had gone in. He lifted up the camera and started shooting. Just point and press. Wind on. Press. Just keep taking the pictures. But as he pressed for the second time, the first depth charge went off, some way off the U-boat's bow. There was a pause . . . it seemed to go on for ever. Then suddenly water erupted on either side of the submarine. Great columns of water rose on either side, climbing into the air and then seeming to hang there.

*

The U-boat lifted as if grabbed by a giant hand. She seemed to rise out of the water, pause for a moment, and then fall back. Sheets of water rose around her, marking where the depth charges were exploding. The captain watched as his boat rose beneath him. He watched the great columns of water rise on either side of him. He felt her lurch and stagger as another hammer blow struck from underneath.

At that moment, the U-boat broke in two. The third charge had lifted her, the fourth had split her, split her asunder. The pressure hull ruptured just aft of the control room and, in that moment, all those below knew the last horror as the water crashed in. The captain lived for another seven seconds. Suddenly he was aware he was in the water. He did not know how he got there. His last sight was of the periscope on which hung the Biscay cross swing towards him as the forward half of the submarine turned on its side. The periscope hit him squarely on the head as the boat rolled over and extinguished all life in him.

The rest of the men who had been on the bridge survived another three seconds. By that time they were all in the water and the shock of the sixth depth charge exploding twenty-seven feet underwater and ninety-two feet from them caused such massive internal injuries that they all died within seconds. There were no survivors.

*

Oh, my God . . . my God. The Sunderland was banking hard over and Paul Irving was watching as the U-boat seemed to shudder under the impact of the depth charges. Then his view was obscured by the great shroud of water which hung over the submarine. Then, as it fell back, he could see the forward half rolling on its side and the after half lifting, stern first. Bloody hell, it's broken in two. Intercom drill went to the wall. 'Shit, Skipper, we got the bastard! We got it! It's breaking up!'

As Tomkins hauled the great aircraft round, ready for another attack if necessary, the U-boat came in to view just forward of the port wing. Already the bow section was on its beam ends and the after section was pointing up in the air, poised for a final plunge. The two halves of the U-boat were dark shapes against the welter of foam created by the depth charges. Tomkins eased the turn and circled the spot whilst they all watched. The navigator, engineer, radar operator and Sparks came out of their corners to watch. The men in the turrets watched. The pilots watched. They watched as the after section of the U-boat slid slowly downwards. They watched as the forward section lay over on its side and then sank very slowly and gradually deeper in the water until the waves were breaking over it. Then it was gone.

Tomkins brought them round and they flew over the scene of the attack. There were bodies in the water. Or they appeared to be bodies. None of them waved or anything. He went round again and came in very very low – about fifty feet and they all stared at the half dozen or so bodies. No, they did not move. No need to drop a dinghy. No need to do the humane thing. Tomkins turned away and set course to the north. Then he eased back on the control column and set the Sunderland into a gentle climb.

Only then did he look around. He was in a daze, a state of mild shock. Time to sort things out. Seems as if we took some hits. He looked across at his first pilot. My goodness, the man is covered in blood. 'First pilot's hit. Second pilot take over!' he called into the intercom. There was a bustle of movement beside him. One of the gunners had appeared and was helping Bannister from his seat. Why hadn't the man said anything? Lane, the second pilot slid into the seat, whilst Bannister was helped aft and then down below to be attended too. As Bannister left, Tomkins could see that the blood was all down one side of his face.

Then the chatter started on the intercom. 'We got the bastards!' Beaut attack, Skipper!' because it was and we'll give even Tomkins that. 'Did you see that . . .?' Good shooting

Scotto!' 'Hey Scotto, where are you?' 'Somebody check out Scotto in the forward turret.'

In the forward turret, Tony Scott was aware that he was missing something. Not only was his turret not moving but the intercom seemed to be dead. He had sat in his seat, in a bit of a daze as the Sunderland turned after the attack. Then he had seen the U-boat in its death throes. He had sat and watched as they had flown low over the spot. But no one was talking to him. Slowly the realisation came to him that his intercom was not working. Still in a bit of a daze, he undid his straps and climbed out of his seat. As he straightened his left leg, a searing, jabbing pain struck him in his backside. And he looking down and saw the pool of blood where he had been sitting.

Just then, a figure appeared beside. It was Bluey. The other man put an arm round Scott.

'Hey, you OK?' Bluey asked, above the roar of the engines.

'I think I caught one in me arse,' shouted Scott, bending over to ease the pain. He found whatever it was only got him when he straightened up so he stayed bent and they made their way back towards the midships section where the first aid kit was kept.

Tomkins had flown a perfect attack but he was not taking charge of the situation as they sorted themselves out. His crew did it for him. Below and aft of the flight deck, in the midships section, first aid was administered to Bannister's cut and Scott's backside. No one would notice that he had pissed himself now. His trousers were soaked in blood. Thank God for that! The engineer checked over his instruments. All appeared well. So he left his seat and headed forward to check for damage. He crawled under the forward turret, noted the shambles and the hole in the nose. He noted the damage further aft, just below the flight deck, and the shattered flight deck window. He also looked out and saw the gaping hole in the leading edge of the starboard wing.

Then he headed aft and checked out the midships and tail sections. He was surprised to see that there were also three largish holes in the starboard side of the tail section, ten feet forward of the after turret. He could not tell but they were the result of the final burst from the U-boat's 20mm gun. What did concern him was that there was a large nick out of one of the control rods running to the elevators. The rod was reduced to just under half its normal diameter. He wondered if it would last all the way back.

Finally he came forward and then crawled into the starboard wing. On a Sunderland, it was possible to move around inside the wing. He did not stay long. Air was roaring in through the hole but the fuel tanks appeared OK. It was bloody cold in there.

Tomkins had gone through the motions. He had done what was required of him. He had attacked the U-boat, successfully. He had circled round and watched it sink. He had flown over the spot to check for survivors. He could do that. That was something you could think about beforehand. An attack you could practise. Now his aircraft and his men were damaged. He had never experienced that situation before. He was the captain. He ought to be doing something about it. Come on, man!

'Captain to . . . errr . . . Captain to Navigator. Course for home . . . Give me the course for home.'

'Zero one five,' answered the navigator. That was the direct route home. Passes a bit close to Ushant but we've taken a few knocks. Might be pushed to make it back. That'll do for now.

'Errr, Captain to Galley. How many wounded? Errrr . . . How are they?'

'Only two, Skipper. Scotto and Phi . . . errr . . . Flight Lieutenant Bannister. Both minor. Lot of blood. Looks spectacular but they'll be right.'

'Captain, roger.'

Half a minute later, the engineer plugged back into the intercom. 'Engineer to Captain. Nose turret is out of action. Couple of holes in the nose section. Hole in the leading edge of the starboard wing. Engines and fuel tanks OK but the hole's pretty big.' Only then did Tomkins realise why he had had to wind on rudder trim. It was the drag from the hole in the starboard wing. That was going to slow them down. The engineer went on. 'There's damage back aft as well. Few holes. And some damage to the elevator control rods. I recommend you take it easy on the elevators.'

Tomkins acknowledged and ran his mind over the situation.

Men were OK. No one killed. He could be gentle with the elevators. That was OK. But the starboard wing. Extra drag. Slow them down. Use more fuel . . .

'Captain to Navigator, I want a direct route home, or as direct as we can.'

'You've got it. Zero one five is direct.'

Oh, how did the man know? thought Tomkins to himself.

VII

'That's it, boys. Time for home!'

Mick Hargan grinned to himself as a quiet 'Hurray!' was heard over the intercom. No more U-boats. They had spent the rest of their time with the convoy searching out the stern sector. Nothing more had been seen. The U-boat they had seen had not stuck its head up again. They had swept backwards and forwards across the imaginary box astern of the convoy where any shadowing U-boat might be found. They had done their bit and now it was time for home.

'Skipper, X-Xray's just come up on the circuit.'

'Goodo. Thanks, Sparks.' They were down to the limit on fuel anyway but it was nice to know the next aircraft had arrived. He glanced at the clock on the instrument panel. They're a bit early, he thought to himself, but then they've had the wind up their tails coming out here, just like us. Now we'll have it on the nose going home. Prudent limit of endurance. And a bit in the pot for luck.

'Mug of tea, Skipper?' It was Tiny who had appeared on the flight deck, two enamel mugs clasped in his enormous hands.

'Thanks, mate. Just what I need.'

Bill Newton was bringing them out of the final turn and setting course for home. They'd keep the lookout going, just in case they came across a U-boat homing in on the convoy, or one on its way out from the French coast. No problems about fighters out here, though. Too far west for them.

*

Schafer lead them round in a long sweeping turn to port. They were spread out in a line of search. No point in trying to fly close together. Stay apart and you can watch the sky around you rather than watching the leader's aircraft all the time. Stay apart and just glance at the leader from time to time. That was the way. And, as leader, he could keep watching all the time, he and his observer. Search the sky above and below, but mainly below. Bloody boring but that's what we are here for. Keep looking and looking and looking, and, one day, you'll find one. Except it was always someone else who found the Tommies. Always someone else who spotted that shape moving across the sea below.

Keep sweeping to and fro across fifty miles of sky. Cover the route down to the south. Cover the route their Biscay patrols take going backwards and forwards, or at least the route we guess they might take. Nothing is certain. It's our best estimate. So search it out, backwards and forwards, sweeping the sea below, watching for that dark shape against the lighter sea.

*

Tomkins had recovered control of himself. He had gathered the information about the health of his crew, the health of his aircraft. He had sifted that information again. He had checked off in his own mind what needed to be done. Engineer to keep an eye on the elevator rods from time to time. Second pilot to keep an eye on the starboard wing, make sure no extra panels were becoming detached. He had enquired again about the two wounded. They were OK. He had also had time to pass out congratulations. It had taken thirty minutes for him to think of it, but finally he had done it.

'Captain to crew . . . err . . . well done, everybody . . . well done.'

What should you say to them? He was not sure.

*

Mick was down in the galley. Time for a breather. Let Bill and George do it for a bit. We're away from the convoy now. If they see anything, they'll shout. Time for a hunk of bread and jam. A big tin of jam was standing open on the small surface by the cooker. Aussie comforts. Good stuff. He dug his knife deep into the tin. There was not much of the jam left. Greedy buggers have had most of it. But a big enough lump of strawberry jam came out on the end of the knife, with a whole strawberry embedded in it. Goodo. He spread it none too evenly over the hunk of bread in his hand. Putting down the knife, he took a big bite, holding the bread carefully so the jam did not run off. Yeah, good stuff. He grinned as he chewed on the somewhat solid bread. As he put the kettle on the stove, Tiny smiled back.

'Beaut jam, ain't it, Skipper? Must come from Victoria.'

'Naw, Western Australia, mate. She's right. Western Australian jam, this.'

'Piss off, Skipper. Best Victoria that.' Mick was unable to answer as he chewed another chunk.

*

Tomkins was aware that they were staying a long way to the east. In fact, he had given up his seat for a few moments and left P-Peter in the hands of the second pilot whilst he went back to look at the plot with the navigator. Together they had looked at the fuel figures, checked the distances, noted the air speed showing on the panel in front of them. The navigator had juggled with the figures, tried a couple of options, checked again. The sum was always the same. They had to go straight back. The extra fuel they had used plus the drag from the hole in the starboard wing meant they would only just have enough fuel to get back. And that was only if the winds had not strengthened. It was going to be tight.

*

The sea below was flecked with white. The wind was steady from the east. The cloud cover was patchy. Sometimes it was quite thick, other times they had blue above them. Sometimes shapes seemed to materialise in the shadows of the clouds, but there was nothing there. The three Ju88s held their open formation as they flew east. The sun, when it shone through a break in the clouds, was over their right shoulders, casting shadows on the instrument panels. Six pairs of eyes searched the sea and the sky. Four pairs of eyes were experienced in the business. Schafer was an old hand. All the observers were old hands as well. Only the two green pilots were new to the business. Well, in fact, Elman had flown a couple of sorties already, but he had much to learn. Bruckner had everything to learn, although it did seem he knew how to handle an aeroplane. He had always followed promptly through the turns. His formation keeping was good, even though they were flying well spread out. Elman was far more ragged, sometimes slightly ahead of the other two, sometimes behind, sometimes above, sometimes below.

Schafer held his right arm up and stretched it backwards. He was starting to seize up. He wriggled his toes in his boots, sat up straighter than normal for a few seconds, tensed the muscles in his thighs and relaxed them, just to try and ease the aches and pains which were building up. Something was digging into his right cheek. He shifted his bottom for the thousandth time but it made no difference. Bloody aeroplanes! Damn-awful seats. He moved his neck and head round in a circle. A rough patch on his collar was rubbing below his left ear. Bloody war!

*

Mick was back in the left-hand seat. He did not know it but there was still a trace of strawberry jam on his lips. They were in a bit of a no-man's land now. Probably clear of anywhere a U-boat might be. Hopefully clear of where German fighters might be prowling. Clear of convoys. Clear of the war, just for a while. However, you could not escape the fact that the Sunderland was a war machine. Might have grown up from a civilian flying boat but this was a war machine. All frills, all luxuries removed. She was stark and functional inside. She was big, yes, but functional. Too big, really. Considering the size, the bomb load is not great. Not enough power in the engines. The bloody things have been going very nearly full belt ever since we took off. Ease back any more and we'll start losing height. No wonder they have to keep changing the damn things.

A war machine. She was showing her age. Scuff marks and scratches on the panels. Bare shiny patches where the throttles had been caressed for the ten thousandth time. The odd screw on a panel hanging loose because the instrument fitter could not get it back in any more. The port throttle was always creeping a bit. The starboard inner luboil pressure gauge always vibrated more than the other, the needle jumping around. The landing light switch was dodgy. The port outer fuel cock was stiff. The lap strap buckle was always a bastard to get in. She always seems just a touch nose heavy. But she's ours. She's D-Dog and we're taking her home for the twenty-seventh time. Good on yer, old girl.

*

There is a point on the maps about sixty-five miles south-west of Ushant. On the map it is just marked 48°02′ North 06°10′ West. It has no other name. P-Peter flew through this point at 1432, heading north-north-east. Three Ju88s flew through the same point at 1436, heading west. The closest the starboard aircraft of the three came to the Sunderland was seven miles. Elman did not see the mere speck in the sky which was the British aircraft. The tail gunner of P-Peter did not see the three fighters cross his line of vision. They were too far away.

Mick Hargan was one hundred and twenty miles north-west of this point at the same time, enjoying his eleventh cup of tea since take-off. Time for one more before we get back but I must have a pee. . . .

*

Phil Bannister took over the right-hand seat as they crossed the latitude of Ushant. The wound over his right eye was still leaking blood from time to time but a small field dressing was containing most of it. His clothes were still blood-stained and would remain so until they got back. If they got back. They were conscious that they were much further east than normal. You could sense that the French coast, the outermost edge of Brittany was just over . . . there. All the turrets were manned. No point in manning the radar so the extra man was in the astrodome, the small perspex dome perfectly placed just aft of the flight-deck, nominally for taking sun and star sights through, but also providing an excellent lookout position for fighters.

The nose turret was manned but would not move again. Not until it had been lifted out and the hydraulic pipes replaced. The tail turret was manned. Bit dodgy going back there to relieve someone. You were made very aware of the holes in the tail section because the wind was roaring in through the gaps in the aircraft's skin. Get in the turret and shut the door quick. Don't try to think about the damage to the elevator rods that the engineer keeps coming back to have a look at. Just hope they hold out until we get back. Trouble is, the elevators probably have to work hardest when you're on finals for landing. Lose the elevators then and you've got a whole heap of problems. Bit close to the ground, or the water, or both. Keep your fingers crossed and hope we make it back. Meanwhile keep watching for those Jerry fighters. Dead dodgy it is, coming this far east. Navvy says we can't spare the fuel to dog leg out to the west, to tiptoe round this bit where a finger of France sticks out into the Atlantic. Skipper ain't said much on the way back. Then he never does. Good piece of flying over that U-boat. Clobbered the bastards first time. Didn't get much reaction out of him though. Cold-hearted bastard, he is. Just went in there, hammered the Jerries and then headed for home. Hardly said a thing to the rest of us, but that's the way he always is.

Tomkins found himself sweating. It was three hours since they had left the scene of the attack. Three hours in which he had recovered from the impact of what he had done. His crew had done what was necessary. The first pilot was patched up and back in the right-hand seat. The engineer had checked out the damage again, and had kept going back to the tail to check the elevator controls. The nose gunner, Scott, was nursing his backside. The other lads were all posted as lookouts, watching for fighters.

But what could he do if they were bounced? Could he throw the aircraft round the sky, at low level if necessary? Would the elevators stand the strain? Could he afford the fuel to do it? He would have to afford the fuel. They couldn't just fly on if fighters appeared out of the sky. He would have to try and evade and dodge and weave. They had practised it enough times. But this could be the real thing, with a damaged Sunderland to handle. Not badly damaged, but enough to be worrying. Use up too much fuel and they might not make it back. So Tomkins was sweating and working out that, perhaps, in thirty minutes, they might feel a bit safer. Then they would be well to the north-west of Ushant and only thirty minutes or so from home. Just another thirty minutes.. . . .

*

Schafer lead them round in a turn to starboard. Enough. The
Ju88's endurance was limited. Couldn't stay out here for
hours. Somewhere in the overall pattern, other aircraft would
be on their way out. To north and south other aircraft would
be searching. They were not the only ones. They had done
their bit of the jigsaw. The parts fitted together. Or at least
they fitted together on a neatly-drawn map in some Ops
Room. Out here they were only searching a small radius
around them. Whilst they were on a westerly leg, something
could have slipped through to the east of them. It was a game
of chance. Today nothing. Tomorrow? Who knows.

They steadied up on one zero zero magnetic. Forty minutes
and then I can have a bath. Then I'll have to look at the flying
programme for tomorrow. See how many aircraft we have,
how many crews. Go through the juggling game again. Never
enough of anything. Not enough aircraft in his Staffel, in all
the Staffels added together to really cover the Bay. How many
Tommies were getting through? They would never know.
Perhaps, after the war, someone would find out, go through
the records on both sides, add it all up? Now it was just
statistics. U-boats who did not come home. Did they die at the
hands of a British aircraft? Were they sunk by escorts? Did
they hit a mine? Fighters who did not come back – what
happened to them? Some they knew well enough. Seen shot
down by others who came back to tell the tale. But what of
those pairs who flew out over the sea and were never seen
again? On the other side, the Tommies would wait for aircraft
that never came back and wonder what happened. Shot down
by a U-boat? Shot down by German fighters?

They were all expendable. In order to further the overall
conduct of the war, men had to die. U-boats, aircraft, tanks,
soldiers. All expendable. But if we can kill his men, his
machines, faster than he is killing us, then we will win. In the
end. Fighters to kill the Sunderland, the Liberators. Sunderlands and Liberators to kill the U-boats. U-boats to sink the
merchant ships. Corvettes to protect the merchant ships. Who
was really winning? Them or us?

He brought himself back to reality with a jolt. He was aware
that his eyes had been searching, but the brain had seen
nothing. The brain was far away. Has a Tommy crossed my

gaze whilst I have been daydreaming? Have I missed one in the last two minutes, in the last four miles of distance flown? Probably not. There's nothing to see out here anyway.

*

'Land ho, Skipper! Looks like Ireland. It's all green.' It was an old joke, but it was comforting to hear it again. The old routine. The familiar – comforting. The little habits which bring security. Tuck that little Teddy Bear in your tunic. He always comes. Lucky mascot? Naw, he likes to come for the ride. Go without him? Not bloody likely.

The Lizard peninsula was off the port bow. Always there. Nice to see it on the way home. Not far now. Then we'll be heading ashore. Get cleaned up. Bit of supper. Any chance of a pint tonight? Bloody hell, then we'll have to be thinking of the next trip. Tomorrow? Next day? Now the weather's better, the breaks are shorter. Might get a bit of fog though, like the other morning. Goodo!

'Aircraft, two o'clock!' The call from Bill Newton brought everyone to the alert. Had to be friendly . . . didn't it? They all waited whilst Bill grabbed the binoculars. . . .

'Sunderland!' he announced, eventually. 'Heading our way.'

As the two aircraft converged, the other slightly ahead of D-Dog, they could read the marking.

'It's Tomkins and his boys.'

'Oh, shit, better let him go first. He's back a bit early, ain't he? He went after us.'

'Had a long way to go,' conceded Mick. 'Get low on fuel, you feel like heading for home. They've been all the way down the Bay.'

They ended up about a mile apart. So Mick eased off the power and let P-Pom draw ahead. No point in trying to get in right behind him. We'd have to wait until he had taxied out of the way anyway. No formation landings on our strip of water. So he slowed down and took a slightly wider route to swing in over the land. They would swing inland and then come round in a wide sweep, descending over the hills, but not too far, lads, 'cos we havn't got wheels. No problems with cloud base now. It's lifted quite a lot so we'll swing over the land. No need to drop down over the sea and head up harbour low. We can see where we are going.

They came in over the steep cliffs of Cornwall, over the small fields and narrow lanes. Mick watched the other aircraft, noticed that Tomkins was also taking a bit of a wide swing at things. Seemed to be taking things gently. Prick though he was, Tomkins could fly a Sunderland. But even from this distance, he seems to be taking things a bit gingerly, seems to be easing her round the corners. Real shallow turns, they are.

Mick found himself quite a long way inland as he lost time waiting for P-Pom to drop down into the valley and follow the final stretch of the river leading into the wider waters of the harbour. Instead Tomkins took her in a straight line, over the hills, a long, steady descent on finals. Then the other Sunderland was lost against the land. Plenty of time.

Mick banked the Sunderland round to starboard. Quite a long way out of town. Keep the revs on for the moment. 2300 revs all round. He brought her round in a long turn. Further out than normal. Get over the village like we usually do. Then ease back on the power and let her slip down into the valley. Wonder why Tomkins went in over the hills?

The familiar village crept under the nose, the church set off to one side just visible out of the port window. Usual place. We always come this way. His hands moved to the throttles and pulled them gently back. After so many hours, the note of the engines suddenly seemed to die as they throttled back to idling revs. He let the nose drop, as it always did as the power came off. Bit of trim just to hold her in the glide. Flaps down. One third. Bit more trim. Bit of power just to hold her. Wind from the east. Come five degrees left to catch the drift. Over the wood, just over the corner. Follow the usual line. Let her drop into the valley. Not right in but that hill to starboard is only just below us now. Come ten degrees right to follow the river. Not far now.

The Sunderland came in over the place where the river widened out, over the final spit of mud. Gently he brought her round to port, to line up down the harbour. Come round a bit more, catch the drift again. Let her ease down. Throttles all the way back now. Glide approach. All clear ahead. No one in the way. Glimpse of a Sunderland, engines running, in amongst the buoys. Must be Tomkins.

Twenty feet above the water. Kick off the drift. Hold her. Check her above the surface. Hold her in the planing attitude and let her settle gently. He felt the tremor as the keel bit the water. As they dropped another foot, the drag of the water started to bleed off the speed. Hold the nose. Hold her how she is. Then she settled fully and the speed was coming off rapidly and the spray was thrown up on either side, a glint of sun catching the water drops.

She dropped off the plane and settled into the water. Just like a duck landing. One moment a graceful flying machine, next a rather awkward water bird. The forward turret was already moving as the lads wound it back so they could get the mooring gear ready. Mick turned off to the side and headed for their spot amongst the buoys. Tomkins looked like he was moored up now. Better not balls this one up with him watching.

They got the buoy first time, just this once. The lads in the bow got the bridle on. The engines stopped. Peace at last. Eleven frigging hours of that racket. The instruments wound down. There was a steady ticking noise from the port inner as it cooled. It always did that. D-Dog was at rest.

'Shit, Skipper, Tomkins has got a bloody great hole in his wing. And some more back aft. Wonder what they've been up to?'

*

Jilly Johnson had watched them come back. She was sitting amongst an outcrop of rocks below the house which the officers now used as a mess. The rocks were about thirty feet above the beach and she had a good view across the harbour. When the sun was out, it was really quite warm, especially if she got down behind the big rock out of the wind, but then she could not watch what was going on.

An MTB had been out in the harbour earlier, doing an engine test or something. The rest of them were in their usual place, alongside the Navy pier. The Sunderlands swung at their moorings, except for those away on sorties. She had seen one go and now two were coming back. She watched P-Peter

land. Golly, were they only just getting back? It seemed an age
since they had gone. She had had time to finish the long night
watch, have a quick bath afterwards, go to bed for the
morning, have dinner, write a couple of letters and then take a
stroll along the beach. And they were only just coming back.

She watched the Sunderland taxi in towards its buoy and
then swing with a burst from its engines to put the nose
alongside the buoy. She could just make out the figures in the
bow. They had called the tender alongside and she could see
ropes or something being passed across. As P-Peter had taxied
in, she had been surprised to see another Sunderland land.
Was this a training sortie which had gone off in the morning?
Then she saw it was D-Dog. John Williams's crew! With that
realisation, there was a stirring of interest, and then, at the
thought of what she had been doing two nights before, a
feeling of sexual arousal. Just the thought of him turned her
on. But he went to bed with all the girls, didn't he? But he was
very sexy, nevertheless.

*

The three Junkers 88s swept in low over the beach, wheels
already down, flaps down. Schafer lead them in, a straight in
approach to runway 06. The wind was still out of the east. A bit
of crosswind. No problem. They came in over the road which
lead to the town, over the final field, the last hedge. He flared
out over the end of the runway, held her off, kicked off the
drift and let her settle. There was a jolt and a slight screech as
the tyres bit. He let her roll on. Give the others room to land.
Don't put the brakes on just yet. The speed came off, the tail
dropped and she was slowing of her own accord. He gave her a
touch of brake, then let her run on down the runway until they
reached the point where the two runways crossed. He led
them round to the right, along the cross runway, and then
back round the taxiway to the apron.

As the engines died, he hit the quick release on his straps.
He grabbed the handle above his head and hauled himself up.
His aching muscles protested. Thank God he could get up off
that seat, though. His arse had long ago lost all sensation.

'Thank you, Ernst.' He always said 'Thank you'. Thank you
for what? the other man wondered. Thank you for coming

along for the ride? Thank you for finding the way back? It's only my job. I'm supposed to find the way back.

They climbed stiffly down from the aircraft. The other two crews were doing the same. Should he have a word with them? They'd debrief quickly in the hut anyway. Should he say anything to Bruckner, who had flown a competent sortie? Probably not. Should he say anything to Elman about keeping formation? What the hell. The lad, for all his arrogance, was still learning. We all had to learn once. He led the way across the tarmac towards the huts.

*

Tomkins was waiting in the Ops Room when Mick and Dinger walked in. Mick greeted the Ops Officer first.

'   Hello, Dickie, old mate.'

'Hello, Mick, Welcome back.'

Only then did Mick turn to Tomkins and gave him a nod. 'Hello, sir.'

'Afternoon, Hargan. Errrr, good trip?'

'Yeah, fine. No problems. No problems. Saw a U-boat. Twice in fact.'

'Did you attack it?' asked Tomkins quickly.

'Had a go but the bugger dived before we could get over the top. There was nothing to attack.'

'Oh, I see . . . I see. How far away were you spotted?'

Mick shrugged. 'Dunno. Four, five miles maybe. Very clear, it was. They had plenty of time to get down.'

'Mmmm.' It was so good talking to Tomkins. You never knew what the bugger was thinking, but you could guess. Hargan . . . takes too long to get in an attack. Misses his chance. Failed to kill. Well, bollocks to him. He wasn't there. I was, thought Mick to himself.

Tomkins was on his way out. 'I'll see your report in due course, Hargan.'

Yeah, sure thing, prick. I'll tell you how it really was. Mick watched the squadron commander leave and then turned to Dick Smiley.

'Right, Dickie, what's up?'

'Tomkins got one today,' answered Dickie simply.

'Got one what, mate?'

'A U-boat.'

'What! Bloody 'ell. Any other bloke would be telling it to all and sundry. How? Where?'

'Down here apparently.' Dickie was pointing to a spot on the map in the southern Bay. 'Chap was heading east. Stayed on the surface to shoot it out. Tomkins got him first run. Took a couple of knocks and some minor injuries. U-boat broke in half.'

'Shit!'

Just then the door opened and one of the Wrens came in.

'Ah, these might be the photos. What have you got there, Janet?'

The girl handed Dickie two photographs which she had carried carefully across from the phot section, because they were still wet. Dickie put them down on the table.

'Wow!' was all Mick could say.

The first one showed a U-boat surrounded by columns of water where depth charges were going off. You could pick out four separate points of explosion, straddling the U-boat. The second photograph showed the U-boat in two halves. It was a bit blurred, as if the camera had been a bit unsteady, but the front part of the U-boat seemed to be twisted over and the stern section was sticking slightly up in the air.

'Hey, that's bloody good,' Mick acknowledged finally. 'Has Tomkins seen these?' His question was directed at Dickie but the Wren answered it.

'Yes, sir. He met me as I was coming across from the phot section. He was on his way there to see the rest. He was saying something about why was the second one so blurred. . . .' The girl realised she was saying too much and lapsed into silence.

'This calls for a party,' announced Mick, and then quietly to Dickie only, 'even if it was Tomkins who got the bastard. It's still a good enough reason for a party.' He looked again at the photos. 'Good attack, that, I'll give him that. Hey, who from his crew was injured, Dickie?'

'Oh, err, Phil Bannister caught a splinter above his eye, but he's OK. And one of his gunners, lad called Scott, caught one . . . in his backside,' he added quietly.

'Poor bastard. Straight up the arse, eh?' replied Mick in a normal voice. Hell, Wrens knew what arses were. They had them too. Nice ones, some of them. This girl's not bad. Bit quiet. I've seen her before. Doesn't have much to say for herself.

Janet did not have much to say. She was not too fussed about the U-boat either. She was more worried about why her period was late. It was always so regular. Now it was two days late. That was what really fussed her.

VIII

The car stopped at the barrier. The sentry came across to the driver's door. 'Off to the station as usual, I suppose?' he asked.

'Yeah, same as ever,' answered the girl behind the wheel.

'OK, love, off you go.'

He walked across to the barrier and raised it and waved her through. The car started off a bit shakily. Hell, I haven't been driving all that long, thought the girl behind the wheel. She swung out of the gate and turned right to go up the hill.

The car started on the long climb and negotiated the first bend. Almost immediately after that, it swung into a gateway on the left, pulling just off the road, and stopped. Without a pause, four girls, two Wrens, two WAAFs detached themselves from the cover of the hedge, stepped quickly across to the car, and climbed in. Three of them squeezed into the back. Jilly Johnson jumped in the front. Within seconds, the car was on its way again.

'Thanks, Annie,' said Jilly as soon as they were under way. The girls settled down in the leather seats.

'Off to the pictures, then?' asked the driver.

'Yeah! It's the new Clark Gable. We've got to see that!' called one of the girls from the back.

'Certainly have,' added another. 'He's wonderful.'

The banter went backwards and forwards as the car ground up the long hill, through the village, and then levelled out at the top. After another half a mile, they reached a crossroads. Annie, the driver, looked both ways and was about to swing out when she called, 'Look out, there's a lorry coming the other way!'

They all knew the drill. The three girls in the back ducked down as low as they could and Jilly did the same in the front. The lorry approached the crossroads, slowed and turned down the lane beside them. Annie made sure she already was moving as it passed so the driver would not be tempted to stop and chat. The RAF lorry straightened up and headed on towards the base.

'All clear!' called Annie, and the others sat back in their seats. By way of explanation, she added, 'You never know when an officer or that miserable sergeant might be out and about. That was OK. That was Ralph Bates driving. He wouldn't tell on you.' The other girls knew the score anyway. Just don't get caught in the officers' transport, that was the rule. But use it from time to time to go the pictures, nevertheless.

*

Jane Phillips was thankful that the long train journey was almost at an end. Lincolnshire to Cornwall by train in war time. What a way to travel! At least she had had a night in London. But all she had wanted to do was have a decent bath, wash her hair under really hot water, borrow an iron to press some clothes, and fall into bed. The train down from London seemed to take an age. The ticket inspector had assured her that they were running to time. It did not seem possible, after what seemed like endless stops at stations along the way. However, when she checked her watch, it showed just on seven and they were due in at two minutes past.

The train drew in at five past. Quite a number of people got out. Jane climbed down from her carriage and pulled her big suitcase out after her. Then she had to step back up for her kit bag and another small case. As she turned to climb down again, a voice behind her said, 'Need a hand, miss?' She looked up to see a porter standing there, a kind, old, weather-beaten face.

'Oh, yes, thank you . . . thank you.'

The porter picked up her suitcase and placed it carefully on his trolley. He balanced the kit bag on top and set off along the platform. Jane followed along behind, adjusting her cap as she went.

'You'll be going to the base, miss?' It was more a statement than a question. 'Come far?'

'Oh, er, from Lincolnshire.'

'Ahh . . . that be far enough. Never been beyond Plymouth

meself, 'cept in the Great War, that is.' They reached the ticket barrier.

Jane fumbled in her bag for her ticket and then followed the porter out. He was already heading towards a car parked in the station yard.

As the porter stopped by the car, the driver who was standing beside it came smartly to attention and saluted. Jane realised she had her case in the wrong hand, thought for a moment whether to return the salute or not – it always seemed silly, women saluting each other – decided she ought to, put down the case and raised her hand to her cap.

'Good evening, ma'am,' greeted the driver. Then, without further ado, the driver helped the porter put the large case on the luggage rack at the back of the car and between them they pushed Jane's kit bag inside.

'Right, that be you ready then, miss.'

'Oh, yes, thank you.' Jane realised she ought to give the porter something. She opened her handbag and reached inside for her purse. What should she give him? Sixpence? A shilling, maybe?

'Don't you worry about that, miss,' he said, touching her arm. 'You've had a long day. You be getting off now.' With that he held open the door and watched Jane climb in. She did not notice the merest glint in his eye as her skirt rode up as she got in and she exposed a flash of stockinged thigh for half a second. As she sat down, the door was shut for her. The driver climbed in the front and started the engine. The clutch went in more smoothly this time and the car drew easily away.

'Come far, have you, ma'am?' asked Annie, even before they were out of the station yard. Jane explained she had come from Lincoln. Was everyone going to ask the same question?

'Bomber station was it, ma'am?' The car turned onto the main road.

'Yes . . . yes, it was.'

'This'll be a bit of a change, then. I was on a fighter station for a bit. Very different it is here.'

'In what way? By the way, what's your name?'

'Anne Jones, ma'am, 'cept everyone calls me Annie.' The girl paused to negotiate the turn off the main road. 'Well, ma'am, for a start there are no runways here. It's all down on the water. It's nice in the summer. Bit bloo – Very cold in the winter. But it's OK. Not too bad. And the aircrew, nearly all of them are Australian, of course.'

'Yes, I'd heard that. Are they very different? I don't think I've ever met an Australian.'

'Ooooh, they're different all right.' Then she added, quickly, 'Not that I know about the officers of course. But the lads . . . they're very casual, like a joke. Don't like any spit and polish too much, if you see what I mean.'

'Mmmm, I see,' answered the officer in the back.

Oh, hell, thought Annie, I'm saying too much. Better shut up for a bit. So she concentrated on driving and let the WAAF flight lieutenant watch the countryside go by.

*

Mick was one of the early ones in the bar. He had walked across the lawn with Dinger. The sun was setting behind the hills. The wind was dropping as the sun went. It was a perfect spring evening.

'What'll it be, skipper?'

'Better make it something weak, Dinger old mate. Got a long way to go tomorrow. Just a beer will do thanks.' On the way across, Mick had told Dinger they were on again the next day. Off about lunchtime, Uncle Dickie had said. Probably all the way down the Bay. What a bastard!

Two pints appeared on the bar. Mick picked his up, raised it to Dinger, said 'Cheers, mate!', and took a sip off the top. 'Bloody hell, steward, you been putting this on to boil?' The steward had heard it all before and ignored it. Mick shrugged and led the way across towards the French windows.

'Come on, let's enjoy the evening whilst we've got some decent weather for a change.'

'Be with you in a minute. Must go and have a pee.'

'Bloody 'ell, mate. You've had one sip and you need a piss? I know this stuff goes right through you but that's ridiculous!' They both laughed at the joke as Dinger broke off and headed towards the main door of the bar.

Mick stepped outside and walked slowly across the lawn. There was still enough light to illuminate the view across the harbour to the hills on the other side. Nothing was stirring on the water. This particular part of the world was at peace – just for the moment. But the gaps in the line of Sunderlands at their moorings showed where crews were away, flying out over the Atlantic, over the Bay, fighting their bit of war. Mick stood and contemplated the peace of the scene as he sipped his beer.

'Evening, Skipper!'

Mick realised he was miles away. He turned to face the voice. It was Bill Newton, with young George Kemp with him. 'What are you having?' Bill was aking of George.

'Oh, pint please,' replied the younger man. With a nod to Mick, Bill headed on towards the French windows, leaving George standing rather awkwardly.

Mick broke the silence. 'Good spotting today, young George. It's not every day you see a U-boat.'

'Oh, yeah. Skipper, there was something I was meaning to ask you.' He paused. 'I mean, those U-boats. . . . Well, we didn't . . . ummm, we didn't drop anything on them, did we? I was . . . I was wondering why not, you know. . . .'

Mick could sense the unease of the nineteen-year-old. He was trying to question what his skipper had done, without really questioning. Mick took another sip of his beer whilst he thought of an answer.

'I've got a question for you. How many ships were sunk while we were out there with the convoy?'

'Well, errr, none, I guess.'

'That's right, mate. None. . . . None at all. That's what it's really all about. It doesn't matter how many U-boats are out there, as long as they don't sink any ships. Now, that one we put down second. How far from the convoy was he?'

'Pffff. About twenty miles, I suppose?'

'Right. Nearer twenty-three actually. Long way behind. Even if we didn't get the bastard, he would have to leg it to catch up, see. On the surface, flat out. Good chance he'll be picked up on radar either by another aircraft or one of the corvettes. Gets put down again. Never makes it back to the convoy. That's what it's all about.'

George thought about this for a few seconds. 'But . . . umm . . . wouldn't it have been worth dropping a couple of depth charges?'

'Well, maybe. But what would it have done? Our depth charges are set to go off shallow. Get the one who is just diving. That's what the boffins have worked out. All scientific, this business. So if we drop a couple, they're going to go off too shallow anyway. He'd be way down by the time we got over him today. Might rattle his coffee cups but that's all. Then we would have thrown away a few bombs which we might have needed later for a chap we really bounced.' Mick paused to take another sip of his beer. 'See, you don't need to be dropping bombs all over the place to get the job done. Keep their heads down, they can't get an attack in anyway. How many of them dive before we see them? How many pick up our radar and duck down 'cos they know some bastard like us is on the prowl? Hard to tell. But if we keep their heads down, we're doing our job.'

Bill Newton appeared, a pint in each hand. Mick went on. 'If you can get the bastard, that's fine. Looks good when you get back, but half our job is just being there. Like the escorts. We're all there just to put Jerry off his stroke. If we manage to clobber the bastard along the way, that's good. It doesn't work every time. I've been in this game a long time,' (He had a small captive audience of two by this time.) 'And that is only the second sortie when we've spotted something. But how many times has us just being there stopped Jerry doing what he wants? We'll never know. But what I do know is the merchant ships and escorts like having us around. They get a sniff of something, something like a DF bearing, give us a call and ten minutes later we've checked it out. Might just have forced the U-boat concerned to dive. That's good enough. Those guys in the Navy are out there for days, weeks. They are the continuity men. We are the glory boys. Get in there fast, do our thing, back home for tea. 'Cept it's not really like that, is it, Bill?'

Mick looked at Bill over the top of his glass as he took a longer swig from his beer.

'No, Skipper. Most of it's bloody boring, with the odd bit of excitement. George, you'll have to get used to the fact that today was a bit unusual what with seeing those U-boats. Might have been the same one. Don't count on seeing one every time we go out to a convoy. Luck of the draw. Like the Skipper says, we're just there to keep the bastards' heads down.'

'Mmmm, I see,' was all George could think to say to all that.

Mick was surprising himself with his analytical approach to their business but he found himself continuing, 'You see, George, we are just a small part of the big picture, the big anti-submarine battle. It goes from bombing U-boats in their bases to searching for them on the way out across the Bay to clobbering them if they get amongst a convoy. Just us being there is part of the battle. Like I said, keep their heads down. You have to fly lots of sorties with lots of aeroplanes to find one U-boat. We found one today but couldn't get in an attack. The boss was luckier. He found one that stayed around to argue the toss. So he got the bastard. It could have been us there . . . but it wasn't. But don't worry, George, we did our bit today and you did a good job as well, mate. Tell you what, as a prize, I'll let you do the take-off tomorrow!'

'Oh, great Skipper! Good on yer!' George lifted his glass and took a good mouthful. His first take-off in a Sunderland at operational load. It was OK at the OCU. They never had to go out heavy. But tomorrow he would have to get Dog in the air fully loaded. . . . Shit!

'Now what we want is a good party tonight, lads. Not too many beers 'cos we're flying tomorrow but we'll celebrate a kill in the squadron anyway, even if it was Tomkins who got it.' Mick turned to Bill. 'Where is he, anyway? Any ideas?'

'I hear he's going off to some dinner party tonight. Won't be here.'

Dinger joined them at last, having been caught in the bar by someone else for a few minutes. Mick called to him as he approached.

'Dinger, you hear that? Tomkins is ducking out on us tonight. Going to some other piss-up.' Then in his awful imitation of an English upper-class accent, 'Damn bad show, I call it, chaps, what?' Then, reverting to pure Aussie, 'Never mind, lads, we'll have a few beers with his crew anyway.'

*

The car drew up outside the house. Jane could see, even in the failing light, that it was a handsome house. She could also see a number of officers making their way towards it from huts set in the grounds. A few were standing on the lawn which faced towards the water, glasses in their hands.

The car door was opened and she climbed out of the car. 'Thank you, Annie,' she said as she straightened her skirt. One of the mess servants had appeared out of the main door of the house and stepped down to the car. 'Flight Lieutenant Phillips, ma'm?' he asked.

'Yes.'

'You are expected, ma'm. Your quarters are in the house here. I'll see to your bags if you'd like to step inside.'

Jane took the advice and climbed up the few wide steps which lead to the main door. Inside, the hall was impressive, with a fine staircase leading to the upper floors. The ceiling was rather ornate, perhaps a bit too ornate. Off to one side, through a door, she could hear the hubbub of conversation. It sounded like the bar. Off to the left she could see into an ante-room, with a few magazines and papers scattered around on the armchairs. That room seemed deserted.

She turned as the mess servant brought her bags in. 'I'll just tell the adjutant you're here, ma'm. He wanted to say hello to you.' With that, he put down the bags and headed over towards the door leading to the bar. A few seconds later he reappeared, followed by a slightly-balding officer with a moustache.

'Hello, welcome,' he called as he approached. 'I'm John Weston.' He held out his hand.

'Hello. Jane Phillips.'

'Good . . . good. Well, welcome, Jane. Nice to see you got here OK. Good journey?'

'Not too bad.'

'Fine, fine. Now, it looks like there's going to be a bit of a party tonight. But I expect you'll want to get unpacked and sorted out and things. Do join us if you want to. Meet some of the chaps.'

'Well, I'd quite like to get sorted out. . . .'

'Yes, of course, of course. Now, have you had anything to eat?'

'No, not recently.'

'Well, look, why don't I get Moore here to bring a tray up to your room or something. How would that be?'

'Thank you, that would be nice.' She wondered if she had missed dinner or something.

'Well, I'll leave you to it, then.' With a smile and a nod, he turned and headed back to the bar.

Jane turned to Moore who was picking up her suitcase. 'Have I missed dinner, Moore?'

'Well, not really, ma'm. But if there's a party on tonight, those that wanted to eat have been through already. If you wanted to eat in the dining room, you could, but I think you'll be on your own.'

'I see. What's the party for?' she asked as she followed him up the stairs.

'Oh, squadron commander got a U-boat today, ma'm, so the squadron are celebrating.'

'Oh.' Yes, it was going to be different from a bomber base. 'How many other female officers are there?'

'Well, ma'm, usually three. Plus you, that is. But one is on leave at present, one is going to some naval dinner party tonight and I think Pilot Officer Shaw is on duty.'

They had reached the main landing and then he took her off down a short passage. 'Female officers along here, ma'm. Bathroom there. Toilet next door. And this room here is a sort of little snug the ladies use.' He opened the door to reveal a small room with a settee, a couple of armchairs, a rather worn carpet and a radiogram. He turned to the door opposite. 'This'll be yours, ma'm.'

*

Yvette placed the two glasses and the bottle of wine on the tray, then picked up the tray and carried it across to the table. It was a quiet evening but the Staffelkapitän had come in with another officer who she thought was an engineer. Despite her good understanding of the German language, she still got confused by some of the ranks and technical terms she heard. It was not always easy to follow the conversations as she flirted with the Germans.

But that was not her concern that evening. What did concern her more was the two men seated at a table in the far corner. They had Gestapo written all over them. She knew the Gestapo men who worked in the district. These two were new but they had that look, that certain something, yes, that smell. They were sipping at their drinks and talking quietly in the corner. She was being very careful to do everything normally, perhaps exaggeratedly so. She could feel herself acting her normal job, and also felt that they were watching her every move.

Tonight she did not flirt with the Staffelkapitän. She delivered the tray of drinks, nodded curtly to the two Luftwaffe officers and withdrew. The Staffelkapitän, for his part, made no attempt to pass the time of day, which is the least he would have done normally. He too had sensed the nature of the two men sitting in the corner and was playing things strictly by the book. Officers may make use of French facilities, may use the cafés, restaurants, bars, but should not fraternise with the French people. Relationships were to be as between conqueror and conquered. How did you explain to the Gestapo that the only female company for miles around was French? How did you explain that, if the men wanted a whore, there were no loyal German girls to serve the needs of the youth of Hitler's Germany. But the French girls had a living to make.

Helmut and Hans sat quietly at their table, talking about this and that but nothing very serious, aware that two men in the corner would be watching. They noticed that the bar staff were being very formal and standoffish. They could understand why. It would be a very quiet evening. Just a couple of glasses of wine each, then back for a reasonably early night. There was more flying to do the next day.

*

Tomkins waited for the driver to open the car door, then climbed out. The girl saluted as he stepped across the gravel towards the door of the house. Another country house taken over by the services 'for the duration'. This one the Navy had moved into, to establish an administrative headquarters. The operational headquarters would remain on the base. Tomkins was not quite sure why the naval presence was increasing – he had heard something about a landing craft base being established and amphibious training being carried out. Could be something to do with the invasion which had to come sometime – this year, next year, when? Whatever the Navy were up to, it seems they now needed a commodore in charge. He had taken over the house as his headquarters and residence and this was his first official dinner party – a chance to meet my opposite numbers on an informal basis, as he put it.

A steward greeted Tomkins at the door and took his cap. He also pointed the way through into the drawing room, whose door stood open. Tomkins entered the room to be greeted straight away by the host, a short, dapper man with the one broad ring of a commodore on his sleeve.

'Good evening, sir. I'm Peter Tomkins from the Sund. . . .'

'Tomkins, my boy, welcome. I've been hearing all about your exploits today.' He nodded to a group captain in another group who raised his glass in greeting to Tomkins. 'Well done, indeed,' continued the commodore. 'Got a U-boat, eh? Jolly good show. Just what we need. Now, what'll you have to drink?'

Once Tomkins had a gin and tonic in his hand, he left his host who was greeting other guests and moved over towards the group captain's circle.

'Peter! Good to see you. Many congratulations on your attack today. Great news.' He turned to a naval commander who was standing beside him. 'James, let me introduce Peter Tomkins, who commands the Sunderland squadron here. He got a U-boat on the surface in the Bay today. Peter, James is in operations in Plymouth.'

Tomkins held out his hand. 'Congratulations!' responded the naval man. 'We have been a bit short of killings in the Bay of late. Did your chap try to dive or stay on the surface?'

'Oh, stayed on the surface, all right. Put up quite a lot of flak but we managed to get through. Got him first time, which was lucky.'

'Good show!' voiced the group captain. 'Once we get settled down, you'll have to tell me about your tactics. We chaps at Group need to know more about what it is like at the coal face.' The naval commander was turning aside to acknowledge a remark from someone who had just walked in.

The group captain added quietly to Tomkins, 'We need to show the Navy that we are playing our part in the Bay so your success today could not have come at a better time. Well done indeed!'

The gathering settled down to the familiar routine of pre-dinner drinks, not that there were all that many formal dinners these days. The gathering was almost entirely service. The commodore wanted it that way. He had a separate dinner arranged in a week's time to meet some of the local people. Tonight he wanted to get the feel of the service people he would have to deal with. He had asked one of the WAAF officers and his own Wren personal assistant to be there as well, just to make sure it was not all male. They were both quite pretty girls. They brightened the place up a bit.

The commodore made a point of circulating around to have a chat with all his guests. Presently a steward came in to announce quietly in his ear that dinner was served. So, with always an eye for a pretty girl, he sought out the young WAAF pilot officer and escorted her into dinner. However, she was not seated next to him. He had placed the group captain and the naval commander of the MTB base next to him. There was shop to be discussed over dinner.

*

The bar was rapidly filling and beer was flowing freely. Mick had migrated in from the lawn and was now tucked in a corner by the bar, holding forth on the subject of the English weather, not that he had had much cause for complaint in the last couple of days. Just then, a group of officers in the navy blue of the RN burst in through the door. 'Hello, chaps, the Navy's here!' and other greetings rang forth. They might be Brits but the MTB boys knew how to drink.

'Sorry, we can't stay long. We're going out in an hour or so,' announced a lieutenant leading the group. Pints were passed across from the bar and eagerly grasped. 'Where are the heroes, then?' asked the same lieutenant.

'Not here yet, sport,' answered one flight lieutenant. 'In fact, the skipper of the crew ain't going to be here at all. But his crew should be along shortly.'

Right on cue, Phil Bannister walked in through the door. His forehead was covered in a large plaster which gave his face a slightly lopsided appearance. As he walked in, a cheer went up. Cries of 'Phil, you beaut!' and 'Good on yer, mate!' came from all sides. The other officers from P-Pom were right behind him.

Once pints had been supplied and hands had been shaken and backs slapped, Mick realised he was probably the senior crew skipper there that night. He detached himself from the small group in his corner, took up an empty glass and thumped it several times on the bar. At the signal, conversation died away. Mick grabbed a bar stool, stepped on the rung at the side of it and then climbed onto the bar.

'Lads,' he announced to the assembled crowd, 'we are here tonight to celebrate one of our crews clobbering a U-boat. Doesn't happen too often. But it's nice to know this squadron's still doing its bit. Now, unfortunately, the skipper of the crew, who you all know well, cannot be here tonight.' There were loud jeers of 'Shame!' from around the room. From the tone of them, no one was actually missing Tomkins' presence. Mick held up his hand for silence. 'So, instead, we have the first pilot, our mate Phil Bannister, and the rest of the officers from P-Pom here tonight. Phil, old mate, congratulations to you and the rest of the lads!' With that he raised his glass as the signal for a toast all round. There were more cries of congratulations from around the room. With that, Mick stepped down from his perch and pushed his way across to where Phil Bannister was standing. He held out his hand 'Good one, Phil! How's the . . . err, injuries.'

'No sweat, mate. The Doc stitched me up and stuck this bleeding great plaster on it. Should be right in a few days.'

'Goodo,' answered Mick, slapping Phil on the shoulder.

The banter went backwards and forwards, no conversation of any consequence. Another cheer went up when Dick Smiley, Uncle Dickie, walked in. He was not often seen in the bar but he would celebrate the sinking of a U-boat with the rest of them. Jokes were exchanged, Phil Bannister and the rest of his team were supplied with beer, a pall of cigarette smoke built up above the assembled crowd, pools of beer started to form on the bar, the ash trays started to fill.

Mick and Phil Bannister found themselves together at one point but with no one else with them.

'Mick, can I have a word for a moment?'

'Yeah, sure, what's the problem?'

'Well, it's all very well us celebrating sinking this U-boat and the boys are making me feel like a bleeding hero. But the honest truth is that I did bugger all. I was just there for the ride. Tomkins flew the aircraft. I was just shit scared and sat in my seat waiting for a bullet to get me. Lucky I just got a splinter in me forehead.'

'Don't worry, Phil me old mate. We've all been in those situations where we've had to watch someone else actually doing what needs to be done. It's worse having to sit there and watch rather than doing it yourself. I remember once during training. Flying a twin. We had an engine failure. The instructor took over from me and I just had to sit there and watch him take us back on one engine. I tell you I was scared, mate.' He paused to try and light his pipe again.

'Yeah, OK, I suppose that's true,' responded Phil after a moment or two's thought. 'But I'll tell you the other thing, Mick. After the attack, which I have to admit Tomkins flew beautifully, it was bloody good . . . after the attack, we circled round and watched the bloody thing sink and went back over the top for a look-see. Then we peeled off for home. Tomkins seemed to go into a sort of daze. There were things to be done. I did not really realise I had been hit. We couldn't talk to the lad in the front turret because his comms had been shot away and he'd caught one in the backside and was sitting in a pool of blood. We had taken a few hits which needed checking out. Tomkins appeared not to appreciate what needed doing. He didn't take charge of the situation. The lads rallied and did what had to be done. Tomkins was flying us heading for home. But for the first thirty minutes or more, he seemed totally detached from what was going on around him. The lads patched up me and Scotto, our nose gunner. The engineer checked the aircraft out and identified the damage. It was only after a while that Tomkins finally twigged what needed doing and checked with the Navvy the route home and things like that. I was down below being patched up part of the time but a couple of the others have mentioned it to me. It doesn't give you too much confidence, does it, Mick?'

Mick puffed on his pipe which he had actually got going. 'Yeah, it's a bit worrying, mate, but you've got a good crew there. You do a good job keeping them up to shape, Phil me lad. Tomkins just comes for the ride. You're the mainstay in that crew. You keep it that way. If you hadn't been hit, I'm sure you would have been in there, getting things sorted out. But it seems from what you have said that your lads did a good job anyway, so you've obviously got them well trained.' He was trying to be as encouraging as possible because the man sitting opposite him was looking a bit glum. He had never really found himself in the role as father confessor before, but he realised that he was fast becoming a senior crew captain and must expect the younger lads to turn to him for advice. Veteran pilot at twenty-three. Shit!

*

Port was being passed. Nice to see that the Navy could still keep up standards. Tomkins was seated between a lieutenant-commander who was busy setting up the landing craft base, and the group engineer on the other side. Tomkins had been able to have a valuable conversation with the latter about engine hours and how often they had to do engine changes and some ideas Tomkins had for speeding up the procedure. He had not noticed the look of slight boredom on the other man's face. A pleasant dinner and he has to listen to a squadron commander going on about engines. How tedious.

After port, they rose from the table and returned to the drawing room. It was a pleasant room. A fire burned in the grate. Despite the warmth of the last few days, the house had a chill air about it and the fire brightened the room. Tomkins found himself next to the group captain. 'You wanted to discuss tactics, I believe, sir?' volunteered Tomkins.

'What, oh yes . . . yes. Perhaps . . . perhaps it's a bit late, don't you think? Thank you, Tomkins, but perhaps you could put some ideas on paper and forward them to Group. Yes, that would be the best way.'

'Oh, well, yes, sir, but I thought you might like to hear—'

'I certainly would, Tomkins, but perhaps in the cool light of day . . . perhaps best on paper. Give you time to gather your thoughts and so on.'

'But I can tell you now, sir. . . .'

But the group captain was turning away. 'Excellent, Tomkins, we need ideas from people like you. Drop me a line will you? . . . Commodore, that was a splendid meal. And so good of you to put us up for the night. It's quite a long trip down here from Plymouth. But a welcome break, I do assure you and so useful to be able to come and exchange ideas. Most welcome, most welcome.'

Tomkins felt it was time to have a word with the WAAF officer. She had been at the other end of the table. He wanted to talk to her about the behaviour of some of the girls with the men from his squadron. . . .

*

The evening was getting more boisterous. Mick, true to his word, was taking it easy and was only on his third pint, sipping slowly. However he had been roped in to lead a rendition of 'Waltzing Matilda', which had been the signal for the Navy to leave. They had to be out in the Channel that night. A short trip. A party with the Aussies was a valid reason for making the night's hunting a little shorter than usual. Just a hunt for E-boats over our side tonight, lads, no pissing about off the French coast. Not enough time to get there now.

A cry went up from somewhere in the middle of the crowd. 'New South Wales versus the Rest! Aussie rules!' New South Wales this side!' A great cheer went up and men started stripping off uniform tunics. This was going to be serious. Furniture was pushed back to the wall, bar stools were stacked up on top of the bar, glasses were carefully sent aside on mantelshelves and window ledges, tucked behind the blackout curtains. Shoes were taken off and carefully stacked behind the bar. Mick studiously avoided joining in. That's all I need – a busted leg before a sortie tomorrow.

'Come on Mick!'

'No way, mate. I'm going for a piss. But put a fiver on the others for me!' A jeer rose from the New South Wales team who were forming up at the French windows end and rolling up their sleeves. A ball had appeared. The referee, a Tasmanian who was the only one present who was reckoned to be even the remotest bit impartial, was standing on the bar, the only safe place, his whistle poised. Mick slipped out of the door before they started. There would be a few cuts and bruises, a few sleeves ripped off, some torn trousers, perhaps a broken toe or two, and a pile of broken glass by the morning. And a bollocking from Tomkins, no doubt. Hargan, what were the officers up to last night? Having a bit of fun, prick. Letting off some steam twelve thousand miles from home. Something you wouldn't understand, mate!

He retired to the toilet as the whistle blew in the bar and a great cheer went up. Five minutes later, he re-emerged. He was just walking across the hall when he heard footsteps coming down the stairs. He turned to look and was surprised to see a WAAF officer slowly coming down, both her hands on the rail as she looked towards the sounds of revelry.

'Oh, hello, love.'

She started. 'Oh, you made me jump. I didn't see you down there. What's going on?'

'Game of Aussie rules.'

'Aussie rules? What's that?' she asked uncertainly.

'Oh, sort of our version of football. Sort of a bit like rugger and football mixed together.'

Oh, I see,' she answered rather hesitantly.

Another cheer came through the bar door, followed by a great crash. The girl had reached the bottom of the stairs. 'Hello, I'm Jane Phillips. I've . . . I've only just arrived and I've been sorting out my things and I heard this noise. . . .'

'Michael Hargan, but Mick to everyone.' He had never called himself Michael before. He held out his hand. Nice-looking girl. Dark hair, big dark eyes. Nice smile. Nice figure from what he could tell under her uniform. She, for her part, felt herself being inspected, but he smiled back. Not bad-looking. Shortish, bit stocky, but not bad.

'It's a bit of a party . . . celebration,' Mick volunteered. 'One of the crews got a U-boat today.'

'Got a U-boat? Does that mean they sank one?'

'Right first time.'

'Oh!' She paused. 'Yes, I see. It's a bit different from a bomber base.'

Her last words were drowned by a great roar and two figures came hurtling through the door, skidded to a halt in the middle of the hall, shook themselves down and headed back into the fray. Mick turned to her and shrugged.

'Bit different from where?'

'A bomber base,' Jane answered more loudly.

'Oh, right.' He nodded his head towards the bar. 'Want to watch?'

'Mmm, not really. Not tonight. I've had a long day.'

She knew the moment she walked in she would be surrounded by young men. She knew she was attractive and that a bar full of men. . . . Well, she just did not feel like taking on that crowd – not yet.

'Stroll outside?' Mick was not sure why he asked. It was not his usual style. He would have been back amongst the game, standing on the bar, cheering with the rest. Something drew him to this girl and he felt he could not just abandon her. 'Can I get you a drink first?'

'No, it's OK thanks.'

He led the way across to the main door and opened it for her. Just that small act was not necessarily the usual Mick Hargan. She stepped out into the darkness and he followed. He led her across towards the lawn, but keeping well away from the French windows. The blackout curtains were shut but light was creeping through. It was quite likely that the French windows would burst open at some stage to eject a body or two. . . . So he led her to the far edge of the lawn. There was just enough light for them to see their way and the outline of the hills and the harbour below was just discernible.

'Tell me about this place,' she asked as they paused at the edge of the lawn.

'Want a seat?' He showed her one of the garden benches and they sat down. 'This place? Commanded by a senile group captain. Nice chap but that's about all. Squadron's Australian – you might have gathered. God's chosen men, except for the CO who's a Brit.'

'So am I!' she protested.

'We fly occasionally. Go out there, bag a few U-boats, come back, get pi . . . have a few beers, play a few games. We're all six foot three, blue-eyed, handsome Aussies. 'Cept for me. I'm the small one in the middle.'

She laughed. Then her tone went serious. 'Now how about it

straight, Mister Mick Hargan? I didn't even notice what rank
you were.'

'Me? Squadron leader, me. I sweep out around here.
That's all squadron leaders do. Sweep out.'

'Oh, sir, I am sorry.'

'You can forget the sir cra . . . sir bit for starters. We
Aussies don't stand on ceremony. Mick will do fine and I'll
call you Jane. OK?'

'OK. But seriously, what happens here?'

'Real serious?'

'Real serious.'

'Right. Well, squadron of Sunderlands. Big aeroplanes.
Flying boats. They are all moored down there in the harbour.
Aussie crews, except for one or two Brits, including the CO
for some reason, and a tame Kiwi.'

'Kiwi?'

'Gentleman from New Zealand.'

'Oh!'

'We fly out over the Atlantic and the Bay of Biscay looking
for U-boats. We fly round the convoys, we fly patrols over the
U-boats routes to and from their bases. Sometimes we get
one. Often we don't.' He paused. 'And what about you, Jane?
Where have you sprung from and what do you do?'

'Me? Communications. Radio. I've just come from Lincolnshire. North Consby. Stirlings. Not very pleasant. You
never got to know the crews.' She was talking quietly but
earnestly. 'They kept getting the chop. You'd meet a bunch
of boys. Get to know them a bit. Perhaps a drink in a pub.
Then, next night, they wouldn't come back. Some nights the
losses were horrible. So you started not talking to the new
crews. One girl was nicknamed Chopper. They reckoned any
bloke who went out with her got the chop on his next trip.'
Mick could sense that what she was saying was upsetting her,
although he could not really see her face in the dark, but he
also found himself letting her continue, getting something
out of her system. He really was becoming the father confessor all round. And he had only met her ten minutes
before! 'She was very upset and had to be sent somewhere
else eventually. It was a pretty bleak place as well. All huts
and very muddy in the winter. And that winter! The wind

used to howl across that airfield.' She paused. 'No, it wasn't a
very nice place to be.'

'Mmmmm, I see. Well, welcome to sunny Cornwall.'

'Thank you. But seriously, Mick, what's it like here? What do
you do?'

'Me? I'm just a simple Sunderland skipper.'

He could hear her faint gasp. 'Oh! I didn't realise . . . I
should've done. I'm sorry.'

'Well, hell, I'm not really much like your film star image of
the aircraft captain. We don't go in too much for that *Target for
Tonight* stuff here. We're just ordinary joes doing a job.'

'Believe it or not, so are nearly all the bomber boys, whatever
the press and newsreels may say,' she replied.

'Yes, I suppose they are. No different from us, then?'

She laughed. 'They're not Australian, or not the ones I met.
There are some people from the Commonwealth and Colo-
nies in the bombers . . . but I suppose you know that already?'

'I had heard,' he said kindly. 'Tell me a bit more about a
bomber station.' He was not sure it was the right thing to say, as
talking about it had been upsetting her, but he felt she wanted
to say more.

'It's all geared to whether or not there's an "op." on. If there
is, then a routine swings into operation. The bombers are
checked out during the daylight hours and bombed up. The
route is planned, they do the weather forecasts, sort out the
signals and so on. Then in the late afternoon, they brief the
crews in a big briefing room. A hundred or more of them.
Then they have a meal and head out to the aircraft. I used to
see them off sometimes. A group at the end of the runway to
give a wave.' She paused and he could hear a faint gulp. 'It was
the waiting through the night that was the worst. Then they
would start coming back perhaps one or two at a time, and you
would start counting. Sometimes they all came back. More
often than not, some did not. In the end, you got used to it. But
I hated it. *Hated it!*'

He sensed she was crying and found himself stretching out
an arm. He put it round her shoulder and pulled her gently
towards him. Mick, what are you doing? Having women crying
on your shoulder is not your bit. She responded and leaned
against him. He just held her there. She cried quietly to herself

for a few minutes and then she stirred and fumbled in a pocket of her tunic for a handkerchief and blew her nose. Eventually she spoke again. 'I'm sorry, but I wanted to tell someone. You can't talk about it on the station. You're the first person I've had a chance to talk to since I left. I didn't mean to unburden myself. I'm so sorry.'

'No need to be sorry, love. It gets to us all from time to time. No problem.'

'Thanks, but I've only just met you and here I am crying all over your tunic.'

'I said, don't worry, love, and I mean it. No sweat.'

Just then there was a crash of breaking glass behind them. It was one of the windows. There were sounds of mild confusion, some swearing and then the noise subsided to just the rowdy cheerings and general row which the game in the bar engendered. It broke the spell for two people, one of whom had felt the need to talk to someone, anyone, to release her from the stranglehold of life on a bomber base. She had turned to the first person who would listen. She would be surprised to find he was not normally the listening sort. He was surprised by his own reaction to the presence of this woman. She was attractive, yes, but there was something else about her. He was not sure what it was. A certain vulnerability but also the air of a woman who was confident in herself. But then again, she had expressed a lack of confidence in the situation she had found herself in at a bomber base.

He did not like to tell her that some of the same things applied at a Sunderland base. Crews went out and did not come back. New faces appeared and were gone within a week. But not all the time. You could go for weeks without losing a crew. Then two would go within a couple of days. In some ways that was worse, because you expected to survive a tour in Sunderlands. It was only when you arrived and started to learn that U-boats could shoot back and German fighters could appear out of nowhere over the Bay that you realised that the odds were not always on your side. But it was not as bad as bombers, of that there was no doubt.

The moments of silence passed. 'Where do you come from?' she asked. It was a standard conversation opener. It was as if all that had been said before did not exist.

'Me? Western Australia. Near Perth. Well, very near Perth really, like right in it.' There were not many people he admitted that to.

'Is it a nice place?'

'I reckon. Sunny, hot. But it's a city. Nice beaches, though. It's OK.' Again, there were few people he would admit that somewhere in Australia was only OK too. 'What about you?'

'Oh, I come from Surrey. Frightfully boring.'

The conversation went on along conventional lines for a while. What neither of them realised was that, in fact, they were two lonely people. One had just come from a job where she found it difficult to relate to the male company. The other had never really had a female friend, someone he could talk to, someone in whom he could confide and, indeed, someone who was willing to confide in him. His view of British women as frigid was coloured by the fact that he had never really been able to relate to a woman, British or Australian.

Nevertheless, the spell had been broken, for the moment. After the intense feelings of their early conversation, they had resorted to the standard 'where do you come from?', 'What did you do before you joined up?' sort of questions. But it allowed them to learn a little more about each other. The noise from the bar was dying away. It seemed as if the game was wrapping up. There was also a chill in the air. Suddenly Jane felt cold, and tired.

'Mick, I'm rather tired. And I'm getting a bit cold as well. I think I'm going to head for bed.'

With another woman, his answer might have been 'Can I come too?' but not with this one.

'I need to head for bed as well. I'm flying tomorrow.'

'Oh, what time?'

'Sometime around midday, probably.'

They walked together back towards the house. As they approached the door, she took his arm and gently pulled him to a halt. Quickly she leaned over and pecked him on the cheek. 'Thanks, Mick. Thanks a lot. Good night.'

'No problem, love. See you t'morrow. 'Night.'

With that she walked on ahead and disappeared through the main door. He followed slowly on behind. Some girl! He pushed open the door. She was just turning the corner at the top of the stairs but did not look back. He walked across towards the bar. Sticking his head round the door, he noticed that quite a lot of people had left already. In one corner a group of young pilots was trying to construct a pyramid so that one of their number could write his name on the ceiling. They must have seen fighter boys doing that on the newsreels or something, he thought to himself.

'Skipper, where have you been all night? We dicked New South Wales. Want a pint?'

'No, thanks Dinger old mate. I'm actually going to bed. See you in the morning.' With that, he turned and departed through the main door and headed over towards the huts and the room that was home.

*

Yvette found her hands shaking. She was trying to dry glasses behind the bar but her hands were shaking too much. It was those men in the corner, the Gestapo men. They just seemed to be sitting there and watching. There were no other Germans in the bar by now. The few who had been in had left. There were one or two locals from time to time but they too sensed the nature of the men in the corner and only stayed for one drink.

The Germans from the airfield she could tolerate. Despite the fact that she passed on all that she heard to the man from the Resistance, L'Hibou, she did not mind the young Luft-waffe men. They were cheerful, they treated her with courtesy although they liked to slip a hand up her skirt when they could, and she felt a certain affection for them in a funny sort of way. But the two men in the corner, they were on the other side of the glorious Third Reich. They were the state machine. They were the evil which the Third Reich was imposing on much of Europe. She was very frightened of these two men. They just sat and watched and talked in a low murmur. They seemed to be watching her. That was why her hands were shaking.

*

'Bloody man!' She thought she had said it to herself but the voice behind her made her jump.

'Who?' She turned. It was the lieutenant-commander who had sat some way down the table. He was a bit dishy but she had not had much of a chance to talk to him.

'Oh . . . errr, well, I was hoping Wing Commander Tomkins might give me a lift back to the base. He knows I live there.' Bloody man had just spent ten minutes complaining about some of her WAAFs so he certainly did know she lived there. 'But he's gone off without me.'

'Oh, no problem. I'll give you a lift. I'm Henry Cassell by the way. We haven't had much of a chance to talk this evening.'

'Helen MacDonald.' As soon as she said MacDonald, you could detect the Scottish lilt in her voice.

'Hello, Helen. I've got my car here . . . I live in a cottage we've taken over in the grounds but I can run you back.'

'That's a long way for you to go.'

'No problem. Come on, it's parked down the way there.'

As they walked away from the house, down the drive into the darkness, he added, 'Of course, if you'd like a nightcap or something before we go? I think I've got something in the cottage.'

IX

'How was the film last night?'

How did he remember these things? wondered Jilly. Here he was, running all the operations and doing briefings and reading all the signals and writing them like crazy and he had time to remember what the girls were up to. What a nice man he was!

'Super, thank you, sir.'

'Good, good,' replied Dick Smiley as he returned to the signal from Group which the girl had just handed him.

Jilly turned back to her previous task before she had been called to fetch the signal — cleaning up the tea boat. It really was getting very messy. Sugar had been spilled on the small table they used which had then got wet so it hardened and stuck to the surface. It was a horrible job but she would be pleased when it was done.

Just then, the door opened and a small group of naval lieutenants came in. MTB COs. She recognised most of them. There were 'Morning, Dickie!' and 'Has the RAF won the war yet?' noises from them as they hung up their hats. They then gathered in 'Navy corner', around the large-scale plot of the Channel, and started discussing options for the coming night. Oh, hell! she thought. Time to put the kettle on.

No sooner had she done that than the door opened and two WAAF officers came in. One she recognised. Helen Mac-Donald. Golly, she looked rough! She looked as if she had been up half the night. The other officer was new. She saw her introducing herself to Squadron Leader Smiley. Then the two officers moved over towards the wall plots.

'This is where it all happens,' Pilot Officer MacDonald was saying.

'The plot shows the areas aircraft are going out to patrol and where the convoys are and the best guess as to where the

U-boats are and so on. It's worth coming in here quite often to see what is going on. That way you can understand more about the signals coming in and out and what radio watch is required and so on. You'll find yourself popping in once or twice a day at least. You're on the list of people who can come in without asking.'

They turned towards Jilly. 'And this is Leading Wren Johnson.'

'Good morning, ma'm.' Helen MacDonald was looking distinctly pale.

'Because we are a combined ops room, we have Wrens working here as well as WAAFs. How many is it now, Jilly?'

'There are eight of us now, ma'm. Four who work in here and four in signals.'

'Yes, you've got Wrens on radio as well,' Helen explained to Jane Phillips. 'They mainly look after the Navy side for the MTBs and so on. But in here, the girls do everything, whatever their service. Isn't that right, Jilly?'

'Yes, ma'm. Would you like a cup of tea? I've got the kettle on.'

'Yes, please,' answered Jane. 'Just with milk, please.'

The two female officers moved across to discuss the system for handling signals in the Ops Room whilst Jilly set to to make the tea. She counted how many there were – she needed ten but there were only nine cups. Guess who would go without . . . again.

*

Helmut Schafer was in his own ops room, talking to Bernard, his ops officer.

'We're not finding them where we're searching. I reckon we need to get further west.'

'It's a long way to go, Helmut. There's not enough fuel for you to do a search if you go any further west,' answered the older man.

'Yes, maybe, but if we just do a long leg out to the west and back again, we're covering a pretty wide swathe.'

'But only once. You search out, you search back. That's it. Ten minutes either side and Tommy gets through without you seeing him.'

'Maybe. . . .'

'You search more to the east, you have time to patrol the search area, more chance of catching one.'

'But only if they are there in the first place. They can plot it out the same way we can. They dog leg out to the west, stay out of range of us. We've got to push further west. I'm going to give it a try. We'll send out aircraft in twos or threes, about an hour apart. We'll all sweep the same route. That way one area will get good cover for a short but intense period.' He paused for a moment, studying the plot. Then he took up the coloured pencil and drew in a line which went eighty miles further to the west than the search areas already plotted. 'Let's try that.'

*

Mick was the last to arrive. Dinger was already there, chatting to Dickie. The other two pilots, Bill and George, were quietly sipping cups of tea. The naval party had gone but the two WAAF officers were still there, also with cups in their hands. In the corner, one of the Wrens was clearing up some other cups. He noticed it was the small, freckle-faced one. Then he also noticed one of the WAAFs was Jane Phillips. She had had her back turned as he came in.

'Morning, Mick,' greeted Dick Smiley. 'Didn't see too much of you last night.'

'Morning, Dickie. No mate, I wasn't there all the time. Decided I'd take it easy. Thought you might want me to do some flying today!'

'Certainly do . . . certainly do. Mick, this is Jane Phillips. She's just arrived. She's going to listen to the briefing, get the feel of things. . . .'

'Yeah, we already met. Morning, Jane, Helen.'

The girls smiled back. Mick turned away towards the plot and then, as the group moved towards the wallchart, he glanced back at Jane, caught her eye and gave her a wink.

'Right, lads. Down the Bay for you today,' started Dickie. He was pointing to a route marked on the plot which ran all the way down to the Spanish coast. It was almost a repeat of Tomkins' route the previous day. 'None of our own activity down there. No convoys, nothing. No known U-boats but the spot where the CO found one yesterday, as you'll recall, was down here. Tucked in quite close to Spanish waters. There were a lot of fishing boats about, as well, apparently.'

He turned to the forecast board. 'Weather's good. There's another ridge of high pressure building up from the Azores. Should give you good vis, light winds, not much cloud cover. Signals . . . nothing special. I've got the usual gen for Sparks. Nothing on your route out, no coastal convoys. There's one prohibited bombing area for when you are coming back – one of our own submarines.' He handed Dinger a slip of paper.

'On the more general front, this thing about U-boats staying on the surface more to shoot it out could be building. Tomkins' target did not try to dive. A Liberator had a similar experience a few days back. It's not much to go on but just bear it in mind. On the tactical side, if you can get ahead of one, you reduce the arcs over which his guns can fire. Gives you more of a chance. Fuel? You've got a full load. Full load of depth charges as well. Fully ammunitioned. Any questions?'

Dinger was busy writing down the details of the route and looking in more detail at the weather forecast and the winds. He also checked they had been given the recognition signals for the day. Mick waited whilst Dinger made sure he had everything. Dinger was the brains of the outfit. Had to make sure the navigator was happy.

Dinger looked up from his bits of paper at Mick. 'I'm happy, skipper.' Mick raised an eyebrow at Bill and George. They both shook their heads.

'Right, lads. Thanks, Dickie. That was quick. See you when we get back, then.'

They collected up their gear and made to leave. Mick noticed Jane was standing slightly apart from the other WAAF, Helen. Quickly he stepped across to her. 'You all right today, love?' he asked quietly.

'Yes, thanks, Mick. Good luck!' she added and smiled at him. Nice smile, nice face, nice girl. Those eyes!

'Thanks, love. See you.' With that, he followed the rest of the team out of the door.

As they walked down towards the water, Mick turned to George.

'Got all me gear, young George?'

'Sure thing, Skipper.'

'Good on yer. Now, I promised you the take-off today, didn't I? Piece of piss today.' He looked up at the sky and at the trees off to one side. 'Not much wind. We'll be heavy but that's all. She'll be all yours, mate.' He patted George on the back, who had a slightly worried look on his face.

The rest of the crew were waiting down by the jetty as usual. There was a chorus of 'Morning, Skipper!' as the two groups joined up.

'Morning lads. Nice quite one today. Down the Bay and back. Two and six a trip round the harbour. See the sights! No sweat.' He was met by groans. Oh, shit, down the Bay!

'On the town last night then, Johnno?' Mick asked the senior air gunner.

'Nah, Skipper. Me girl had pissed off to the pictures without me. Early night last night.'

'Who with?' chipped in another voice from the back.

'By meself, for once,' called back John Williams.

'That makes a change,' answered another voice. The banter went on as they got the gear down the steps into the tender. Ginger almost dropped one of the water drums. Tiny managed to catch it as it started to roll down the steps out of Ginger's hands.

'You on the piss last night, Ginge. Dropping the bleeding water. . . .'

'Get stuffed!' The lads were in good spirits.

The tender took them out across the water. It was a lovely morning, the sun shining out of a nearly clear sky, with a few small, puffy cumulus building up. Just an occasional ruffle of wind ran across the water and there was warmth in the air. The hills around stood out in the clear air. They seemed that much closer when it was so clear. Mick pushed back a few strands of hair blown in his face by the wind created by the boat's movement.

'Good day for flying, Dinger.'

'Sure thing, Skipper.' Dinger was not so sure though. Good visibility like this, fighters could see a long way. Give me a bit of murk, a bit of cloud to hide. Let's just do the search on radar. But don't say it. Got to keep the lads cheerful, whatever your inner feelings, thought Dinger to himself.

The tender drew alongside the Sunderland. She looked good with the sun shining on her. The patches of oily exhaust on the wings, the dirty patches on the hull, they did not matter. She was a mature lady who knew her job. She'd put the hours in. Why call her D-Dog? That was not a lady's name. But Dog she was and Dog she would remain, and she's all ours lads.

'Anymore for the *Skylark*?' Another familiar joke, a talisman. Go through the old routine, the things we know. It makes us feel safe. One by one they climbed onboard. The gear was passed in, food, water, a new frying pan, a couple of cups stolen from who knows where, binoculars, recognition flares, charts, navigator's box of tricks, Skipper's gear, couple of spare Aldis bulbs. Pile it all in and get it sorted out.

The familiar pre-flight routine started. There was a short argument between Ray and Banjo as to whose job it was to pump the bilges that day. John Williams stepped in and sorted that one out. Mick took up station on the flight deck and let them get on with it. After a few minutes, Dinger came up to the flight deck, chart in hand.

'You happy with this route, Skipper?'

'Yeah, I reckon. It takes us well out to the west, don't it? Then a straight run down. Looks good.'

'OK.' Dinger retired to his table to work out courses and times and distances.

George climbed up next and sorted himself out on the right-hand side.

'It's all yours, George. You check her out, you get the show on the road. OK?'

'OK, Skipper.'

Where do I start? thought the young man to himself. It looks so easy when the Skipper does it. It all just slots into place. But what do I actually need to do? Mick let him think it out for himself. It was the best way to learn.

Engineer's checks. Radio. Navigator. Turrets. Bilges. Bombs. Flares. Ammunition. Hatches. Flying controls. Slip rope. The reports came in and after some thirty minutes George found they were ready to go. He strapped himself in and Mick followed suit, seemingly letting George get on with it but actually watching his every move.

'Ready to start engines,' George called over the intercom,

once he was settled in his seat. 'Errr . . . port outer, then starboard outer.' The engineer acknowledged, reported that the engines were primed and waited for the first engine to burst into life, his eyes on his instruments. Fuel pump pressure OK. Let's go!

George went through the starting routine. The port outer turned over, caught, missed, caught twice and then burst into life. He gave her a bit too much throttle as the engine fired and the revs wound up rapidly, swinging the aircraft on its moorings. Quickly he snatched back the throttle and the engine died. 'Shit!'

'Just take it easy, young George. Just ease up on the throttle when she catches.'

I did it plenty of times at the OCU, thought George to himself, and now I balls it up! But he got it right the second time and the engine caught and settled at just above idling revs. The starboard outer followed. The instruments came to life. The artificial horizons erected and levelled. The tachos and luboil pressures were steady. Electrics were OK, the batteries were charging. Quick final check before we go . . . he let his finger lead his eyes over the instruments, over the controls. 'Right, stand by forward. I'm just going to ease up on the buoy. I'll bring it up on the port side.

George eased the throttles forward, gave a burst on the port outer so the buoy swung in under the port bow, held her there and nodded to Bill who was ready with the whistle. At the blast, the two gunners in the nose let go of the slip rope and the Sunderland was free. George swung her further to starboard on the engines and moved slowly out of the mooring. If the truth were known, he did it better than Mick's previous effort, in fact better than most of Mick's efforts, but no one was going to tell him that.

The Sunderland taxied slowly up harbour. They started the inners on the way. Get them warmed up before we go. As they approached the far end, they went through the engine checks, vital actions before take-off and a careful look over the hills to make sure there was no one coming in on finals before they lined up for take-off.

'Just remember she's heavy, George. She'll take a bit longer to get up on the step. She'll be slower accelerating so you'll need to steer with the engines longer than you're used to. And don't give her the inners too early.'

George nodded as he eased the port outer forward and starting swinging her round. He kicked on full rudder – it helped a bit but not much. Slowly she came round. He caught her as she completed the turn to line up down harbour, over corrected a bit and swung a few degrees back. Meanwhile Bill had a quick final check down the harbour with the binoculars to make sire there were no small boats in their path.

'OK, lads. Taking off!' called George over the intercom.

He pushed both outer throttles forward and she started to move. Golly, she was sluggish. He saw what the Skipper meant. The nose was swinging to starboard. He brought the port outer back a fraction. The swing stopped and the nose moved back to line-up down the harbour. Keep her just to the left of the church in the distance. Let her run. Come on, baby!

The speed came up slowly. She was very heavy. He had his hand on the inner throttles. Should be OK now. He pushed them slowly forward and could feel the power coming on. The spray from the bows was clear of the inner propellers. 4260 horse power in unison. It felt good. He could feel this big aircraft through the controls. Air speed was coming up. He felt a slight pull on the control column. He glanced across at Mick who had one hand on the controls. Mick signalled with his finger, an indication to hold the nose up a bit. George applied the slightest of pressure and the nose rose fractionally. As it did so he could feel that they were in a much better attitude. The bow had been tending to dig in, he realised. In only a few seconds, she rose up on the step, into the planing attitude and then she was really going. Now she was accelerating, the main drag of the water gone. The hull was doing its job, holding her on the water, rather than in it. Air speed came up. He eased back on the control column too early. She would not fly yet. He held her a little longer, speed came up another ten and then she was ready. She lifted off the water and was airborne again. And as the last drag of the water fell away, he felt what a beautiful aeroplane she was. Even heavily loaded as she was, she flew like a lady, gentle to the touch, light on the controls. He held her slightly nose up and let her slowly climb away. Two hundred feet a minute. Not much but enough.

Ashore two WAAF officers watched them go and waved. But the lads in D-Dog could not see the distant figures just above the beach.

*

In France the weather was very similar. Just a little more wind but that would die as high pressure built from the west. Spring flowers were out across the airfield. They seemed to grow in clumps and the clumps showed up as patches of colour amongst the grass. Birds were singing and, all of a sudden, western France, occupied France, did not seem a bad place to be.

Helmut Schafer stepped into the briefing room. The routine was almost exactly the same as that followed an hour earlier in Cornwall. Routes, areas, U-boats, convoys, any attack restrictions, other aircraft movements, an FW Condor to be aware of, on its way out, signals, weather, recognition flares. It was much the same list of things to run through. But after that, he discussed tactics, again. He had run through it with them yesterday. He would do it again today. It was Bruckner and Elman he was flying with, again. That was his decision anyway. They would learn with him before he sent them off with someone else.

'Now, gentlemen, if we find a Tommy, remember the tactics. We split. I go behind him. You go either side of me, on the quarters. We synchronise attacks. That way, he may turn to avoid one attack but the aircraft coming in from the other side has a good target. We divide his fire. If you can, get underneath him. But he'll probably go low so you cannot. Get in close. Use your cannon to good effect. Once you've done one attack, pull out and reform astern. Same formation. Then we do it again. If we go in together, we can get him. If we go in one at a time, we are vulnerable. Understand?'

'*Jawohl!*' they both replied. Did they really understand? Did they really know it was no easy shooting out there? Did they understand that they had to use these tactics if they were to succeed? Time would tell.

He led them out towards the aircraft.

*

'Cuppa tea, Skipper?' The familiar routine. Take-off, climb

away, put the kettle on. Test burst on the guns but get the
kettle on too. Need to start thinking about dinner too. Chops,
spuds, baked beans. Not bloody beans again! Always give me
wind, they do. No beans for me. Double whacks of spuds
though.

They had levelled off at a thousand feet. No point in going
higher. The search started, well, not as soon as they left the
English coast but not long after. You never knew when you
might find a U-boat trying to sneak into the Channel to patrol
off the Lizard or down by Wolf Rock. So stay at a thousand feet
and start the other familiar routine, the lookout. In the
turrets, in the cockpit, get the old eyes searching. Only eleven
hours or so to go. And keep your eyes on the sky as well. Some
cheeky sod of a Jerry might sneak across from France, have a
quick bit of fun over the Channel and be back in time for a late
lunch. So the turrets were manned, safety catches off, and the
eyes were searching. The nose turret tended to spend most of
his time looking down, with an occasional sweep of the sky
ahead. After all, they could see the sky ahead just as well, even
better in fact, from the flight deck. The midships and tail
turrets tended to search the sky. The midships turret could
hardly see the sea anyway. The tail was where an attack was
likely to come from so keep watching the sky, Ray my boy, and
keep us safe from some Jerry fighter.

Mick took out his pipe and placed it in his mouth. He did not
light it. He just puffed gently on nothing, but it was comforting in its way.

George was still in the right-hand seat, looking a little more
relaxed. Not too bad, that take-off. Only balls up was with the
engine but he wouldn't do that again. Now the autopilot was in
and he could let his eyes do the work, do the search, sweep the
sea and the sky.

'Anyone want their chops well done or anything?' asked a
voice over the intercom.

'You mean there's a choice?' asked another voice. 'I thought
it either burnt or black, the way you do them, George.'

'Any mint sauce, then. Proper job like we have in New South
Wales.'

'Piss off, when did New South Wales know how to do a
proper job?'

'Hear you officer types had a game of Aussie rules last night, then, and NSW got hammered. That right?'

Mick interjected, 'Ease it down, chaps. Keep your eyes open, not your mouths.' Mild bollocking from the skipper, but Mick's OK. We'll take it from him.

The tea arrived. It looked a bit strong. Mick tried it. Hell, it was strong! He put the cup in the holder by his seat. 'I've just got a Gee fix, Skipper,' came Dinger's voice. 'The wind's a bit lighter than forecast. Come right five degrees. New course two two zero.'

'Two two zero,' George acknowledged and set the new course on the autopilot. Gently the aircraft came round to the new course and steadied.

*

The three Ju88s wandled along the taxi way like three ducks on the way to the water. They always looked ungainly on the ground. They were all engine and a big, solid wing. Rather narrow fuselage. That was where the resemblance to ducks broke down. They were the wrong shape at the back. The front one and the second one taxied in a nice straight line. The back one was weaving around a bit, rather like a young duckling learning to walk. The pilot might have been a duckling, young and inexperienced, but the aircraft was fully fledged fighting machine, armed with 20mm cannon. The aircraft was very able; the pilot still had a lot of learning to do.

Schafer led them onto the runway and they lined up. Already it was becoming a familiar routine for the three of them. Elman was reminding himself not to get too far out on the outside during the turn after take-off. Don't be afraid to tuck in close. You've got the widest turn of the three anyway. Suddenly the leader was rolling. Elman gave a quick, final tug to his straps and then pushed his throttles all the way forward. The roar of the engines deepened, the aircraft started to roll. Touch of right brake to straighten her up.

He glanced to his left to see Bruckner level with him. Quickly he switched his eyes to Schafer's aircraft ahead. Watch the leader. Keep your side of the runway. Don't worry about the other wingman. The tail lifted and he had rudder steering. A touch of right boot to hold her straight. Check the speed.

Glance at the engine instruments. OK. Check ahead. Nicely in formation. He saw the tail of Schafer's aircraft drop, the nose rise and the leader was climbing away. He waited two seconds, checked his speed and followed through.

As the wheels left the runway, his hand went out for the undercarriage lever. He felt the thump as the locks came off and the gear started to come up. What a bastard of a job that had been, changing the undercarriage he had managed to write off. And with those coarse, sweaty mechanics as well. They were a product of the Third Reich? They ought to be ashamed of themselves. Their language! And their conversation was so crude. Schafer's aircraft was banking. Elman followed round, holding her in a tight climbing turn to port. Much better than yesterday. Neatly tucked in. Bruckner was inside him turning more tightly. The leader came out of his turn, the two wingmen steadied up behind him and they headed for the beach and the sea.

*

An hour out. Time to change round. Mick stayed where he was but Bill took over from George. Dinger stayed at his table. Navigators stayed put for ever. No breaks for them, but they didn't have to keep looking out of the window, feeling their eyes going funny with the strain of just looking at nothing, hoping and praying that it would continue to be nothing, in the sky that is. See a U-boat down below, now that's different. See one early in the trip, drop all our bombs, then we can get home early. 'Cept then the hours don't add up so quickly. It's not the number of trips that count, like it does with the bombers, it's the hours that matter. Make it a long, cushy trip and that quickly adds to the total. Be nice to get a U-boat, though. Wonder if there's any of the bastards down there watching us go by?

Dinger plotted another Gee fix. It was so easy, this close to England. The little electric box of tricks told you the answers, told you where you were . . . within a certain tolerance. And depending on conditions. When it was good, it was very good. Rather like the girl in a nursery rhyme. But when it was not so good, when radio reception was poor, when there were thunderstorms around, then you had to know what you were doing and treat the answers with caution. Keep a dead reckoning running as well. Check your winds. Keep a note of them. You never know when Gee is going to let you down. A station might just go off the air. The Jerries might be jamming it. You might be out of range. And you were out of range most of the way down the Bay. Then it was back to basics, back to steam navigation. None of this new-fangled stuff. Just the sun and stars, estimate of wind and dead reckoning. Keep your hands in at astro, lads. That's what they had taught him at navigation school. If you go to Coastal, that's what you'll be using. Treat your sextant as a friend. Look after it. Clean it, polish it. Guard it from knocks. Check its errors. One day, it's the only thing that will get you home. Oh, you need an accurate time piece as well, so look after that. Check its error regularly, make sure it is gaining or losing at a constant rate. Doesn't matter if it is slow or fast, just so long as you know by how much and can predict the change since the last time check.

So Dinger checked the Gee fix against his dead reckoning. Looked OK. He worked out the wind again. Much the same as before, which again looked OK. He wrote it down carefully in his log. When we come back, later today, tonight, that wind estimate which I've carefully written down might make the difference between getting back and getting lost.

Hank Jones, the engineer, was also writing in his log. Take the engine readings every hour. Log the fuel readings. Compare that with the rate of consumption. Estimate how much fuel is really left. Fuel gauges – not the most reliable of things. So work it out all the ways you can, take the worst figure and knock off a bit for luck. That way there will always be a bit left when they get home. He wrote his figures carefully in his log and made sure his tea did not splash on it. He'd got a mild bollocking for turning in scruffy logs not so long before. Might as well try to do it properly. It saves all the bother of another bollocking. Don't know why we have to send the logs in anyway. Something about being able to monitor engine performance.

Load of balls. I know how my engines are doing. I fly with the bloody things. I make sure the plugs get changed on time. I make sure the oil changes are done, the levels checked. I know how many hours each one has done. I don't have to look it up. I can tell you, mate! I know the starboard inner always runs a bit hot. I know that luboil pressure always jumps around a bit but its only this gauge 'cos the one of the flightdeck is OK. I know that fuel cock is a bit stiff but we know how to do it. I know the bloody throttle actuators always need bleeding. I also know this aeroplane is underpowered, mate, and we really have to hammer those engines to keep the bloody thing flying. Full chat most of the way. Might be able to ease off a bit when we've used some fuel, but not much. Those Pegasus really take a hammering. Perhaps they'll put something else on the next Mark of Sunderland, if there is a next one, if we haven't won, or lost, this bleeding war by then.

In the galley the spuds were just coming up to the boil Always a bastard getting those to boil. Bloody great saucepan. No wonder it takes so long. Spuds for eleven. That's a lot. What a job it is peeling the bleeding things as well! Which is worse, being stuck in the turret or having the trick in the galley? At least you could get a smoke down here. You could in the tail turret as well. Strictly illegal, having a quick fag in the tail turret. But who's to know? No one came back there except at the change-round. An hour on your own back there. At least you felt you belonged when you had the midships turret, or a spell on radar, or in the nose turret. You were amongst the others then. But down in the tail, that was lonely. What about those poor sods in bombers who were stuck in there for hours on end? At least it was only an hour at a time here, then a swap round. Turn the spuds down a bit, lad. Just let them bubble gently. Time to think about frying some of the chops and putting the beans on. Not too popular, the beans. 'Cept for Johnno and Sparks. They'd eat a mountain. Must be immune from wind, those two.

*

The Junkers were level at two thousand feet. The Tommies usually fly low so we'll just get a bit above them. Schafer had considered flying really low so they could look up at the sky and see other aircraft against the sky rather than the sea. But low flying was hard work and they tended to get a lot of salt in the engines. Although the latest modifications which Hans had been working on should ease that problem. Two thousand was a compromise height. A chap down low might still be difficult to see against the sea but at least he would not be too far below them. He leaned over to check on Ernst's chart where they were. Making progress although the line which ran across the chart, the line he had decided himself, seemed to stretch a long way ahead of them.

He looked back over his shoulder to the left. Bruckner was still there, some five hundred metres out on the quarter, the spread formation. His aircraft rose and fell gently relative to Schafer's, a restful sight reminiscent of a quiet afternoon's flying over the hills of Bavaria. Oh, to be able to do that again! What a summer that had been! 1938. Before Poland, before France, before this bloody war in the Atlantic. Weren't the British calling it 'The Battle of the Atlantic'? Must be the world's largest battlefield. And he was one small soldier in the battle. But he was no infantry man walking to war with a rifle over his shoulder. He was the modern knight in armour, riding the latest steed which modern technology could breed, armed with the sharpest of lances, the 20 mm cannon. His lance could cut through metal like a knife through butter and from three hundred metres as well. His lance could explode inside another aircraft, cutting it to ribbons, setting fire to it. He liked the metaphor. Perhaps he would have a Teutonic knight painted on the nose of his aircraft?

X

The two young women were sitting together in the small snug on the first floor. On the small table before them were two cups of tea. The clock above the fireplace said twenty to two. There was no fire. It was getting too warm, and anyway coal was scarce.

It was Jane who spoke. 'When the crews go out, what . . . what dangers do they face? Surely it's pretty safe out there, isn't it, away from fighters and flak and things? But they were saying something about the U-boats shooting back.'

'Mmmm, the U-boats do have guns. Deck guns and anti-aircraft guns. I sat in on a lecture a few weeks back. Know your enemy and all that. They put machine guns and things on the U-boats for shooting at the aircraft.' Helen paused to pick up her cup. 'There are fighters over the Bay as well,' she added, taking a sip of tea.

'Oh!, exclaimed Jane, startled. 'Many? What sort?'

'Junkers 88s, I think. They go out hunting for the Sunderlands and Liberators and so on. From time to time crews don't come back. We put it down to fighters. Some have seen them but not been spotted. Some have been shot at but survived to tell the tale.'

Jane had broken out in a cold sweat hearing this. That poor man! She had been telling him all about bomber boys getting the chop and it happened here too! How awful! How could she have been so thoughtless? How could she think that there might not be dangers in flying the Sunderlands as well? How could she have been so selfish as to pour out all her woes when he was faced with the same sort of dangers?

'Does it happen often?' she asked quietly.

'No, fortunately. Just from time to time. Quite a lot of them finish their tours.' She paused. 'I hear it's quite unusual for a bomber crew to finish a tour?'

'Yes, yes it is,' she answered without really thinking. She was still thinking about Mick and all that she had poured out last night.

Helen changed the subject. She could sense it was upsetting Jane. 'I'm sorry none of us were here last night to greet you but I had to go to some Navy dinner party.'

'Lucky you.'

'Not really. It was mainly older men and a bit boring. Then that man Tomkins. He's the squadron CO. No one likes him. He started on at me about the way some of the girls carried on with the men. I ask you! What does he expect, people stuck down here in the wilds of Cornwall? Of course the girls and the men are going to get together!' Which reminded her of the remainder of her evening, well, the remainder of the night. Some night cap! Golly, she had felt rough. He was dishy, that Henry Cassell. And a cottage all to himself! He had said something about others moving in in the near future. She would have to make use of the time before that happened. That was, if he rang her, as he had promised. Perhaps this evening? I could really do with an early night after last night! But. . . .

She was miles away. she came back to reality. 'Come on, there's more to do! Have you finished your tea?'

*

Ushant was abeam to port, well down over the horizon, a hundred odd miles. One day, after the war, he'd go and see it. Perhaps stay on in England for a bit, if he could, after they had finished with him in the RAAF. Or would he have to go all the way home before getting out. Oh, shit! It would be rather nice to spend a bit of time seeing France. Mick chewed reflectively on his pipe. That was the way it would go, wasn't it? They would win, wouldn't they? The invasion would come, one day? They would march into France? They would push the Jerries back, same way they had in North Africa? The Allies would win, wouldn't they? Bloody hell, man, we had to win. There was no thinking about a world where they did not win. With the Russians and the Americans in this thing, they had to win. But they had to win the Battle of the Atlantic along the way. That came out in every brief, every lecture, every pep talk they had. It is a battle we cannot lose, men. That's what the staff on

the ground kept telling them. Why don't we get more aircraft
then? the lads asked. Need to strike a balance, was the answer.
We need to take the war to Germany as well. Need the bombers
to win the war over Germany. Meanwhile the convoys get
hammered and that's OK, is it?

Doesn't make sense. We've got to beat the U-boats first. That
was obvious to anyone in Sunderlands. They saw the figures of
merchant ships sunk. Secret, they were. Not released to the
great British public, or Australian public come to that. Beat the
U-boats first, then we can go and beat the shit out of Germany.
Give us the aircraft out here for a while and we might do it.
Continuous cover over the Bay, that's what they needed. Get a
few Mosquitos down here, give the Junkers what for and that
would help. Then we really could give the U-boats a hard time.
Pin them down all the way across the Bay. That's what was
needed.

Hell, I'm miles away. Come on, man, you're supposed to look
out of the window! His attention returned to the present and his
eyes started another sweep of the sea ahead and to port.

Sparks was having problems. The morse kept fading. It was
only routine stuff but it was nice to know you could stay in touch
with base. Don't transmit unless the Skipper tells you to. Just
listen in, listen to any messages from base, like 'Come home'.
They only sent that one if it looked as if everywhere was going to
be socked in by bad weather or something. Even then, for a guy
way down the Bay with four hours to fly to get back. . . . Crews
had been lost trying to get back in the middle of blizzards in
winter, blizzards which had not been forecast before they went
but which came out of the Atlantic whilst they were away. So
keep listening to the morse, even though it faded in and out.
Listen for our call-sign. And make sure the transmitters on top
line, just in case we need it. If we do need it, it's likely to be in a
hurry. A sighting report. An attack report. A distress message.
But everyone prayed it would not be the latter.

*

Bruckner was finding the flying very tedious. There was no
excitement in this, just cruising across the Atlantic on the
off-chance of seeing some lumbering Allied aircraft. It was a
needle in a haystack. The chances were so remote. It was crazy.

How did he ever get into this situation? Volunteered for
front-line operations! This was no front-line. This was about
as far as you could get up a back water. There were no medals
here. He would never become an ace. Not out here, over the
Atlantic. What about night fighters? Fly a 88C-6b. He'd been
shown over one once. He'd seen the Lichtenstein radar aerials,
seen the displays in the aircraft, discussed with the pilot how it
worked and the tactics they used. There was a challenge.
Shooting down bombers in the night sky over Germany. It was
still a job for a Ju88. At least he was an 88 pilot. What a versatile
aircraft it was turning out to be. Bomber over Britain, fighter,
tank buster in Russia. And he had also seen the plans for
something called *Schrage Musik*, an upward firing cannon to be
used against the bombers. Tiptoe underneath a bomber where
he cannot see you, get in his blind spot, then fire two 200 mm
cannons into his belly. That was going to be some weapon.

Meanwhile here he was droning out over the Atlantic, the
sun beating down on them, the cockpit like a greenhouse. He
was sweating, his observer, a young man he had not really got
to know yet, was sweating. All they were going to do was fly a
long way to the west, turn round and come back again. What a
boring day.

*

The Sunderland's cockpit also was getting warm. The big
windows trapped the sun's rays. It was all right for the Navvy,
for Sparks, for the engineer. They were in the shade of the
fuselage. But the cockpit could get roasting. It was only Spring
and it was getting bad already. Bill Newton adjusted the fresh
air vent so it blew directly in his face. That was better!

In the nose, it was John Williams on watch. Slowly he
traversed the turret backwards and forwards. Use the guns as
pointers. Follow them. Search the sea with them. Draw a
search pattern across the sea with the barrels of the guns. Let
the eye follow. No day dreaming. Well, perhaps the occasional
thought about the other night, in bed with Jilly. Bit inexperienced she was. But fun. Keen to learn or so it seemed.
Keep searching the sea. Forget the black stockings for the
moment. Good idea, black stockings. That's where the Wrens
had an advantage over the WAAFs. Very sexy. . . . Shit! What

was that! His hand went for his microphone switch. A streak of white in the sea! Adrenalin started to flow. Switch on intercom. Report . . . then another porpoise broke the surface and then another. . . . His voice was already saying 'Splash in the water ahead. No. . . . No, relax. It's porpoises.'

Mick was already upright in his seat, hands reaching out for the controls, ready to take over. The engineer was already flicking switches to get the bombs out. Reflex actions. Then the anti-climax. But hearts were already pumping, palms were already sweating, breathing was already faster. It only took a second for the body to react to possible immediate action. It took four or five minutes for it to wind down, for hearts to return to normal, for breathing to steady. The adrenalin took even longer to disperse.

Nobody said anything. Johnno had done the right thing. Call what you see. A second or two's hesitation might mean we miss it. Call what you see, even if it does turn out to be a whale, a porpoise or the Flying Dutchman.

Back to searching, lads. The second round of dinner came up. You could not get all the chops in the frying pan together. Do them in two whacks. Meant the spuds were going a bit mushy for those who had the second lot. Couldn't be helped. Ginger brought up the skipper's. No beans. Chop and spuds. It did not look all that exciting. Now, tea would be better because Mick happened to know they had some more of that good jam on board. Big wedge of bread with jam an inch thick on it. That's some tea. And a decent cup of tea as well. That would be good. He balanced the plate on his lap and stuck his knife into the chop. At least it felt nice and tender. That was a good start.

Down in the galley it was time to clean up. Always a bit of a game, washing up. Heating the water on the two burner stove took ages, just like getting the spuds to boil. No one waited long enough. The washing-up water was always lukewarm. Give the plates a go over. Most of the dirt comes off when we dry them. At least our Mum's not here to see what's going on. We seem to survive. No one's gone down with food poisoning yet. Then the frying pan. Try to get the grease off. Go through the motions. But why bother, really? We're only going to use it again next trip. Let the grease build up a bit. Does no harm. At least this new pan is a bit more level than the old one. The old one had a great bulge in the bottom, a hill from which all the fat drained away. Things in the middle always burned. This one was much better. Good job we 'accidentally' dropped the old one over the side.

In the astrodome, Dinger was busy with his bubble sextant. He adjusted the filters to reduce the brightness of the sun's light until it was just a dim image. Then he carefully adjusted the image until it sat neatly in the centre of the bubble.

'Now,' he called.

Hank would note the time. Dinger read out the sextant altitude. He did it three more times. Average the readings, get a better result. Then he ducked down from the clear dome in the top of the aircraft, returned to his desk, carefully stowed away the sextant and sat down with the slip of paper Hank had passed across.

Ten minutes later he had a position line plotted on his chart. Just a line. They had been somewhere on it, ten minutes ago. Take another one when the sun has moved a bit, run on the first line to allow for the distance flown between sights, plot the second line and where they cross is where you are, give or take a bit. Simple in theory. Took practice to do it well. But he ran on his last fix and made that cross with the position line. He marked a position on the plot. He added a time neatly beside it. That's where they had been ten minutes before. Now they were nearly twenty miles further on, twenty miles further to the south. Still along way to go. Just about half way.

*

The three Junkers had reached the western limit of their search. Time to turn. They were not down to half on fuel. Schafer had made sure they turned back with a reasonable margin. What if they found something on the easterly leg? It would be embarrassing if they did not have enough fuel for combat. So he had turned back with some thirty minutes margin of fuel for combat. Plus a bit for luck, and head winds, and delays in landing, and just feeling comfortable. In fact, they had used only a third of their fuel. But that was how the sums worked out. It was about what he had expected. They had got nearly to the end of his line. Not quite. There were a few miles to the west they would have to miss out, a few miles where a Tommy might slip past, outside the search. But it meant the Tommies would have to go a long way round.

How far west did they come? If only they knew more, had built up some sort of pattern. It was still very uncertain. He had studied the reports of aircraft who had found Allied aircraft. He had seen the reports from other squadrons. There was not a definite pattern but they all seemed to indicate that the searches needed to be pushed as far as possible to the west. They had been messing about too far to the east previously, of that he was sure. It was out here to the west that they must be coming.

He leaned across again to look at Ernst's chart. Now the pencil line which lead back to base looked a hell of a long way to go!

*

'Change round, lads!' They did it one at a time. Don't all change at once or we end up with no one looking out of the window. Nose gunner to radar. Takes time that one, coming in from the bright light in the turret to the dim lighting around the radar. We ought to get the galley to take over radar, thought John Williams. He hasn't been in the sun light down there. His eyes will be better adapted. I'll fix it for next time. Radar to Tail. Tail gunner to Midships. Bastard that one. Two hours in the turrets. Midships down to the galley, galley up to the nose. All change round. It was better if Sparks was in the roster as well. They could all read morse. They could stand a trick on the wireless. But he was having trouble reading the signal and had dropped out of the change-round. Fair enough. He was the best operator.

The pilots changed as well. Bill Newton slid out and young George dropped into the right-hand seat. Then Bill took over from Mick in the captain's seat. Mick probably wouldn't stay out of his seat for long. 'I'm going for a piss, Bill. Keep her steady so I don't do it all over me desert boots!' With a chuckle, he headed aft for the Elsan. Perhaps he'd have a puff on his pipe back there as well.

*

Squadron Leader Weston stood in front of Tomkins' desk.

'Adjutant, just what was going on in the mess last night?

Broken windows, broken glasses, beer all over the carpet, I gather. Were they fighting, for goodness sake?'

'No, sir. Just having fun.'

'Fun! You call this fun, breaking up the mess. I call it irresponsible and typical of this Australian rabble. Who was the senior officer there? Who was supposed to be in charge. . . . You?'

'Well, I was there, yes, sir, but the senior officer was, errrr, Squadron Leader Hargan.'

'Hargan! I might have known. The most irresponsible of the lot. . . .'

'No, actually sir, I'm wrong. The senior officer was Squadron Leader Smiley. He is senior to all the aircrew squadron leaders.'

'Smiley?' That's got you, you bastard, thought Weston to himself.

Tomkins mulled this over for half a minute. Then he looked at Weston again. 'Will you ask Squadron Leader Smiley to come and see me.'

'Yes, sir!' With pleasure. If only I could be a fly on the wall at this next interview. John Weston had got to know Dick Smiley quite well over the months. Dick could give as good as he got when roused. He was not often roused but. . . .

Dick Smiley entered Tomkins' office five minutes later. John had told him what it was about. Might as well get it over. . . .

'Ops, I understand you were present in the mess last night.'

'Certainly was. Don't get in there often enough. Good party.' Attack was the best form of defence.

'Good party, Ops? But they broke the place up!'

'No. Bit of minor damage maybe.'

'Minor damage! They broke windows, glasses, bottles, I hear. There was beer all over the carpet. And two of the officers have contrived to sign their names on the ceiling!'

'Oh, they succeeded, did they?' answered Smiley mildly. Keep your man off balance.

'Succeeded? Ops, you seem to be condoning what went on last night?'

'Yes, of course.'

'What? You do? You allowed this sort of thing to go on and did not try to stop it?'

'No.' Dick Smiley kept his voice quiet and even. Tomkins' was rising all the time. Play it gently, thought Dick, like a fly before a fish.

'But . . . but you were the senior officer present!'

'Oh, yes, I suppose I was.'

'You should have stopped it. They have no right to do this sort of thing. What were they doing exactly?'

'Oh, I think they called it Aussie rules. Sort of football and rugger combined. New South Wales versus the rest. The rest won. . . .'

'They were playing football in the mess! And you let them! It's outrageous. They are just a bunch of irresponsible, coarse, indisciplined . . . oafs. I shall stop all leave for a month!'

'I shouldn't do that, if I were you,' replied Dick very quietly and evenly.

'What?'

'I said I wouldn't advise that course of action.' Dick was looking directly at Tomkins' face which was slowly turning red with rage. This is fun, thought Dick to himself.

'And who are you to question my decisions?'

That did it. It's time, thought Dick Smiley. It really is time. He kept his voice at the same quiet, even pitch but there was now a certain venom in it. 'I'll tell you who I am! I was flying aeroplanes before you were even born, Tomkins. I may only have squadron leader's stripes on my shoulders but I held the King's Commission in 1915. I've come back to help out in this war. I may be too old for flying but I believe I can offer my experience to help in this conflict. I work long hours because I believe the aircrew deserve a good service, whatever time of day or night.' Tomkins was about to say something but Dick held his gaze and continued. Nothing was going to stop him now.

'You have one of the best bunch of boys I have ever come across. They take their jobs seriously.' He saw the look of surprise in Tomkins' face. 'They do a very good job. They may be a bit scruffy, they may appear casual to you, even offhand. But these are not Hendon cadets you're dealing with. They have not been brought up on spit and polish and air displays and "Anyone for tennis?" after tea. This is a war, in case you had not noticed. You have a bunch of boys who have come a long way from home to play their part. They come from a land where the values are different from ours. They take people for what they are, not what school they went to, not what club they belong to. They call a spade a spade and they don't go in for social airs and graces but they get on and go out there and take on the U-boats and the fighters and the weather, and the RAF red tape from time to time. They steal the cups and plates and knives and forks for their aircraft.' Again more surprise registered on Tomkins' face. 'They beg, borrow, or steal if necessary, the parts for their aircraft. They scrounge extra food from the kitchens. They call each other by their first names. They dress for comfort rather than the parade ground. And they do a bloody good job. And you're too stuck-up to see that. You just don't understand, do you? This war is about morale. We live in bloody awful conditions. The huts they live in are dreadful. The aircraft they fly are pretty spartan but they love them. And they love that mess. They love that house. That house is what England is all about for most of them. A bit of history. Something with a bit of background, tradition, maturity. Not like Australia. That's a young country. They look to us as the old country, something established, permanent, a mother country to turn to, and they're not going to let Hitler or anyone else spoil that.

'Last night they were actually celebrating your U-boat, for God's sake. They were celebrating something you had done! And it was Mick Hargan who suggested it. If you had been there, they would actually have bought you beer and said, "Well done, sir!" because they recognise when a job has been well done. You chose not to be there so they bought your crew drinks instead and congratulated them and the squadron celebrated the fact that we had a U-boat kill for the first time for quite a while.' He was in full flood now and there was going to be no stopping him.

'They let their hair down. They had an evening when all that were here had gathered together for the first time for a while. They were celebrating just that, just all being there together, sharing jokes, hopes, fears maybe. They were young men having a good time. That game was great, to see them all mucking in together, forgetting this war for just a few minutes, forgetting that they might never see the end of it, forgetting that one day they might have a watery grave. Last night was the best thing that could possibly happen. And the best thing you can do is forget it, just put the cost of replacing the glass and so on on their mess bills. It'll only be a shilling a head or something. They won't mind that. Just forget it. OK?'

With that, he turned and walked out of Tomkins' office. As he shut the door behind himself, he had a broad grin across his face. Golly, he enjoyed that! As he walked towards the ops room, to his world, he even allowed himself to break into a laugh. A passing aircraftman looked at him a little strangely. What the hell! I enjoyed telling Tomkins where to go. Stuck up prick, that he was. Yes, I really enjoyed that!

*

D-Dog crossed the imaginary line at 1417. The line was the one marked on the wall plot by Staffelkapitän Schafer five hours before. It was the German search line, a man-made line, a line on a chart. D-Dog crossed it, unknown to her crew. The Sunderland flew on, on a heading of 193 magnetic, indicated air speed 110 knots.

Ju88C, callsign X67T, was on the same line at the same time. Its pilot was the same Staffelkapitän, the one who had drawn the line in the first place. At 1417 his aircraft was nine miles west of the Sunderland, heading east. At that range, they did not see each other. But the Junkers were flying at just over 200 knots. The geometry of the situation dictated that the Junkers would pass only four miles astern of the Sunderland.

XI

Tiny reached the end of his search. His turret was traversed round towards the port side. Slowly, he traversed left, his eyes searching the sky behind them. Keep looking, boyo. God, this is boring, but keep looking. His eyes swept over a small puffy cloud, sitting all on its own in the sky. Wonder why that's there? he wondered. Why does one solitary cloud just sit there over the sea? His eyes moved on. A movement at the edge of his vision, low down, caught his eye. A speck of white, moving above the sea. Some bird, that's all.

His gaze moved back above the horizon, the faint line where sea and sky met. Wonder how many miles away it is, the horizon. We can never know 'cos if we fly to it, it keeps moving away from us. Interesting that. The horizon is something you can never get to. . . . A speck in the distance, just off to the left. Look, stare, focus. What is it? Oh, shit, there's three of them!

'Aircraft! Starboard quarter! Three of them!' Mick was down in the galley when the klaxon went, having a quick chat to Ray. He was on the flight deck in seven seconds.

'Three aircraft astern!' shouted Bill as Mick plugged into an intercom socket.

'Tail, Captain. Report!'

'Three aircraft, starboard quarter. Fair way off. Five miles maybe. Crossing left to right. Seem to . . . seem to be about at right angles to our track. Down quite low. I don't think they've seen us yet.'

'OK, keep an eye on them.'

'Control on the net!' It was Dinger's voice. He had shifted to his control position, to the astrodome. If they were fighters, if they were spotted, it was Dinger who would take over control, he who would direct the battle from his vantage point in the astrodome where he could see all around, where only he could see the whole thing and decide on the best course of action.

They had practised it. Would they need to do it for real? All around the Sunderland, fingers were crossed, breath was held as they flew steadily on and prayed that the fighters would not see them. Twenty seconds had passed.

'They're still crossing left to right. Almost right astern now!' Keep going, Jerry, keep going just the way you are. . . .

*

Lieutenant Elman was doing it strictly by the book, just the way he had been taught. His eyes were doing a precise search of the sky around. Every now and then, his eyes came back to the instruments, check heading, check height, then they would go to the leader's aircraft, check formation, then back to the search of the sky. Beside him, his observer, another earnest young man, was doing the same thing.

*

In the Sunderland, Tiny was watching the three aircraft, his eyes looked to them. And his guns were tracking them. Slowly the turret was moving as he followed with the guns. Silly really. They are too far away to shoot at and we don't want to unless they spot us but it is still comforting to keep the guns following. Just keep going. . . .

*

Where were they? How much further to go? Elman leaned across to look at the chart. His observer noticed his movement and pointed a gloved finger at a spot on the chart. The breadth of his finger covered a large area on the small-scale chart, but it gave Elman an idea of where they were. Still a long way to go back to base.

Still looking to his right, his eyes lifted, and as they did so, a flash of light caught his gaze. Just for half a second. A flash, then it was gone.

Tiny was not to know it but, as he traversed the turret, one of the panels above his head, one of the polished Perspex panels, was angled just right such that the sun was reflected off it and the beam of light reached four and a half miles across the sky to the cockpit of a German fighter. He was leading the fighters with his sight, a bit too far. Instinctively he turned the turret back two degrees.

There it was again! Another flash, another glint of sun. He grabbed for the binoculars, put them to his eyes, found they were miles out of focus, took his other hand off the controls, let the aircraft fly itself for a few seconds and focussed the binoculars correctly.

'Aircraft!' he called as his own aircraft, his hands no longer at the controls, started to bank itself gently to starboard. It was the best way for it to go.

*

Oh, shit! Oh, mother! Oh, God! Please, no. Are they? Yes . . . no . . . yes. 'They're turning!'

'Which way?'

'Towards! They're turning towards!'

Well, this is what it's all about, Mick my boy. How do we get out of this one, eh? Go through the motions. Play it a step at a time. Not much hope against three Jerry fighters, which is what they must be. But we'll have a go, because that's all we can do.

'Captain to Engineer. Jettison bombs!'

'They're on their way, Skipper.' The galley doors were already open, the bombs, the depth charges with fins on, were already moving out along their rails. Once they're out, we'll ditch the bastards. Get rid of the weight, get rid of the explosive. Get a cannon shell in that lot and there won't be anything of the old Dog left.

'Bombs out, Skipper!' Quickly Mick switched the selector switch and pressed the release. He felt the Sunderland lift as the bombs dropped clear.

'Control has the aircraft in sight!' There was a pause. 'Three of them confirmed. Look like three Ju88s.' Oh, shit, this was for real then! 'They're coming in from right astern. They're spreading out a bit. Bit higher than us.'

Height! thought Mick. Get down a bit, lad. Don't let the bastards get underneath you. They'll shoot your arse off that way. Think tactics. Despite the fact that you're shit scared, think, man, think. Height? Get down low. Heading? Which way to go. No point in going south without any bombs. Turn for home? But they're right behind and that's where home is. Turn west? Yeah, turn west, Mick my boy. These lads are a long way from home. Might be running short of juice. You've got plenty of fuel left. Take them west. They might run out of fuel and have to turn for home. That's it! Keep thinking. Everyone in the right place? Bombs have gone. Engines? Well, when it starts, you want full throttle. No, shit, you want full throttle now, mate! He pushed the throttles all the way forward. The engine note deepened. The sound was good. It sounded as if they were doing something positive, like running away. Against three Ju88s? You're joking. They can go at least twice as fast as us . . . but it seems better to be going flat out anyway.

'Dinger, I want to work round to the west if we can. Take them as far from their base as we can. Sparks, send a report. Tell base. Tell them we're under attack!'

'Roger, understood. Just stay as you are at present. They're closing in. All guns, I'll tell you which targets to take. Don't fire too early. . . .' Dinger was watching the three fighters intently. Which one was the leader? Which was the weakest? Which was the one they really had to dodge? Which way to turn when they came in, as they surely would?'

*

Bruckner was flying his aircraft with precision. So there was action to be had out here! Well, well! He admitted quietly to himself that he had been wrong. But it was only a lumbering Sunderland. Quite difficult to see against the sea but, as they closed, the outline was becoming clear. It was a Sunderland. Big and lumbering. Easy shooting. One pass and they could go home. How could that thing stand up to 20 mm cannon? He thumbed off the safety catch on the gun fire button. He checked the gun sight in front of his eyes, checked the illumination. OK. Final check round the instruments. Check engine. Pitch to fully fine. All fuel pumps on. Flaps are in. They've been in since we took off but do the checks. Fuel readings OK. Straps done up tight. Slowly and carefully he pulled down his goggles. The windshield might go. Best to have his goggles on. He pulled his facemask straps tight. You need the microphone ready at all times. He was ready for combat.

*

'They've spread out. There's one right astern, and one out on each quarter. One on the left seems to be lagging a bit. They are still slightly above. Range is closing.' The commentary was continuous now. Tell the lads what to do. Tell the Skipper what's happening. He can't see out of the back. Keep it calm, Dinger my boy, even if your right leg is shaking because, like everyone else, you're shit scared of these German fighters. Armed with cannon! Oh my God!

*

Schafer was lining up right astern of the Sunderland. The range was closing rapidly. Go straight in, first pass, get them first time, no time to think. He'd seen the bombs drop away from the Sunderland. Won't help you,Tommies. You're out-numbered, out-manoeuvred and out-gunned. Like shooting the proverbial sitting duck. For just a second, he felt some sympathy for the Tommies, for the men he would shortly kill. How many were there? Nine, ten, something like that. What were they like? Did they have children, wives, families? When did they last have a woman?

Too late to think these things. It is time. He lined his aircraft up on the tail of the Sunderland, let the nose drop slightly, pushed the throttles all the way forward and led them into the attack.

*

'Here they come! Tail, take the one in the middle, midships . . . midships take the one on the right. Skipper! Stand by to corkscrew port . . . stand by . . . stand by. . . . Corkscrew port. *Go!*'

Mick hauled the controls over, banking her hard over to the left. Pull the nose up, full left rudder. Just like they taught you in OCU. 'Cept you did it at two thousand feet there, not three hundred. Bugger the sea, just stay out of it. Haul her over, hard. Pull the nose up. Give her full left boot. Heave her

round the sky. She'll fly. Meanwhile, Sparks was tapping at
his morse key.

*

Bruckner was watching his leader and saw his nose drop.
He flew on straight and level for a few more seconds. Let's
get up on the quarter of this Sunderland then I'll turn in
and shoot them in the side. Five hundred metres . . . four
hundred . . . now. He pushed the nose down, held her
straight for two more seconds and then banked her gently
to the right.

Come round in a curve and pump shells into the side . . .
two hundred metres. My God! Before him the shape of the
Sunderland was changing. His side-on view was changing.
The big aircraft was rearing up, and banking and turning.
The wing was dropping and the nose was rising. All of a
sudden the big aircraft before him seemed to be rearing up
like some monster. His nicely set up attack was going all
wrong. His aiming point, which would have been the
cockpit, was moving up and round. Bloody hell! The Sunderland was turning towards him . . . they were going to
collide!

*

Tiny followed the fighter astern with his sights. Don't worry
about the fact that your stomach is in your mouth as the tail
drops as the Skipper hauls the nose up. Don't worry about
the fact that the horizon is tilting and the aircraft is screwing
into a tight left turn. Just follow the target. Don't worry
about the fact that he's going to shoot first 'cos he's got
cannons and you've got machine guns. Just keep
following. . . .

The Junkers was firing. The tracer was going high, over
his head. Just keep it that way, Kraut! Just a little closer. . . .
He squeezed the trigger and the four Brownings fired in
unison. Four streams of bullets arched forth, gravity curving
their flight path the moment they left the barrels. Four
streams of bullets went low. Up a bit, up a bit. . . . Then the
fighter was breaking right, its three second burst spent, its

moment gone as the range closed right in and the fighter had to break off.

*

Bruckner pressed the fire push but he knew he was not aiming anywhere near the Sunderland. Instinct had taken over. He was already hauling back on the control column, hauling back so he would go over the top of the aircraft, hauling back to avoid colliding with the bloody thing. The Sunderland flashed by ten metres beneath him.

*

Dinger watched it all. Mick had thrown the Sunderland on its side. The fighter astern got in one burst which went just past the tail. In fact there were a couple of holes in the tail fin. . . . The one to port was completely thrown by the corkscrew and had come bowling in over the top, with a burst from the midships turret to help him on his way. And the third fighter had to break hard left to avoid colliding with the other two. . . .

*

Elman could not believe what was happening. First Schafer's aircraft had come sweeping round in front of him, forcing him to jink left and then he had spotted Bruckner coming over the top of the Sunderland and had to break hard left to avoid him. He had got nowhere near having the Sunderland in his sights. What a balls-up!

Angrily he kicked off the rudder, hauled the Junkers straight and looked around. Where was everyone? From a near collision with all the other aircraft, he was suddenly alone! He craned his head left and right. Ah, there, over his left shoulder. He brought the Junkers hard round.

*

Tiny was feeling more confident. So, the Germans were not so good. And he had the feel of the guns now, had the feel of how much he had to raise them to allow for the stream of bullets dropping. He had the feel of how much to aim ahead. Got close to the first one, right at the end. And that one that broke across the tail, might have winged him as well.

Mick was hauling her straight. Where are we? Where's the compass? Still spinning. Where's the sun then? Get the sun on the port side if we can, take these jokers out to the west. Survived the first pass. How many more?

'Any damage, lads?' he called over the intercom.

'Couple of holes in the tail fin. Nothing else I can see,' came back Digger's voice.

'Tail's OK.'

'Midships OK.'

'Noise OK. Can I have something to shoot at next time. . . .'

'Control, keep the chatter down. They're forming up again.'

*

Not so good, that, thought Schafer. In fact, a bloody shambles. If they all tried to go into together, they were sure to meet. He looked around to see where the other aircraft were. Elman was on the left, coming round in a tight turn. Bruckner was taking station on his right. Already they were closing the Sunderland too fast, the gross difference in speed forcing them closer before they were ready. Got to get this sorted out.

'Circling right!' he called over the radio. 'Open out astern and reform!' Could they really do a coordinated attack? Could they get into a formation, at the right range, in the right place? He led them round in a one-eighty turn. Bruckner followed. Elman was still trying to get into position and slipped even further out to the side.

'Sunderland's turning!' called Ernst, who was craning his neck to watch the target.

'Oh, bollocks!'

*

'They've turned away! But not for long, I don't think. Keep coming round to the west, Skipper.'

Mick brought her round. Steady up. Take a breather. Wipe the sweat off your palms.Give the lads an encouraging word. 'Well done, lads! We surprised the bastards that time!' Trouble was, they might not be so surprised next time.

*

'Throttle back. Slow turn to port!' Schafer called over the radio.

If we don't go motoring round the sky so fast, we might get this next attack sorted out. It was all taking too long. It was a mistake to try it with two inexperienced combat pilots. But if they went in one at a time against this Sunderland, they could be engaged by all the guns. They had to divide the fire, hope that one aircraft could get in a good shot.

They came round the turn. There was the Sunderland. Hell, it has turned and we're not astern of it now. We're all round on the beam. That might work out. . . .

'Bruckner, go straight in, I'll go left. Elman, come under my tail and follow Bruckner. Acknowledge!'

Two 'Understoods!' came back across the ether.

'Go!' ordered Schafer. He pushed his throttles forward, gave a quick wind on the trim to adjust for the power and banked slightly to the left. He glimpsed Elman banking right and turning hard under his tail. That's better!

*

'Hello, something different! They're coming from the beam. One's coming straight in. One's breaking left. The other is behind the first two. Nose and midships take the left-hand one, tail take the right. Anybody take the third one! Stand by corkscrew starboard. We'll turn into the bastards again.' Five hundred yards . . . just a little longer. . . .

In the nose, Ginger could see what was happening this time. He could see the German fighter just forward of the wing tip. It was growing bigger every second. This time, I'll have a go at you bastards, 'cos this time, when the skipper corkscrews starboard, I'll have a clear shot. . . .

'Corkscrew starboard . . . *go*!' Again the great lurch as Mick hauled up and over on the control column and kicked on the rudder. It was like being in a lift in the nose as it rose into the air. Like a roller coaster ride, but I don't care because I can see you clearly now, you Kraut bastard. . . .

*

Bruckner was ready for it this time. He was ready for the Sunderland to rear up in the air, to turn towards him. He was anticipating it. Just follow through, lead him with your guns, then break right. Easy.

At three hundred metres he fired. The tracer shot out in front of his eyes, marking a path from the nose of the aircraft towards a point in space through which the Sunderland had to fly, a point where cannon shell and metal had to converge. But the Sunderland was rising and turning and his shells were going high and he pushed the nose down a fraction but it was too much. The stream of cannon shells sliced across the target but only two hit. One went right through without exploding. The other hit low down, just where the hull turned under, well down from the cockpit, well down from the nose turret. The shell exploded and sprayed fragments round the innards of the lower hull. But it was mainly just space there. Nothing vital.

Then the Sunderland was large in his windshield and he pulled hard back and over and broke right.

*

Ginger saw the fighter open fire. The tracer went over his head. He held his fire . . . just get in range and I'll have a go at you. Fire! He watched fascinated as his bullets curved away. Way high! But leave it there. Come left, come further left, the bastards going to turn, I know he is . . . I just know he is. . . .

Then the fighter was turning. Ginger did not notice a jolt somewhere beneath him. He was watching his bullets as the fighter turned straight into them. He saw the hits. A neat line across the underside of the wing. Then the fighter was gone. Where's the next bastard?

*

Schafer watched Bruckner going in. The Sunderland was responding, climbing and banking and turning. Perfect. He'll be just where I want him, a big target. . . . Bruckner was breaking away. Schafer was five seconds behind him . . . five seconds behind in opening fire, but from a completely different direction. This was working out. He was nicely positioned round on the starboard quarter of the Sunderland with a view right along the top of it as it banked and turned.

But then the Sunderland was suddenly levelling and the right wing was coming up and the nose was going down and the rudder was hard over and what should have been a broad target was suddenly getting smaller and the deflection angle was changing. . . . He kicked on left rudder, skidding round to lead the Sunderland's turn but it put him in a bad position and he was skidding all over the sky and what should have been a long, long burst from a perfect position turned into a panicky two second blast into open space as the Sunderland dropped away before him. And he felt the blows as machine gun bullets tore at his aircraft but nothing happened and the aircraft flew on, climbing and turning out of range.

*

In the midships turret Banjo had swung off the first fighter and was waiting for the third. The third was following the first in, except the geometry of the situation was changing as the Skipper corkscrewed port and what had been a high elevation shot with the Sunderland banked hard to starboard was rapidly becoming a low elevation shot .. . . possibly even out of my arcs if the Skipper leans her over any more. And then he was firing as the third fighter came roaring in, cannons blazing. They were getting a bit bloody close. . . . He felt the blows as the shells hammered into the Sunderland somewhere back aft. . . . Bank, bang, bang . . . bang, bang. But he kept on firing because the nose of the fighter was rising and he was going to come over the top and that's perfect 'cos I'll get you, you bastard. His sights came up and he led the silhouette that was his target, the silhouette just like on the recognition posters, led it and allowed for the speed of the target but not quite enough because a row of bullet holes was punched in the rear fuselage of the Junkers. Then it roared overhead and it really did roar 'cos he could hear the bloody thing!

*

Schafer held her in the tight turn. Come hard round and have another go. Get in again before they expect it and hammer them. Just while they think the second attack is over, come hard round, catch them as they level out and get them. . . .

*

'Good shooting, turrets. We took some hits back aft. Tail, you OK?' No reply. 'Tail, you there?' But he could see the turret moving from the astrodome. 'Control to Skipper. Comms are out withTail but the turret's moving. . . . Hold it, I think one of the bastards is coming round again. Level out. Stand by corkscrew. . . . I'll tell you which way. . . . Yeah, he's coming round again. . . . It'll be a corkscrew port . . . stand by . . . *go!*'

Tiny could see the fighter coming round. The intercom was dead but that didn't matter. All he had to do was shoot at what he saw. It was comforting to hear voices but. . . . It was also nice to know which way they were going to corkscrew . . . be ready for the lurch, ready for the turn, ready to keep the guns tracking as the Sunderland stood on one ear or the other and the tail dropped. . . . The fighter was straightening, lining up again. Are the others coming in as well? Get the bastard you can see. . . .

*

Don't worry about the other two. Just get this attack in. Get in close. . . . Oh, hell! The Sunderland was banking again, but this time I know what you're doing, my Tommy friend, and my sights are following and leading and myhands and feet are moving just fractions of an inch as I keep my aircraft lined up so the sights are following you and I can anticipate your movements. . . .

*

Dinger watched the fighter coming in. Tail would take him. Check where the other two were. . . . Far out. . . . No problem. 'Midships, take the one astern as well!'

The fighter was firing. The tracers were high . . . coming down . . . it was all happening so slowly . . . a fighter closing at a relative speed of over a hundred knots and the bullets, the shells going so much faster but the tracer just hung there . . . then crept down . . . and down.

It was only a three second burst but the last fifteen shells were the ones that counted. They tore through the after fuselage, then the line moved forward and up, ripping through the midships turret and then the last three went over the fuselage and into the starboard outer engine.

Mick felt the hammer blows as the shells struck home. The controls twitched in his hands. She was taking hits. Keep pulling her round, mate, keep moving her round the sky. Moving target, keep at it. Don't worry about the sweat, heave her round, get her out of the line of bullets, just stop those shells crashing home.

Then it stopped. There was a blur out of the corner of his left eye as the German fighter broke away to the side. God, where's the next one?

'Fire! Starboard outer's on fire!' Dinger's voice. 'Fighters are holding back. . . .'

Mick glanced across to his right, then looked properly. Suddenly he seemed far away. Engine's on fire, mate. They got you. Set fire to you. It's over there – that one out there on the right, the far one. You can't see properly from here. You can't see all the engine nacelle. You can only see the prop. The rest of the engine's hidden behind the inner. But take Dinger's word for it. The bastard's on fire. There's smoke and flame and shit coming out of the back of it. . . .

'Fire drill, starboard outer!'

His voice sounded detached. Go through the motions. It won't do any good but do it anyway. Put out an engine fire? No chance, with those tinpot extinguishers they put in the engines. No chance at all, but go through the motions anyway. Throttle right back. Left foot moving instinctively to hold her straight. Asymmetric flying they call it. Unbalanced. Engine out one side. Practise it at OCU. Fuel cock off. Magnetos off. Grills shut. Activate extinguisher. Engineer would have the fuel pumps off. Stop the engine, stop the fuel supply, activate the extinguisher. That was the principle of the thing. Wouldn't do any good. But you're still heaving hard on that extinguisher because you think doing it hard might help. Might as well crawl out there and piss on it. . . .

'I think it might be out, Skipper! Flames have gone. Still a lot of smoke. Yeah, it might be going out. . . .'

*

Schafer was coming round again. He knew he had hit the Sunderland, had seen his cannon strike home. Now he had to see. He could not go in and attack again. His cannons needed reloading. Send one of the others in? No. Hold it. Regroup. Get sorted out. He had been lucky. Get back in some sort of order and all go in again. They might not have to, not after those hits. . . .

But the Sunderland was still flying. Smoke was trailing from the right wing, from the outer engine. But just smoke and it seemed to be diminishing. But the engine was stopped. He could see the blades of the propeller turning slowly in the airstream, but there was no power in that engine. The engine was shut down. That was clear.

*

'Banjo's had it, Skipper!' It was Johnno's voice. 'Had it' was an understatement. John Williams could hardly bear to look at the sight before him. All that was left of the young gunner was a headless torso, a bloody mass, a pulp where only a few seconds before there had been a man, a friend, a mate. He staggered away from the turret and threw up.

'What about the turret?' a voice was saying. He retched again.

'Johnno, what about the turret?'

He recovered himself. 'It's out, Skipper. Shot to pieces.'

Mick was having trouble holding her. He'd wound on rudder trim but that did not seem to help much. Perhaps that was shot away. He called for George in the right-hand seat to help him out, to apply some additional pressure to the rudder pedal. Poor George! Just had to sit there and watch it all happen around him. Just the problem Phil Bannister had been complaining about. . . .

Assess damage. One engine out. Midships turret out. Damage round the tail. No comms with the tail turret. Maybe a hit or two up front but no-one's had time to look yet. One dead. Three fighters still flying. A few hits on them, maybe, but what would machine gun bullets do?

'They're still holding back, still re-forming,' called Dinger. Mick brought them slowly round to west again. Keep going. Use every little bit of help you can get. Boy, do you need it.

*

The three fighters lined up again astern of the Sunderland. Ernst had crawled into the nose to reload the cannons. Bloody awful job, that. He was just struggling back into his seat, trying to get his straps done up. Schafer was throttled right back. Airspeed was way down. She was feeling sluggish but he did not want to close in. Very difficult not to close in on this slow-moving Sunderland. So the three fighters seemed to hang in the air, way below their normal flying speed. . . . Might have to put some flap down but that's crazy. . . . Time to go in again.

'Attack from astern. Bruckner lead from the right, Elman follow on the left. I'll come in behind you. Acknowledge!'

They both answered. 'Go!' he called.

Bruckner's aircraft immediately accelerated ahead of the other two. Go in just a few seconds apart this time. Either side and right astern. Just a short gap between them and they wouldn't mess each other up. . . .

*

'They're coming again! The one on the left is leading.' Hell, he couldn't talk to any turret that could bear. Midships was out. Tail's intercom had gone. 'Nose, be ready for one coming up to starboard! Stand by corkscrew starboard . . . stand by . . . stand by . . . *Go!*'

Again the Sunderland banked and lifted and turned but this time Mick only pulled the nose up a fraction, held it for a second and then let it drop. Let her come, George my boy. Let me get full rudder! Get your foot off the bar! I know you're helping but I want to spin her round that dead engine. . . .

*

It was just as before. The Sunderland was doing the same thing . . . bank and turn, nose up . . . then, suddenly, its nose was dropping, dropping towards the sea and Bruckner had to push his own nose down and lead to the right and follow the target with his sights and keep pushing and. . . . *Fire!*

His guns fired for one and a half seconds and then stopped. It was not enough. He was out of ammunition and had not had enough time to correct his aim. He banked hard right and broke away. . . .

Suddenly there was a series of hammer blows beneath the cockpit. He felt a pain in his leg – a sharp stab. A red hot sensation. No problem. . . . The aircraft was still flying. . . . No

. . . problem. . . . Suddenly everything was moving very slowly . . . the aircraft was banking . . . the wings almost vertical . . . must pull her out . . . turn your hands to the left . . . push with your left foot . . . bring her out of the turn . . . level out . . . there's plenty of time . . . just . . . do . . . it . . . now.

The Junkers continued to roll, to roll slowly over on its back and then the nose went down and, with rudder still on, it started to skid, but you couldn't see that. The nose went down and, in an inverted position, a terrified young observer watched as the sea rose towards him and wondered what was happening. He only had another seven seconds to wonder as his pilot's life blood sprayed over the cockpit from a shattered femoral artery, shattered by a single bullet.

The Junkers hit the sea at two hundred and five miles an hour. It ploughed straight in, its wings breaking off. Just a wheel floated after the splash had subsided, but there was no one to check it out. The battle had already moved on across the sea. . . .

*

Only Tiny saw the Junkers go in. It went in astern of them because the Sunderland was still turning and no-one else could see. And he only noticed out of the corner of his eye because he was busy firing at the next one who was coming in from astern and who was nicely lined up and whose shooting was getting better all the time.

The burst went through the Sunderland's port elevator and then moved left, hitting empty space for 0.8 of a second before it contacted the left wing tip. Three shells hit the wing and then the burst was spent and the fighter was breaking left and Tiny was hosing bullets across the space that separated them but none were hitting. . . . Then the fighter was gone.

*

Elman had seen Bruckner's aircraft turn slowly over and dive towards the sea. But the Sunderland was giving him a good view of its underside. As it was turning away from him, he could see the shape of its hull. Funny looking thing, this flying boat. So squat and fat. He was growing more confident. He watched Schafer going in, watched him fire, saw the hits on the wing, the wing that was banked away from his own point of view. Watched as Schafer broke away, watched that Schafer would come over the top of him. No problem this time. . . .

He fired and his tracers leapt out across the two hundred and fifty metres. Come up a bit, up a bit more . . . bit more. . . .

*

The shells were pouring in on the port side. There was a series of crashes from somewhere behind the flight-deck. The aircraft shook and shuddered under the hammer blows. Just for two seconds. Then they stopped. But there was a stink of cordite. And a scream from somewhere aft, a horrible, blood-curdling scream . . . then it stopped.

Bill Newton was the first one there. What a shambles! What a bloody shambles! There was a gaping hole in the port side of the fuselage. In fact he could see another hole lower down. . . . But the people . . . Hank Jones was dead. Half his head was shot away. But it was Jim Bailey, the Sparks . . . blood was pouring out of a wound in his neck, bright arterial blood. First aid! Shit, what do I do? Stop the bleeding! What with? Just get something on it, for God's sake! He knelt down beside the figure on the deck. Hand! Put your hand over it! He pressed his hand against the man's neck, could feel the warm blood against it, could see the blood oozing out through his fingers, see it running down his wrist.

Then there was someone else beside him, pushing something towards him. What is it? Field dressing. Get it on. Press it into place. Stem the flow. He grabbed the dressing and pressed it hard against Spark's neck. But it had only been there a few seconds and it was bright with blood.

He couldn't stem the flow. But he went through the motions and held the dressing in place and then another one when it was passed to him and he watched the man die before him. Bloody hell! Life just went from the figure as he knelt beside it. He could feel it draining away, could see the blood running out and there was nothing he could do. The man just faded away and there came a moment when you knew it was no longer any good, that all your feeble trying was just that, a feeble attempt at the impossible. And around you the Sunderland lurched and staggered, he knew not why, he cared not why. If it was another attack, it was another attack. . . So what?

*

'They're holding off. There's only two of them. I don't know where the third one went. He's disappeared.'

'Damage? Who's checking the damage?' There was a pause.

'It's Johnno, Skipper. I'm with Bill Newton. He's off the net at the moment. He's trying to sort things out. . . . Hank's caught it. Sparks doesn't look too good. Bloody great hole back here. Radio's shot away. Engine panel's gone.'

'Roger, Johnno. Control, Dinger, you all right?'

'Yeah, Skipper, I'm OK.'

What Dinger did not know was that he had been incredibly lucky. The hits from the cannon had been just below and aft of his position at the astro dome. He had been protected by the presence of the radios, by the engine instrument panels. They had taken the impact of the cannons' explosions. It was a section of radio chassis which had penetrated Jim Bailey's neck. But it was the blast of an exploding 20 mm shell which had removed the left side of Hank Jones' head. One splinter had passed half an inch from Dinger's left leg, but he was not to know that. The splinter had been two inches long, as sharp as a razor and had cut through the starboard skin of the fuselage. If he had not moved his leg a fraction just as the shell exploded, the splinter would have cut through his thigh. Such was the luck of war . . . for the moment.

*

One fighter gone and the Sunderland was still flying! Get them while they're down! But Schafer waiting for Elman, waiting for him to report he was ready, waiting for him to report that he too had re-loaded his guns.

XII

The two young women, the two WAAF officers were together
in the Communications Centre. Around them was spread the
equipment of a war-time signals organisation – teleprinters
connected with Group Headquarters, with Coastal Command
Headquarters at Northwood in Middlesex, telephones, radio
receivers, transmitters, plug boards, files of signals, trays for
signals to go or ones waiting for distribution, cypher machines,
code books, stateboards – and operators.

Jane Phillips was taking it all in as Helen (who still looked a
bit pale) explained the procedures to her. There was a flurry
of activity in one corner where a girl sat at a receiver,
headphones on. The watch supervisor was taking a signal
from her. The WAAF corporal looked at the piece of paper in
her hand, looked at the stateboard which showed aircraft's
coded callsigns against their side letters, wrote something on
top of the signal.

'You might want to see this before I pass it to Ops,' she said
as she handed it to Helen MacDonald.

Jane peered over her shoulder as they both read the words:
'Under attack. Three fighters.'

At the top, against the callsign, the supervisor had written in
red pencil – 'D-Dog'.

*

Mick was not sure he could hold her. The last manoeuvre,
letting the nose drop during the corkscrew, had almost put
them in the sea. He knew he had pushed the old girl to the
limit with one engine out. But the extra drag created by the
holes in the side and in the wing and the tail fin had almost
tipped the balance between managing to stay in the air and
stalling and crashing into the sea.

Now he had her level and was just managing to gain a little

height. Two hundred and fifty feet. He could not contemplate another corkscrew – they had only just got out of the last one. He was having to nurse her, treat her gently whilst, at the same time, having to apply brute strength to the rudder to counteract the drag of the dead engine. He was sure the rudder trim was shot away. Winding on the trim wheel did absolutely nothing. What a bastard! And any moment now they were going to be coming in again. But Dinger said something about there only being two of them?

*

'Come on, come on! Schafer quietly fumed whilst he waited for Elman to reload. The two Junkers were crawling along, trying to stay behind the Sunderland. He was having to weave so as not to close, even though he was throttled back as much as he dare. What were those clowns doing? He'd ordered Elman to check his ammunition supply as it ought to be almost out. No point in attacking again if Elman's guns were going to run out as soon as he opened fire.

The Sunderland was mortally wounded, of that he was sure. It was down very low. Elman had reported getting hits on the port side. It just needed one more go, one more good attack. . . .

*

There was nothing much to be done. Or was there? Bill Newton contemplated the scene before him. Wind was roaring in through the shattered side of the fuselage. There was blood all over the deck. The two bodies were sprawled in the pools of red. There were pieces of radio, engine panel, radar, fuselage skin scattered around. Now it was all dead weight. That was it! Ditch it! Get rid of excess weight. Bugger the Jerry fighters. There's nothing I can do anyway.

He turned to John Williams who had been beside him as he tried to save the radio operator's life. John Williams it was who had dug out the field dressings, who had watched as he tried to save a man's life to no avail. Do something positive!

'Johnno! he shouted above the roar of the wind, the roar of the engines, 'Start ditching stuff over the side!' With that, he bent down, grabbed a hunk of the radio operator's desk and hurled it out through the hole.

*

Tiny was watching the fighters. I don't know what's going on up at the front end. I'm not all that certain I want to know. But I'm all right back here, Jerry, and I've got a little trick up my sleeve for you next time. I'm watching you bastards and I don't know why you're hanging about but I'll bloody get you when you come in next, if you're coming that is. Or have we scared you off? I saw one of you spear in. Caught a glimpse. Looked like a bloody great splash from what I saw. I didn't get that one so it must have been one of the lads up forward. Good for him! Reckon it's my turn now.

*

One man of the crew had played little part in the action so far. Down in the galley, Ray had a mad frenzy of activity at the beginning as the bombs went out and were ditched. He had made sure the hatches were shut securely once the bombs were all gone. Then he'd got the galley secured. Get the stove out. Throw some water on it to cool it down. Nice source of fire that if it all goes over. He'd hurled the pans and kettle into the locker. Not that had done much good. It had come bursting open at the first corkscrew and everything was now scattered round the galley.

He was bloody scared. He was plugged into the intercom. He could hear all that was happening, hear the reports of the fighters coming in, hear the guns firing, feel the hits, smell the cordite. But there was bugger all for him to do except hang on tight as the Sunderland lurched and banked and skidded round the sky. He was feeling very ill and very frightened. And he knew some of his mates were dead. He'd heard the reports. Oh, shit! He had to do something!

'Control, this is Galley,' he called rather tentatively.

'Control,' came back a reassuring voice. Hell, thought Dinger. We'd forgotten all about the galley.

'Anything you want me to do?'

'Yeah, Galley. Get back aft, check the damage and see if the tail turret is OK. Right?'

'Right!' Something positive to do. But when was the next attack coming? It seemed an age since the last one.

*

George knew exactly how long it was. Five minutes by the flight-deck clock. Five long, whole glorious minutes. A lifetime. A lull, a reprieve. But they were going to come back, weren't they? They were just getting ready for the final stroke, the final thrust of the sword. One more attack like the last one and they couldn't possibly stay flying. The skipper was struggling to keep her up. He, George, was having to keep his weight on the rudder pedal as well as the skipper to keep her more or less straight. It was bloody hard work. What had happened to the beautiful flying machine that had taken off that morning? Where were the light, balanced controls? Where was that reassuring feeling of solidarity, of toughness, of dependability? She was in a hell of a mess. He had looked back down the short passage which led aft. Bill and Johnno were working away at something. He could see they were lit by daylight coming in from somewhere back there. And hidden in the roar of the engines was the sound of rushing wind, wind blowing through gaping holes in the fuselage. Could she take any more of this?

*

Ready at last! Nothing too clever this time. One after the other, one on each quarter. 'Elman, take starboard quarter, follow after me. I'll go port. Acknowledge!'

Once again he pushed the throttles all the way forward, the engine note rose to a crescendo and the Junkers accelerated rapidly towards its target. Two Junkers with fully-loaded guns against a mortally wounded Sunderland. The Tommies might have shot down one 88. Man was incompetent anyway. One more attack and they had to go down, to fall out of the sky, to break asunder as they hit the sea.

*

Tiny was watching, watching very carefully. But he was bent over his guns, his head cocked on one side. The barrels of his guns were not following the fighters. They were pointing at the sea and twenty degrees off the target. It looked like he was dead. He was very still but he was watching. Only his eyelids were moving as he blinked.

*

The range was closing rapidly. The Sunderland was still straight and level. No jinking about this time, no throwing the aircraft round the sky, no banking and weaving and ducking. A simple target. And as the range closed he could see that the tail turret was not following. The guns were not tracking him. It was obvious the midships turret was out of action already. Now the tail turret was out as well! No one to fire back. Perhaps no one to tell the pilot they were even coming! Get in close. Fire as close as you can. Finish them off. Pump your shells right into the heart of the thing. He lined up on the point where the wings and fuselage met, the centre of the Sunderland. Firing from slightly above, as he would be, the shells should slam right through to the flight-deck. Just another two hundred metres!

Tiny watched. Come on, you bastard. Just a little closer. . . . Almost in range . . . almost . . . *now*!

He swung the guns up and round. He knew just where to aim, just where to lead off, just where in space to put his bullets. The sights came up and he fired.

The Junkers reared in the air, like a wounded animal, reared up and spat fire. But its fire went over the top. Its nose went up and it banked to the right and smoke started pouring from its starboard engine. Got you, you bastard!

*

Elman was following Schafer in, following in time but taking a sweep round to the starboard quarter of the Sunderland. Line up. Steady . . . target's not manoeuvring . . . this is going to be easy . . . sights on . . . press the. . . . Shit! Suddenly Schafer's aircraft was coming right across his path, two hundred metres in front, cutting across and banking and climbing and blocking the view, blocking the way to the target . . . and pouring smoke from an engine! Oh, my God! He pulled hard over and brought his Junkers tight round to starboard, turning inside his leader. What do I do now?

*

'Tail's hit one! He bloody got it, Skipper! Tiny got the bastard! And the other one's broken away. They've both broken off! The first one is pouring smoke from one engine. You beaut, Tiny!'

Dinger watched as the first fighter climbed slowly away and turned through one eighty degrees. He watched the other go round in a full circle and thought for one horrible moment it was coming round for another attack. But it swung away again and opened out a bit and then turned to take up station astern. And there it stayed, for the moment.

*

A Ju88 was one hell of an aeroplane to fly on one engine. Schafer was struggling. He was also very lucky. It might be pouring smoke but there were no flames. But it was no longer any use to him. The engine was shattered by the stream of bullets which had gone into it. Slowly the Junkers clawed for height and slowly he brought her round to the east. East was home and that was the only way to go. There was no way he could attack with one engine out. And his radio was out. He couldn't call Elman, couldn't call him and tell him to get on and finish the job. He'd just have to leave him to it. The only thing to do was head for France. Any bit of France would do.

*

Suddenly Elman was alone, he and his observer, two young men, two products of the Hitler Youth, and a single Junkers 88. Now it was one against one. One Junkers against a Sunderland. But cannon against machine gun.

Elman suddenly felt fear, real cold sweating fear. Fear that took away all reason. Fear that made you shake and shiver and your mouth run dry and your pulse race. Suddenly he faced the prospect of death. And it made him very frightened.

Somehow the Junkers had flown itself in a wide arc so it came up astern of the Sunderland. Somehow it had throttled back to maintain station. Somehow it was weaving gently from side to side to avoid closing the range. Elman was not sure how it had got there. But one part of his brain was saying, 'You're just lining up for your next attack.' Another voice was telling him, 'You need an excuse to go home, a reason not to go in again.' Fuel! That was the reason. He checked the fuel gauges. Hell! It really was a reason to go home. He was down to nearly a third and the action had been dragging him further and further from base all the time. It was time to go. He made a great play of pointing the readings out to his observer. The message was clear.

But he could not bring himself to just turn away. There had to be one more gesture, one finale. His hands went to the throttles and the Junkers accelerated towards the Sunderland yet again.

*

The bastard was coming in! Just the one, all on his own. No clever tricks this time, thought Tiny. You'll get everything I've got. His guns were following the fighter as it came in from slightly above and on the starboard quarter.

*

He fired early. He was far too far out. His shells were filling empty space. His aim was miles off. The sight was on a point somewhere behind the Sunderland's starboard wing and the range was long. His shells were dropping well below the target. He didn't care. It was a gesture. Yes, sir, I attacked again but had to break off due to lack of fuel. That was what it was all about. An explanation. An exoneration from blame. You did your best, Elman.

The tail gunner was firing back. He too was firing at very long range, but, in a few seconds, his fire could be effective. Five more seconds and a bullet could come smashing in through the windshield, could get me in the head, the guts, the balls. Already his hands were moving in response to an instinct for survival and the nose of the Junkers came up as he started to break away to the right.

*

Mick could only sit and wait and listen to the commentary. No evasion, no corkscrew, no nothing. Just sit there and take it, boyo. Suddenly there was a bang, bang, crash . . . and then nothing. She shuddered slightly and flew on. Three hits. You could count them. Then nothing.

'He's breaking off . . . turning away . . . turning . . . opening on a one eighty . . . didn't come all that close.' There was a long silence. . . . 'I think he's finished. I think he's going home. He's opening astern. Still opening. About a mile now, still going . . . still going.' Fingers stayed crossed, silent prayers were muttered, hopes not raised too high.

Mick broke the spell. 'Where were those last hits?'

'Starboard side, I think one on the hull and a couple on the wing. There's a hole just inboard of the starboard inner but otherwise everything looks OK.'

Dinger again, Dinger who had led them through. Mick had just been the driver. And now they were waiting, hoping, praying for Dinger's pronouncement.

'He's gone!'

*

Schafer was nursing his aircraft. She was climbing slowly, very, very slowly, but she was climbing. But he had two other, more important, concerns. Ernst was dead. Sitting quietly in his seat, as he always did, he had died. Schafer was not quite sure when or why. From the pilot's position, it just looked as if he was resting. It was only when Elman leaned across that he could see that the whole of the observer's right side was soaked in blood. The man just sat there, held by his straps, his head lolling. All I have to do is touch his shoulder and he'll wake and tell me the way home. But I've tried that and it didn't work and now I'm not sure where I am so all I can do is head east. France is a big place.

But I'm not sure I'm going to get there because there's something wrong with the fuel situation or the gauges are all cocked up. They say I'm down to a quarter but that can't be right because I checked it during the attacks and I was only just under a half. The gauges must be wrong. . . .

*

They took stock. They checked her over and Bill noted it all down and worked it all out and then told Mick about it.

'Three engines. As best we can tell from the remaining

instruments, those three are OK. No sign of re-ignition on the starboard outer. Fuel appears to be OK. Damage. Tail section a bit of a mess. Most of the rudder is OK. Control links OK except for rudder trim which is shot away. Holes in the rear fuselage. Bit draughty but that's all. Port side aft of the flight-deck. All the gear's finished. No engine panels, no radios or radar. Starboard side, few splinter holes. Port wing . . . from what we can see, damage to the wingtip. Can't see what exactly. Starboard wing is a bit of a mess round the starboard outer and there's some damage inboard of the inner. Midships turret extensively damaged. And, errr . . . three dead, Mick. Hank, Sparks and Banjo. Oh, and Johnno caught a splinter from the last attack. Bleeding a bit from his guts, that's all.'

'Thanks, mate. Sorry about Hank and the others. . . .' His voice changed to something more positive. 'Dinger, which way's home?'

'Trying to work it out, Skipper.'

'OK. Now, listen in, lads. We've taken some knocks but that was goodo that we got those fighters. Well done, the gunners. You on the net, Tiny?'

'Yes, Skipper.'

'Good on yer, mate! Now, we've brought Tiny out of the tail turret 'cos he's bugger all good as a lookout if he's got no intercom. So, I want a lookout in the astrodome all the time. If something crops up, we'll man the tail turret. Now, George and me will keep the old girl flying but we need some help. I want those who are spare to carry on ditching stuff from where Bill and Johnno left off. Anything that's loose that we don't want, ditch it. We need a bit of height to play with. Right, let's go!

He brought her very, very slowly round to the north and then a bit east of north. Home must be about this way. Dinger would tell him shortly. But did his left leg hurt! Heaving on the rudder to hold her against the dead engine. Me bleeding leg's seizing up! We'll have to take it in spells, get the lads in the right-hand seat, make them do it for a while.

'Skipper, try zero two five for home.'

That was the best he could do at the moment. Dinger played with the figures again. Just thirty minutes the action had lasted. Where were we when we started? What was the general direction when we went in? What speed did we make in that general direction? Call it west although we were all over the place. Say we only made forty miles due to all the zigging around. We must be about there. Allow twenty miles on that position. Course for home? Go too far east and we bump into Ushant. Go too far west and we miss Land's End and go up the Irish Sea. And all I can do is make the best guess, the best DR and go on that, 'cos the Gee is shot away and I'm not going to get anything else out of that, and me sextant's smashed as well. I've got a chart and a pencil and dividers, and my log with the winds on. And we've still got a compass. Zero two five. Best guess. That's all I can do.

Stuff was going over the side. Elsan, food, pots, pans. They got the mooring ropes out from forward and ditched those. That's when they discovered the holes in the lower hull. Sorry, Mick, but she's not going to float for long when we get back. Smashed seats and the rest of the radio gear. Flares, markers, tins of jam, they all went. But not the water drums. And what about the bodies, Mick? A quiet whisper, not on the intercom. A quiet whisper, as much as you could above the roar of the engines. Do we ditch the bodies, Mick? No, Bill, it's not that desperate yet. It's the least we can do, take the lads home. Things aren't that bad. She's just starting to climb a bit and we're burning off fuel as well. We're right, mate.

But he did not know about the damage the very last shell had done in the final moment. One splinter, only half an inch in diameter, had penetrated the starboard inner engine nacelle and, just before it came up against solid metal in the form of the engine block, it had nicked one of the luboil pipes. A very fine spray of luboil was now being forced out of the minute hole by the luboil pump, a spray which coated the inside of the engine nacelle. As it built up, the airstream through the engine blew it aft as a virtually invisible mist.

XIII

She had hardly taken in a word in the last forty minutes. She had followed Helen around as things were explained, people introduced, but she was just going through the motions. I met a man one night, a man who listens to me, who listens to my troubles, my doubts, my fears. I tell him stories of bomber crews not coming back, of men getting the chop. And he listens and says little of himself. Then, after that, I find he is facing the same sort of dangers, the threat of being shot down, the possibility of not coming home one day. Then I watch him take-off and wave as he goes. What do I see next? I see a signal saying he is being attacked by three fighters . . . in daylight! Even I can see no one comes back from that. Oh, Mick, I'm so sorry, so bloody sorry!

*

Two thousand four hundred feet! Bloody marvellous. Height gives you time, time to think and react if something goes wrong. Height is comforting when you're nursing a crippled aircraft home on three engines. She was still a cow to fly but they'd rigged up a rope arrangement on the rudder pedals on the right-hand side and that took a lot of the load. Made steering a bit difficult but she would turn if you banked her without the rudder. Bit sloppy. She'd slip into the turn but we're not here to give flying lessons. We're just here to get the old girl home.

She's flying bloody slowly. It's all that drag from the holes and bits knocked off the wings and so on. No longer did she have a smooth skin, like a virgin. She was flying like an old lady. But the engines were good. Steady readings all round. Plenty of fuel. No sweat.

'Cept Dinger tells me he is not sure where we are. Well, he says he can draw a circle on the chart and guess we are somewhere inside it. All he's got to do is get the circle over England without any part of it going too near France. If the circle crosses England, so do we, and that's all we want. And we'll be back before dark, which is bloody goodo 'cos when I try to land the old girl, she ain't going to float for long and it would be nice if the tender crew could see we have a spot of bother and come and pick us up. And get the bodies out before she goes down.

Mick clamped his pipe firmly in his teeth and sucked gently at it. It was unlit as usual.

*

A hundred miles away another pilot was trying to gain height. Height is distance, and if the fuel runs out I need the height to make it to the coast – maybe. But I burn more fuel by climbing but the engine's at full power anyway, so it doesn't make too much difference except that climbing reduces speed. It's a balancing act, thought Helmut Schafer to himself, and I'm not sure I'm getting it right, but I'll have a try because that is all I can do. Problem is, the fuel gauges are still going down and I've still no idea whether it is just the gauges which are defective or whether I really have lost fuel. Only time will tell.

Slowly the Junkers climbed, fifty feet a minute. It was nothing but after forty-five minutes that made 2,250 feet. Like Mick Hargan, he found it comforting. Trouble is, a Ju88 glides a bit like a brick. Lose that engine and I'm heading down fast. And they don't ditch too well either.

*

Dick Smiley was contemplating the news. Poor old Mick. But there was hope. Hope would not really run out until you knew that the Sunderland could not possibly still be airborne because its fuel must have run out. Even then, you hoped they might have landed away somewhere and that the message had just not got through. Or made it into some deserted bay. That had happened before. Trouble was, it was going to be another ten hours or so before all hope of them having any fuel left ran out. And another twelve hours before you were pretty sure they had not landed somewhere else. One signal, that's all they had. There might be another . . . might. If the truth were known, there was not much hope against three fighters but he would go on hoping for another day. How many times had he done it before? Far too many. But he felt especially sorry that it was Mick this time. The new boys, well, you didn't really know them so you did not care so much. But one of the old hands, someone like Mick who'd been around a while, worked his way up, that was different. Mick was part of the squadron, far more than Tomkins was. A guy like Mick was what the squadron was made of. What a bloody awful war!

*

They tended to congregate just at the back of the flight-deck, the ones with nothing to do. There was one in the nose turret, one keeping lookout in the astrodome. Johnno was lying down, down below and they were taking it in turns to be with him. His wound in his belly was still bleeding, well, more sort of oozing blood. You couldn't seem to stop it. You couldn't really get any pressure. And he had this pain in his guts, kept moving around, couldn't get comfortable.

Dinger stayed at his table, so that only left two of them without a job. So they hung around the back of the flight-deck, which was probably the best place for them anyway. One of them was ready to race back aft to the tail turret and they took it in turns to go the rounds, crawl round the old girl, see if anything was coming apart anywhere. But the flight-deck was the focus of attention. It was all down to simple flying now. Just get us home, Skipper. That's all we ask. You're doing a great job. And they could look over Dinger's shoulder and see how far they had to go. His dead reckoning positions were moving slowly across the chart. Soon have Ushant abeam. Downhill after that, mate.

*

Elman was watching his fuel gauges carefully. It was part of a fighter pilot's life, watching fuel, particularly over the Atlantic. It could be close. His observer was doing the calculations. Should be OK but not much to spare. He really had had to break off because of the fuel situation. Another attack and he might not have made it. He still might not make it. He too had been slowly gaining height but he had the power to do it. He was at eight thousand feet and had failed to see Schafer's aircraft pass six thousand feet below and three miles to one side. Now Elman was opening out ahead of Schafer. Not that he could have done anything to help. Except watch where Schafer bailed out.

*

The gauges read zero. He hoped and prayed and flew on. Five minutes he was given. Then his one remaining engine coughed twice, ran, then stopped. Instinctively he put the nose down. Convert height into distance. Something you learned early in training. Engine failure. The instructor pulling back the throttle. Nose down. Adopt best gliding speed, the best speed which meant the aircraft would glide as far as possible. Then the height became time and space. Time to find a field to land in, space in which to comb the area to pick that field out of the jumble of landscape below. It didn't work over the Atlantic. Fifty miles short of the French coast, it was all one big field, cold and wet and uninviting. You couldn't land on it anyway. She would go down like the brick she was. Time to get out.

He was not entirely sure how he got there but it came as something of a surprise to find himself dangling from his parachute as the inverted aircraft glided down at a steep angle to crash in the sea below. Four minutes later, the cold Atlantic came up to meet him.

*

Tomkins had seen the signal. So it looks like Hargan and his crew might have had it. Never did like the man. Awkward, undisciplined, uncouth. Not officer material. Probably got what he deserved. Too cocky. Sure to happen at some stage. Not professional enough. Insufficient attention to detail. But even so, bad news to lose an aircraft and a crew. Letters to write to next of kin. Explanations to Group. Squadron reputation, his reputation went by the events of the day. Yesterday they got a U-boat. Good show, Tomkins! Today? Tomkins, I hear you've lost an aircraft and crew. Bad show! Sure the route they flew was suitable? Who approved it? Were you in on the decision? Bad show if your outbound routes are going too close to France. Shows lack of judgement. He could hear it all now. And his ideas for new tactics would merit scant attention.

Tomkins? Got a U-boat a while back. Must have been lucky.
Been losing crews as well. Not too good, that.

And what to do about that party in the mess last night?
Bloody rude of Smiley, that outburst of his. Quite uncalled
for. Man should know his place. Might have been around a
while but still only a squadron leader. Not his position to
question my judgement. Discipline, that's what is required
from the Australian rabble. Got to bring them up to standard.
Can't have them doing it their own way. I'll have to tighten
things up. Need to give that some thought.

He started writing a note to the mess treasurer: 'In the
circumstances, I consider it would be appropriate to spread
the cost across the mess bills of all those present. . . .'

*

The crosses on the chart said Ushant was abeam. Give or take a
bit, but it looks OK on the chart. She's still going and the
skipper says we're OK for fuel and the weather's OK and vis' is
good. Piece of piss, mate. Downhill from here. Just lob across
the Channel and we're home.

Time for another look round the old girl, decided Ray.
Didn't really do much in that last lot, did I? Rather got left out.
So I'll do my best now and have another look around. He told
Bill Newton, who was now in the right-hand seat that he was
going for another check around and headed aft. There was a
sort of no-man's land only a few feet aft of the flight-deck. Get
past Dinger's table. Starboard side's not too bad. Port side very
bare now where we've heaved gear over the side. Then the
bodies. No man's land.

Hank and Sparks laid out on the deck. Covered over now,
but still blood around. And don't look at the midship turret.
Don't look at the headless torso in there. Sorry, Banjo, old
mate, but you understand. . . .

He hurried on by and headed for the tail. Quick check of the
tail turret, make sure it's ready to go, guns still loaded, turret
control still OK. If we need it, it'll be in a hurry. Check the tail
section. No change. Rudder and elevator controls OK. Can't
do anything about the holes in the fuselage skin but at least
they're not getting any better.

Down below. Say hello to Johnno, who looks pretty rough,

and to young George who's down here with him. Check the lower hull, all the way forward. Not too good. The water's going to come pissing in those holes when we land. They're not any bigger but they ain't going to get any smaller. On the way back, check the clips on the main door. We might have to climb out in a hurry when we get back. Make sure the door ain't going to jam. As long as Mick can get us down back at base, they should pick us up pretty quickly. But nice to know the front door will open.

*

Yvette noticed. She noticed that one of them came back alone. She was working in her mother's garden, as she did most afternoons after the bar shut. The vegetable garden was essential if they were to have enough to eat. The two pigs did not take much looking after but there was always something to do with the vegetables. So she had seen them go out and she saw only one come back. She was pretty sure it was one of the three. She might have been mistaken – it might be a training flight coming in from somewhere or another aircraft being delivered. So she waited but only one came back. After a while she was certain two had not returned. They had to come close by on their final approach when the wind was in the east. Two did not come home. There could be a simple explanation. They could have landed elsewhere. It might all have been planned that way. But it was worth noting.

She returned to raking a strip level before she cut the narrow furrow in which to sow the carrots.

*

Elman taxied back in, swung his aircraft into its normal slot, applied the brakes and shut down the engines. Peace at last. He climbed stiffly from his seat, slowly easing his aching limbs. He climbed slowly down from the aircraft, followed by the observer. The ground crew were approaching. So was Hans the engineer.

'You're back first. Problems?' called Hans as he approached.

'Bruckner's had it. And Staffelkapitän Schafer was hit and retired with one engine knocked out. I saw him turn for home but that was the last I saw.' His speech was slightly slurred. He felt light-headed.

'Hit by what? What happened?'

'Oh!' Elman realised the other man did not know what he was talking about. 'A Sunderland. We attacked a Sunderland. Bruckner was hit and crashed into the sea. Schafer had an engine hit and had to retire.'

'And the Sunderland?'

'Errrr . . . still flying when I broke off.'

'Broke off? Why?'

'I was running low on fuel. The . . . errr, the target took us a long way west. I was running low. I had to return to base. My tanks are almost empty now. You can check for yourself,' he added, challenging the other man. I really did have to break off. It's true. . . .

Hans turned away without a word and headed for the operations room. Bernard would have to sort this out. It's his job, not mine. He checked his watch. How long can I give Hans? One engine out . . . maybe thirty minutes . . . maybe.

*

Shit! Luboil pressure was dropping and the temperature was rising. Starboard inner. Can't see any reason for it. But looks like she's starting to run out of oil. Losing lubrication. Temperature starts going up. How long will it run? Luboil pressure only just out of limits but it is dropping and the temperature is going up. Bill agrees we are probably losing oil. No other explanation. Nothing much we can do. I've sent one of the lads into the wing to have a look but he's not really sure what he's looking for. You can't really get amongst the engine anyway, just look from a distance. Funny that. You tell visitors you can get inside the wing of a Sunderland and they don't believe you. Not doing us much good now anyway. The engineer's bought it so we're on our own. Just keep going, baby, just another forty minutes or so. Then you can pack up, but not just yet.

*

Jilly had heard the news. It travelled fast. Like another woman, her afternoon was passing in a daze. She had gone through the motions of finishing her washing but her mind had been elsewhere. Confused thoughts. Did I love him or was it just a bit of fun? Was I one of the many conquests of John Williams or was I a bit special to him? Does it matter? I went to bed with him so he's always going to be someone special in my life. He wasn't the first but he was certainly the best. He made it fun. Sex was to be enjoyed, by both partners. That was his attitude. Not like some. Not like the slam, bam, thank you ma'm brigade she had heard about and come across from time to time. Not that she ever fell for their crude advances. Even she, inexperienced though she was, could recognise that sort.

But now the day had to move on. She had to get cleaned up, maybe grab some tea, maybe not, and then go on watch. That was going to be the worst bit. In the Ops Room they would be wondering, wondering what happened, hoping they might come back, and she would have to be there with them.

She hoped there was no one else in the room so she could wash and change in peace, but it was not to be. Irene was there and so was Janet. Irene was sewing a button on her jacket. Janet was lying on her bed reading a magazine. Jilly entered quietly and headed for her locker. She gave Janet a quick, forced smile but ignored Irene. That was a mistake.

'Oh, hello,' piped up Irene. 'You're looking pretty miserable. What's the matter? Isn't lover boy taking you out tonight? Not going to get it toni. . . .'

Jilly ran from the room, tears streaming down her face, hearing as she went Janet screaming 'You stupid bloody cow! Can't you keep your bleeding mouth shut? Have you got bugger all brains? He's been bloody shot down, hasn't he?'

Jilly was not there to see the look of horror on Irene's face. She also missed the look of surprise on Janet's face, surprise at her own outburst. But perhaps that's what happens when you are really beginning to think you might be pregnant and that was the last thing in the world you wanted, thought Janet to herself as tears ran down her own cheeks.

*

The pressure was dropping back steadily and the temperature was going up. It's going to stop. It's going to seize up. Not enough lubrication so it's going to seize up. Problem is, when? And what when it dies? Two dead engines on the same side. No way can I hold her against two dead engines. I'll have to pull the power off the other two and then we're on our way down, fast. With all that drag, I'm going to have to push the nose well down to retain flying speed. That means the rate of descent is going to be high. Shit! We won't have much time when it happens. Get ready for it now!

'Captain to crew! The starboard inner is running a bit hot. Just in case we lose it,' (sound optimistic, he thought to himself) 'just in case, I want you to prepare for ditching now. Get Johnno strapped in. Get the dinghies ready. Errr . . . get the water drums by the dinghies. Then all of you get strapped in, except the lookout. We'll keep the lookout going for the moment. And Bill, I want you in the right-hand seat. Everyone acknowledge!'

There was a chorus of replies. Oh, bugger. Don't tell me we've come this far and the engine's going to go. A quick glance at the chart. It's not far now, is it? Surely we'll make it, won't we. Skipper's just being cautious, ain't he? Just in case.

They got Johnno moved and strapped in. He looked pretty rough but he could move if he had to. They got him up near the escape hatches and strapped him in. Bit of a problem, strapping in with all the seats on the port side gone. They found just enough places left. Five minutes later, they were all in place, except for Ginger who kept the lookout in the astrodome. If the engine went, he'd have a minute or two. Plenty of time to duck down from the dome and get into the one remaining set of straps. Bill Newton was in the right-hand seat, armed with a knife, ready to cut the rope on the rudder pedals. If the engine went, Mick wanted to be able to move the rudder fully. If he pulled the power right off the port engines, he should have more or less normal rudder control. They would need it if they were going to ditch. Thank God for the weather. Clear with light winds. Sea should be pretty calm. No problems about ditching. Shouldn't be too bad.

*

Helmut Schafer could tell them what conditions were like, a bit further south admittedly. You suddenly realise how small these bloody dinghies are when you are in one somewhere in the Bay of Biscay. Even though there was only a slight sea, a swell was running in from the west and was lifting his dinghy and then lowering it gently into the troughs between the long, low waves of the swell. It was like being in gently rolling downland, except the hills were moving past you. One moment you were on the crest of a hill, a wave, and could see the far horizon; next you were down in the valley and your horizon was limited to the hill tops around you. And it was cold, so bloody cold. He'd not been in the sea long. A quick struggle to release his parachute harness. Get the dinghy inflated. Scramble in. Even so, he was soaked right through and now his wet clothes were cooling in the gentle breeze and he was getting chilled. There was a bit of warmth in the sun but not enough to dry him and warm him.

Would they come looking for him? Would they know where to look? What had happened to Elman? Did Elman actually know I had headed for home? He must do. He must have seen me break off and head east, surely? Did Elman survive? Had he got back to tell the tale or was he, Schafer, the only one left of the three? They had tangled with a porcupine and got a bloody nose for their trouble. What a balls-up!

*

Bernard and Hans and Elman, and another pilot, Otto Brun, were gathered round the plot. From Elman's account and his observer's record, they had worked out roughly where the running battle must have taken place. Now there was a strip of water marked off, a corridor leading from the battleground back towards the coast, a wide swath, somewhere in which they thought a downed crew might be. Allow for navigational errors, allow for the fact that he might not have known exactly were he was, add a bit for luck and you end up with a very big area to search. Is it worth it, just for two men? A disproportionate amount of effort, just for two men who might be dead anyway. But you try, don't you? You try because, one day, it might be you out there, and, if it was, you'd want them to come looking. What if we find them? Drop food, water, dinghies if they need them? Call up the Navy, get them to go there? That was it.

Two aircraft were ready to go, the two who should have done the last sortie along Schafer's line, as it had become known. Now they would be diverted. Bernard would take the

responsibility. Get some extra dinghies and food and water
into them and get them away. It's the best we can do but we'll
go through the motions. Then we can say we tried. But that's a
hell of a big area and two aircraft will only be able to scratch at
the surface of it.

*

He'd telephoned! Supper, at his cottage! Wonderful! He'd
pick her up. Helen MacDonald was feeling distinctly more
human. Despite what rumour suggested, the night before had
only been a nightcap, or three. Despite her Scottish upbring-
ing, she really did not have a head for alcohol. Three whiskies
had been far too much. He'd got her drunk but he hadn't
taken her to bed. Instead he'd brought her back and she'd
made it through the gate and then very slowly and carefully
along the drive towards the house. She hadn't made that bit.
She'd been overtaken by a great sinking, churning feeling in
he stomach. She had known she was going to be sick. Oh, my
God! She had staggered off into some bushes and thrown up,
not once but three times. And then, the final indignity, she had
found herself wetting her knickers and she had to drop them
fast and just squat there, shivering and shaking and sobbing
and retching. Never again! Fortunately, no one had been
about to see the state she was in when she made it back to her
room.

And it was all his fault! But she still wanted to see him again,
desperately. Tonight would be different. No drinking. But if
he wants to take me to bed, I'll let him. She lowered herself
carefully into the bath. Second bath that day. She had really
needed one early in the morning. What a state she had been in!
What a morning it had been, showing Jane round. Lunch had
been a trial. A sit down afterwards with a cup of tea was better.
Now she was feeling far more human. Another bath would do
the trick. Pity about that Sunderland which appears to have
been shot down. There's been no sign of them so they must
have had it. Pity. This water's wonderful!

*

Forty miles to go. Less than thirty minutes, even at the speed
we're flying. But the luboil pressure's down to virtually

zero and the temperature's off the scale high and she's going to go any minute. But a minute is a mile and a half nearer home, and it all counts. Trouble is, we can't tell anyone about it because we've got no radio. So, if we have to ditch, there's no guarantee we'll be picked up. But we'll face the problems one at a time.

Five and a half more minute they got. Eight and a bit miles on the long leg from Ushant across the mouth of the Channel. Thirty-one miles short of the English coast. There was a terrible screeching, screaming sound from the engine, a dreadful sound of whirling metal being dragged to an abrupt halt as lubrication ceased and she seized up solid. One moment the engine was producing virtually full power, the next it was dead, the propeller shuddering to a halt.

Mick was already hauling back on the throttles. She was swinging wildly. Get the power off on the other side. Hold her straight. And get the nose down, boyo! Bill pressed the klaxon push but it was not necessary. The engine was its own klaxon. They all knew they were going down.

As the nose dropped and he set her up in the glide, it was, in some ways, a relief. Just for her last moments, she felt like a lady again. The rudder responded, the drag of a dead engine no longer trying to pull her round. Effectively, all the engines were dead now. OK, those on the port side are idling, ticking over. All they're doing is providing the final bit of power for hydraulics and electrics, just enough to see us down. Now she was gliding, rather than being heaved through the air by the engines, she felt much easier, as if to say, Peace at last, let's do the last bit gently. Put me down nice and easy and I'll give you time to get out. I'll float for a while. My hull will fill but not too quickly. You'll have time to get out, to stand on my wings, get your dinghies out and climb in. She seemed to be saying, I'll see you right, Mick old mate.

Fifteen hundred feet. Best way to land? Into wind. Must be. Lowest landing speed. Least impact. Bits won't drop off. Use the flaps, hold her right off, let her stall just above the waves and drop in. That's the best way. But keep going north and a bit east, just a little bit longer, just a little bit closer to home. Try to get as near as you can. Won't make any difference but it feels better that way. Only turn off, turn into wind, at the last moment.

Thousand feet. Bill's hand was on the flap lever. He's reading my mind. A nod, that's all it needs. He gives you half flap. Just right. Eight hundred feet. Time to turn. Ease her round. Gently he banked the Sunderland round, holding the nose down to maintain flying speed. Four hundred feet as he came out of the turn. Another nod. Full flap. Feel the brakes come on. Great slabs of flap going down into the airstream. Extra lift and extra drag. Lower the stalling speed but when she does stall, she'll drop like a stone. Just what we want.

Two hundred. Start easing back. Check the wind direction from the ripples, ripples that are now turning into waves as we drop nearer the surface. Check the little patches of white on the sea. Kick her round five degrees. Put her right into wind. Bring the nose up. It's coming anyway because instinct and a lot of flying time have taken over. Forty feet. Rudder pedals moving to hold her straight. Hands moving to hold her level, to hold her above the surface. Nose up some more.

Twenty feet, back a bit more. Ten feet. Now hold her there! Hold her above the sea, keep hauling the stick back. Classic way to induce a stall. Keep hauling back. Don't let her drop. Speed bleeding off, fast. Flaps acting as bloody great brakes. Hold the wing up, don't let it drop. Keep the floats clear. Put a float in and we'll spin round it. Hold that wing up! Keep coming back, right back . . . all the way. The control column was all the way back. All he could do was hold it there and wait . . . wait for her to stall.

Her final moments were those of an innocent young girl. She just stopped flying and from just five feet above the surface, she dropped in, delicately and gently like a young girl. There was a pause as she skidded along the surface, as the rapid deceleration threw them against their straps. Then the nose dipped. She stuck her nose in and, at the same time, the port float, weakened by the damage done in the area around the wingtip, broke off. The wingtip dug in, she started to swing and a great dash of spray crashed against the windshield. But it was a gentle, final pirouette, like the final moments of a ballerina's dance, a graceful, final sweep, a final flourish. It was her finest moment. Here you are, boys.

Automatically Mick stopped the port engines. No fancy shut down. Just switch off the ignition. Then they were moving. The hatches were opened and they were scrambling out onto the wing. The dinghies went up, but there was plenty of time. She was settling but only very slowly. She'd take a while to fill. Don't hurry, lads. Let's do this properly. They helped Johnno up top, willing hands pushing him up through the hatch. Mick saw them all go. He and Bill were the last two. Bill was looking at the bodies. It was the first time Mick had seen them. He had not left his seat all the way back. A last few moments with the lads. Bill raised an eyebrow as if to say, shall we put them in a dinghy? Mick shook his head.

'They'd rather go with the old girl.'

So he said a silent, final farewell, to his men, his aeroplane. Sorry you didn't make it, lads, but thanks for everything. . . . And thanks, old girl. Sorry we got you in such a mess but thanks for all those hours. . . . He had one more quick look round the flight-deck. Then he followed Bill up through the hatch and onto the wing. The lads were getting the dinghies inflated. Plenty of time. Do it right. They'll just sit in them and wait for the old girl to go down and float off. Piece of piss, mate. No sweat.

*

They found him on the first leg. A lone dinghy out in the Atlantic and they found it first time. Bloody marvellous! Trouble was, they couldn't go down and pick him up. All they could do was drop the food and water, circle round for a while, note the position very carefully, waggle their wings in encouragement and then head for home. We'll be tucked up in warm beds tonight while poor old Helmut has to float round the Atlantic for the night. It'll take a while for the destroyer to get there, once we can get the Navy off their backsides.

*

They'd come. He'd only been in the water about two hours and they'd come. He knew he was lucky, incredibly lucky. Perhaps Elman had been there. Perhaps Elman had seen him go down but could not linger due to lack of fuel. Perhaps Elman had marked the position on his chart and been able to tell the two Junkers where to come.

They'd dropped two drums to him, coming down on small parachutes. To the aircraft, it probably looked as if they had dropped close. To him, they might just as well dropped them on the other side of the Atlantic. Fifty metres upwind. Only a gentle breeze but it was enough, enough to push his dinghy away from the canisters. He tried paddling with his hands, he tried leaning over the front of the dinghy and doing a sort of swimming motion. It was no good. He lost his sense of direction and had to keep stopping to see where they were. Even that was difficult. The canisters bobbed up from time to time and, as a swell swept by, occasionally they appeared as if on the side of a gentle hill. But he had to stop paddling to look. He thought he was getting there at one stage, thought he was making progress, but when he looked, the canisters were well off to one side. All he had done was swing round in a small circle. He could not make progress against the wind. And he was getting wet again. As he leaned over the front of the dinghy, an occasional wave caught him and now his tunic was soaked.

Finally he leaned back and rested. Preserve your strength, Helmut. You do not need whatever is in those canisters. Food? He could go without food for a long time. Water? A couple of days without water. He could survive, survive until a ship or boat or float plane came out to pick him, up. At least they knew where he was, that was the main thing.

*

She floated for an hour, by which time the wings were awash. The waves started breaking over the wings. The lads were in good heart, considering. They'd had time, time to get sorted out. Not that there was much to sort out. Get the water drums in, get themselves in. Pump the dinghies up hard. Top them up after the air bottles have inflated them. Get in and get settled down. Get Johnno comfortable. Blankets and things? We haven't got any. Nothing onboard which will do. Nothing in the old girl we can bring along. No sweat. It's Spring. Shouldn't be too cold. They didn't realise that the water in the Channel was at its coldest in Spring. It had cooled all through the long winter and the warmth of Spring had not yet had time to start raising the temperature of the sea. They laughed when Bill Newton got splashed and got soaked all the way up one side. Anyone for the skylark, a trip round the bay? Messing about in boats.

The dinghies floated off and started to rock and pitch and sway to the motion of the sea. It was not long before they found it was a very uncomfortable motion. Oh, to be sitting back on the wing. But she'd gone. The old girl had sunk. She'd given them time, lots of time, whilst the hull filled with water. The wings had held her for a long time but slowly the cannon shellholes had let the water in and filled the voids in the wing. The fuel tanks were intact and they provided buoyancy, but in the end, it was not enough.

She had gone very gently and quietly, her tail lingering above the surface. Then she had slowly slipped from view, the last tattered section of the tail slipping beneath the waves. Sorry, boys, I've got to go but I'll take Hank, Sparks and Banjo gently to their final resting place. They and I will slip quietly to the bottom, to rest for evermore.

XIV

The juice ran down between her breasts, across her navel and was caught by the first line of hairs. He leaned across and licked some of it up. She laughed as she held up another spoonful of peaches for him. A whole tin of peaches! A treat she had not had since the war began. She did not ask where Henry had got it from. And now she was sitting up in his bed, stark naked, sharing it with him. It was not the only thing she had shared with him that evening.

What an evening! What would her mother say? No longer a virgin. She giggled at the thought. So this was what sex was all about. He had been kind and gentle. A light supper. No drinks. He'd offered but she had said no. He understood. She was nervous. Will he ask me to bed? Will I really go through with it if he does? What if he doesn't ask? What if he just offers to take me back? Does he find me attractive or is he just being polite, asking me to supper? I'm no beauty. I'm short but not dumpy. Round face. The dark hair of the west of Scotland. Some would say a typical Highland lass. How does he see me? How does this dishy man see his women? There must have been lots, surely? Experienced. He was a charmer, of that there was no doubt. Polite, considerate, leading the conversation but drawing her out, letting her speak. His cooking was good. Simple but good. The cottage was sparsely furnished. He'd only just moved into it and was making do with what was already there.

And then after dinner they'd sat on the small sofa. There was only room for two. She'd felt very self-conscious. He looked very handsome. He was wearing uniform but had taken off his jacket and had put on a sweater. She was still in her uniform. Nothing sexy about a WAAF officer's uniform.

But he had leaned over and kissed her gently on the cheek and she had turned and let him kiss her on the lips. It was not like the fumbling kisses with the boys at home, behind the church hall. And even that only in the holidays. A convent school for her. What an introduction to life! Convent school in term time, round the back of the church hall in the holidays. Oban! Hardly the place to learn the ways of the world. Teenagers fumbling through life's lessons together. Nothing from her mother, except something about periods. Sex was, something to be endured, something necessary to have children, but that was all.

Like so many others, the war had brought her, dragged her, from a sheltered world into the reality. Life in the south of England. So different. London. Even in war, an amazing place. But her training had been a woman's world. Women ruling over women. The women's services. Almost as cloistered as a convent whilst you went through the training mill. Then release, release into the big world of a base, with men, real men, men from all over the world. It had been a shock and she had tended to withdraw. The impact had been too much. She was the shy one! Didn't say much. Not one for chatting to the aircrew in the bar. That was because she did not know how to do it. She had never been in that situation. How she had been selected as an officer, she did not know. Good school, well-educated. Nice girl. Steady. Dependable. Maybe. Was that what they had looked for? Hardly a leader. Hardly one to instinctively take control of a situation. She knew her limitations.

His kisses had been different from any other kiss before. He knew what he was doing. No one behind the church hall had the faintest idea what they were doing. She found it arousing. She had felt that first spark of arousal. And she enjoyed it. She relaxed slightly. She tentatively put her arm round him and tried kissing him back. It was not good. She lacked skill. Then she had nestled her head against his shoulder and let him hold her whilst he talked gently about nothing in particular. They'd kissed again and she had felt his fingers slowly unbuttoning the front of her tunic. Should she say no? Should she move his hand away? She felt a flutter of her heart. To go on or not? But he was gentle and she was enjoying it . . . she thought, but was also very nervous. He slipped his hand inside her tunic and gently ran his fingertips across her breast. Trouble was, the armour of a uniform shirt and a bra beneath it did not allow much sensation to penetrate.

'Would you like to change?' he whispered quietly.

'Change? Into what?' she asked, a little startled.

'Go in the bedroom and you'll see.' The commitment. The bedroom. To go or not? She did.

He let her go in alone. The bedroom was at the back of the cottage. That she knew. She opened the door. What a wonderful little room! There was a fire burning in the grate. The room was warm, warmer than the sitting room, if you could call it that. More like a parlour. A warm, snug little bedroom. Plain but an attractive room, nevertheless. And on the bed, carefully laid out, was a nightdress. She picked it and held it to her. Silk! How many others had worn it? How many other girls had had the same technique? Should she fall for it? Why not? It was what she wanted.

She stood in front of the fire and took off her clothes. She laid them carefully on the one chair in the room. For a few seconds, she revelled in the sensation of standing naked before the fire, its heat playing on her body. She turned back and forth, letting it warm her. Then she slipped the nightdress over her head and pulled it down. What a lovely sensation! The smooth silk slid across her skin, its light touch sending a thrill up her spine. So this was why rich people wore silk! It's wonderful. She found herself running her hands across her belly, across her breasts, just enjoying the sensation.

There was a knock on the door. 'Can I come in?' Do I get into bed or stay here? What the hell!

'Come in!' she almost whispered.

He came in, a smile on his face. He had changed. He was wearing a dressing gown. It looked like silk as well. He shut the door carefully, stood and looked at her in the light from the fire. She had not put on any other light. Then he came across and took her in his arms.

In bed, he had whispered at one stage, 'You haven't done this before, have you?' She had shaken her head. 'I'll show you how,' he had answered. And he did show her how. He had caressed her body and kissed her. He had slid the strap of the nightdress from her shoulder to reveal her breasts. He had kissed her nipple and let his tongue run across it. What a feeling! It was so different when a man did it. She had stroked her own breasts as she lay in bed many times. A girl at school had kissed them once, when they were going through that phase of exploring each other's bodies. It was the only way to learn about sex. Stories from other girls' elder sisters, elder sisters who had actually 'done it'. A phase when they had climbed into each others' beds after the lights were out and the nuns had gone. A time of whispers in the dark and fumbling under each others' nightdresses and looking at other girls' breasts when they washed and comparing sizes. A time of touching each other's bodies . . . there. Old wives' tales about if you touched yourself there, it would make you blind. Modern girls knew that was not true. And when he had touched there . . . that was fantastic. Doing it yourself was . . . fun? Another girl doing, back in those cold, dark nights in the dormitory was . . . sexy? But a man doing it, oh so gently, his fingers lightly stroking. . . . She wanted him, wanted him to enter her, to feel him inside her. And when she was ready, he did. A glorious feeling of fulfilment, of abandon, of animal lust. The sheer lust she felt had shocked her. As he slid back and forth within her, she was not sure what to do. There was a basic instinct to move with him, to match his rhythm. He had brought her to a fantastic crescendo as his rhythm quickened, his thrusting deepened. Then he, too, had come and she was certainly no longer a virgin. What a way to go!

She carefully tipped the can and the last of the juice ran into the spoon. She held it out to him. He took the spoon from her but did not put it to his mouth. Instead, he very slowly placed it against her breast and tilted it gently so the juice ran down her skin. He put the spoon aside and leaned down to lick the juice from her.

Ten minutes later the bed was creaking to their rhythm as they did it all over again.

*

It was so bloody cold. A gnawing, sapping cold. He had never been so cold. It was spring but they were bloody freezing. With the onset of darkness, the cold had come. Every whisper of the breeze was a cold blast, biting through their clothes. Wrap up warm in a Sunderland. It can get a bit parky, lads. Now those same clothes were as if nothing against the chill of a night in the English Channel.

Mick had tried to rally his lads. But the motion of the dinghies, the two of them held together by a lanyard, and the chill of the night had damped all spirits. They kept a lookout. A pair of eyes to watch. Someone to let off a flare if something passed in the night. A patrol boat, a destroyer, E-boat, anything. English or German. We're already past caring. Anything will do. Anything at all. So we'll keep a lookout whilst the rest sleep. But sleep did not come. They were too cold. Natural inhibitions went by the board. They moved close to each other. A joke or two to hide their embarrassment. 'What nice perfume you're wearing, Ginger!' But they wrapped their arms around each other and tried to keep warm.

Bill was in the worst shape. His wet uniform was freezing him. They'd helped him off with his tunic and Tiny had lent him his big sweater. But there was nothing they could do about his trousers. Poor old Bill. Bill, the quiet one. Bill we can rely on. Nothing special about Bill. One of the crowd but he's steady as they come. Now he's not too good. Getting bloody cold. If they had known the word, known the symptoms, they would have known he was rapidly developing hypothermia.

*

The end of a long watch. Midnight. Jilly walked slowly across towards the hut and bed. No news, no hope. No real hope. They must have run out of fuel, wherever they were. Squadron Leader Smiley had said something about they might have landed away somewhere but she knew he was just trying to be kind, to boost her morale a little. She had hardly said a word all watch. She just looked at the stateboard. D-Dog. Captain's name Hargan. A time. The time they took off. Who was going to rub the name from the board? Who was going to pick up the cloth and wipe the name off, remove them from this world? Not her.

*

Schafer was absolutely frozen. If he had known, he would have understood the agonies the Sunderland crew were facing. But he was alone and that was worse. No one to share the discomfort. No one to try and raise morale. No one he could feel responsible for. Just himself. Being slightly further south than the Channel meant it was fractionally warmer. The fact that he was wearing wet clothes negated any advantage. He knew Bill Newton's agony as he felt himself freezing. He shivered uncontrollably but it did not help. He curled up in a tight ball, the foetal position. That helped a bit but soon his limbs were aching and he had to move. But the agony of moving, of feeling cold, clammy cloth against him as his body moved inside his clothes! Oh, my God, please come quickly and pick me up!

*

It was one-thirty in the morning. She would stay the night. He would run her back very early, before people were about. She would get him to drop her up the lane and she would walk across the fields and sneak through the wire behind the house. No problem. Everyone knew about the hole in the wire. Even Groupie used it for a stroll in the woods.

'What are you doing tomorrow?' she asked, tentatively. It was the question he should ask but she wanted to know, wanted to know if this was a one-night stand for him, a quick fling with a lass from the Highlands, or would she see him again? She knew as she said it she might be spoiling the magic of the night.

'Ah, well. . . .' Her heart sank. 'I've got to go out with the MTBs. Actually, not got to, want to. You see, when my landing ship is finished, when they've finished building her at the local yard, I'll become the squadron commander. We're going to build up a squadron here. They're building some of the ships here, some at other ports. But we'll build up to twelve or so. I want to learn more about the Channel so I'm going out for a night with the MTBs tomorrow. Should be rather fun!'

Fun! She had heard about what the MTBs got up to and he called it fun. 'Henry Cassell, you will be careful, won't you, because I love you.' She had said it. She had told him.

'Yes, I'll be careful, my darling Helen. Then I can come back to your pretty little bottom.' With that he playfully tried to smack her but could not get much of a swing under the bedclothes. Instead he took her in his arms and five minutes later she was asleep.

*

The dawn came slowly. There was a faint lightening of the sky but daylight came so slowly. When it did come, they could see why. Fog. Bloody fog again. No wonder they were so cold. With the light, they could see droplets of water clinging to their clothes. A fine dew covered them. As the light came they stirred from their cramped positions. Eight men. Mick looked at his lads. You're the leader, mate. You've got to keep this lot going. But what for? No bastard's going to find us in this lot. The whole German Fleet could pass us by and we'd never see them. Real pea souper, this one. But I'll go through the motions.

'Right, lads. Water ration. Ginger, do the favours will you. One cupful each, eh?' At least they were not short of water. One full five gallon drum, one third full. Plenty. Ginger took the latter and unscrewed the top. Carefully he took a cupful and passed it towards Mick. 'Naw, do the others first, mate!' Carefully, Ginger swung the cup towards Johnno, Johnno with the wound in his belly. Mick had read something about you shouldn't give a man with a belly wound anything to drink. But, hell, Johnno had to have something. Tiny was next to Johnno and helped him with the cup. The wounded man looked pale, but so did most of them. He drank his fill and then Tiny had a cup.

Mick leaned over the side and pulled in the lanyard that held the two rafts together. Dinger was the leader in the other raft. God, he looks rough, thought Mick. But then perhaps I look the same.

'Morning, Dinger. How goes it? Water ration, mate.'

He helped Ginger pass across the first cup. Ray had the first one, then George. Another two quiet ones, those two. Beside them, Bill was lying back, his legs pulled up. He was asleep. He had not stirred with the others.

'Do I wake him?' asked Dinger, his voice dry and croaky.

'No, leave him. If he's asleep he's the lucky one. Best thing for him.'

The water ration done, the two rafts drifted a few feet apart, to the extent of the short lanyard.

'Right, lads,' Mick announced to the other three in his raft. 'Time to wake up, get some life into us. Get your thinking caps on. I'm going to call a letter and I want you to call the name of a place in Aussie. All of you, different place. We go round. Then the next one calls a letter and so on. And as you call a name, you move a leg. Next round you move an arm. OK?' It sounded crazy but it was a way of getting them to move, to do something, and perhaps, to warm up a bit. Shit, it was so bloody cold!

'Right, let's go! A!' He moved his leg out as the replies came back – Adelaide, Alice, Augusta. Ginger was next. 'D!' Darwin, Derby, Denmark. Legs moved. There was not much room but it was something. 'T!' Townsville, Tenterfield, Tennant Creek. 'Where the bloody hell's that?' 'Northern Territory, mate!' 'Might have known.' 'Bloody Queenslander.' Morale was picking up.

The morning moved on. A quiz. Competition against the other raft. Leave Bill, if he's sleeping. Three against four. But, shit, man, our three brains beat your four any day. What's the capital of Scotland, then, smart arse? Glasgow. Bollocks, mate, it's Edinburgh. Oh, shit, is it?

A song. There was only one song they could sing. Waltzing Matilda. The song of the swagman and the billabong and the jumbuck sounded faintly across the grey, misty waters of the Channel.

*

Henry Cassell was standing at the back of the group. This was the briefing. More a planning discussion. Put an idea, hack it around, throw in a few ideas, then let the leader gel the plan. Ushant tonight? If the fog clears. The Jerries must go inside Ushant. We'll get away early. Get over there just after dark. Patrol across . . . here. Anything that comes out of Brest tonight has go to come round the corner if it is going up Channel. Focal point, just here. Take it to their doorstep. Right, agreed. Then the details. Route, times, callsigns, radio frequencies, which boats to go, a relief for a sick man.

Then a cup of tea from the Wren. A word with Dick Smiley.

Sorry you lost one yesterday, Dickie. Oh, by the way, this is Henry Cassell. He's taking over the Landing Ship squadron, when it's built that is. He's coming for a ride with us tonight. Dickie tried to smile back but his heart was not really in it.

*

The same fog lingered over the Bay of Biscay. It hung like a shroud across the waters. The wind had gone. Now just an oily swell rocked him. But he could not see the hills and the valleys. His horizon was only a hundred metres away. The fog was thick and it stayed even after the sun was up. There was no welcoming glimpse of the sun through the mist, no golden ball in the eastern sky, starting to appear as it burned off the fog. The fog stayed all day.

The cold was weakening him. He tried to keep warm but there was nothing he could do. His damp clothes clung to him. There was no warmth in them, none at all. He lay and drifted, both physically and mentally. His mind was drifting, was wandering off. A day at school, so long ago. A walk in the hills. His first girl. The day he fell in the stream when he was only four. The memory of that made him feel even colder. Think of warmer things. Think of summer days. Think of a holiday on the North Sea coast. Hot summer days. Playing on the sand. Digging holes and building sandcastles. Great fortresses to guard the Fatherland. Fortresses proof against the guns and archers and knights of old. Fortresses proof for evermore, or until the tide came in and washed them away. Oh, well, you could build another one the next day. Days on the beach, playing with his sister. Two years older than him. A life time. The day she had taken him into the sand dunes and undone the top of her swimsuit to show him her breasts. The breasts of a fourteen-year-old. They seemed amazing at the time.

Hot days in the Alps. High in the mountains. Sun beating down but snow all around. No, don't think about snow. Sand is better. Or sitting round a log fire in the winter. That's a warm thought. Keep thinking that one. Keep thinking warm things. Hot sun or fur coats or big log fires. Food and drink. Don't need food. Could do with a drink. Even a cup of hot coffee, revolting through the wartime coffee is. No, don't think drink. That only makes you feel thirsty. Think warm, that's the main thing. Think of the sun which is blazing down somewhere above this cloud. Think of the sun which could be roasting you in your cockpit. It'll do it again. Next time you fly, you'll be cursing as the sweat runs down your brow. Oh, for a bit of sweat now. Oh, for that warm sticky sensation of sweat pouring off your body. He would revel in the sensation next time it occurred. Hot bath. That was the thing. A nice hot bath. Not in the draughty huts they lived in. He'd go into town. The hotel where he drank. They had a bathroom. He'd ask to use that. Lie back in the hot water and just soak it all in. Warmth all over his body. Get Yvette to wash his back. Now, there was a thought. . . .

*

The other raft came alongside as Dinger pulled in the lanyard. He leaned over to whisper to Mick. 'Mick, it's Bill. He hasn't moved all morning. I think he's dead. But I haven't checked him out. Didn't want to alarm the others.'

'Oh, shit, mate.' He thought for a moment. 'OK, you'd better check on him.'

Dinger moved across the raft, ignoring the looks of the others. He felt Bill's hand. Very cold. He felt his forehead. Same. He sought for a pulse at his wrist and then at his neck. Nothing. He tried to see if he was breathing. Nothing. He turned to Mick and shook his head. Oh, bollocks, thought Mick to himself. Oh, shit, Bill, I'm sorry old mate. We just thought you were sleeping. Oh, bloody hell!'

Dinger came back and leaned over where the two rafts were rubbing together. 'What do we do now?' he asked quietly.

'Leave him. Cover his face but leave him for the moment. We'll take a vote later.' Why later? Because everyone had lapsed into their own worlds. Leave it that way for the moment. They were there, watching, but they were not part of what had just happened. Let them lie. He looked at his watch. Four o'clock. We'll have a water ration at five. Tea-time. Then I'll ask the lads what they want to do.

*

The engines roared into life. Henry Cassell stood on the bridge of the MTB and watched what was going on around

him. He had never been in MTBs before. Cruisers,
destroyers, a battleship once, but never anything this small.
Different world. Less formal. Destroyers were less formal
than cruisers or destroyers' MTBs were another step on from
destroyers. You knew who the captain was. He was the
skipper and he was God. But only a minor god. A young man
leading even younger men. He, Henry, was by far the oldest
on board. He was a very senior officer. A lieutenant-
commander. Theirs was a world of lieutenants and sub-
lieutenants. A young man who had been an accountant
before the war was the captain. His sub-lieutenant had been
at university, reading geography. That much he had learned
from a short chat over a cup of tea in their minute wardroom.
He had made it clear he was just there as an observer.

The first of the MTBs backed away from the pier. They
followed in quick succession. A long run tonight, all the way
to Ushant. Get away well before dark. Bit of a balance. Not
too early or we might arrive whilst it is still light enough for a
patrolling aircraft to see us. But early enough so we can be in
place as soon as possible after dark. Then we'll sit and wait
and see what comes round the corner. With a bit of luck, we'll
find a coastal convoy. Quick, short, sharp attack and away.
Probably just guns. Might get a torpedo away but it's bloody
difficult amongst those convoys at night.

The six boats turned in the harbour and lined up one
behind the other. At a steady ten knots, they headed down
harbour. Thank goodness the fog was clearing. Bit of wind
picking up from the west. The forecast said the fog should
disperse as the wind freshens but we might still get the odd
patch on the way across. It was more likely to linger near the
French coast apparently.

It was good to be back at sea again. An open bridge, the
wind in your face, wrapped up in a duffle coat, tucking in
behind the bridge screens to stay out of most of the wind.
The men on the foredeck stowing away the ropes and
clearing the gun for action. The steady roar of the engines.
Ensigns fluttering proudly in the wind. It was good to be
back. This was the next best thing to a night in bed with a
woman. Shy little thing, that Helen, but willing to learn.
Mmmmm. . . .

*

It was only as the sun was going that the fog started to clear. The vote at water ration time. A hard question to ask. Do we tip Bill's body quietly into the sea or do we keep him in the dinghy? He did not need to add, to keep him in the dinghy to remind us all of our own vulnerability, our lack of immortality. But they wanted to keep him. We can't just tip him over the side, Skipper. He's our mate. We'll take him back when we get picked up and give him a decent burial. No one said, if we get picked up.

Johnno was in a bad way. He was moaning and occasionally crying out with pain. His wound was not bleeding much, as best they could tell. But he was in a lot of pain and was not really with him. They wiped his lips with a damp handkerchief. They put their arms round him. We shouldn've done this for you, Bill old mate. I'm sorry but we did not realise you were in such a bad way. Now we'll try and bring Johnno through. We'll nurse him the best we can but he doesn't look too good. No longer the handsome ladies' man. His hair is plastered down across his face and his tongue lolls out from time to time and he is a pale, slightly greeny colour. But we'll try and get you through, Johnno. After ballsing up looking after Bill, it's the least we can do.

XV

Finally the name, the callsign was rubbed from the board. Dickie did it. He did it, and then walked across towards the mess. He needed a drink. It was not often he resorted to drink in time of trouble. But I'll drink one to you, Mick. I'm sorry you didn't make it.

*

Night came but it made little difference. He went from one world where he could not see very far to another, from one world of grey to one of black. It was still the same cold world, still the same Bay of Biscay. It was still a world where no one could find him because no one could see him. If they had sent out aircraft during the day, there was no way they could find him. If there was a ship or something looking, they would have no chance in that fog. He had heard stories of men surviving days, even weeks in dinghies, open boats, even hanging on to wreckage floating after a ship had been sunk. But not in these waters, surely?

But come on, Helmut. Hell, this is not winter. The summer is coming. It is warmer. You can survive. Come on, man! You can make it. The fog will be gone tomorrow and you'll be able to see for miles and someone will come looking and you can let off one of your flares and they'll come and pick you up. Easy. Just the night to get through. Not a very long night. Not as short as midsummer but not like the long nights of winter. Just a few hours. Then it will be dawn and you can hope again. Just keep going for the hours of the night and they'll find you again and come and fetch you. Then you really can have that hot bath you've been dreaming about.

*

Yvette's fears had been confirmed. Two aircraft missing, but they'd spotted one man in the water. In some ways, she was sorry, sorry they had been shot down. Then she remembered herself. They were the enemy, they were the occupying forces. They were the product of the Third Reich. They were Hitler's men. They were the nation that ran the Gestapo. Thank goodness those two Gestapo men are not in tonight. Only a few locals had drifted in to exchange some words with the owner, to have a quick drink and move on. They'll be no Germans coming in for a party tonight, that she knew. At least she might get an early night.

*

For the second night they wrapped their arms around each other, wrapped their legs together. Don't worry about the fact that your crutch is hard up against mine, mate, as long as it keeps us warm. I think mine's shrunk so much I'd never find it anyway. Tiny had Johnno in his arms. Good man. Tiny. Big and strong and powerful. Really threw those guns about shooting down those Jerries. Seems an age ago now. He had Johnno cradled in his big arms, his broad hands supporting the other man. Poor old Johnno! Still moaning and crying with pain. Bit of a bastard, a belly wound. Bleeding seems to have stopped, though. The dark stain over his trousers is dried blood now, or as dry as anything is in this goddamn dinghy. Don't knock it, though. It's keeping you out of the water. If you'd been in the water with just your life-jacket, you'd have copped in hours ago. This little dinghy is your salvation, mate, so talk nicely about it.

Go through the motions. Keep a lookout posted. You never know. And it might be the only chance. The one ship that passes in the night. Darkened ship. Bloody difficult to see. So keep your eyes, and ears, skinned. You might only hear it, not see it. Listen for engines, for the sound of a ship's wash. Look for that streak of white which might mark where a ship is cutting through the water.

They were not to know about the six MTBs passing twelve miles east of them.

*

Jane Phillips was lying in her bed. She could not sleep. She kept thinking about that evening. Was it really only two evenings ago? Two evenings ago that she had met Mick Hargan? She had heard more about him from others. No one knew that she had spent much of her first evening with him, sitting in the night air, listening to the sounds of a drunken party. So little snippets had come out. Bit of a character, our Mick. Genuine Aussie. Comes from somewhere in the bush. Bush? A Perth suburb doesn't sound much like the bush, but what exactly did they mean by 'the bush'? Doesn't like Brits too much. You could call him bigoted. Women? He'd rather have a pint in his hand. Mick's OK if he's with a bunch of Aussies. Piss-up in a pub, that's Mick's scene. Bit crude, scruffy, undisciplined. Lads like him. Runs a good crew. Bit of a mixture, like all crews. A few quiet ones, a few noisy ones. Mick and his navigator, Dinger Bell, they get on well. Usually go drinking together. Good pair to have at a piss-up. Tomkins hates Mick. Mick hates Tomkins. Women? Mick? As I said, rather have a pint in his hand. No, no regular girlfriend or anything like that. No, not his scene.

Had she got him all wrong? Had she got the wrong man? It was Mick Hargan, the only Mick Hargan she had met, whose shoulder she had cried on? What if there were two? But he had said he was a Sunderland captain. And D-Dog's captain's name was Hargan. Had to be the same. Why did she have to meet him like that? Was it all going to be like this? Another place where men got the chop. Oh, no, would she become the station Chopper? Don't go out with Jane Phillips. Night out with her and you're for the chop next, mate. We call her The Chopper. Give her a miss. Nice-looking, but give her a miss.

The tears came again as she buried her face in her damp pillow.

*

In a room just down the corridor, Helen MacDonald lay in her own bed, thinking of her evening with another man. What if her mother knew? You wicked, wicked girl, Helen Mac-Donald. Just wait until your father comes home. He'll beat you with a hair brush. But not here. Not here in Cornwall, a whole world away from Oban. In its way, Cornwall was a remote part of England, but it was the people who had moved in who had

changed it, or at least this small part of it. The RAF and the
Navy had changed many things.

No longer a virgin! I've had my first man. And I enjoyed it.
She felt a tingling feeling deep down. I would take him here
and now, if I could. But I'll have to sleep alone. But before I
do. . . . She turned over to lie on her stomach, pulled her
nightdress up a little and slid her hand down. Her fingers
slipped between her legs and she stroked herself gently. The
waves of an orgasm swept over her and then she slipped into a
deep sleep. She dreamed of silk night dresses and warm
fires. . . .

*

They were in position. The MTBs were spread out in a long
line, about half a mile apart. Allowing for how far the ones on
the wings could see out to the sides, they covered just over
three miles of sea. They hoped it was enough. Three miles of
search line, through which a convoy would, hopefully, have to
come. Navigation was a bit tricky. One of the boats had a Gee
receiver on board. They had scrounged it off the Sunderland
boys. It made a hell of a lot of difference. They could navigate
accurately round the Channel without having to feel their way
in the dark. For the most of them it was a magic box. For the
leader, in whose MTB the Gee set was installed, it was a box he
had got to know and love. He had learned of its foibles from
the Sunderland navigators, had learned when you could trust
it and when you should not. He had learned of its range
limitations. Tonight, because they did not have the advantage
of the height of a Sunderland, they were pushing the range to
its limits, and a bit beyond. He'd taken the last decent fix as his
datum and they had run on from there on dead reckoning.
Then allow for tide, take a quick check with the echo sounder
to see if the depth ties in and then hope that the spot marked
on the chart is about right. Change your mind and keep the
echo sounder running all the time. Dodgy coast, this bit of
Brittany. Rocks and shallows. Play safe. Keep an eye on the
depth. And remember the tide. Fair woosh runs round
Ushant. So work it out, like you have to every time you're in the
Channel. Stem the tide. It's on the turn. Soon you'll have to
turn the line north-east and point your bows into the ebbing

tide. Just keep the engines ticking over. Keep nosing into it. Don't let it take you south, onto the rocks off Ushant.

In another MTB, Henry Cassell was leaning over the tiny chart table, listening to an explanation of the same problem. The dim red light illuminated the chart, a masterpiece of the engraver's art. He'd seen them making the masters for printing the charts before the war. This was a pre-war chart. There had been no surveys done in this area for a while! Not that it made much difference. Rocky coast. Nothing changed. Not like the shifting sands of the North Sea.

He listened to the explanation of the tidal flow in the Channel. He had traversed the Channel many times and knew its strong tidal streams. But he needed to learn more about flows close to the coast, the way the tidal stream was deflected by headlands, by underwater obstructions. One day, when he took his ships across the Channel as part of the invasion force, as some day he surely must, he would need to know these things. He would need to know how to take his ships into an enemy-held coast at night. Trouble was, he had no idea which bit of coast. Where would the invasion be, if there was an invasion?

*

Mick had the lookout. No one else stirred. Were they really asleep or were they just lying there? He swept his eyes around them for the hundredth time. Shapes in the dark. His eyes played tricks. Lights appeared. He blinked and they were gone. He was looking at nothing and his eyes were playing tricks. Look at something close, the dim shapes of the men around him, then look back. Nothing there. No lights. Just a dark night. But there were one or two stars above. The fog had gone, or so it seemed. Now it was the westerly wind.

Not as cold as an easterly. Comes in from over the warm sea. That's what the met boys had told him, sitting in those lectures all that time ago. Warm sea! There was nothing warm about this sea. Had he really been able to sit out on what seemed a warm evening with Jane Phillips? Had they not felt cold? But out here, on the sea, only thirty miles away, it chilled you to the marrow. Went right through. But you started not to notice after awhile. Perhaps that was good. Or perhaps it wasn't.

When you no longer noticed the cold, perhaps that was the danger sign. He stuffed his hands deeper in his pockets, hunched his shoulders more against the cold and swept the horizon yet again.

Suddenly there was a long, chilling groaning sound from Johnno. It seemed to come from somewhere deep inside him. Then the pitch of the sound rose and he was crying out with pain. It was a piercing cry which had them all awake. Tiny was holding him close without squeezing him and talking quietly to him. 'It's OK, Johnno, just take it easy. You're with your mates. You're safe. We'll get you back, mate. We'll get you seen to, have you right in no time. Just take it easy. . . .' The crying rose to a piercing scream and then stopped abruptly. They sat and waited and listened to Tiny still talking quietly, comforting his mate. But then Tiny stirred and moved. 'Got the torch, Mick?' No skipper, this time. It was 'Mick'. Mick pulled the small torch out of his pocket and passed it over to Tiny. Gently the big man laid Johnno down so the back of his head rested on the side of the dinghy. He was checking for a pulse. Then he checked the eyes. Quietly he said, 'Reckon he's gone, Skipper.' They were not to know that it was internal bleeding which killed him.

*

The lighthouse was flashing. The lighthouse on Ushant was flashing. It looked like the light had been shaded so that it only shone towards the channel between the island and the mainland. They could faintly see where the beam was cutting the air, a beam sweeping across the water two miles to the south of them. It could only mean one thing. Something was moving.

Quietly the men moved to their stations. Half the crew were closed up all the time anyway. Now the rest joined them. Guns crews. Tubes crews. A fair variety of guns. 2 pdrs the main armament. Twin 0.5 inch machine guns. .303 machine guns. 20 mm Oerlikons. And the torpedoes. All were ready. All they could do was watch and wait. Wait for the first glimpse of a darkened ship. It might be a destroyer, an E-boat. Or a small merchant ship. It could be someone looking for them. Perhaps the Germans had radar and had spotted these six echoes sitting off the coast. But surely they would not put on the light

for someone trying to sneak round from Brest to catch the
MTBs unawares? Unless they thought the shading was protec-
tion enough. But the beam was visible as it swept across the
narrow channel and the light was reflected off the minute dust
particles and drops of water in the atmosphere. It was enough.

*

The German destroyer was heading west-south-west. Some
flyer in the water. Needed picking up. Risk a whole ship just to
pick up one man? But there's not too much risk down here,
well south of Ushant. Unlikely to be attacked by aircraft.
There could always be a submarine out here, though. Yes, we
are risking a whole ship to find one man. And do we really
know where to go? The Luftwaffe has given a position but
we've known their positions before. Could be miles out. Wind
and current. Could take him miles away. Pity we couldn't get
out sooner but the port engine needed fixing. Couldn't have
done anything yesterday anyway. Thick fog all day. Never find
a thing. It's clearing now. Freshening from the west. Few stars
out. Should be OK when dawn comes. Should be in the area
soon after that. Might even find him. Best chance he's got. No
one else is going to pick him up.

*

'Romeo two has a ship in sight to the south. Two thousand
yards.' 'Romeo force, immediate execute, course north, speed
ten.' Then, one minute later, 'Close in on Romeo Two.' They
knew what to do. Move the line along ahead of the ship which
Romeo Two had spotted and shorten it in. They had done it
before. Get in close together across the front of the enemy
force, whatever it was. Attack together. After that, it's every
man for himself.

The note of the engines deepened as they came round to the
north east and increased speed slightly. Romeo Two would
become the focus, their guide. The other boats would slant in,
increasing speed slightly so they kept on the same line of
bearing. They would reduce the distance between them.

'Romeo Two is losing the ship astern!'

'Romeo force, guide speed seven.' Slow the guide, slow the

line. Let the Germans come to us. But we've got our backs to them at the moment.

Henry looked very carefully out on each side to where the other boats should be. Bloody difficult to see them. Their camouflage always looked too light in daytime, but, in fact, at night, the boats were very difficult to see. All he could pick out was the line of their wash, a white scar on the water. He could see a boat on each side. Each boat could see only one boat on each side, so they had to keep station relative to what they could see. It meant the line was pretty ragged in practice, but they would all be roughly in the right place.

'Romeo three has something in sight bearing two zero zero.'

Was that the same ship as Romeo Two or was this another one? He found this night fighting fascinating. Not that the fighting had started yet, but the tactical problems . . . something completely new. Short range, limited visibility, darkened ships. Racing round at high speed. Except they were creeping along at seven knots at the moment. . . . He always imagined MTBs racing in at 40 knots or something. He had been surprised to hear they could only do thirty. Hell, battleships could do that.

The line had shortened and now the MTBs were creeping along ahead of the enemy force. What if it were two German destroyers? How did destroyers and MTBs compare? A destroyer might be a torpedo target, if the torpedoes were set to run shallow enough. What depth were they set at? Could a 2 pdr gun do anything to a destroyer? What use were the machine guns? There was so much to learn.

It was time. 'Romeo force, X-ray attack. Go!' It was only afterwards he would find out what an X-ray attack was. Three boats go left, three go right. Pincer movement – simple really. Keep the tactics simple. Nothing clever in the dark. It was confusing enough without trying to do anything clever.

The MTB swung round and accelerated. Up to 20 knots. Not flat out, not yet. He could just make out another on their flank doing the same. But it was only by keeping an eye on the compass repeat that he had an idea where they were going. Somewhere to the south, two, three thousand yards could be a convoy. Probably small, just a handful of ships. Could be. Only two ships had been sighted, type unknown. Could be they were just about to run into a force of E-boats sent out for just this very thing – to take on the British MTBs. They came round in a wide sweep which would bring them in somewhere on the bow of where the convoy might be, if it was there at all.

Suddenly there was a burst of tracer off to their right, a line of bright dots moving across the night sky. Then others joined in and dots could be seen moving in both directions. The sound of rapid gunfire came across the water above the roar of their engines, followed by the deeper boom of 2 pdrs firing. Around them, all was dark. They were running blind into the unknown.

There was a glimpse of white to starboard, a white scar in the water. The wash of something. . . . 'E-boat, stern on. Leave it!' the Captain called, his binoculars to his eyes. Other eyes were looking ahead, binoculars striving to pick out the dark shape of a ship, to gather in what little light there was. Four look-outs searched back and forth. Thirty seconds . . . a minute, a very long minute. It seemed like an age. 700 yards a minute at 20 knots. Nothing. . . .

'Ship ahead!' The look-out's cry brought everyone's eyes swinging to look ahead. The captain's glasses went to his eyes. 'Starboard thirty!' he cried. The wheel went over and the MTB leaned hard over as they swung, swung close under the bow of a ship which had appeared out of the dark. He just had time to glimpse that it seemed to be a small coaster before they were crossing its path and opening out on the other side.

Then he watched as the captain ran out roughly at right angles to the course of the ship. Forty seconds. Then the captain ordered the wheel hard over and, at the same time, throttled back slightly. So, he knew roughly where a target lay. Run out on its beam. Not too far mind. Swing round, slow down a bit to give yourself a little more time. Then they were round on an almost reciprocal course. Allow for the fact that the target was moving, aim off just a bit. Tubes ready. Tiptoe back in towards where you think the target is, assuming it has not turned right away. Keep your eyes skinned for escorts. Look-outs watch their own sectors. Don't worry about what's going on around you, lad, you watch your bit. Never know when a bloody E-boat or even a destroyer is going to come charging out of the night.

'Got it!'

A shape in the dark ahead. The MTB came left ten degrees. Aim off the torpedoes ahead of the target. There was a sudden, loud whoosh as the first torpedo left its tube, followed two seconds later by a second. Just two. He could just make out the splashes as the torpedoes entered the water and then the MTB was leaning hard over and the throttles were going forward as they broke off. They turned to the south, towards the stern of the convoy. Around them, tracer was criss-crossing the night sky and the duller boom of the heavier guns could still be heard.

Confusion. The fog of war. Everyone in their only little corner, limited by the distance they could see another ship, a darkened ship, on a dark night. That said, suddenly a flare burst in the sky somewhere behind them. Beneath it, he could see the shape of two small ships. Bloody difficult to see what they were. MTB-sized. There was a sudden bright flash from one, followed by flames. Theirs or ours? Impossible to tell. But in the faint light of the flare he saw a torpedo strike home, a column of water rising up the side of the target. Then the flare was gone. They raced on.

'E-boat starboard bow!' a voice screamed.

Then he saw where the machine guns came in. There was no time to swing the 2 pdrs onto the target as the German ship swept by only two hundred yards to port. But the lighter machine guns were able to swing round and pour tracer into the German. He could see hits striking home, little flashes in the dark. Impossible to see where. The German was caught off guard. There was no return fire for fifteen long seconds. By this time, they had swept past and the E-boat was just abaft the beam. Suddenly a machine gun on the E-boat opened up, fired briefly and then stopped abruptly as tracer poured into the point where the machine gun was firing from. Good shooting! As quickly as the German appeared, it disappeared, but, just as it did so, there was a loud crash aft and the boat shuddered and lurched . . . and slowed. They had been hit.

The wheel went over. Someone's shooting at us. Might be a lucky shot from that last one, could be someone we haven't spotted yet. So keep ducking and weaving. We've lost an engine but keep going full chat on the others; after all, we've got four all together. Jink around to spoil their aim, if anyone is aiming at us. . . .

Another shape in the dark, to starboard this time. Guns swinging. A scream of 'Hold fire! It's one of ours!' Then the shape was gone.

Then they were out in the open. The sights and sounds of battle were still evident on the starboard quarter. No more shapes in the dark. Another flare astern. Something on fire. A bright burst of light, as of something exploding, then nothing. The battle eased. There was another sudden burst of tracer on the starboard bow. Two boats exchanging fire for just a few seconds. Then it stopped. As suddenly as it had all begun, it stopped. Somewhere in the dark, the MTBs were withdrawing. Nothing on the radio. North the compass read. Home. Time to break off and head for home, but, even as they did so, he could feel them slowing again. They slowed but kept going. Difficult to tell how fast. Men were coming up to the bridge to talk to the Captain. Guns crews were still poised, ammunition numbers were ready. The battle was still not over . . . not until we are a good five miles or so from this lot. Keep your eyes skinned. There might still be an E-boat or two out there. We're going north and the convoy is off to starboard and hopefully we're clear. But keep looking whilst we sort out these problems with the engines.

Henry stayed tucked in his corner at the back of the bridge, watching and listening. One engine was out. Another one had a bad cooling a water leak and had been shut down whilst they fixed it. One hit back aft, that was the damage, but enough to penetrate to the engine room and right off one engine. Lucky there wasn't a fire. Bloody lucky. Nineteen knots they were making. That sounded pretty good on two engines. A hundred miles to go. Five hours. But first light would come in two and a half. Only fifty miles from the French coast at first light. Would it be enough?

*

There were lights in the night and voices, but the voices were laughing. He shook his head. An illusion, a dream. There was nothing there. Must keep going. . . . Must not give in. . . . He forced himself to look, to look out into the night. He could just make out the shape of the low waves as they swept by him. He could pick out an horizon, a line between the slightly lighter sky and the darker sea. There was no one there . . . there was no one to find him . . . must keep going . . . must keep going until daylight . . . then they would come.

But I'm so cold, so incredibly cold. I dare not move. If I move, a new wave of coldness hits me. I must stay curled up in a ball. I must not worry that circulation to my legs appears to be cut off. It's just an illusion. You can't feel your feet but they're still there. Must keep going. . . .

Schafer held his knees close into his chest and waited for the dawn to come.

*

The Ju88 followed the taxi way carefully. Difficult to see the way in the dark. Just one. We'll send one. The destroyer's on its way. Forecast looks hopeful. Fog's gone. With a bit of luck, the aircraft will find him and can call the destroyer in. Just one aircraft. I think we can justify that. After all, the Navy have sent out a ship for just one man. We can pull one aircraft out of today's sorties to go and look for Helmut. After all, he is the Staffelkapitän.

The Junkers turned onto the runway. A green light flashed from the control tower and the aircraft roared down the runway. It lifted off and climbed away, heading west. Behind it, there was the faintest glow of light in the sky as the new dawn approached.

*

The stars in the east were starting to go, starting to disappear as the sky lightened just a fraction. To the west, it was still dark. But the fog had gone! Thank God for that. Mick lay back in the dinghy and hoped and prayed that, with the improved visibility, someone might spot them.

Each man lay in his own cocoon of discomfort, of cold, of shivering. They lay huddled together. An illusion of warmth. That was all it was. But they were making it through the night. Pity about Johnno. Great pity. Good lad. I'll miss Johnno. But the rest seem OK. We should get some sun today, a bit of warmth. We're OK for water. Don't need food. Could do with losing a bit of weight anyway. Just a bit of warmth today and there was hope. Stay warm during the day and the night was bearable. Trouble with that fog, they stayed cold all day, the day before. Thirty-six hours they'd been cold, so bloody cold. Not the crisp coldness you got on a frosty morning, the crisp coldness which made it nice to slip into the mess and sit by the fire with a pint in your hand. This was a damp, penetrating coldness which chilled you right through. It sapped all strength, all the will to do anything. That was the trouble. That was what killed you.

Once the sun is up, once there's some warmth in the air. I'll get the lads talking, singing, anything just to get some life back into us. Otherwise another couple of days like this and we'll all be dead.

*

He was leaning over the chart with the captain. 'We're just taking the straight line home,' the young lieutenant was saying. 'My radio's out so I can't tell Romeo leader we're on our way back but limping along a bit. So we'll just have to make our own way home. We've done it before. Always bloody difficult to join up again after these night actions. But comforting if you can,' he added. 'Aircraft. They're the biggest problem. They usually send out a patrol or two after a bust up like this. That's why we like to be well over our side before the sun is up. It gets more difficult in the summer – shorter nights. This may be the last time we come all the way down here for a while.'

Henry studied the chart. A straight run back across the Channel. Minefields were marked in but they would pass clear of them. No problem . . . except for the possibility of aircraft.

'Why Romeo force?' he asked the Captain, suddenly.

'Oh, the boss is a Shakespeare buff.' He laughed. 'We were Brutus force the other night. We've had Othello, Falstaff, even MacDuff!'

'Not Bottom?'

'No, not Bottom!' He laughed. 'He's been told to stop. The intelligence boys say it's too predictable for the Germans listening posts.'

He ran his dividers across the chart and marked the dead reckoning position on the chart for an hour ahead.

A wonderful feeling of warmth came over him. At last he was feeling warm! Wonderful! All sensation of cold had gone. He felt warm and snug and comfortable. Now he could just rest and wait for them to come and pick him up. . . . Just a short sleep, now I'm feeling warm again. . . . Schafer's eyes closed.

*

It was getting lighter. There was a red glow in the east and they could see the horizon all around. There was nothing in sight. No MTBs, no E-boats. They were alone, for the moment. Now the danger lay in the air. Now the look-outs concentrated on sweeping the sky, watching for the first speck in the distance which might be an aircraft coming out to look for them. Those bloody Ju88s. Bastards they are. Got cannons. Shoot this lot to matchsticks. We're only made of wood. Cannon shells will go straight in. Quick burst from an 88 and we've had it. We've seen it happen to others.

*

He was imagining it. A faint sound. Like an engine. Aircraft! Quickly he shook the others. 'Ginge, Tiny! Aircraft engines!' They stirred reluctantly. He called to the other dinghy. 'Dinger!' His voice was faint and croaky. '*Dinger!* Engine noises! Aircraft somewhere! Get your eyes skinned!'

They all stirred and tired eyes searched the sky above. Not really enough light yet. Where is the bastard? Worth firing a flare? Not yet. Could be miles up. Never see us. Save it till we're sure. Keep looking, lads, there's something out there. Not getting much louder. Well, perhaps a bit, but only slowly. Must be bloody high then. Oh, shit!

'Skipper! *Skipper!* A mast, over there! It was Tiny. Pointing. A mast? Then the big man, was trying to stand, to balance precariously in the dinghy as he tried to stand. He got into a sort of half crouch. 'Yeah, it bloody is, Skipper! Give us a flare!' Mick grabbed the nearest flare and passed it. Tiny attempted to fire it.He fumbled and almost dropped it over the side. He tried again. Nothing. Slowly he tried again, made sure he was doing it right. 'Bugger's duff! Got another, Skipper?'

The next one went first time.

*

Henry Cassell was leaning over the back of the bridge, a cup of cocoa in his hand. It was good to be back at sea. Quite a life in these MTBs. Quite a night! Lot of fun. He watched the wake astern — a timeless thing, the wake of a ship. He watched the interaction between the bow wave and the waves being generated by the light westerly wind. Patterns ever changing. Waves rose and fell, broke and died. Always moving, never still.

A bird caught his eye, sweeping low across the waves. Difficult to see as it flew low over the surface. Effortless. No movement of its wings. It just floated along, another timeless thing, the flight of a sea bird. Then it rose and turned, rose high and then dropped down again. His eyes followed. . . . Hell! What was that? A flare or something! A red light curving into the air. 'Red flare! Starboard quarter!'

*

The MTB was coming alongside. A rope was thrown. Tiny took it and hung on tight as they were hauled alongside. A scrambling net was down. Mick grabbed it and held them against the MTB's side. The other lads were pulling the other dinghy alongside. Helping hands came down and grabbed his arms. He was about to protest about getting the lads out first but he was already being hauled up. Two sailors heaved him up onto the MTB's deck. Someone else threw a blanket round his shoulders.

'Good on yer, mate!' was all he could say.

Then he looked around. Hey, it's one of the MTBs from home. Good o—! A familiar face or to. He recognised one of the petty officers. A sub-lieutenant appeared at his side.

'Are you the senior officer, sir?'

'Senior officer? Yeah, mate, I suppose I am.'

'Would you like to come to the bridge, sir? My men will look after yours.' Yeah, leave the decisions to someone else! Mick followed the young officer forward and then up to the bridge.

A tall officer was standing at the back of the bridge. Another young one was coming forward to greet him, but he turned to the older man. But the young one was saying, 'Welcome, sir! I'm the captain.' Bit confusing this.

'Yeah, right. Good on yer, mate. Thanks for picking us up.' Come on, Mick, even you're getting this stiff-upper lip disease. You're bloody glad to see these blokes. Bloody say so!

But the captain was turning away, turning to look over the side of the bridge to see how things were going. Mick moved to his side. 'There's two dead in the dinghies. I'd like to take them back.'

'Yes, well . . . I want to get moving as quickly as . . .' but then he saw the look on Mick's face. 'Of course.'

Getting the bodies on board was not easy. Five extra minutes. Five extra minutes of vulnerability. Let's get going! But they picked up the bodies and put them on the after deck and covered them over. Then they moved away, a quick burst of machine gun fire going into the dinghies as they left, to sink them.

Then the two throttles went all the way forward and they headed for home.

*

An aircraft was circling twenty degrees off the port bow and about five miles ahead. Ju88. Position looked about right. Must be over the dinghy. Can't contact him on radio. Don't know his frequency. Another balls-up. Don't know each other's frequencies, but it's pretty obvious what he's doing.

The destroyer came twenty degrees left and headed for the spot the aircraft was circling. Fifteen minutes later, they were a hundred yards off the orange-coloured dinghy. One man in it. He hasn't waved. Probably too weak or cold. The sea boat was lowered and slipped. The men bent to their oars and slowly the boat closed the gap. It drew alongside the dinghy. They were pulling the man in. The dinghy floated clear. The boat headed back towards the destroyer, the blades dipping in unison.

The destroyer captain leaned over the side of the bridge as the boat manoeuvred under the falls. Quickly it was hooked on and they started to haul it up. He turned to the officer of the watch and nodded. The man leaned to the voicepipe and, a few seconds later, the destroyer started to gather way.

Five minutes later the first lieutenant stepped onto the bridge, having supervised the hoisting and securing of the sea boat.

'Wasted journey, Captain. He's dead.'

XVI

Mick was down in the chart room, just forward and down from the bridge. Out of the wind. Warm. He had a mug of cocoa in his hand and a big wedge of bread. Out of the wind, warmth. Simple things. Survival.

'Bloody good of you to find us, mate!' he was saying to the captain.

'Well, bit of luck really.'

'You out here on your own?'

'No, there's another five MTBs around somewhere. Should be ahead of us. We got slowed down by our engine problems. . . . Tend to get scattered after these nights, we do. The others may have passed you but just a bit further off.'

Mick thought about this. 'You come out the same way?'

'Yes . . . yes, we did.'

'So you could've been quite close to us on the way out?' Had they missed the MTBs passing in the night? Was there a chance they could have been picked up, perhaps saved Johnno?

'Maybe,' the captain was saying. 'Maybe, but, of course, the tide's been on the ebb for a while now. It would have swept you a few miles west in the night. That could have been the difference.'

A yell from the bridge. 'Aircraft!' The young officer was up the ladder immediately. Mick followed. Not a bloody Jerry! Not an 88 to come out of the morning and balls it all up. 'Twin-engined!' He felt a sinking feeling in the pit of his stomach. Oh, shit! Nearly made it and one of those sods appears. A long wait. It was coming from the north-east. No, not it . . . them. About three thousand feet. Had they been spotted? Were the Jerries going to come swooping down and blast them with cannon? So near and yet so far.

He stood on the bridge, off to one side whilst six men with

binoculars watched the aircraft. He could just see them with
the naked eye against the red sky of dawn. The sun was just up
and the aircraft were dark specks against some distant cloud.
A perfect morning. A good morning to be alive, not have some
bastard come roaring down shooting you out of the water. He
looked around. Plenty of guns, this things got. Might be able to
take on a pair of Ju88s. MTB. Manoeuvrable. Could jink about
a bit. Bit more than a Sunderland. There's chance yet . . . if the
bastard's spot us. But the rising sun is illuminating us. They
will be looking at our sun-lit side. If they've got their eyes
open. . . .

'It's OK. They're Mossies.'

'You sure?'

'Yeah. I can see the shape of the tail. Yeah, they're Mossies,
for sure.' Thank God for recognition lectures! Mosquitos.
Ours. Tension went. A great relief. His hand was shaking but
he was still holding the lump of bread in it. The next mouthful
tasted better.

*

Land. A familiar piece of land. The Lizard. Almost home.
Looks different from the sea. Takes longer to get home too.
Not just a few minutes flying time. More like thirty minutes.
But it's England. Land of Poms. Looks pretty good today.
Perhaps I won't knock it quite so much in the future. Looks
grey and solid and friendly from here. Perhaps the beer's not
so bad. A quiet pint in a pub would go down well.

The other lads were up on deck. Goodo, these Navy chaps.
Loaned a few clothes, done us proud with cocoa and then soup
and bread and then a fry up. Eggs, bangers, beans, more
bread. A feast for a king. Great! And they're taking us home.
Their home is our home. Bloody convenient. We'll ask them
up to the mess for a piss up. This bastard is going to be worth a
party. Boy, we'll have a party and a half after this lot. And I'll
be in the middle of this one. Wonder how she's getting on, that
young Jane. Not bad, that one. Could brighten the place up a
bit. Be nice to see her again. Not a bad looker. Not bad at all.

Thirty minutes later the MTB passed through the entrance,
the steep rocks rising on either side. Plenty of room. Get a
battleship in here. MTB can cut in close. No problem. The

people at the signal station came out to wave, up on the cliff above. Recognition signals had been exchanged a while before. It's OK, it's one of ours. Give the base a ring, tell them there's a straggler coming home. That's all six. Nice to see them back.

Men stopped work on the decks of the other MTBs as they came round the corner. They were busy re-ammunitioning and loading fresh torpedoes. Do the jobs, then everyone can get their heads down. Been a long night. As they pulled alongside, sailors exchanged banter. 'Where have you bastards been? Late again!' The heaving lines went across. The ropes went out. Bit difficult screwing her alongside with only two engines. Bit of juggling with the throttles then she was there. Shut down. Silence. Great!

They had not been able to pass the message that they had survivors on board. No radio. And Mick had agreed it was not worth the bother of passing a message by light as they approached the signal station. 'No sweat. It's a nice morning. We'll walk up. Thanks a lot, mate. We really appreciate it. Oh . . . I'll get some transport down for the bodies. Can you. . . .'

'Yes, sir. We'll look after them.'

So Mick led the team ashore. Six of them. Six out of eleven. Could've been worse. Could've been a whole lot better. Once ashore, they started walking up the slight hill away from the jetty. What do we do now? What do you do when you've just come back from the dead? Eight-thirty in the morning. Breakfast? No, we'd better get the medics to check us out. But I'm going to the ops room first. 'OK, Dinger, take the lads up to the sick bay. I want them checked out. I'm going to see if Dickie's in.'

Dick Smiley was reading an intelligence assessment which had come in overnight. It was a long signal, giving all the figures for ships lost, U-boats sunk and so on, plus a whole lot of words about German industrial capacity and their ability to keep building U-boats. He thought the figures looked a bit optimistic. U-boat building should be slowing. That was the theory. Trouble was, it did not seem to be working in practice.

The door opened. Dick glanced up. A ghost walked in. Mick Hargan! All he could do was sit and stare, his jaw dropped.

'Morning, Dickie, old mate. Don't look so surprised. It's only me back from a trip! It sounded like the usual Mick, except it wasn't.

There was a brittleness in his voice.

'Mick. Where the devil. . . . How. . . .?'

Mick came forward to shake his hand. The two men exchanged smiles. They did not notice the Wren in the corner, a look of hope on her face.

'Long story, old mate. Hey, this ops room still do tea?' He turned to the young Wren. Oh, it's that freckle-faced one again. 'Hello, love. Got any tea in the pot?'

'Yes, sir!'

'Goodo!' He turned back to Dickie. 'Yeah, bit of a long story, mate. Got bounced by some 88s over the Bay. Three of them.'

'Yes, we got your signal.'

'Oh, you did? Right. Managed to get two of the bastards. Well, we saw one of them go down and me tail gunner knocked out an engine on another. Then the third one packed it in and headed for home. But they made a bit of a mess of the old girl. Knocked out me starboard outer. Bit of a fire but got it out. Quite a lot of damage, really, but she was still flying. So we headed for home. Nearly made it, but the starboard inner packed up about thirty miles short. Had to put her down. Jumped in the dinghies. Then one of the MTBs came by first thing this morning, picked us up. No sweat!'

'Glad to see you back, Mick. Glad to see you. Now, where were these fighters?'

'Long way out. Hell of a long way. Dinger will tell you better than I but . . .' he walked over to the wall chart, 'must've been right out here. Bloody long way from a Ju88. Unless they're putting drop tanks on them or something.'

'Mmmmm,' mused Dickie. 'I'll pass that one on. If they're coming that far out, we might have to re-think out routing.'

In the corner the kettle started to sing. 'You OK, Mick?'

'Bit tired, mate. Need a bath and some fresh clothes and a bed.' He paused. 'Tomkins about?'

'No, he went about seven. He's doing a convoy south of Ireland. He's going to land away at Milford Haven. Liaison visit or something. Wants to talk to the COs up there. Be back about lunch time tomorrow. By the way, Mick, are your crew OK?'

'Oh, shit, Dinger, I lost five of them.'

'Mick, I am sorry.' Dickie picked up a pencil and pulled a piece of paper towards him. 'Can you give me the names. We'll have to inform next of kin and so on.'

'Oh, yeah, sure. Yeah, we'll have to do all that, won't we. But, I mean, are we down as missing already?'

'Errr, yes, yes, you are. We'll inform next of kin of those who are safe and those. . . .'

'Right. OK, we lost Jim Bailey, me Sparks. Hank, that's Henry Jones, the engineer and Banjo . . . errr, James Patterson. They all bought it during the attack. Then Bill Newton died in the dinghy . . . the first night, and Johnno . . . John Williams . . . we lost him the other night.'

The kettle in the corner was boiling but the girl did not take it off. They could not see that her face had crumpled and tears were streaming down her cheeks. She ran from the room and the door banged as it swung shut behind her.

*

'Bloody silly, this. Putting us in bed, Doc. I don't need to be turned in in your sick bay. I'm fine.'

'It'll do you good, Mick. Best thing for you. You'd be surprised what it's taken out of you.'

'Oh, bollocks, mate. I'm fine. No problem. And get that bleeding needle out me arm.'

He did not notice the nurses undressing him as he lay on the bed. He was out to the world.

*

A face by the bed, coming into focus. Girl's face. Going again. God, I feel tired. Sleep. . . .

Later, the same face. Seen her before. Nurse? Coming into focus.

'Hello, Mick.' A voice. Heard it before. When? 'It's me, Jane.' Jane who?. . . . Ah, got it!

'Hello, love.' A whisper. Eyes closing. Come on mate, say hello to the girl properly. The feeling of a kiss on the cheek . . . sleep.

*

It was dark. Where the hell am I? In bed. Where? Not me own bed. Somewhere else. Shit, where am I? Dying for a piss. Got to get out. Sick bay . . . that's where I am. Got it! What time is it?

He climbed slowly from the bed. Moving like an old man. A voice. A nurse. 'What are you doing out of bed?'

'Need a piss. What time is it?'

'Two o'clock. Come on, I'll help you.'

'Two o'clock when?'

'In the morning.' She helped him along between the short row of beds. Other figures sleeping. Dim lights.

'How long have I been asleep?'

'About eighteen hours.'

Eighteen hours! Does that make to today or tomorrow? When did I come in here?

He did not care as the nurse held him up as he stood before the urinal. Bloody embarrassing normally, but I'm too bloody tired to care. . . .

*

Morning. Fully awake. Know where I am now. Funny dreams. Faces in the night. Dream about going for a piss. Someone holding me up.

'Would I like a bath? Yes, I bloody well would, love.' A nurse running the water. That's service for you.

'What about the rest of me lads?'

'They're OK, sir. They've all had a good night.'

'When will I get out of here?'

'When the doctor's seen you, perhaps.'

Bloody medics, run the place like a prison. But the bath was good. So was breakfast. Breakfast sitting in bed. Rare treat, that. Then the Doc coming round. How you feeling? Fine. Blood pressure. Temperature. Look at me eyes. Stick a thing down me throat. In me ears. Reflexes. Stethoscope. Bloody cold, that. Why don't they ever warm the thing. Urine sample.

'You're all right, Mick. You can go. Take it easy for a few days. You'll be off flying for a week. Come back in three days, I'll just give you another check.'

Clothes. Fresh clothes. From his room. 'Got any scales, love?'

'Yes, they're in the room at the end of the corridor.'

Half a stone, that is what he had lost. No bad thing.

Dinger, in the next bed. He's up and about now. Getting dressed. Docs given him the OK. Young George is still asleep. No sweat. The rest of the lads are in the 'other ranks' ward. Officer country, this. Bloody air force. Even divide you up in hospital.

'Dinger, you OK?'

'Sure thing, Skipper. How about you?'

'Yeah, mate. I'll be right. Look, there's a few things I need to sort out with Dickie and the adjutant. Meet me over in the ops room, will you? Dickie will want to know exactly where we met those bleeding fighters.'

*

The morning was bright and clear. A good morning to be alive. The last twenty-four hours were lost. A blur. He could remember coming to see Dickie. He could remember their conversation. Then he could just remember seeing the Doc in the sick bay. After that, it was a blur. But now it was a new day, a wonderful day. A spring morning. A spring morning in England. Not a bad place really.

He walked in through the ops room door. Bunch of Navy blokes in there. A familiar face. He went over.

'Hello, sir,' the young lieutenant greeted him. 'How are you?'

'Fine, fine. Look, thanks again for what you did for me and me mates. That was goodo.' He looked at the chart they were studying. 'You off again tonight?'

'Yes. We had a stand-down last night. Off again tonight.'

'Oh, right. Well, look, when you've got a free evening, give us a shout and we'll have a few pints together. Least we could do for you.'

'Oh, right, thanks.'

Mick left them to it. No Dickie yet. Better go and see the adjutant.

There were funerals to arrange. What a bastard. Letters to write to next of kin. Could take ages for a letter to get back to Aussie. All they would have would be a telegram. Two telegrams. Missing in action. Then, sorry, but he's dead. Two pieces of paper, twelve thousand miles away. And then a letter, weeks later. What could he say to them?

He got it sorted out with the adjutant. The man knew what to do. Done it all before. Knew the form. Good advice. Don't worry, Mick, I'll take care of that. Leave that to me. . . . I'll get my chaps to sort that out. Personal effects. Records to be annotated. Killed in action. Died of wounds. He knew the routine. Seen it before. John Weston. Not a bad sort. Admin and all that crap. Not my scene but he seems to know what he's doing.

Dickie was in when he got back to the ops room. Dinger was there too. 'I've run through it with Dinger, Mick. Now, you'll have to write up a report. Can you do it this morning?'

'Oh, yeah, I suppose I'd better.' A report. Official. Tell them what happened. The facts. Not how it really was. The sweat, the fear, the way the lads hacked it. Three Ju88s. Had they really taken on three of those bastards and come back to tell the tale? But it would not be the true tale. Official report. Official language. Evasive action was taken. Not – I stood the old girl on one wing and nearly dropped her in the sea. An engine fire was extinguished. We returned fire. One enemy aircraft was seen to crash. One enemy aircraft was hit with machine gun fire and was seen to disengage. Load of crap. How could he tell them the way Tiny got the bastard? How could he tell them that they took on three fighters and hacked the bastards? How could he tell them that they were bloody lucky to be picked up. MTB whatever number was sighted at whatever time and a distress flare was fired. Official language. Load of balls.

'Yeah, I'll do you a report, Dickie.'

'Doc says you're all off flying for a week, I see.'

Was that good or bad? Did he really want to fly again? Bit like riding a horse. What did they say? Get back on as soon as you fall off. Would he want to get back on in a week's time? What about a crew? Have to get five new faces. Wouldn't be the same again. New aircraft. Wouldn't have the feel, the familiarity. Might not be so lucky. Lucky aircraft, D-Dog. Never be another one. New aircraft would not be the same. Not much of his tour to do. Might just see it out with some new faces in the crew, and a new aircraft. Five or six more sorties and that might be it. Might hack it.

'Dickie, I'm going to go over to my room and put this report together. Dinger, can you write down the position and time when we saw the fighters and the position where we reckon they broke off? I'll have to put those in. Oh, and get me the MTB number will you? I never bloody noticed.'

He picked up a pile of blank paper from Dick Smiley's desk. And a couple of pencils. With that, he headed out of the door and walked across towards his hut, deep in thought.

'Mick!' That voice again. He turned. 'I heard you were up and about. I came to see you last night but you weren't really with it.'

'Hello, love. How are you?'

'I'm OK. And much better for seeing you.' She had a lovely smile. And those eyes . . . 'I missed you, Mick.'

Did she? Bloody hell!

They were walking together towards the hut. She was saying, 'I'm sorry you lost some of your. . . .'

'Yeah, me too. That's the bastard of it all. Some of the lads didn't make it. Real sod, that.'

'Mick, I'm glad you got back . . . I really am.' She had a very serious look on her face, just for a moment. Then she gave him a little smile.

They reached the door of the hut. 'Come in, for a moment.'

'But it's men's. . . .'

'Oh, bugger that.'

He opened the door for her and she climbed up the two steps into the hut. He led her down the narrow passage to his door. He opened it for her and ushered her inside. Home. The only home he really had. It wasn't much. He pushed the door shut and turned to face her. They stood looking at each other for a few seconds, then he moved towards her. He took her in his arms and held her tight.

He held her tight for a long time because he did not want her to see the tears running down his face.

*

A quiet beer at lunch time. Not bad, this English beer. Bit warm but I'm getting used to that. Some familiar faces in the bar. Word gets around. Quite a lot of the lads were flying or sleeping. Just a few there to say 'Good to see yer, Mick!' 'Hear

you shot some of the bastards down.' 'Where were they, Mick?'
'How did you get them, Mick?' 'What evasive tactics did you
use?'

Then lunch. Sit down lunch with a white tablecloth and mess
servants there to serve it. Not the chops and beans of an
operational sortie, thrown together on a two-burner stove.
Proper grub, this. Bit limited by wartime rationing. Roast lamb
today, sir. Cabbage and potatoes. Sounds good. Spotted dick
and custard. Good English cooking. Couldn't be better.

A message. Tomkins is back. He'd like to see you in his office
. . . when you've finished lunch.

*

Tomkins was still in his flying gear. Dick Smiley was with him
in his office. Mick's report was on Tomkins' desk. '. . . So they
were brought back by the MTB about, oh, eight-thirty, I
suppose. Pretty tired, they were. If you want my opinion, sir, I
believe they did a very good job.' I'll say my bit now, Tomkins.
Whether you want it or not.

'Mmmm, thank you, Ops. I'll have a quick read through the
report.'

Fifteen minutes later he had been through it once, and parts
of it twice. It made good reading. He would have to change
some of the wording but it would then go up to Group. Good
report from your man, Tomkins. Jolly good show, dealing
with those fighters. Reflects well on the squadron when you
have men like that. Reflects well on Coastal Command.
Reflects well on you too. Must be running a good show down
there if your chaps can pull off this sort of thing. Good bunch,
these Australians, are they?

*

Mick took the precaution of calling in at the ops room. Dickie
was back from seeing Tomkins.

'Hello, Mick. Tomkins wants to see you.'

'Yeah, thanks, Dickie. I got the message. How is he?'

'Much as ever. Oh, by the way. Message from Group. They
have said that's it for you. End of tour.'

'What?! But I haven't got all me hours in.'

'New rules. That's it, Mick. They said it wasn't worth you

getting together a new crew. You haven't got long to go anyway. You and Dinger. End of tour. They want you to go to a training unit. Not sure where yet.'

The relief. A release from it all. The end. No more going down the Bay. He and Dinger. Great. And no more bloody Tomkins. Get away from that Pommie prick. Better go and see him.

'Thanks, Dickie, old mate. Better go and see Tomkins, then. Hey, was that report OK? I'm not too good at all this official writing.'

'Looked OK to me. I don't know what Tomkins will say about it. . . .'

'Look, Dickie, I've had Tomkins up to here. If he says one thing out of line, just one thing, I'll bloody hit him.'

*

'Jolly well done. Hargan. Good show . . . good show! Splendid shooting down those Huns. And you almost made it back. Unlucky that engine went when it did. . . . You've no idea why?'

'No, sir. She just lost luboil pressure and over heated. Seized up.'

'Yes, I see. Well, I'm glad you made it back. Oh, sorry about the chaps you lost. Have you seen the adjutant?'

'Yes, sir. All taken care of.'

'Good, splendid. Now I've only had a quick read of your report. I'll have to go through it again more slowly. But I notice you've recommended one of your gunners for a medal. DFM. Timms, is it?'

'Tiny Timms. That's the one. Deserves a medal. Bloody good shooting.'

'Yes, yes. We'll have to see about that. I'll have a think about it.' He turned over the top page of the report and studied it briefly.

'Now, about this report, I did notice there were one or two spelling mistakes in it. . . .'